euphoria

euphoria

a novel

Connie GAULT

Edited by G. Hollingshead.
Cover image,"Broken cup and saucer on the floor," by Soren Hald/Stone Collection/Getty Images.
Cover and book design by Duncan Campbell Design.
Printed and bound in Canada by Friesens.
This book is printed on 100% recycled paper.

Library and Archives Canada Cataloguing in Publication
Gault, Connie, 1949–
Euphoria : a novel / Connie Gault.
ISBN 978–1–55050–409–5
I. Title.
PS8563.A8445E96 2009 C813.'54 C2009–902671–6

10 9 8 7 6 5 4 3 2 1

2517 Victoria Avenue
Regina, Saskatchewan
Canada S4P 0T2

Available in Canada from:
Publishers Group Canada
9050 Shaughnessy Street
Vancouver, British Columbia
Canada V6P 6E5

The publisher gratefully acknowledges the financial support of its publishing program by: the Saskatchewan Arts Board, the Canada Council for the Arts, the Government of Canada through the Book Publishing Industry Development Program (BPIDP), Association for the Export of Canadian Books and the City of Regina Arts Commission.

Canada Council for the Arts
Conseil des Arts du Canada

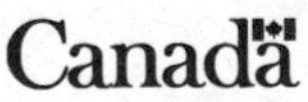

Regina
CITY OF REGINA

For Joanne

The best thing, after wisdom,
is a merry heart.

prologue

the promise

Toronto, November, 1891

The earth tipped and she was gone. The lodgers sat dazed around the dining-room table and avoided looking at her chair, a straight-backed wooden chair in every way like theirs except for being empty. It was the evening after Jessie Dole had her baby and walked off the wharf into Lake Ontario. Everyone in the house had been interviewed by the police, the Children's Aid Society and every newspaper in Toronto, and they had all run out of words. Thinking about young Mrs. Dole was itself an impediment to speech. Gladdie McConnell took the thin-sliced bread and the cheap butter with its whiffy fumes into the dining room, and then refused to carry more. The lodgers waited and waited for their supper, and Mrs. Riley called and called, but it wasn't Mrs. Riley Gladdie wanted to hear yelling her name.

"Gladdie! Gladdie!"

All Gladdie could think, over and over, was *If only.* If only it was morning instead of night, if only it was Jessie Dole calling her, if only she'd asked for help. Gladdie could have saved her. But she hadn't called, she hadn't asked and now she never would. Gladdie shut out Mrs. Riley's caterwauling. She had no room in her head for Mrs. Riley and her demands.

With Gladdie refusing to budge, Mrs. Riley had to finish serving the supper, and to say she wasn't pleased would be putting it mildly. She had to trot back and forth like a servant, herself, while Gladdie McConnell sat on her cot in the corner of the kitchen with her eyes on the far wall. It wasn't a situation that could be allowed to continue. As soon as the lodgers had eaten their meal and drifted off to their chilly rooms, Mrs. Riley returned to the kitchen to jolt Gladdie out of her grief, though when she plunked herself down beside the girl it was to console her, she said.

Gladdie was mad at Jessie Dole and had no energy to defend her. She had to listen to Mrs. Riley go on and on. Gladdie McConnell was twenty-four years old that November evening, which meant she'd lived with Mrs. Riley and worked for her in the boarding house over half her life, and she was well aware there was no method that would make the woman stop talking if her mind was occupied with any thoughts at all. To Mrs. Riley a thought was not complete until it was said aloud to someone else, and even that wasn't enough. The other person had to agree with it before she could ever let it go. Gladdie clapped her hands over her ears, and still the tirade went on and on, louder and louder, until finally Mrs. Riley got the picture.

"Have it your way," Mrs. Riley said. "Sit on your tush all night. See if I care. But I'm deuced if I'm clearing the table or washing the dishes for you." She looked down on Gladdie a minute before she stood up, as if there had ever been a chance she would clear the table or wipe a plate that Gladdie had washed. She heaved a sigh of such force it struck Gladdie's neck and made the fine coppery hairs at the bottom of her bun stand on end. Gladdie didn't move in any other way, so at last Mrs. Riley hoisted herself off the cot and sailed out of the kitchen.

Gladdie could have crawled right into bed, she was so exhausted, but after the house was dark and silent and only the gleam of the stovepipes saved the room from utter blackness, she remained on the edge of the cot with her bare feet flat and freezing on the linoleum – she had got as far as taking off her boots and stockings – and she could feel herself not moving a muscle. Numb as a post. It felt like she wouldn't ever move again. And if she was to move again, she couldn't tell what muscle it would be she could rejuvenate first to get herself back into the way of motion.

Then the baby cried and she was up before she knew it, rooting around among the dirty pots and pans for the stockpot where she'd boiled the bottle they'd borrowed. She had to let the baby cry while she warmed the milk. It reminded her of the gulls she'd heard down on the wharf, that cry, how they wheeled in the sky above the lake, trying to screech that they were lonely. Their cries were always strangled, or so it seemed to Gladdie, as if someone had told them to quit, crying would do them no good. But there was a difference in the way the baby cried. The sharpness of the sound was similar, and the distress, but there were no half cries here. Wee little voice that it was, it went on and on, like an emergency that wouldn't ever end.

What Mrs. Riley had been saying was true, though Gladdie hadn't wanted to hear it. Mrs. Riley herself had three childbirths before, as she said, she knew any better, and she was only talking about women's bodies, how the messages a body sends a woman can get mingled, and the mind follows the body into confusion. Gladdie knew it was true because she'd helped Mrs. Riley deliver babies more than a few times in that very house, and she'd seen how the women themselves, their first time, didn't know what was happening. "They usually think they need a good shite, don't they," Mrs. Riley said, though she knew Gladdie didn't like that kind of talk. "And the further into it they get, the more they want out. There's only one way out of this, I tell them," Mrs. Riley said with a snort. "You've heard me say it, Gladdie."

A trail of blood, they said in the papers, led from the bed to the outhouse, and from there out the yard, down the alleys and all the way to the lake. In the papers they embroidered everything; that was something Gladdie had noted. You'd imagine a river of blood running through the kitchen, gathering force on its way downhill through the city and staining the lake red. It was this supposed trail that gave rise to the rumours that Mrs. Dole had given birth to the baby in the outhouse or she'd dumped it there to die. The readers of papers liked to feel horrified.

There were a few drops on the kitchen linoleum, it was true, but the baby was left in the bed. Gladdie told that to the reporters, to no avail. She believed, as she always would, that young Mrs. Dole had thought the infant was dead. It didn't cry, or at least Gladdie hadn't heard it, not at its birth. And Jessie Dole didn't cry out herself, not once. That was like her. Gladdie would have heard her and been there to help in a minute if the unfortunate girl had made the smallest sound in the quiet of the night. Her cot at the back of the kitchen was next door to Mrs. Dole's room. Gladdie didn't know how she could have missed the whole thing. The floor squeaking as poor Jessie Dole slipped out should have woken her, if nothing else did.

The baby didn't cry until morning was almost dawning, and by that time Jessie Dole was long gone. The sound scared Gladdie awake. She ran to the bedroom, and there she could just see in the half-light the bed in a turmoil and on it, in a nest of soiled sheets, this little wizened thing flailing its fists and legs, crimson in the face. Jessie Dole had tied off the cord with a strip of rag and left the infant there. Gladdie left it too, didn't pick it up, didn't stop to think once she saw the bed was empty but for it. She wheeled around and flew out the back door, through the porch, down the path in the thick mauve light of early morning. She banged on the biffy door before she realized it was latched on the outside with the twistable chunk of wood that was worn so smooth to the hand from so many latchings that even that morning she stroked her fingers along its polished raised grain for the bit of solace it could offer. But no one could be in there, and she ran out the gate, trying to think of nothing as she darted through the twisting, narrow back lanes, then dashed down York Street all the way to the lake. It was not quite dawn, but men were working at the railway crossing, and when she passed them one hollered at her, her nightie being a signal to his heathen side even though it covered her as fully as her clothing would have done. Then, at the wharf, they stared at her while she searched the lake as if she expected someone to come walking toward her on water. Standing on the swaying dock she wrung her hands, watching, listening, and lifted her feet, one at a time, to warm the cold soles on her calves. No one came walking over the swelling water, or rose from it. The boats knocked against one another, making a hollow sound, and beyond them the lake looked endlessly dark and sounded greedy, slapping and sucking at the wharf. The gulls screeched. In the dull south sky was half a moon, lit just on the edge of its left side. There was no sign of young Mrs. Dole, no sign that she had ever been there. The police found her that same day, later, with stones in her jacket pockets and nothing to identify her, but they knew by then she came from Mrs. Riley's.

Gladdie blamed herself because she'd never talked to Jessie Dole as she should have. She was a lodger, and Gladdie had let that put a wall between them, forgetting she was a girl first. If other women could live after what they had to do, Jessie Dole could have too. Gladdie thought she should have told her about the others, how a woman can be strong.

One thing occurred that Gladdie didn't know could happen just from feeding a baby. She'd never done it before. The babies who were born at Mrs. Riley's were fed on the breast. Besides, they left soon afterwards with their mothers. Mrs. Riley had them out the door as soon as the mothers could walk. It was part of the agreement, she said, that she shouldn't be burdened with all that puking and puling. So Gladdie fussed a while with getting the bottle and the baby lined up before she noticed what was happening. The baby fastened her eyes on Gladdie while she sucked her milk. She looked at Gladdie hard and wouldn't look away. The nipple was big for her and she sputtered and gasped, but she wasn't going to let it go, not for a second. She seemed to think she might not get hold of it again. In the same way, as if she might lose her if she broke her concentration, she looked at Gladdie and wouldn't look away. It made Gladdie uneasy. She began to think the baby was pulling a promise from her just as much as she was drinking milk from the bottle. There was nothing soft and babylike about it. It was a scowling look. Fierce. She was but a day old. After a time, when she'd drained about half of the bottle, the little pale eyelids drooped and her sucking slowed. The measured rhythm broke a few times and those times she sucked hard again, in a panic, and frowned up at Gladdie again as if to be sure of her, but then after a bit her arms went limp, the nipple lolled on her tongue and she let go and sank into sleep. Gladdie wiped up the milky drool from her chin and put her cheek down against the little cheek. There she was – the little fighter – asleep. And there was Gladdie with a hundred chores to do and two arms drugged with holding her and no idea how to keep the promise she'd been making to her that she'd never give her up.

part one

whoever you are

waking

Regina, July 1, 1912

When Orillia Cooper finally woke, it was like coming from nowhere and breaking the surface of time; it was like being dead and then alive, or as close to that as she'd ever experienced, and the first thing she saw when she opened her eyes was the woman sitting by her bed, alert as a guard, on the white-painted metal chair.

"Is it you?" Orillia asked. Before the woman could answer, everything shifted. "Something's making me swim," Orillia said. It was the morphine, wafting her up past the woman, off to a high corner. She closed her eyes.

"Is it you?" she asked again.

"Yes, it's me," Gladdie McConnell said.

Orillia laughed. It was a high, thin laugh, appropriate to a person suspended near the ceiling. She said, "That's the right answer, whoever you are."

The next time she woke, she didn't open her eyes so soon. She was still half inside a dream; she was standing in the green cave formed by the drooping branches of a weeping willow tree. She wanted to stay there and she wanted to leave. She let her mind dart about in the green-tinged light until she remembered where she was, that she was in the hospital, and surely – this was most important – she hadn't been so silly as to give them *anyone's* name. She was not going to open her eyes and find Gladdie McConnell sitting beside her bed.

At the same time she was convincing herself of that truth, something was distracting her. Something was hurting at the foot of the bed. Pain was down there, jabbing, while she hovered above, reassuring herself that she hadn't really seen Gladdie McConnell in her room.

Her eyes opened on a fat splayed book, a finger tracing along under the lines of print. She knew whose finger that was. Shiny-skinned, dry-knuckled, blunt-nailed. It was Gladdie McConnell's finger. It was Gladdie McConnell. In the flesh. Tiny maple leaf pins ran up the front of her yellow blouse in haphazard fashion, as if they'd been blown there. Some of them were silver and some were enamelled in flame colours like her hair. Under her chin, where the skin wasn't tanned, a pouch sagged, wrinkled a bit like a finger-softened penny candy bag. What a wide froggy mouth she had. What a nice flat nose. What frizzy, coppery hair, and half of it stuck out of her topknot.

"I thought I was dreaming," Orillia said. "I didn't think you were real." Without any warning, pain drilled up her legs. She tried to sit up, but she only pulled against the straps that held her pinned to the bed. At almost the same moment, at the sight of the pain, fear snapped in those gingersnap eyes of Gladdie McConnell's, and she jumped to her feet. "I'll get a nurse," she said. She hiked up her skirt and dashed out of the ward as if her own life depended on her speed. Even through the pain, Orillia watched, amazed, as Gladdie McConnell – a woman she barely knew – ran off with her knees bent close to the floor like a racer.

The hospital room intimacy – the chair sat necessarily close to the bed since she was in a crowded ward with seven other women – embarrassed Orillia, and before she spoke she looked away from Gladdie McConnell. "I'm very sorry," she said in a thin little voice to the wall. "I'm sorry to have made you *hurry*..." The wall made no response, and neither did Gladdie McConnell, for a minute. When she finally spoke, her gravelly voice slipped over Orillia's shoulder and fell into the space between her and the wall. She said, "You looked in pretty bad shape."

"It takes me by surprise," Orillia told the wall. "And only the morphine..."

"I seen how the injections help," was all that Gladdie said.

So it went for a few days after the surgery on Orillia's feet. Sometimes she woke in the night and the ward was dark, the chair by her bed empty. Then, before she knew it, she heard herself shrieking. The nurses came running, starched white cotton flapping, and hung their moon faces and wide-winged caps into the darkness over her bed. Sometimes, because it was too soon to give her another injection, and they couldn't bear the sight of her back arching and her body straining against the straps, and it was worse to look into her beat-up face, they cried. When that happened, Orillia pretended she didn't see them. She didn't believe in tears. She didn't think you'd catch Gladdie McConnell crying.

It was a while before Orillia could take in the information that she'd been injured in a cyclone. Miss Harmon, the matron, told her the details when she stopped during her rounds for a chat. Three floors of the telephone exchange, where Orillia had worked, had crashed down, and Orillia had fallen through those floors, with the entire switchboard, to the basement. Her supervisor and three other girls fell, too, but Orillia was the only one who'd been hurt. The others had hardly been scratched. Miss Harmon said it was a miracle. Orillia had to agree, although during the discussion she couldn't help looking at the end of the bed, where her crushed feet, under covers, were protected by a wide wire cage.

"We had quite a time getting the name of someone to contact from you, Miss Cooper," Miss Harmon said, raising her eyebrows. "You told us there was no one."

"There isn't anyone," Orillia said.

"Miss McConnell isn't a relative?"

"Oh, no."

"A family friend?"

"A family friend? No. No, she's just – well, just a woman from Aquadell."

"Oh, yes. Where we sent the telegram. I hadn't heard of Aquadell."

"It's only a hamlet, west of here. You wouldn't have heard of it; it's just being settled. The railroad hasn't reached us yet. I lived there until I relocated to Regina."

"And Miss McConnell lived there?"

"Yes. She hires herself out, you know, to look after sick people, clean house, that sort of thing. I guess that's why I thought to mention her name."

"I see," Miss Harmon said. Her eyebrows peaked so high her cap twitched. "You were very glad to see her," she said.

Orillia asked if Gladdie would bring her some books from the house where she was rooming, and Gladdie had to tell her the house had been demolished. She asked more questions then, and Gladdie told her the facts. The cyclone had hit Regina the day before Dominion Day. Twenty-eight people in the city had been killed, and hundreds had been taken to hospital.

"It wasn't just out to get me, then," Orillia said.

"No," Gladdie said. "Nor anyone else. Wind's a mindless thing."

"It was only a little joke," Orillia said. "Good grief. The news of it must have spread. It would be in the papers, wouldn't it? I'd better send a telegram. I wonder if you would do it for me, please?"

Without a word, Gladdie McConnell opened her handbag and drew out a stubby pencil and a piece of stiff paper the size of a visiting card, and waited with the pencil poised.

"Just say: 'Cyclone puny. No, cyclone overblown. I'm fine. Love, Orillia.'"

Gladdie McConnell put her head to one side as if thinking that over, but when Orillia said nothing more, she licked the pencil lead, and wrote down her words. Orillia gave her the address in San Francisco, where her mother was on her honeymoon. "To Captain Samuel Hagan and Mrs. Cooper Hagan," Gladdie wrote, and Orillia thought about the message transferring, as if by magic, from Gladdie's hand to her mother's hand. She saw it happening, the card passing between the two hands, accomplishing its mission so her mother wouldn't have to think for a moment it was her duty to return.

Once the card with those words was safe in the handbag, Orillia squirmed. She didn't know a blush couldn't be seen through the bruises, and she turned her head away before she spoke again. "I was under anaesthetic; I didn't know what I was doing," she said. "When I gave them your name."

"That's all right," Gladdie said.

"You must think I'm odd." Nothing, in Orillia's thinking, could be worse than being considered odd. "Asking for you like that, out of the blue."

"You look better today," Gladdie said in her sensible way. "Your eyes are clearer."

Unexpected, happiness lifted them both to the ceiling.

a lie

Miss Harmon checked with Gladdie McConnell. "Miss Cooper's supervisor at the telephone exchange tells us she's twenty. Can you verify that?"

"Yes," Gladdie said. "She'll be twenty-one in November."

"And she has no family?"

Gladdie thought about Orillia lying strapped to her hospital bed. Where the poor girl wasn't bandaged, she was so battered and beaten you had to put your hand to your mouth to stop the words that might have described her. She thought about the bruised face that was so swollen the flesh under the eyes lay scalloped over the cheeks. And about the telegram she'd sent off to San Francisco.

"No next of kin?" Miss Harmon went on, trying to peer into Gladdie's reticence.

"No," Gladdie McConnell said, evading the sharp eyes and the eyebrows, and half-expecting the roof to fall on her head.

rescue

When the telegram from the hospital arrived in Aquadell, Gladdie McConnell had been minding Mabel James' toddlers and cleaning her hot kitchen over the general store while Mabel lay on the couch nearby with a wet cloth on her forehead. The telegram came to the post office special delivery, because it was a holiday, and Em Knelson brought it, climbed up the outside stairs and knocked loud enough to be heard over the din within. Mabel groaned, so Gladdie answered the door with the middle James infant riding her hip and howling from a slap he'd just received from his mother.

"This is for you," Em said, holding the telegram up and not smiling. Gladdie's heart nearly stopped.

"Close the door. Keep the heat out," Mabel whimpered.

Gladdie stepped out into the glare of a determined sun, and shut the door behind her. There was barely room for her and Em and the baby on the small wooden landing that overlooked the town's few dusty streets and its false-fronted rooftops. The little boy rubbed his slimy hot face into Gladdie's cheek and blubbered while she tried to focus on the words. The baby seemed to know he was getting even less attention than was his small due and arched his back as if to leap out of her arms. She handed the telegram back to Em and asked her to read it aloud. She jostled the baby, clucking at him until he laughed and bubbles came out of his nostrils.

"Orillia Cooper injured in cyclone. Please come." That was all the telegram said. They'd heard about the cyclone that had ripped through Regina the day before, but it was still a shock. After the first few seconds, Gladdie decided Orillia could not be seriously hurt, or they would have notified her mother.

"The hospital sent it," Em said. "She must have asked for you." Em Knelson was Gladdie's closest friend in Aquadell. She could make a statement that was more a question, and expect an answer.

"Her mother's away, that's why," Gladdie said immediately. "I'll go on the next train," she said, squinting into the sunlight behind Em's face.

Em said, "Mr. Pomeroy's returning to Rose Creek in half an hour. He can give you a ride to the station." Mr. Pomeroy had hitched his best mare to his two-seater democrat to deliver the telegram. Having read the message, he'd assumed Gladdie would be returning with him. It was a good thing the railroad had moved closer to Aquadell. She could get to Regina before the day was over.

She didn't have many possessions, and it didn't take long to fill her valise once she reached her room. That morning she'd laid out the clothes she'd expected to wear to the Dominion Day fair and supper in the late afternoon. She washed and changed into them, keeping her mind on getting out the door in time to catch the afternoon train from Rose Creek. People watched her as she strode the wooden sidewalk down Main Street with her bag. Bunting flapped overhead, red, white and blue, and at the empty end of the street, by the ball diamond, tables were already being set up to sell sandwiches and pies. Mr. Pomeroy had taken a cup of coffee at the café while he waited for Gladdie, so the whole town knew that Orillia Cooper had been injured in the cyclone and had asked for Gladdie McConnell to come to her aid. That was fine with Gladdie. It meant she didn't have to explain where she was going. It left her free to think the one thought that mattered to her: She asked for *me*.

logic

Doctor will be here soon," the nurse said, fussing, snapping the softened bedding into lozenge shape. She wasn't quite careful enough with Orillia's feet this time, so she got vomited on.

"All in a day's work," the nurse said when she'd swabbed down her arms and the bed was pristine again. "And here he comes." The patients in the next beds saw him too, and sat up to watch.

Every day he came to her bedside, the young, the good, the handsome Dr. Kitely. He was making a valiant attempt to save her feet, but they weren't saved yet. Infection was the enemy. Dr. Kitely and Orillia were collaborators in the fight against it, or so he let her believe. As soon as he'd seen her, unconscious, in emergency, he'd taken her to surgery. To get her in, he'd had to push aside two of Dr. Graham's cases. With his face set, not like himself at all, he'd yelled at the nurses for more light over the operating table and at the other doctors for more time. Then he'd painstakingly debrided the wounds, tweezing splinters of wood and granules of brick from the flesh, and excised the traumatized tissue. He'd aligned the small broken bones and fastened them with pins. He'd buried the ends of the cut nerves in muscle. All this he'd done with a textbook open beside him. He was young and hadn't come across these injuries before, and he didn't intend to take unnecessary chances. He'd left the wounds open, loosely packed with Vaseline gauze. The left foot looked clean, but the right had been partially degloved before being crushed and he'd had to leave it a bit of a mess. Dr. Graham, coming into the operating room to see how much longer he'd be, had pulled him aside and told him no matter what he did the girl would be dead within hours from shock and renal failure. Dr. Kitely had proven him wrong in that.

On the wards he was the very personification of elegance in a tweed suit, a light summer weight, a greyish tan with flecks of coffee brown, the colour of his eyes, and he was a self-effacer. He hid behind procedure and let the nurses bully him. It was his way, the way he'd found to keep impersonal, to disarm expectations so he was free to concentrate on his work. He was known to be committed to surgery as some men were to religion. He was also known to be married.

His nice brown eyes darted over Orillia's bed. His black hair slanted over his forehead and a muscle in his cheek twitched. He laid the back of his cool hand on her cheek.

"Any fever?" he asked in his reserved murmur.

"A little over normal," the nurse said.

"I have to look at your feet," he said. "I'll be as gentle as I can."

He was always gentle and he always looked pensive. Opening the bandages, he ritualistically unwound the gauze and stared at the results of his reconstruction of her feet. As usual, the nurse held a sheet up to block Orillia's view, but whose feet were they, anyway? One quick grab pulled it down, and there they were, at the end of the bed, with pins as ugly as nails piercing the flesh. He'd put them in to hold the bones together. "I look like a martyr," she said. But her feet were not the pale, limp feet that might have hung at the end of a cross. The left, like the bloated belly of a poisoned pup, gleamed with a plummish sheen; the right oozed blood like a badly butchered or half-gnawed hunk of raw beef. The pins sticking up looked cruel. She vomited again.

"She's been complaining of the pain, Doctor," the nurse said, after she'd dealt with the mess.

Orillia opened her mouth to protest. It was unfair. She might throw up, but she never complained.

"Is it worse?" Dr. Kitely asked.

"It seems to be bothering her more. Throbbing, she says."

Not once in her whole life had Orillia Cooper said the word "throbbing." She vowed on the spot she never would. Tears seared her eyes.

"There's some new swelling," he said quietly. His hand grazed hers. "That's why they hurt more."

"They're getting better," she said, finally speaking for herself.

Accidentally, he looked smack into her eyes and saw them brimming with frustration. He blinked, rapidly, and in that split second betrayed himself. Maybe he loved her for her broken feet, not for herself, but every woman in the ward could have told him he shouldn't have looked into her eyes.

It was up to the nurse, who'd been trained in the art, to rescue him, and she intervened with the first topic she could muster. "Her friend from Aquadell comes to visit every day, doesn't she, dear?" she said.

"Aquadell?" Dr. Kitely said absently. He patted the bedcovers before he left, as if to say a general benevolence was all he'd ever intended.

"Do you like Dr. Kitely?" Orillia asked Gladdie McConnell.

"Anybody would like Dr. Kitely," Gladdie said.

The other women in the ward got up a discussion on falling in love with your doctor. Apparently, for reasons the women enjoyed exploring (the intimate nature of the relationship, the helplessness of the woman patient, the authoritative status of the doctor), it was almost bound to happen.

Gladdie didn't believe things were bound to happen, and she knew it was more than a way of talking to say so. It was a dangerous slant of mind that could lead a person into error. She'd been tricked, herself, into following that easy logic. Coming to Regina, on Dominion Day, she'd fallen into its trap. She'd been so sure Orillia couldn't have been badly hurt. Whenever that thought had crossed her mind, she'd told herself the girl was young – as if being young would be a protection. And she'd let herself be happy. While the train took the flattest, quickest route over the prairie, barely stopping at the little towns strung along the rail line, she'd let herself believe fate had intervened to bring them together at last.

Only when the engine slowed, and they entered the city, did she see the enormity of supposing nature could ever act on her behalf. The other passengers jumped up and disfigured their noses against the windows while the devastation from the already famous cyclone rolled by. "Look," they said, and Gladdie looked – at buildings and houses smashed to the ground, at part of a train lying on its side in the yard like a prayer going nowhere, at a pair of men's striped pajama pants drooping from the leg of an upside-down table. "Imagine," they said, and she wondered if you could imagine what it was like, being in the midst of that terror. She didn't think you could create in your mind the fear you'd actually feel trying to round up children and find a safe place for them when there wasn't a safe place.

The engineer whistled the approach to the station, and people started gathering their belongings. A picture flashed into Gladdie's mind, of Orillia when she was six years old, back in Toronto. A little girl with big black eyes, stepping out from under a huge weeping willow tree on her great-uncle's front lawn – a tree like the largest live umbrella you could imagine, big enough to shelter her from anything – stepping out as if she'd known it was safe because Gladdie was standing at the gate, waiting for her.

But it was another child Gladdie was seeing outside the train window, a real child superimposed on the remembered, a real child right in front of her eyes. She had to give her head a shake, the conjunction of two times so threw her. And she knew the white-haired woman waiting on the platform was Hilda Wutherspoon – she'd sent her a telegram from Rose Creek, asking to stay at her house in Regina – but for a second she thought it wasn't her old friend, she must be mistaken, because Hilda had that skinny little girl in tow. They swept past the window, Hilda and the child in a blue polka-dot dress, then all Gladdie could see were the others waiting there and the piled-high luggage carts and the sign saying this was Regina. She tried to look past the windowpane, but it stopped her from seeing them until they popped up alongside again, Hilda hurrying the little girl, her eyes searching the cars for a sight of Gladdie, and strangely the child's eyes searching too.

She sat on while the other passengers pushed by, in a hurry to get out and begin their lives again. She had her valise beside her; she could easily have stood and gone with the crowd, but she needed to wait. The sight of the little girl with the searching eyes brought her back to her own childhood, as if the little girl had been set on the platform to remind Gladdie of everything that counted.

"A moment more won't matter to the child," she thought as she sat in the quickly emptying car. She shook her head again at that. Here was a little girl who didn't know her at all. Gladdie's coming or going could hardly matter to her. She'd only thought it because Mr. Riley had once said that exact thing about her in her early years at Mrs. Riley's house. "A moment more won't matter to the child."

Well, he knew better. Everything matters to a child.

"This is Susan. She's staying with me for a while," Hilda said. She put her hand on the skinny little girl's shoulder, and those worried brown eyes peeked up.

"Did you think I'd had a daughter and not told you?" Hilda went on, beaming down at Gladdie, for she was a good foot taller. It had been four years since they'd seen one another, almost long enough for Hilda to have had the child, and she was obviously pleased with the idea, so Gladdie said she had just for a second thought that. All of a sudden she felt like hugging Hilda, but they'd never done that sort of thing. They'd been good friends, they'd travelled west together, but they hadn't ever lived in the same house. They'd both worked for Mrs. Riley, but not at the same time. They'd only got to know one another when Gladdie had gone back for visits and had to give Hilda advice on how to handle the old dragon. How young they'd both been then, a dozen years ago.

Susan didn't make a peep, even when Gladdie knelt and said hello to her. She put her head down and shrugged her tiny shoulders.

"You haven't changed a bit," Hilda said when Gladdie stood up. "Your hair's as red as ever. And just look at those gingersnap eyes, snappy as ever. Peppery. Remember Mrs. Riley used to call you that?"

"You'll find, Hilda," Gladdie said, imitating Mrs. Riley, "that men will go out of their way to avoid a peppery woman."

"You'll notice *I* haven't changed, either," Hilda said, sounding a lot like the gloomy old dragon too. They were both good at it, having lived with Mrs. Riley all those young years. Hilda had changed quite a bit. She'd put on weight and her hair had all turned white, but her face looked as fresh as ever, and she had the same softness about her that she'd always had, that would make you excuse her if she couldn't be firm. Gladdie said she'd been thinking of Mr. Riley, strangely enough, as the train pulled in. "And just before I saw you and the little girl, I had a picture in my mind of Mrs. Riley preening."

"Oh yes, preening," Hilda said. "I can vouch for that." She wouldn't be able to vouch for anything Gladdie said about Mr. Riley. Mr. Riley was before her time.

"Why did she ask for you?" Hilda asked when Gladdie told her about the telegram the hospital had sent. In spite of a near fatal tendency to go limp in the face of bossiness, greediness, viciousness and even simple foolishness, Hilda could see to the heart of a situation before anyone else. And she couldn't be indirect to save her life. She was like that always, asking the most important question out blunt.

"Her mother's in San Francisco, on her honeymoon. And in Aquadell I go out to look after sick people," Gladdie told her. "As well as clean house."

"Of course," Hilda said in a way that showed she wouldn't pry if Gladdie didn't want to tell the whole truth. She pointed to the brooches on Gladdie's blouse, and said, "You always did like those maple leaf pins."

"I put them on this morning, in honour of the day," Gladdie said, which was true, but she added something that was not quite true: "And I was in too much of a hurry to catch the train to take them off." She hadn't really been in such a rush. She'd wanted to leave the pins on her shirt front.

"You told me you wore them for good luck. The last day I saw you, you were wearing some of them," Hilda said.

Then Gladdie felt she really could have given her old friend a hug.

"You'll be able to find the house when you're done at the hospital?" Hilda asked.

"I will."

"I'll take your valise."

"Are you sure?"

Hilda put out her hand and Gladdie passed over the valise. "Goodbye, Susan," she said, and the child ducked behind Hilda's long skirt.

whoever you are

To anyone who really knew Orillia Cooper, if there had been anyone who really knew her, it would have seemed an odd choice of occupation, that of telephone operator, a joke to think of her stringing lines across a switchboard, connecting people to one another. She wasn't a person anyone would have called communicative.

The job at the Regina exchange had come to her more by happenstance than option. There was nothing for her in Aquadell, just as her mother had said, so she'd come to the city to look for work. Being uneducated, she'd expected to apply at the few places where an inexperienced young woman might find employment: at shops, at the banks, the lawyers' offices, realtors. She went to the telephone company first, as her mother had advised, and got hired as an operator because it was June, and June, as everyone knew, was Wedding Month. Two of their girls were getting married and would have to quit, and Orillia had the qualifications. Her voice was clear and pleasing, she could enunciate and she knew how to talk like a lady.

As it turned out, it was an ideal occupation for her and respectable, though the pay was low. A great many rules had to be followed and that had been a plus. The rules limited the possibilities and thus the potential for error. She was happy in that narrow sector, in the row of girls on high chairs at the switchboard. The mechanical nature of the work and the need for accuracy made her feel efficient, and the limited authorized socializing among the girls kept her from being lonely. She liked the snips of people's lives she heard over the lines. She liked having a neutral voice and set phrases to say.

"Let nothing surprise or anger you," Miss Brown, the chief operator, said. "But don't put up with a curse. One curse," she said – with a light in her eyes – "and you hand them over to me." Orillia hoped for curses. She aspired to Miss Brown's job. She decided she shared Miss Brown's relish for human exasperation. She thought she could hear herself, as she got more confident, slowing her words just slightly as Miss Brown did when she answered calls, letting the pauses speak, driving the arrogant businessmen crazy.

Inside the telephone exchange, the girls and Miss Brown hadn't known what was happening when the storm to the south of the city screwed itself into a tornado the third Sunday Orillia worked at the switchboard, though all afternoon the air had been close, and the windows set high into the wall above them had let in a heavy, pearly light. Rain hit the panes about four-thirty, and the thunder and wind increased in volume.

Later, when the building shook and the walls responded with a noise like a person screeching, Orillia Cooper calmly said, "God."

"Quiet," Miss Brown said, out of habit, then the lights went out and the switchboard died. The girls were left with their arms in the air. It was just as if in the middle of semaphore they'd forgotten the message.

Gladdie hadn't been inside a hospital before; she'd only imagined what it would be like from listening to Pearl Fink, one of Mrs. Riley's lodgers, who'd worked at the Toronto General. Pearl had cleaned up after surgeries, and was always spouting the kind of details you couldn't help picturing in the violent hues of pus and blood. Orillia's ward was the whitest white. The walls, the metal bedsteads, the coverlets were white, and down the middle of the long room were small white tables covered with white, lace-edged cloths. The windows were curtained in white, too, and a misty, milky light came through them. And the nurses wore long white aprons and bright white winged caps. The whiteness was a form of bravery, and Gladdie took her cue from it and stayed dry-eyed, even when Orillia's pain was hard to bear. She didn't race from the room for help anymore, either. It wasn't good for Orillia to see panic; she needed reassurance. It would be weeks before they'd know if the operations were successful, if her feet would heal. Even among themselves the nurses, superstitious, didn't speak of amputation.

Gladdie didn't speak of it either, not even to Hilda. She told Hilda the good news, the small signs that might mean progress. In the same way, she didn't mention the path the cyclone had mowed through the city, though you couldn't help seeing the evidence. No matter which way she walked between the hospital and Hilda's house, she had to look at buildings with their roofs sheared off and their windows gone. She didn't want to gawk at others' misfortune, but she was curious, and a few times she walked down Lorne Street to see what was left of the telephone exchange, where Orillia had worked, and the library and the big Methodist church. She'd seen half a block flattened, the last house leaning against its neighbour as if in despair, and the whole second floor of another house that had detached and flown across the street to land in somebody else's front yard. She'd seen houses that had collapsed completely, and lay like piles of pick-up sticks. People still combed them, searching for their diaries and photograph albums. The big church had been gutted. The telephone exchange had just one wall left standing. But she exclaimed over the new legislative building, that had missed being razed, instead. "Like a Taj Mahal," she pronounced it, to Hilda's satisfaction. Hilda's house, which she'd bought only that year to run as a boarding house, was directly across from the legislative building, a few blocks into a new neighbourhood where streets had been laid out on the flattest land imaginable and where only a few houses, so far, had been built in an unorganized fashion. "Like summer teeth," Gladdie said. "Summer here, summer there." It was an old joke of Mr. Riley's.

They talked about the past often, joking like that, as they washed and dried the dishes or mopped and dusted, for Gladdie insisted on helping out. They chatted about the kinds of things that didn't matter to either of them but joined them.

"What's Aquadell like?" Hilda wanted to know.

"I'll tell you," Gladdie said. "When I first arrived there and saw the tents and shacks, and not a proper street or sidewalk anywhere,

I didn't realize what had brought people there, or what a privilege it would be to live in that new place they were building. It took me a while to see that from the start it was a hopeful place. You couldn't find a place more hopeful."

Hilda nodded, and cut them each another slice of her raisin pie, and poured them each another cup of tea, and thought about her own hopes, which centred on a little girl whose parents hadn't been found.

The girls from the telephone exchange came to visit – Harriet, Maud and Isabel – and all the women in the ward smiled at them, they looked so sweet in their matching navy skirts and the wide green cummerbunds that they must have cut from the same length of material, and their yellowy-ivory blouses, and their straw sailor hats. Unfortunately they didn't recognize Orillia. They had to search the beds twice, with a slower sweep the second time at the heads on the pillows, and when they saw her, they looked scared stiff.

Gladdie McConnell went stiff, too, at that expression on their faces. She got up as if to leave, or maybe to block their entrance.

"No, please stay," Orillia told her, so she sat down again.

"Come in, girls, come in," Orillia called, and beckoned them to her. She'd had her injection just before visiting hours and after a few minutes' nap she was riding high on it.

"Get yourselves some chairs," she said.

"Do you think we can?"

"Certainly. Everyone does it." So the girls dragged chairs from around the ward and brought them up to the bed. The other patients watched, expecting to be entertained.

"This is Miss McConnell," Orillia said.

The girls fussed with seating themselves and looked more at the gloves in their navy blue laps than at Orillia. "I'm so glad you've come," she told them. "I can't remember a thing about the cyclone. Everyone asks me about it, and all I can remember is you, Maud, saying the thunder could make us deaf if it went through our headsets." The girls discovered three spots on the wall to the left, the right and above Orillia's head. Then they looked at the bump in the covers at the end of the bed where her feet were enclosed in the wire cage.

"I really am all right now," Orillia said. "My feet are healing. But it's been embarrassing not being able to make a good story of it. People expect it. So – what in the world happened?"

They tried to tell her. They stumbled through the story they'd rehearsed dozens of times by then. Eventually they turned to Gladdie, who wasn't saying a word. "It's a miracle no one was killed," Harriet told her.

Isabel said, "We were so lucky."

"Yes, it was a real miracle," Maud said. "We came out of it with hardly a scratch." Her voice ended on a high note. The word "scratch" hung in the air while the whole ward dropped into a wary silence. Afterwards, on their way home, everyone knew, the girls would talk about it. "Wasn't it awful?" they'd say to one another. "When we said we were lucky, and her crippled."

Isabel finally ended the silence. "What will you do when you get out of the hospital?" she asked.

"Oh, I'll take the rest of the summer to recuperate," Orillia said. "I hope to get a room in a boarding house, with some kind people." She grinned at Gladdie McConnell. She lifted her chin with a look of triumph.

"Your life is changed forever," a young nurse said to Orillia one day, her voice full of awe.

"I suppose it's a test," Orillia said to Gladdie. "Though sometimes it feels like a punishment."

"It's just bad luck," Gladdie said.

"Unless some good comes of it?"

Orillia didn't say good had already come from it, in the form of Gladdie herself. It wasn't the kind of thing she could say to another person. But she felt it often. So when Gladdie left the ward and the girls from the exchange asked who she was – let them wonder, Orillia thought, let them guess to their hearts' content. The truth was there was nothing to tell. Gladdie McConnell wasn't a relative or even a family friend. They were only acquainted because they both lived in Aquadell and it was such a small town. In fact, as she told them, she hardly knew the woman.

a good name

Although she didn't ever foresee having the chance to do it, Gladdie sometimes imagined telling Orillia about Jessie Dole. She knew where she'd begin. With Jessie Dole's arrival at Mrs. Riley's door. It was logical to begin there, with the cold, wet night she'd appeared out of nowhere as if the storm had blown her to the door. Starting there would mean her own first vision of Jessie Dole would be Orillia's too. She knew how important that first sight would be, introducing Jessie Dole to her daughter. She went over and over that evening, reliving her own pleasure in young Mrs. Dole's arrival, seeing her again shining in the black night at Mrs. Riley's door, sheltering under her umbrella while the rain pounded down around her, splashing out of the overflowing gutters, running in dark rivers through the streets. The long beginning put off the sad ending; she knew that too.

"One October evening," she would say, "in a hard rain, a young woman of good family. . ." Yes, that's how she'd begin, and put Jessie Dole where she belonged, at the centre of Orillia's life. Gladdie thought everyone needed someone at the centre of her life.

Like she had Margaret. Never to be displaced. Never to leave in that way, though nearly forty years had passed since Margaret had really left her. A rocking chair was about all Gladdie remembered of the big house in Toronto where they'd lived, an old wooden rocking chair that sat in a corner of a little upstairs room, with a doily-covered cushion waiting on the seat. Where she'd been raised to the age of six – raised to be good, to work, to be Gladdie.

Margaret used the Proverbs of Solomon to teach Gladdie the alphabet and life. Certain verses, that is; not all were suitable. She'd sit in her rocker, resting at the end of a long day, with the little girl on her lap, and read aloud from her Bible. By lamplight she explained the letters and guided the small pointer finger over the type on the thin pages, and Gladdie heard and learned to repeat: "Heaviness in the heart of man maketh it stoop: but a good word maketh it glad." And Margaret told her, "That's why your name is Gladdie. It's a good word to make the heart glad."

"As an earring of gold," Margaret read (and Gladdie traced the letters), "so is a wise reprover upon an obedient ear." The wise reprover and the obedient ear came together in the rocking chair in the upstairs corner of the big house, and two lists, of things that were good and things that were bad, grew side by side in Gladdie's head. The best of the good things was wisdom, and just as importantly the worst of the bad was foolishness. A fool said everything he knew. A fool shut his eyes or even *winked.* Moving his lips, he brought evil to pass. And a naughty person had a *froward* mouth. Gladdie would not, for the world, be considered froward, but she knew what it was to wish to be perverse. A momentary thrill shot through her body to her fingertips whenever the possibility of doing exactly the opposite of what Margaret asked occurred to her. Of course she did everything Margaret's way, but that only tested her secret power of refusal and strengthened it, for Margaret was authority. The highest authority. Sitting in the rocking chair learning the shapes of the alphabet, the structure of words and their message-bearing abilities – but not yet understanding the influence of rhetoric – Gladdie didn't notice that Margaret and Solomon had merged.

"Keep my words," Solomon said. "Bind them upon thy fingers, write them upon the table of thine heart." And Gladdie did, with every one she traced, but to her, sitting on Margaret's knee, it was Margaret's words she was binding on her fingers and Margaret's words she was writing on her heart, and when Margaret read, "I was set up from everlasting, from the beginning, or ever the earth was," Gladdie only understood better the feeling she'd always had that Margaret was eternal.

"When there were no depths," Margaret said, "I was brought forth; when there were no fountains with water abounding, before the mountains, before the hills..." her voice rolled on, sonorous and grand with the music of the phrases. "Blessed is the man – or child," Margaret said, "that heareth me, watching daily at my gate, waiting at the port of my doors. For whoso findeth me findeth life. Gladdie, will you remember that?"

Gladdie, in her rough little voice, said she would.

When Gladdie was six, Margaret left her, and she was taken from the big house to another house to live with a family by the name of Tupper. Much later, when she was older, she understood it must have been death that had separated them, but at the time she was only told that Margaret had gone, and she'd believed she would return. One day, soon, Margaret would return to the big house to ask them what had become of the little girl who'd lived with her there. She'd talk to Beryl and Mr. Travis in the hallway. They were the two Gladdie remembered. She'd go no further into the house, she'd keep her hat and her coat on, she'd have no time to stop and visit. She'd be bound and determined to find Gladdie that day.

Three years Gladdie lived with the Tuppers, all the while abiding in the certainty that Margaret would show up someday at the door. Day after day, in the first months, before she learned the ways of that house, she held her breath whenever she heard a knock at the door, and listened hard. She was used to hearing things wrong. At that stage of her life her ears were prone to infections, and at times hardly a sound would come through. But a knock – she'd never miss that. She was always lying in wait for it. When anyone knocked at the Tuppers' door, wherever she was, whatever she was doing, her head went up, and if that knock chanced to sound as if it meant business, she'd stand up fast, prim as you please, and fold her hands together. She didn't know she was doing it, but she was mirroring how Margaret would have looked if she'd been standing there, on the other side of the door. This was a great joke to the Tuppers. A knock would bring them all to the hall to see her, Mr. and Mrs. Tupper, Uncle Tiny and Sarah Tupper, who Mr. Tupper said was his morganatic wife. In certain moods Uncle Tiny went round the side of the house, rapped on the front door like a policeman and scuttled to the window to see the fun.

The Tuppers took Gladdie in and fed and clothed her, but they never liked her. They said she put on airs. Too many times she mentioned Margaret and how Margaret liked things done. They said, "If the woman's so wonderful, why don't she come looking for you, why don't she show up at the door?" They said, "She's forgotten all about you." Even after Gladdie learned to shut up about Margaret, she never fit in with the Tuppers, and she knew she shouldn't. They were scornful and slothful and terribly, deliberately froward. They were glad at others' calamities. It was a good thing she had Margaret inside her as a way of fighting them. The problem was, the further inside her Margaret went, the harder it became to remember her. "Keep my words," Margaret had said, but there were few of them Gladdie could recall. She thought it was from never speaking of her anymore. She thought it followed if you never spoke of people you were liable to forget them. When she finally closed the door on the Tupper household, on a foggy, cold winter's day, her last day among them, she decided she'd not so much as mention them ever again.

She had to leave once she saw the truth. "Watch daily at my gate, wait at the port of my doors," Margaret had said, but the Tuppers' gate was not Margaret's gate, and their door was not her door. Gladdie could watch and wait a lifetime, and Margaret would not return to her there. She took note of the address, however, in case her bad luck was incremental. She wasn't a foolish child. She knew it was a house she should shed like a coat full of fleas, but she also understood she was still only a girl and she needed a bed to sleep in. In case she had to turn back, she knew enough to pay attention to street signs and look for landmarks, although at first she didn't see any. She stepped out into a wintry, anonymous world, block after block of narrow brick houses crammed close together, some with fat, flat roofs, some with sharp, pointed roofs that poked into the dull sky, all with only snippets of yards around them, not at all like the green, treed spaces she remembered around the big house where she'd lived with Margaret. She had no idea where that house could now be found. She saw no neighbourhood like it on her travels that day as she trudged out of one working-class area into another, past a whole street that had been razed to the mud, where men were constructing even narrower houses, attached to one another to save even more space. The half-finished houses, framed but without walls, made her envision families with lots of children gathered around dining-room tables. She knew they weren't real families, though she saw them in such vivid detail she knew how each head would feel if she patted it, passing by each chair to serve their potatoes. They weren't real children; they didn't live there and they never would. All they were good for was for making her feel a bad trick had been played on her. She felt better when she left that block behind and got her bearings by lining up her course with a high church spire with a cross on its top. Then she began marching on the sugary snow at the sidewalks' edges for the pleasure of hearing her boots crunch.

It wasn't the smartest escape in the world, setting out on a cold day in January, but at least Gladdie had taken the precaution of pulling a pair of Sarah Tupper's woolen hose over her own thinner stockings, and she'd exchanged her slippers for Sarah's sturdy button-up boots. The boots were boats on her feet, but at least they were higher, thus better for walking in snow. She'd also helped herself to Mrs. Tupper's brown and tan plaid shawl, and draped it about her from head to shins. Most prudently, she'd accepted contributions from the pockets of both Mr. T. and Uncle Tiny, while they were napping.

Gladdie was proud of the things Margaret had taught her. She was proud she knew better than the Tuppers what was right and wrong. But some of the things she did, like stealing, Margaret would never have pardoned. Gladdie had to pardon herself. The pardon for taking Sarah and Mrs. Tupper's things was not having warm clothes of her own; the pardon for taking the money was food. The Tuppers were always saying she ate as much as a horse, but it seemed to Gladdie she'd never had her fill. That day she left them, she hadn't walked more than an hour southward through the slushy streets, taking care to turn some corners yet watch her route and keep the big spiked church tower ahead of her, before she stepped into a dark little restaurant to find out what it would feel like to do just that.

At first, going into the restaurant, she couldn't see at all. Even though the snow was melting in the streets and was dirty more than white, and the sky was the soft grey of old Mrs. Tupper's gruel (with about the same viscosity), it was brighter by far outside than in. Gladdie had to wait until a counter and stools, made of the same molasses-coloured varnished wood as the walls, appeared out of the gloom. When bottles of syrups and ales on shelves behind the counter started gleaming at the corner of her eye, she stepped forward into the room. The figure of a woman seated on one of the stools at the counter separated from the shadows and was Margaret for an optimistic second or two before becoming a person Gladdie hadn't ever met.

A pale face and a pale apron walked toward her from the depths of the restaurant. The woman was talking, Gladdie could tell, but her words didn't make it through Gladdie's ears. She came right up to Gladdie, her eyes drawn to three frown lines over her nose. Gladdie had known on entering she'd have to answer questions, and she'd rehearsed what she'd say. "My Granny give me money for dinner." Mrs. Tupper had always wanted Gladdie to call her Granny.

"Let's see it," the waitress said, scowling into her face.

Gladdie gave her a look right back, as she did those days, not knowing or caring that it made her look bold because looking straight ahead was a virtue and kept a person from evil. The woman held out her hand for proof that she had money, so Gladdie hitched up the small purse she'd hung on a string around her neck and opened it for view, and the waitress slapped a menu on the counter. When she came back later and saw Gladdie still poring over the one page, she thought the child couldn't read. As Gladdie didn't pay her any mind, she poked her.

"I'm deciding," Gladdie said. She didn't hear what the woman said to that. Her hearing trouble came and went, her ears plugging up whenever infected. It came in handy now and then to be thought deaf, and she'd got into the habit of pretending she couldn't hear even when she could. The problem was that her right ear especially would sometimes hurt so fiercely she had to believe it was a punishment for fibbing. Until the boil in there burst, she'd go a while with a hum in her head, and only if a person shouted could she tell what they were saying, which had its drawbacks.

"I'll have the roast," she said.

"Aren't you the one?" the waitress said, speaking as much to the woman sitting two stools down as to Gladdie.

The woman down the counter got her meal before Gladdie did. From the moment that plate was set down, Gladdie had her eye on a wedge of fruit that was lying on the side as a garnish, that glistened like a light in the dark room. Gladdie took it to be a variety of orange and imagined how it would taste. They'd had oranges at the Tuppers' only at Christmas. Her mouth watered at the thought of the treat. The woman and Gladdie were the only diners in the restaurant, it being past most people's dinnertime and not yet suppertime. The woman smiled at her before she started to eat. Pretty soon a bowl of soup got plunked in front of Gladdie as the first part of her own meal. A slick of lukewarm fat covered the soup, and when she dipped her spoon in, oily bubbles ran out to the edges of the bowl. The grease coated her lips. She licked them. The soup was gone in no time, the cabbage flavour remaining at the back of her throat as the main reminder that she'd eaten. The slice of lemon – she did learn eventually what it was – stayed at the side of the woman's plate.

The soup wasn't hot, but it made Gladdie realize she'd forgotten to bring a hanky. Margaret thought a girl shouldn't be caught without a hanky, but they were hard to come by at the Tuppers'. It made Gladdie feel dirty, her nose running. It made her see and feel, on the palm of her hand, one of the nearly weightless, sharply pressed and folded, cool-feeling squares a girl should be able to pull from her sleeve. She pushed her sleeve up, and when no one was looking she wiped her nose along the plushy part of her forearm. She had long thin reddish hairs lying side by side over the flesh of her arm. She didn't believe they'd always been there. They seemed to have appeared one day and got worse daily since then. She pulled her sleeve back down so as not to have to see them or the evidence of having no hanky, the shiny track of dried snot left behind. In the restaurant the wall panelling and shelves and counter had been smeared with so many coats of varnish the surface of the wood was a half inch from touchable, and Gladdie had an awful picture of her arm gleaming with its own casing of gummy golden brown. Down the counter, on the plate, the lemon was still uneaten. She finally couldn't stand it anymore. She slid off her stool and went to the woman's side. The woman was wearing a lovely, long skirt of a shiny dark blue material that gave off different-coloured lights and a tight black jacket with the top buttons open so you could see her throat.

"Ain't you going to eat that?" Gladdie asked when the woman looked down at her. And just like that, the woman held the plate out. Gladdie took the lemon slice. It felt wet and cold. It looked the prettiest thing, glittering like liquid light, putting even the shimmery skirt to shame, and as soon as she had it in her fingers, the scent came to her. She brought it to her nose and smelled so hard she nearly inhaled the thing. She couldn't smell it enough, it smelled so good. The waitress came along while she was sniffing at it and said something sharp. Gladdie thought she meant she couldn't have the garnish off the woman's plate. She popped it into her mouth before the waitress could grab it from her, and sucked on it. Both the women laughed to see her face.

The nice woman who'd given her the lemon said, "It's sour." But Gladdie would have none of that. She shook her head. She pulled out the rind and stripped the fruit from it. When she swallowed, she shuddered, and that made the women laugh again.

"Oh, it's not sour, oh no," the waitress said.

The nice woman said, "Most people find a lemon sour."

Gladdie got back up on her stool. There was her plate, heaped with what just might be more than enough, and steaming. She grinned at the women. "It may be sour to you," she said. "But it's sweet to me."

Oh she was cocky. Pride she counted as her biggest sin. God knows where it came from, she often thought in later life, as she'd never done a thing to earn it except keep on living. And it wasn't the most useful quality. It went before destruction, pride, as a haughty spirit goes before a fall. But sometimes it helped her, as it certainly had in prompting her to leave the Tuppers and strike out on her own, feeling almost like a heroine, which was what the Tuppers called her when she got on her high horse with them.

When Gladdie grew older, if the Tuppers ever came into her mind, she used them as a hallway to Margaret. She made herself see them lined up either side along the walls, leering. But they could leer all they liked, Mr. and Mrs. Tupper and Uncle Tiny and Sarah. It didn't matter to Gladdie, because at the end of that hallway was the corner room in the big house where the empty rocking chair waited for Margaret, and where Gladdie left the Tuppers behind, just as she left them behind that winter day, intending to have them vanish from her memory so she could be her better self again.

Many times Gladdie tried, and failed, to bring Margaret stepping up into her mind like the others who came later would do whether or not she wanted them, but she was too young when Margaret left to be able to recall her clearly afterwards. She didn't have Margaret's face or form in her memory; all she had was what Margaret had left inside her, which besides the belief that there was a right way to be and a right way to do a host of things such as fold linen, was the feeling that Margaret loved her. It wasn't the knowledge that she loved her, nothing as definite as that. Anyway, a feeling is enough to go on.

infection

As there are different kinds as well as degrees of pain, so there are many sources and avenues of infection.

"It's euphoria, dear, not happiness," the nurse said. Two of them were bathing Orillia. They were middle-aged women, past thirty anyway, and both were overweight in the way of dumplings that puff over the edges of the pan. Their fat arms in wrinkled cotton – starched cuffs removed – swayed over top of their patient while they nattered to her and to one another as if they didn't notice their cloths were anywhere near her body. They barely touched her, since her skin was bruised and broken in about a thousand places. They worked in sections and never exposed more than a few inches of flesh at a time. For her part, Orillia tried to stay above the necessary pain and humiliation.

"It'll end when we take you off the morphine. The euphoria. Best to be prepared."

"We're only warning you. You'll fall harder if you're not ready for it."

"Never mind, dear."

She must have blushed, she thought, or looked away, and that was the wrong way to handle the bath. Direct, that was the way to be, and rise above it.

"Under the arms now."

"You should be used to this by now. It's only the first few times it seems strange to have someone wash you."

Their amused eyes met above her.

"We see all kinds, you know. No need to be shy."

"Nothing surprises us anymore."

"Tell her about Mrs. – you know, the one we had in here last month."

"Six breasts."

"What?"

"'I'm a bit of an oddity,' she said before we started. And you could say that again."

"You surely could. There they were, six of them, and they marched down her chest to her abdomen, like a dog's teats."

"They got smaller as they went down."

Orillia experienced a spectacular vision of the phenomenon of the six breasts as they might have occurred on her own chest and belly.

"Your friend from Aquadell's rather odd, isn't she dear? So fierce. Nobody's going to hurt you while she's around."

"Like a bulldog, isn't she? With that growly voice."

"You're lucky to have her, dear. Since you don't have your own mother."

"Is my face as black and blue as my arms and hands?" she asked.

Of course they said it wasn't.

She couldn't sleep. How could anyone sleep with all the heavy breathing that was going on in the ward. Not to mention snoring. Women – snoring. It was disgusting. You couldn't hear yourself think. Not that she wanted to think. How foolish she'd been, imagining people cared about her, inventing connections where none existed. Dr. Kitely. Gladdie McConnell. Just as her mother had often said, she put her own construction on everything, on everyone around her. She imagined things. Happiness, when it was nothing but euphoria.

It meant nothing that Gladdie was here in Regina. She'd come when asked for, that was all. Gladdie McConnell was only doing a job, just like Dr. Kitely was only doing a job. She hired out to look after sick people in Aquadell, after all. Orillia should be paying her! She hadn't once thought of that, but of course the woman would expect to be paid. She must be wondering what was wrong with Orillia, not even offering, assuming she'd give up her home and livelihood to sit by a hospital bed in Regina and not even have her expenses paid.

The nurses thought Gladdie McConnell was odd. They would think *she* was odd too, if they knew. What could be odder than to ask for a woman you hardly knew to come and look after you?

She wasn't going to worry about it anymore. She was going to think about something else. About being outside. She was going to lie perfectly still until she could pretend she was outside where there might be a chance of a cool breeze. And she could almost do it; she could almost feel the blessed coolness on her skin. But no, it wasn't any good. The others' breathing dragged her back to her bed, and now she felt even hotter. She wasn't strapped down any longer, but she couldn't get out of bed; she couldn't get away from the breathing. In and out, sigh and snore. It was like a nightmare ocean, ebbing and flowing in tune with the pain, pressing on her, crowding her mind.

The image of herself with six breasts came back to her unexpectedly. She saw them again, as she had when the nurses had told her about them. And as soon as she envisioned them they tingled, the length of her chest and belly. Magically, her hospital gown became one that opened down the front and tied at the top, and two nurses appeared beside her bed. Each pulled one end of the ribbon that undid the loosely knotted bow and the gown fell apart, revealing the breasts to the man standing in the shadows just past her bed. Dr. Kitely blinked when he saw them, in a most gratifying way, and climbed onto the bed. "Oh, Doctor," her own voice whispered huskily in her ear. After that she didn't have to move a voluntary muscle (luckily, since she wouldn't let herself do such a shameful thing). No, she didn't have to move a muscle, just let it wash over her, the doctor, his hands, the breasts – goodness!

Afterwards, she slept until morning, and all the next day she felt calmer than she had since she'd been injured. It was hours before she started to fuss about who Gladdie McConnell was and why she loved her.

a heroine

As every child knows, if you're going to make a new life, you must look for a job. Once she'd eaten, Gladdie set out again in high spirits and better weather. The sun had poked out of the fog while she was inside the restaurant, and she was soon too warm with Mrs. Tupper's shawl over her head. She couldn't pull it down, though, in case her hair would give her away. If Mr. Tupper came looking for her, he'd be able to pick her out from blocks away. Sweating, she hiked along the slushy sidewalks, keeping out of people's way and dodging the spray from the busy streets as best she could, and most of the time forgetting to look up and note the signs at intersections, as she'd told herself she should. Every once in a while she checked to the right to be sure the church spire that rose above the rest of the tall buildings was still there so she knew she wasn't walking in circles, and once or twice, feeling a hand about to clamp down on her shoulder, she looked behind her to be sure Mr. Tupper's black top hat and his froward face wasn't floating over the other heads. None of the other Tuppers went out much into the city. It would be Mr. T. who'd look for her and take her back if he caught her.

But she saw no one who looked like him, no one with a mustache big enough to hide buck teeth, dripping from fog and exertion, no one with what Sarah Tupper called the constipated look in his eyes. For more than an hour she continued in the direction she'd been heading, which was south, though she didn't know it was south, toward the bigger buildings of the downtown area and the wharfs and the lake, and with every step she felt freer. Before her, everything was larger than she'd ever seen before, and grander. Above the roofs of the huge buildings, smoke from the factories down at the lake puffed and billowed into the sky. But she was still walking through streets of smaller establishments, little privately owned businesses selling cigars or hats or stationery, and it was exactly where she wanted to be. She'd seen children as young as she was working in shops. She thought if someone hired her they'd have to feed her as well, and give her a place to sleep. She didn't know how ignorant she was of the ways of the world.

All at once the church with the big spire gleamed only a few blocks to the right, and she saw that it wasn't a cross on top, it was a weather vane. A higher class of pedestrians strolled the streets here, the sidewalks were paved, the windows glittered, and the walls were decorated with the stone heads of men and animals. Even the horses that pulled the carts and carriages along here stepped with a daintier air than their counterparts on lesser streets. As Gladdie hoped to find work in a fancy place, she was drawn to the establishments that advertised themselves in gold script on their windows. The further she went toward the big church, the more standoffish these shops looked, until she reached one of the fanciest of them all: "Monsieur Armand: Hair Goods, Hair Dressing, Perfumery." She put her face to the glass and peered into a long room. Women were sitting aloft in a row of elevated chairs, having their hair cut and crimped by men who flitted about them in white coats. The men all looked haughty, and the women, she could see, tried to match them, though it was obviously tricky to look haughty with your hair soaking wet. The stylists talked to one another through the big mirrors in front of the ladies. The ladies sat still and looked at themselves and the men. It was like a dance where only the men moved. The floor was messy with hair. The men trod in it and carted it about on their shoes. Gladdie found the door and stepped into a stink of scorch and pomade.

In the big room she looked right into one of the fancy mirrors and into the eyes of a lady with two chins who was getting her hair curled. It was a new way for Gladdie of looking at someone. She felt as if she'd caught the lady doing something she shouldn't have been doing. Not that it bothered the double-chinned lady. She didn't find Gladdie interesting, and turned her eyes back on herself. The hairdresser didn't look up from his curling iron. No one paid her any attention. She waited a bit out of shyness, then walked down the length of the room to the back, where two children were getting shampooed, lying side by side and squalling. The two older girls who were doing the shampooing stared at her. They were both stylish and had their hair done up in identical grown-up frizzes, but she stared back at them anyway.

"Here. What do you want?" said a man's voice behind her. It was the first hairdresser, from the front of the establishment. He had a natty moustache that curled up at the ends and a contentious forehead that wrinkled like wicker.

The only thing she could think of to say was, "Sir, would you like a girl?"

"Hah!" the hairdresser said with a bitter half laugh, and he bent over and whispered loud enough for the shampoo girls' amusement: "Would I?"

"I see you've a broom and dustpan back in the corner and a quantity of hair on your floor," Gladdie said. "I'd say you could use a girl."

"Oh?" he said. "You're offering to sweep the floor?"

"For pay, Sir."

"For pay, Sir?"

She kept her mouth shut as she'd learned was best when taunted.

"Do you see these girls here?" the hairdresser asked. The shampoo girls and the two children were all looking at her, their hands and heads dripping. "These girls do the sweeping," the hairdresser said, not unkindly. The big girls turned to one another and raised their eyebrows in a way you could tell they did a lot because it gave them pleasure.

"Thank you, Sir. I'll not trouble you further," Gladdie said.

When she'd got nearly out of the room, the man bounded up behind her. "Wait!" he called. "Girl!" And when he caught up to her he said, "Would you like your hair shampooed? Tell you what. We'll wash it and dress it on the house." His whole face crinkled as he looked down at her, trying at the last to be kind.

"No thank you, Sir," she said. "For I like to pay if I get something."

"Sure?"

She nodded, though it wasn't strictly true.

"Henri!" the woman in his chair called. "Have you completely forgotten me?" Henri and Gladdie turned together to see the lady's full face glaring at them in the mirror, trying to look imposing under curlers.

"Try Spain and Gowans, down the block," Henri said before he took himself and his comb to his client. Gladdie saw his left hand glide in a careless-seeming way into the crook of the woman's neck while he leaned forward and placed the comb on his table.

The sidewalks were busy when she stepped outside again, and people seemed to be hurrying more. The sun had disappeared behind the fuzzy grey sky. Her skin shrank from the damp cold air that crept under Mrs. Tupper's shawl, but what could she do but go on down the street to Spain and Gowans, whose door, in gold letters but plainly, said they were Merchant Tailors. After wiping her feet on the mat just inside, and sniffing a peculiar scent she imagined would be the smell of clean dust, she passed by stacks of rolled fabrics in masculine patterns and the colours of tabby cats. This time when she saw a gentleman she asked, "Sir, do you need any help?"

"No," he said. He was carrying a bolt of trousering and didn't stop.

On the next block, a fat gentleman in a tall gleaming black hat nearly knocked her over on his way out of a flower shop. They dodged one another. He had a wrapped bouquet in his arms and had to poke his red face out around it to see her. "Can't you tell you're in my way?" he said.

Third time lucky, she said to herself, and went in through the door he'd been blocking.

She saw the end of the room first, where the staff worked, cutting the stems off roses and chrysanthemums and making arrangements for weddings and funerals. Then she stopped, seeing the banks of blooms along the walls. It was so beautiful she was afraid to be turned down. She wanted to stay there forever. The scent of all the blossoms mingling was sweeter than anything she'd ever smelled. It was even better than the lemon, and got stronger as she stood there thinking how much she'd discovered already just by going out in the world on her own. The colours beat along the walls as if the petals were wings, and gave her the feeling she was rising or could rise off the floor if something inside her could let go, and the word "arabesque" formed in her mind. She had no idea what the word meant, but it made loops and opened a space that was already connected with flowers and light and a man it would be good to love.

Arabesque. She heard it in a man's voice and strained to remember. A man's jacket, she thought she remembered that, the fabric rough and soft at the same time against her cheek. But then she thought of Spain and Gowans and all the suiting she'd just seen. Maybe it was something she'd made up, that cheek against that chest. Or she'd once seen – that was more like it. She was probably remembering seeing a man lift a little girl into his arms – a father it would be, lifting up his daughter – but where this was she didn't know. It couldn't have been at the Tuppers'. Her hand went to her cheek. The skin there was colder than her fingers. She decided she'd made up the man and the girl to fit with the loveliness of the flower shop and with the charm of that word arabesque. But the word, she clung to it. It was a real thing. And who knew where it had come from? None of the Tuppers would have said it. Nor did it sound at all like the words that popped into her mind now and then from the proverbs in Margaret's Bible.

"Well?" said a woman from the back of the shop, and Gladdie had to put her thoughts away and forge her way through the hall of flowers to ask her question.

"Now look here," the woman said, laying down a sheaf of spicy smelling pinks. "You're only a little gal. You belong in school so's you get an education and don't become a burden on society. You don't look healthy. Not at all healthy. You'd best go on home and don't bother people about jobs. You'll not get anything in shops, child. You're too little. And too dirty to boot."

When she got to the door, the woman yelled, "It's getting dark. You go on home now."

The sky was darkening when she stepped outside again, and snow had begun to fall. The flaring gas street lamps lit swaths of dancing flakes, and behind them was the wonderful ivory-coloured church with its huge arched door and all its pieces pointing upward to the heavens. Gladdie turned westward and soon found herself in a maze of long streets, inside the shadows of tall buildings. Fewer people were out walking now; the shops and offices were closing. She tried to move noiselessly, even invisibly, along the sidewalks, and because the image of the little girl being lifted up in the man's arms had made her feel a lot more like a lost child than a heroine, without knowing what she was doing, she began to seek a man who looked fatherly, at least to her unaccustomed eyes.

euphoria

Orillia told Gladdie the nurses had said it was euphoria she was feeling, not happiness. Her black eyes flashed at Gladdie, then looked away.

"Euphoria's a good word," Gladdie said, though she'd never heard it before. "It has a nice lilt to it."

"It's like happiness," Orillia said. "But it's over-optimistic. It's the morphine that causes it. Really, I thought I was hiding how happy I am. They treat me better if they think of me as a tragedy."

Gladdie tried to see what Orillia was thinking behind the talk. "How happy I am," she said, in the midst of her affliction. But it's only the morphine, Gladdie remembered. "There's a word I've always liked," Gladdie said. "It's kind of like euphoria, the sound of it, I mean. Arabesque."

"Arabesque," Orillia said. "I like it too."

"I never did find out what it means."

"I'm afraid I don't know either. Maybe it means Arab-like, whatever that would mean."

"It has a cheerful sound," Gladdie said. Another quick look from those black eyes made her realize how determined her voice had sounded. Nothing was worse than false cheer, and now they were stranded. What else was there to say?

Then she remembered Susan. She could tell Orillia about the little girl, Hilda's temporary ward. "At Hilda Wutherspoon's house, where I'm staying, there's a little girl. I don't think I've mentioned her," Gladdie began.

Orillia's face calmed; her eyes took on a faraway look while Gladdie talked. She was thinking of her own childhood, maybe, as Gladdie often did when Susan came to mind.

"Of course she can come here when she gets out of the hospital," Hilda said when Gladdie asked. "We'll make room for her." Hilda's whole intention in buying the house in Regina had been to take in boarders, as much to keep herself busy as to supplement the income from her late husband's pension. Mr. Wutherspoon had died in the fall of 1911, and soon afterward she'd packed up her belongings and the few things of his that would remind her of him, and left Vancouver, where they'd lived next door to his two elderly sisters. His sisters had been dismayed by her decision; they'd expected Hilda would take care of them after Albert was gone. But Hilda had been trapped once in her life. She'd wasted her youth in a situation she hadn't known how to escape. She wasn't about to sink into another and lose the vigorous years of her middle age.

"Good for you," Gladdie said when Hilda told her. She knew what a rough life Hilda had led before Mr. Wutherspoon had carried her off.

"I did pity them," Hilda said, and her pale blue eyes turned luminous behind her spectacles.

"Of course you did, but they'd have taken advantage of you dreadfully."

"Yes, I'm afraid they were counting on it."

That made them both laugh. They were sitting in lamplight at Hilda's kitchen table. The house had electricity, but Hilda liked to light the old lamps sometimes for their peaceful glow. They both still enjoyed the soft light of the coal oil, the fluttering sound and even the bitter smell that wrapped around them while they sat together in the evenings after Susan had gone to bed.

"I still want you to come in with me," Hilda said. "My idea in moving here was to get you to help me run the place." They'd been through this before. Hilda had written to Gladdie to ask her to join her in Regina, but Gladdie hadn't wanted to leave Aquadell. Hilda didn't press the matter now. If Gladdie's young woman was going to recuperate here, that meant Gladdie would spend the summer. And who knew what would happen after that?

"But your bedrooms are all taken," Gladdie said when Hilda said she'd be delighted to have Orillia stay. Gladdie and Susan occupied the top floor, in what were really attic rooms, and on the second floor the two rooms besides Hilda's were taken by an elderly woman by the name of Lettie Pringle and a man named Mr. Best, who used his room as an office and paid half board. "Unless Susan's gone by then," Gladdie added. The child had got separated from her family somehow in the cyclone. While the police tried to find them, the Anglican church had made her a temporary ward and arranged with Hilda to look after her. Susan hadn't been hurt at all, but she hadn't spoken a word since they'd found her, not even to say her name. Hilda had given her the name Susan. She had to call her something.

"Oh, we can give Susan's room to Miss Cooper," Hilda said, happily ignoring Gladdie's comment. "Susan can sleep on the little couch in my room. It won't be any problem. She'll fit on that little couch just fine, she's so tiny. And I have lots of extra bedding."

Gladdie thought the third floor wasn't the best place for a young woman who couldn't walk, but she decided not to worry about it yet. A lot could change in the course of a few weeks.

"How are *you,* Susie Q?" Gladdie said to the little girl every morning, and got a shy smile in return. Privately she worried that Hilda was getting too attached to the child. It would be best if they found her parents soon, in Gladdie's opinion, though it was a pleasure to see Hilda's face light up when Susan took her hand or grinned at her.

at mrs. riley's house

Mr. Riley was a short, sandy-haired man with an inclined nose and a notable stoop. He would put his head sideways to look at you. Mrs. Riley was a big-headed, overblown woman who liked to wear wrappers around the house as she was never comfortable in stays. Mr. Riley let it be known they ran a boarding house together on the more respectable edge of a district in those days called Macaulaytown and later more notoriously known as the Ward, but it was Mrs. Riley's house. She'd bought it with her own money, and no one resided there long without knowing who ran it.

Mrs. Riley spoke her mind in anyone's presence, whether they were deaf or not, if they were, to her thinking, inferior to herself. Most people belonged in that category, and she didn't consider their feelings of much account. Mrs. Riley said they would have to notify the police. Although Gladdie was ragged and not clean and her hair was red, Mrs. Riley said her manners raised her above the level of the common riff-raff and made keeping her dicey. Mr. Riley said she'd only run away again if she was returned home.

"You'll be up for kidnapping. Is that what you want?" Mrs. Riley asked. But in the end she did nothing. She saw Gladdie was quick to learn and though Dorrie, their housemaid, got it into her head at first to dislike her, Gladdie made sure to make herself useful. She knew she was, as Mrs. Riley called her, "a mouth to feed," and in the circumstances didn't ask for wages.

"Let me tell you how I found this little gal," Mr. Riley said one evening, some time after she'd come to live with them. He had a friend there that night who'd escorted him home and sat for a bit with him and Mrs. Riley and Dorrie in the circle of lamplight at the kitchen table while Gladdie struggled to stay awake on the stool.

"It'll be his own invention," Mrs. Riley warned the friend.

"Not at all," Mr. Riley said and began. "It was early morning. The lodgers had left for work, and as I'd had the pleasure of a fried breakfast, I went out to the back porch – for social reasons, you understand. As soon as I opened the door Mrs. Riley shouted to me to close it, for God's sake."

"That part's true," Mrs. Riley said. "The cold was billowing in."

"And since I'd stepped out to the porch for social reasons," Mr. Riley said, at the same time turning to Gladdie to focus the others' attention on her, "I closed the door as I'd intended to do."

Gladdie perked up, seeing the story was going to centre on her.

Mr. Riley paused. "And there on the floor," he said, "was a little blue girl."

They all looked hard at Gladdie and imagined her blue. But why did he say on the floor she wondered, for that part was untrue.

Mr. Riley went on to tell them the sun was just rising on a hoary day; frost had patterned the porch window and rimed the wallboards. His slippers had slithered across the iced linoleum toward the child who was curled up on the floor in the old rag rug, and was either sleeping or dead. Mr. Riley said he held his breath while he looked on her; he knew he was in the presence of beauty. They all looked at her again, and Mr. Riley hastened to add that it was not the child who was beautiful but the indigo stain on her china doll cheeks and the gleaming arc of powdery snow that had blown in under the porch door and made her look as if she'd been rocked to sleep in a quarter moon. He told them he'd said "Jesus," as a person will, speaking to himself in a confidential way, knowing no one else is with him, but with the feeling someone might be right there, close enough to be nudged by his elbow – someone special like Jesus himself – if he looked quick.

Mr. Riley's account nearly put Gladdie into a trance. She sat there half forgetting it was supposed to be her and half loving that it was.

"Are you going to tell us Jesus Christ Almighty come to stand beside you in your back porch?" Mr. Riley's friend asked.

"Not Himself," Mr. Riley said. "But if you won't taunt me, I'll tell you the truth. A presence come to me there. And looked down on the little gal with me." He nodded at Gladdie and she nodded too; it really seemed it had happened.

"Mary, was it?"

"No, no."

"Joseph then?"

"It might have been Joseph, now you mention it. He had a practical aspect to him."

And how did that manifest itself? Mr. Riley's friend wanted to know. Mrs. Riley suggested it was in contrast to Mr. Riley. Mr. Riley didn't take offense. He was always agreeable to interruptions and even encouraged laughter at his own expense. While Mrs. Riley was giving her opinion, Mr. Riley grinned just a little as if he wanted to keep his amusement to himself, or maybe he was remembering something the presence had said. Mr. Riley appreciated a friend to talk to. He was a man who did not like to experience life alone.

"Just take a moment, now," he said, "to see Joseph and the frozen child, if you can, there in the back porch in the glimmery cold. And then you'll understand the feeling that stole over me, while I stood there, that I didn't want to go on to the next tick of the clock." It was the quiet, Mr. Riley said; the air held quietness. "A moment more won't matter to the child," he told himself; he couldn't have said why it mattered to him. He'd seen himself teetering, the girl far below him as if at the bottom of a deep well.

She could see it herself – Mr. Riley way above her, peering down with his head on one side.

"Of course she was only on the floor, a few feet from my face," Mr. Riley went on. "And if she wasn't dead she soon would be. I knew that from the waxy look of her. I bent over to investigate, concentrating, you know, on her condition and having forgotten entirely what I went out there for, and I accidentally farted, not very loudly – and the little gal's eyes popped open."

They all laughed and Mr. Riley's friend said, "Say, what happened to Joseph?"

In a slow voice as if he was puzzled, Mr. Riley said, "It was soon after that he faded."

They all laughed harder. Mr. Riley leaned back in his chair and his good friend slapped his knee.

"I carried her in and put her down on that stool where she's sitting now," Mr. Riley said. "Dorrie had set it by the stove. Then we all got talking and forgot about her and she fell off. Didn't you?" he said to Gladdie. But she'd put her head down and was tugging at the wrinkles in her stockings. "She don't hear well," Mr. Riley informed his friend.

"She can hear when it suits her," Mrs. Riley said.

"Look at her," Dorrie said. "She's blushing."

The truth of Gladdie's arrival at the boarding house was different from Mr. Riley's account and wasn't a story Mr. Riley would have told, at least to anyone of consequence. Later on he told it to Gladdie and Dorrie one night when he'd had more than a few and got sentimental. Gladdie supposed he'd changed it the way he had to overlay the real event that he was happy to forget. On the other hand, he did always like to dress life up and make it more attractive.

Another thing Mr. Riley liked was to relieve tensions that arose from living with Mrs. Riley by frequenting some of the popular bars in the city. As he was an amusing companion, good at telling stories and ready at all times for a joke, he was popular with a certain male crowd. That same evening Gladdie appeared on his doorstep, they'd been discussing bastards in the Bay Horse. Bastards had come up at the Bay Horse in a punchline, then the coarser of them had got round to wondering how many of that ilk they had amongst them, how many of their own young might be, unknown to them, walking through the streets and passing them without recognition. They'd bragged a bit about the possibilities. Mr. Riley wasn't superstitious, and when the conversation ended he gave it no more thought. He didn't know what he was in for that night when he came home, a little unsteady on his feet. He didn't know a little girl was out on her own in the city, looking for a man like him.

Gladdie had tried to walk through the downtown area as if she knew where she was going. She hadn't done a very good job of it. A collection of tattered newsboys had started following her, teasing her, and a woman with spectacles and tight lips had stopped her and asked what her business was and why she was on the street alone. Gladdie didn't want to start worrying, but the buildings had gotten taller, and it was hard to see any distance. The shops and offices had closed and the night was drawing down. Then she saw Mr. Riley, the most convivial and innocuous of a circle of men. When he took leave of them, she followed him home.

It was a good thing he whistled while he walked. In and out they went, through so many snaky alleys she was soon lost. Most of the houses were dark, though a little gleam from the snow, where it wasn't too trampled and dirty to reflect light, showed them to be small cottages with shared walls. Every passageway was narrowed with a tipsy conglomeration of barrels and sheds and outhouses, and Mr. Riley was always disappearing behind piles of unused lumber and unusable junk that looked ready to shift at any moment and crash down on a person's head. Only his whistling kept her hopeful he wouldn't vanish into some crooked doorway before she could turn the next corner after him.

At last they came to a few taller houses and she saw him go inside a fence that had two additions sticking out into the yard, like two long front teeth with a gap between them. A low fence ran down the middle of the gap. Mr. Riley took the path to the left and went into his biffy. Gladdie waited behind a shed till he came out, whistling more in a whisper now, and zigzagged up the skinny path between snowbanks to his door. Once he'd gone inside, she opened the gate and used his facility herself.

Stars had begun to poke through the night sky when she came out, and she stood for a minute looking at the house. It was a poorer house than the Tuppers,' but that didn't mean it was a worse house, and though not a single window nor roof nor chimney nor wall in the entire neighbourhood wasn't on a slant of some degree, the people inside could still be kind. She took the path to the back door and knocked her cold knuckles against it. She pulled the shawl off her head and looked back at the yard. There was nothing to see within the rickety fences but the path and the lumpy snow. The city beyond the back lanes had disappeared. Up above only a spatter of stars burned in a not quite dark sky. No one came to answer the door, so she opened it and entered a small, chilly porch, and knocked again.

Mr. Riley opened the inner door, tilted his head and wiped his ginger mustache down his face. "And who the devil are you?" he said. Then fear jumped all over his snub-nosed face.

Mr. Riley had a simple way to handle life. Before he ever understood what was the matter, he was prepared to take the blame. "Jesus," he said, in a private way, and he closed the door to the kitchen behind him. In the cold bluish light he examined Gladdie's hair and her freckled face. His mother had been a redhead.

Gladdie grinned up at him, unaware, of course, of the uppermost thought on his mind. She'd started out thinking she'd ask for work, but as soon as she said, "I'm looking for–" Mr. Riley put his hand over her mouth and stopped her. Then he wrapped her in his coat and hid her for the night in the pantry. Before he left her there in its stale-smelling fastness, he made her promise to make no sound and to eat only a few bites out of numerous foods in the larder, if she was lucky enough to find any, so no missing items would give them away. She didn't find much to eat, once she was alone in the dark little room, only withered carrots and some dry bread – and she nibbled no more than a mouse would have, at the edges of them – but she did sleep, in spite of being half frozen.

In the morning Mr. Riley came downstairs before anyone else, sneaking by Dorrie's bed in the kitchen. He wakened Gladdie, shushed her and bundled her out the door. Before sending her off, he slipped her a few coins – it was all he had – and said he couldn't for the life of him remember her and didn't think he knew her father.

She wasn't lying on the floor when he went out to the porch after breakfast. She was just standing there.

That first morning in the Rileys' kitchen, when Mrs. Riley let her come in and warm up by the stove, Gladdie thought of something that had never occurred to her before. It happened as soon as she saw Mrs. Riley drinking her tea at the table, and Dorrie taking orders – as soon as she saw the relationship between them. While she was watching them, trying to hear them, trying to figure them out, in the back of her mind she was wondering why, if Margaret was so proper, she had let a child call her by her first name.

Gladdie had no time to contemplate an answer because she'd walked right into a situation. Of course it was all Mr. Riley's fault. And it was lucky for her that the fuss had begun. It took attention from her, so that by the time Mrs. Riley had a clear chance, later, to wonder if it would cause them trouble to keep her, she'd already established herself as a helpful addition to the household.

Mr. Riley was always willing to take responsibility for anything he might have done if it would make life simpler and the sword of justice swifter. He called this facing things head-on, and it was a useful habit, but it was a shortcut and it blinded him to the dealings between others. In his mind, there was himself and Mrs. Riley, there was himself and Dorrie. He never did see that other link, between the women.

Mrs. Riley was the opposite. She was never at fault, in her mind, standing as she did above the rest. And even her connection to Mr. Riley was on sufferance. But Mr. Riley could overlook all he wanted and Mrs. Riley could deny all she wanted, their lives were inextricably intertwined with others', and at the very moment Mr. Riley had to confront Gladdie's determined little face in the back porch, Dorrie, their servant, had been confessing to Mrs. Riley what should have been obvious to all eyes. She was pregnant – for the second time. This misfortune was a nuisance in itself to everyone involved, but what Mrs. Riley couldn't stand, and she said so, was that the girl was a liar.

"You can boo-hoo on your own time," Mrs. Riley yelled at her, for she always said Dorrie would get out of work however she could. And there she was, standing in the middle of the kitchen, with her apron to her eyes and the most offensive part of her person protruding behind the bulging seams of her housedress, a big girl with bones you could lean on for a lifetime if you were, like Mrs. Riley, prone to take advantage. It was at this moment that Mr. Riley had opened the back door and returned to the kitchen in a plume of ice fog, saying "Georgina," in a light and lively manner, with a jerk of his head toward the porch.

Mrs. Riley pulled her kimono tighter over her fat breasts and allowed Mr. Riley to hoist her to her feet, then she followed him to the porch.

"Stop your snivelling," she said to Dorrie as she passed her. At the doorway, she said, "Oh Lord, some riff-raff."

"What'll we do with her?" Mr. Riley asked, stooping over the child to examine that face again. For her part, Gladdie wrung her hands and trembled without having to try too hard.

"Do with her?" Mrs. Riley snorted. "What do you think? We're Christians, ain't we? Bring her in and Dorrie will give her tea to thaw her."

"Ah, you're a big-hearted woman," Mr. Riley said, watching her with admiration, for he did think her grand. And she returned to her place at the table and absentmindedly and comprehensively scratched her left breast while she sipped her tea, reinforced in her own high opinion of herself.

Mr. Riley took Gladdie's hand and led her into the kitchen. Dorrie put her apron down and fetched a stool while her red-rimmed eyes leaked their tears, unchecked, down her broad cheeks.

"Set that stool by the stove," Mrs. Riley said. Dorrie was already putting the thing about as close to the range as a person could sit without scorching, but Mrs. Riley liked to give orders even if they weren't needed, to keep her number one spot in the household. Mr. Riley set Gladdie down, whereupon she felt faint all of a sudden and swayed unsteadily. He propped her up momentarily, holding her not quite by the scruff of the neck but by a fistful of serge at one shoulder. "Here," he said to Dorrie, indicating the little girl was her responsibility.

"Oooh," Dorrie said as she took over. "She's cold as sin. And dirtier."

"You'd know about that," Mrs. Riley said.

"See how she picks on me," Dorrie said to Mr. Riley. She turned from Gladdie to appeal to him, and that's when, out of drowsiness and frozenness, for she'd waited in the back porch a long time, Gladdie fell off the stool to the floor. She curled up there on the rug, all unnoticed by the adults because Mrs. Riley stood up to her full height and took on the look of a giant. What a fury she was in. How dare Dorrie petition Mr. Riley? In Georgina Riley's kitchen. She pointed to the door and roared: "Out!"

Mr. Riley, you could see, truly appreciated the performance. His eyes lit up. He'd often say Mrs. Riley was no common woman. He hadn't any idea what the cause of her anger was. It almost seemed as if she could bear only three of the human race, herself included, in the kitchen at any one time, and with the little girl coming in, poor Dorrie must go. He was not ignorant of Dorrie's condition, but he thought his wife hadn't seen it. He'd been telling himself the girl only looked like she'd put on weight. He was ready to admit any day of the week that hope often did him in.

"Wipe that silly grin off your face," Mrs. Riley told him. She advanced on Dorrie and whispered: "Do you think I don't mean it?"

"I've nowhere to go, Mrs. Riley," the girl said.

"Pitiful. You're pitiful."

Mr. Riley's intestines squeaked. "And you," Mrs. Riley said. "Well. You're the most pitiful thing in God's green earth!" And she walloped him a good one, right in the eye. "Well," she said again. She'd startled herself, as she always did when she turned to violence, but she didn't want anyone to know it, so she swept a cool look over the others and sailed out of the room. Mr. Riley hopped up and down a few times and spun around the kitchen, holding both hands to his eye and grunting with pain until the fear that she'd done irreversible damage sent him dashing off to check in the hall mirror. Dorrie sat down on the recently vacated stool, pulled her apron again to her face, and sobbed so hard into it that Gladdie, lying at her feet, felt the floor shake as much as it had with Mr. Riley's hopping.

Mrs. Riley was trying to teach Gladdie to shine the lodgers' shoes, to see if she'd be useful enough to rescue from a life of deprivation. "Spit! Spit!" Mrs. Riley was yelling, while she waved a boot in the air.

"She don't understand English," she said to Dorrie in disgust. "What's her name again?"

"Gladdie."

"Gladdie, you look at me now."

The fire in the range had been allowed to die down, it being midmorning. Gladdie was sitting hunched on the stool again, in Mrs. Riley's cold kitchen. She was shivering and whimpering with chilblains, but at least she knew she wasn't suffering alone. Mr. Riley's eye socket had erupted in several iridescent hues, and Dorrie had a headache, she said, and sat by Gladdie, snivelling over a basin of unpeeled potatoes. Mrs. Riley, however, had reappeared on the main floor looking magnificent in an emerald green silk dress she'd confiscated from a long-gone tenant, and on entering the kitchen she exhibited the outward effects of an inner glow.

"Does she not speak the language?" she inquired.

"She can't hear, I think," Dorrie said.

Mrs. Riley and Dorrie together contemplated the flat, freckled face and the matted red hair. Gladdie's nose was running something awful, and not being able to stand it any longer she did a quick swipe along her arm when they turned away to sigh to one another. Then Mrs. Riley took her sharply by the chin and pulled her face up toward her own. Peering into Gladdie's eyes and forming the word with care, she yelled: "Spit!" She did shove the boot in front of Gladdie's face pretty quickly and Gladdie did aim for it, but it was unfortunate for them both that she was eager to please. And even more unfortunate that Dorrie laughed. Mr. Riley, luckily for him, was absent. He'd gone to see somebody about something, his usual employment. Spittle dripped from Mrs. Riley's hand and a spot stained her satiny bosom. For a moment she stared at her hand, then the boot hit the wall. Mrs. Riley's language, when she was aroused, was hot enough to scald any but a child frozen near to death *and* mostly deaf, and it was evidence of Gladdie's true state that she still shivered after Mrs. Riley's poise had finally returned and Dorrie had retrieved the boot.

Settled again, but more suspicious, Mrs. Riley resumed her questioning. "How old is she?"

"She says she's nine," Dorrie said.

"Nine?"

"So she told me."

"You're small for nine," Mrs. Riley said to Gladdie. "What's her last name?"

"She says she hasn't got one."

"What do you mean, hasn't got one?"

"It's what she said."

"Come now." Mrs. Riley handed Dorrie a potato, as she'd stopped peeling to talk. She turned to Gladdie. "What's your name?" she shouted.

It was a thing Gladdie didn't like, giving her name. Her throat closed up when she tried to speak. It didn't want to let go of that information. But with Mrs. Riley glaring at her, she had to give it. "Gladdie," she said, her voice rough.

"I know that. Last name, if you please."

"I have none," she said.

"Yes you do," Mrs. Riley shouted. "Everyone has a last name. You were born with one. Didn't you have a mother?"

After a bit Gladdie nodded, as she knew she must have had one.

"I don't suppose you were encumbered by a father?"

Gladdie ignored that question, and Mrs. Riley didn't wait for an answer. "Your mother'd have a name," she said.

Gladdie gave no opinion on that, and Mrs. Riley was tiring of the topic and the strain of speaking at a high volume. "You have to have two names in this house," she said, though it was obvious to each of them this wasn't a long-term rule. "We'll give you Dorrie's," Mrs. Riley said, perking up at the inspiration, "and you can be sisters."

Sisters. Gladdie could hardly believe the word had been said. She felt her heart leap painfully in her chest at the idea of a bond between herself and the big girl. She was sure Dorrie had it in her to be loyal if you could get her on your side.

Mrs. Riley smiled, herself, at the concept of sisterhood. She could picture the two girls side by side, happily scrubbing her floors. But Dorrie scowled at her potato, stabbed it with her knife and popped an eye up into the air. That made a question pop into Gladdie's mind. "What is it?" she asked Mrs. Riley.

"What is what?"

"My name."

"McConnell."

"What?"

"You tell her," Mrs. Riley said to Dorrie.

"McConnell," Dorrie said in a heavy way that Mrs. Riley didn't care enough to heed. It was nothing to her, after all. It was just one more resignation on Dorrie's part. Gladdie had taken her name. She now had nothing in this house, and therefore in the whole world that was entirely her own.

Mrs. Riley rose from her chair. She had better things to do than chat with servants. She was pleased to have two now, though she warned Gladdie from the start that she'd remain wary of her if she showed too much spirit for the benefit of the household and for her own good.

Upon Mrs. Riley's leaving, Dorrie put the knife into the basin with the potatoes and asked Gladdie what she was grinning about. Gladdie was rocking back and forth on the stool with her arms hugged around herself. She couldn't say. Knowing Dorrie's distress, how could she explain how happy she was to be there, sitting beside her and sharing her name?

acquaintance

Hilda was peeling potatoes at the sink when Gladdie walked into the kitchen after a long day at the hospital.

"One lodger, one spud," Gladdie said in perfect imitation of Mrs. Riley.

"The more they get, the more they expect," Hilda said.

It was good they had Mrs. Riley to laugh about. It was good they could laugh about those days in that low house, because they couldn't agree on everything. Hilda had a lot more backbone than she'd had in the old days. Marriage had given her confidence, Gladdie figured, and maybe it had made her see her own worth. Hilda never pried, but she had her opinions. She thought Gladdie should write to Florence Cooper, even if Orillia didn't want her mother informed that she'd been hurt.

"I think it's wrong not to let her know," Hilda said. "Her mother would want to come and see that she's all right, if she knew. And Orillia needs her, no matter what she says. A mother's different from anyone else, more of a comfort than anyone else can be."

As Gladdie had no personal experience of mothers, she let Hilda have the last word. But she didn't write to Florence Cooper. She just tried not to be pleased that Orillia had asked for her instead of her mother. Of course, she thought, you'd have to squeeze Florence Cooper hard to get any sympathy out of her. Even if she was your mother you wouldn't think of calling on her. That was something she couldn't tell Hilda, just one of the things.

She couldn't say she'd lied to the matron, either, backing up Orillia's claim that she had no family to contact. She knew what Hilda would think of that.

"I've had a letter from Percy Gowan," Gladdie said as soon as she walked into the ward, and she grinned from ear to ear. She couldn't help it. If Percy Gowan wasn't the most eligible bachelor in all of Saskatchewan in the year of 1912, she didn't know who was. She started to pass the letter to Orillia, but Orillia waved it away.

"He wants to come and see you."

"I don't want to see Percy Gowan. I don't want to see anyone from Aquadell," Orillia said, lowering her voice so the other women in the ward couldn't hear.

"You want me to tell him that?"

"Why not? He doesn't need to take it personally."

It was Gladdie's opinion that he'd take it very personally, as any young man would, but she didn't say so. Sometimes she didn't understand Orillia. She said things she didn't mean.

"I hardly know him," Orillia said after a minute, in a nicer voice. "You know him better than I do." Gladdie had cleaned for Percy Gowan, as much as you could clean a one-room bachelor shack with a sod roof, and she'd baked for him twice a month and done his washing.

"He's just a big kid, a big, blue-eyed kid, for all his twenty-some years," Gladdie said, shaking her head and smiling, as people tended to do when talking about Percy Gowan. Percy's ranch was closer to Rose Creek than to Aquadell, but he did his shopping in Aquadell. He was a friendly sort and everybody liked him. He was a runner, which was a thing unknown in Robin Hood District before he'd arrived. You'd see him often loping down the roads in his running gear. They said he won races in big cities. He was always going off to meets, sometimes neglecting his farm, they said, to run. People were indulgent, talking about him. He made them shake their heads, but they liked him for it.

Gladdie unfolded his letter and laid it on her lap and smoothed it out. With her finger under the words, she read it silently again, to herself. Now and then she smiled.

"I know you're fond of Percy," Orillia said after a minute. "But you take an interest in *everyone,* don't you?" She shut her eyes and turned her head away.

Gladdie hardly had time to get over her surprise before Orillia propped herself up on an elbow and said to the wall, "Gladdie, I will pay you, as soon as I can make arrangements with my bank – for your time and everything you're doing for me."

"We can talk about that later," Gladdie said. It was her turn to look away.

"What's Miss Cooper like?" Hilda asked one evening when they were sitting in lamplight while the house settled into darkness around them.

Orillia was so much like Jessie Dole, in looks at least, that Gladdie's happiness got caught in her throat, but she couldn't tell Hilda that. Not when Orillia didn't know the truth. Little Fighter was what Gladdie still called the girl, in her mind, remembering how fierce her baby eyes had been. But she looked like Jessie Dole most when she was content, when her eyes were gentler and looked out with trust. Not that Gladdie had often seen poor Jessie Dole content – far from it. But Gladdie and the lodgers had always been hoping to see it. She'd had that effect on them. Her enjoyment of a single second had been their reward.

"Smart as a whip," Gladdie said in answer to Hilda's question. "You never know what she'll say next. But at the same time she's ladylike."

"Ladylike," Hilda said.

"She could walk into Shaunessey's and no one would blink." Shaunessey's was the ladies' hotel where Gladdie had worked after she'd left Mrs. Riley's.

Hilda waited for more.

"She has a winning manner," Gladdie said, although she knew Orillia wasn't as winning as Jessie Dole had been. She had too many of Florence Cooper's ways and formality to charm others as soon as they set eyes on her. She was a complicated girl, as you'd expect if you thought of her growing up between those two women, pulled one way by whatever she'd inherited from one mother and in the opposite direction by what she'd learned from the other.

"She's a complicated girl," she told Hilda. "Of good family." Talking about it made her remember it was the truth, in spite of the Coopers being unsatisfactory in so many ways.

"Gently raised," Hilda said, almost in a whisper.

"Sheltered," Gladdie said, and her gravelly voice dropped too.

heaviness in the heart

Dorrie, poor girl, was dead tired the morning Gladdie showed up and took her name. With the whole day and a heap of potatoes in front of her, she laid her head down on the kitchen table and fell asleep. Sitting right beside her, Gladdie put her hands on the table and felt it vibrate with the big girl's breathing. The tremor passing through the wood from Dorrie to her reminded Gladdie of what Mrs. Riley had said: that they were sisters now, and the far-flung hopefulness that always came with a tearing feeling in her chest rose in her again.

Gladdie was tired too, and in spite of the hope inside her, she was still cold from her long wait in the back porch that morning, and she leaned her head just a little onto Dorrie's shoulder. Then she pressed closer, to warm against her, and feel her humanness. And here was where, in thinking one house much like another, and the people in it likely to be somewhat the same, Gladdie newly named McConnell made a big mistake. It was partly feeling sorry for Dorrie but more feeling anxious for herself that provoked the mistake. She wanted to make friends, and she knew what Sarah Tupper liked when she got het up. She thought she knew altogether what pleased people. She had no idea what effect she'd have on Dorrie, that Dorrie would look on what she did with horror. The poor girl looked so burdened, even in her sleep. Gladdie thought she could ease that, soothe her. She thought she knew how.

Afterwards she couldn't remember clearly what it was she did. She tried to put it away out of her mind as soon as it happened. Dorrie scared the bejesus out of her, that's why. But she knew it was touching. The way Sarah Tupper had taught her to touch.

What a gasp Dorrie gave out. There was a minute she looked about as surprised as Gladdie had ever seen anyone, then she lashed out, her whole arm and the weight of her full body flung against Gladdie. Then she bolted up and threw herself onto her cot in the corner of the kitchen, screeching and hollering as if she'd bring the house down. Gladdie tried to make her stop. She begged her to be quiet.

"Get out," Dorrie hissed, so Gladdie snuck into the dining room and sank into a corner by the cold fireplace where nobody would see her if they were looking for her, and nobody was. Only Mrs. Riley was home, and all that racket didn't even wake her up. She'd retreated to her bed after the strain of dealing with people, and you could hear her snoring down through the house.

That evening after they'd all had their supper and Gladdie'd had hers, sitting beside Dorrie in the kitchen with Dorrie not speaking to her, and she'd dried the dishes while Dorrie washed, not speaking to her, and the lodgers had drifted upstairs to their rooms, and Mr. Riley had divested himself of his day clothes and crawled into bed in his long underwear, all the while relating his conquest of the Bay Horse bar crowd with some long-winded blasphemous story, Mrs. Riley descended one final time from her bedroom to inspect the kitchen in case any more labour could be demanded of the girls before lights out. She found Gladdie lying under Mr. Riley's coat on the rug in front of the range. It was the best she could manage as no one had given her a bed.

"Can't she sleep with you?" Mrs. Riley said to Dorrie.

"No," Dorrie said. Her cot, in the far corner of the kitchen, was narrow enough for herself, especially now in her expanding condition, but she didn't use that for an excuse. She merely said no so definitely Mrs. Riley was taken aback and said she wouldn't have thought Dorrie had it in her to be so hard.

"You've not an ounce of charity," Mrs. Riley said, nodding in satisfaction. "You'd put a dog there."

Dorrie turned away and looked at the wall. Mrs. Riley shrugged and went to bed.

"I forgot my book," Mr. Shamata told Gladdie. He was sitting on the edge of his bed in the wan beginnings of morning light, looking at his remembrance of the person he'd been the night before. "I knew I'd left it behind in the parlour. I climbed into bed without even thinking about it till my head hit the pillow. It was freezing in the room. I burrowed down and tried not to worry. I told myself everyone knows it's my book and no one else wants it, nobody else in the house ever opens a book, as far as I can tell. Also I told myself I've read it so many times I didn't need the real thing beside me." But that was untrue. He had needed it by him. Mr. Shamata had closed his eyes and waited; he'd thought maybe he was tired enough to fall asleep on his own. A man of sixty-odd, after all, needed his rest, and nature ought to provide it. He hadn't felt himself opening his eyes, but before long he saw that they were open, and there before them was the inky room with only a gleam of light at the edges of the tiny, curtained window making him imagine a moon over the snow.

His boots had been taken for cleaning that morning and had not been returned. By night they should have sat side by side with their tongues hanging out near his bed, but even if they had he wouldn't have put them on. In sock feet he'd be quieter, descending the stairs a step at a time, trying to avoid the squeaks that might awaken others and alert them to his need. He'd left his book on the sofa. He could hardly think how that had come about, but he supposed he'd been flustered by Mrs. Riley as he'd risen to quit the parlour. She'd often say a thing to set him off. She knew how to goad him with mysterious phrases as if she'd ever been educated. Quotes from books no one had heard of that maybe didn't exist. Or worse, from Gulliver. She had no respect for private property or for any sort of privacy at all. The cover of the book, so familiar to his fingers, and the slight weight of it, calmed him. What did Mrs. Riley matter then? It was his last book. He'd pawned the others but this one – Gulliver – he'd never give it up. This book held a world of thought, and when he had it in his hands Mr. Shamata carried that world, too. He no longer read the story; he could look at the illustrations and resurrect the experience of living it.

Dorrie had closed the door to the front hall in an attempt to keep the scant radiation from the stove within the walls of the kitchen, so Gladdie didn't know someone was on the stairs, then in the parlour. It was coincidental that she crawled out from under Mr. Riley's coat, which had taken on so much of the general climate of the room that she hardly felt its lack, at the same time that Mr. Shamata reclaimed his novel. Quietly, so as not to waken Dorrie, she stepped over to the door. She opened it an inch and spied the dark shape of the elderly man as he crossed the hall and took his book upstairs. When he reached the landing, she trailed him, imagining herself his slow shadow so her footfalls would make no sound. She followed him up the two flights to the attic, where the low ceiling peaked over two small doors. Mr. Shamata's door creaked as he went into his room, and creaked again when he closed it. She waited in the darkness between the two rooms and listened to him settle into his bed. She waited and waited until the cold got too keen to bear, then slowly she turned his doorknob and, with two high squeaks of the hinges that didn't disturb his breathing at all, she opened and closed his door. She dithered there, on that side of the wall, but not long. Soon she was in his bed, in the warm space between him and his book.

In the morning she listened while he tried to explain it to himself.

Winter mornings the kitchen clock struck six in blackness and Dorrie woke. She kept her stockings on all night and an old pair of men's woolen socks over them, which was as well since she had no slippers to put on. She'd swing her feet free of the bedding and haul herself and her growing belly out of her cot as quickly as she could to poke the fire in the stove and add wood. Then she'd crawl back into bed until the edge wore off the cold in the room and she could put the kettle on and dress for the day. The realization came to her in small slow stages, that morning, that Gladdie wasn't where she'd left her. Mr. Riley's coat lay huddled on the floor by itself. Dorrie picked it up and hung it by the back door, then she lit the kitchen lamp. Soon the kettle's bubbling drowned out the first sounds of the house coming to morning life, and Dorrie made the big pot of tea and started the porridge. The night before, as usual, she'd set the dining room table for the lodgers. Now she took the teapot in and plunked it down and lit the inadequate coal in the fireplace. When she came back to the kitchen for milk and sugar, Gladdie was seated at the table.

"You're in Mrs. Riley's chair," Dorrie said.

Gladdie gave her a puzzled look, still letting on she couldn't hear. Mrs. Riley was on her way downstairs. You could hear the stair treads protesting and her sighing after each step. "Damnation," Dorrie muttered, and she picked Gladdie up and set her on the stool.

Mrs. Riley said, "Oh look at the princess."

Dorrie sighed.

Gladdie grinned.

"Tea?" Mrs. Riley inquired, and Dorrie brought her the special tea made in her own pot to her precise standards.

"Boots," Mrs. Riley said to Gladdie. And when she didn't respond, Mrs. Riley said: "Dorrie!" And Dorrie screamed: "Boots! Boots!" And Gladdie went and got them.

"Do you think Mr. Shamata wants to go out barefoot into a morning like this?" Mrs. Riley asked her. Dorrie swung the porridge pot off the range and took it and the trivet to the dining room, where the lodgers were beginning to gather to break the night's fast with the gruel.

Mr. Shamata didn't come down to breakfast. Mr. Shamata stayed in bed and let it be known he'd been stricken with something dreadful that was going to confine him to his room for days. Even to Gladdie he'd said he felt sick.

Although she could hear if people spoke up or right at her, the old hum was droning in Gladdie's head that morning, and along with the hum was a thick feeling on the inside of her ears. It wasn't too bad. She was used to it. In any case it was better than the pain that stabbed sometimes for days without end, in the right ear especially, crackling and jabbing until she'd hear a great snap and blood and pus would pour out. While she scraped and polished the lodgers' boots, and the hum in her head kept out the others who crossed the kitchen linoleum on one errand or another, she went into her own mind, where the woman in the restaurant said, "Are you sure you like lemons? They're very sour, you know." She had a kind look on her face. "I do like lemons," Gladdie said, and the woman gave her the slice. She sucked it and grinned, not showing how sour it was, and the woman laughed. "You're an unusual girl, aren't you?" she said.

Dorrie clucked her tongue as she swept around Gladdie, letting the broom clatter against the legs of the stool and rake Gladdie's shins. Gladdie didn't take much notice. She liked cleaning the lodgers' shoes and boots. You could see how much improved they were; some of them were new enough you could go a step beyond clean and make them shine. She liked Dorrie, and she knew she'd offended her. Mrs. Riley was one to watch. She'd put a hand on Mrs. Riley's knee and had that hand slapped. Mr. Riley was staying clear of the kitchen.

At one o'clock sensible people, according to Mrs. Riley, took their naps. The house was meant to be quiet. Dorrie told Gladdie to dust the parlour and make no sound. The room was dark when she went in with her flannelette rag, and it was chilly because there was no fire in the grate or in the dining room at that time of day. Gladdie pulled the heavy drapes back to the sides of the front window and let some weak daylight in through the grimy panes. She dragged the velvet-covered footstool with the silky fringe over to the window and sat there with the rag in her hands until her eyes could get used to the dimness and she could dust things without knocking them over. Mrs. Riley had a number of pictures and photographs on the walls and on the mantle and sitting up on the tables. They hung forward or leaned back at different tilts, crowding the small room. The people in all the pictures looked straight out and, as they lined the room and all faced inward, there was no place Gladdie could look that several of them weren't staring right at her. On a small table near the French doors to the dining room was a pair of tintypes of a man and a woman in bathing costume. The woman seemed familiar. Gladdie went and picked up the flowery frames and took them to the window.

In one oval was a confident, defiant sort of figure, a half-dressed man leaning against a fancy stile with the sea behind him. Hand on hip the man stood, with almost a smirk on his face. He was slender and clean-shaven but for a small moustache. His bathing costume was V-necked and covered his arms and his legs to his knees. The woman, who seemed pleased with herself without smiling, had her foot up on a rock that didn't look real. You could see boardwalk behind her and a high sea that didn't look real either. Her costume appeared to be black, as the man's was, but hers was trimmed with white at the ends of the elbow-length sleeves and along the collar and skirt bottom. The skirt came only to her knees, and she wore black hose. Her hair hung down past her shoulders, and a tam sat flat on her head. She was not an attractive young woman, but she had a slight, pretty figure. Only something mean in the expression of the eyes had travelled from the past to the present and made Gladdie think the girl had transformed into Mrs. Riley. She'd seen pictures very like these before, in which the adults or children, for it could be either, showed off the same air of disdain on their faces, but in the ones she remembered they were wearing no clothes.

She turned to the window and made out the grey silhouettes of the row of houses across the street. She wiped her rag at her eye level over the steamy grime and waited to see someone walk past the clouded glass into her clear space and out again. It wasn't long before two little boys ran by with a box they carried between them. A horse came along, a humble beast, drawing a cart behind it, with a man jolting along on the seat and big canisters behind him. Gladdie watched for some minutes. She didn't see a woman at all, and no one stopped to look at her. She leaned her forehead against the windowpane and might have floated off to sleep, listening to the parlour clock tick, if she hadn't heard someone walking on the floorboards above her head and decided she'd better get to work.

Every day she brushed and scrubbed the dirt from things and gathered garbage and ashes and took them out back and emptied chamber pots and wash basins into a pail and dumped it in the outhouse then swished it out with ammonia, rearing back when she breathed it in, and at night she crawled under Mr. Riley's coat on the rug in front of the stove, and when they were all asleep, she crept up to Mr. Shamata's room and tried to make him feel better.

Mr. Shamata stood outside the door of the Earl Hotel until someone came out. He had no idea why he did that. It seemed superstitious, but his skin felt like it would split and fall off if he couldn't indulge his whim. The man who stepped out onto the sidewalk was just the sort Mr. Shamata would have expected would walk out of the Earl Hotel, a shambling man with a big red nose and watery eyes, a man who smelled of a bad bed. Mr. Shamata went inside and inquired about a room.

"Sharing?" the desk clerk asked. He was a skinny person, too old for his pimples. The difference in price was impressive. Mr. Shamata booked a bed in a room for ten. To his embarrassment, he shuddered in front of the clerk. He'd thought of his father. Gratefully he remembered the clerk couldn't know his thoughts and neither could his father, who'd died before this degradation. Because that's what it was, and Mr. Shamata told Gladdie so that morning. Even though Gladdie liked him very much and he liked her.

Mr. Shamata went directly to the parlour after he spoke with Gladdie, and found Mrs. Riley there by the fireplace, remonstrating with Dorrie about the number of clinkers. "It was Gladdie did the fire," Dorrie was saying.

"May I speak with you, Mrs. Riley?" he asked.

Dorrie left the room.

Mr. Shamata choked when he started to speak, but it had to be said. "I'm giving notice, Mrs. Riley," he said.

"Indeed?" said Mrs. Riley.

Mr. Riley only nodded and said: "Today."

"Leaving today?"

"Yes," he whispered.

"There," Mrs. Riley said to Dorrie when they heard the front door closing. "He's gone."

"Poor man," Dorrie said.

"Good of him, really," Mrs. Riley said. She was in a happy frame of mind and gave even Gladdie a nod. "Saved me the bother of removing him. He'd paid to the end of the month, too. They're more likely to expect, the older lodgers. 'I expect you're wanting your rent, Mrs. Riley,' they'll say, and you know what that means, Dorrie. Means *they* expect you rent rooms as a charity and are grateful for the odd donation. When they get that age, who'll hire them? Didn't you think there was something Oriental about him?" Mrs. Riley went on. "Shamata. You'd wonder with that name. When he first arrived I thought of it, but I didn't ask as he looked respectable."

"Poor man," Dorrie said again.

"If I keep hearing you sigh like that, Missy, after every blooming thing you say, you'll be another one out looking for a pillow to lie your head on," Mrs. Riley said quite cheerfully.

For two nights Gladdie had a bed to herself and then Miss Avis came. By that time Gladdie had got acquainted with the other lodgers and knew she didn't want to bunk in with any of them. Either they shared rooms already, or they were in one way or another distasteful. In the dark kitchen she watched Dorrie taking off her dress and laying it over the chair by her cot. Maybe after all she'd ask Dorrie if she'd let her in, or maybe she'd not ask but wait a while and crawl in beside her when she'd gone to sleep.

"Don't be thinking of sharing with me," Dorrie said at that moment. "Get yourself wrapped up in Mr. Riley's coat and be glad you're not out on the street. I know what you've been up to."

She did as she was told.

In the night Mr. Shamata poked his head into her dreams looking worried, just as he'd looked in the mornings when he'd light his lamp sitting on the side of his bed and turn to wave her out of his room. He'd shown her his book with the pictures of Gulliver and his travels. She'd tried to be friends. She couldn't think too long about it; the chilblains were coming back like they did every time she got cold. Miss Avis it would have to be. Gladdie had seen the old lady in the hall. She'd been sweeping down the stairs when Miss Avis arrived to inquire about the vacant room, a woman about Mr. Shamata's age, Gladdie thought at first, but then she saw she was even older. She held her hand over her mouth while she talked. Gladdie had known a woman, a friend of Mrs. Tupper's, who had a growth on her upper lip as if someone had once slit it open and inserted a small saucer in there. It had been habitual with her to shield it from view. She thought Miss Avis must have something like that wrong with her, but when she picked up her bags to go upstairs you could see she was quite normal. Her eyes were pink and leaky. She'd seemed about to cry if Mrs. Riley had said no to her, or if the room in the attic had cost too much. Mrs. Riley told her there was a man across the hall up there and if she was going to object to that she could take her pennies elsewhere. "Oh no," Miss Avis said in a bewildered way. Mrs. Riley grinned then and Gladdie almost overheard her thoughts: here was a person who wouldn't object to anything as long as you'd let her retreat to a corner.

It was so cold in the house that night, and dark, for there was no moon, and Gladdie's feet were so numb she felt she floated up the two invisible flights of stairs. In the attic she stopped and dissented with herself as to the wisdom of her course. She had a premonition that fearful people would cause trouble, that you couldn't trust them to act in a predictable manner, but she couldn't go into the other room, where Mr. O'Connor slept. Mr. O'Connor reminded Gladdie of another tall, wide-whiskered man whose name and existence she was trying to forget. Mr. O'Connor was fatter than Mr. T and he was greasier, too, the reek of his pomade announcing his arrival before he entered any room, but the two men had more than those wide, wet whiskers in common. Mr. O'Connor had already proven every bit as froward. He was greedy at the table and a boaster, and from her first day in Mrs. Riley's house he'd perceived Gladdie's uneasiness in his presence, and winked at her over the others' heads.

Miss Avis must have heard the doorknob turn. She must have seen the door open. The floorboards creaked when Gladdie stepped in, and Miss Avis screamed. Luckily for Gladdie, Miss Avis screamed so loud and long that hearing her anyone would have believed she was quite far into the procedure of being murdered, and that meant Mrs. Riley wasn't leaving her room. It was up to Mr. Riley to defend the lodgers when they got to extremities. So it was Mr. Riley who watched Gladdie slip down the stairwell as fast as a ghost while he went up to the attic, yanking his pants on over his long underwear.

Mr. Riley came into the kitchen early the next morning while Dorrie was making the porridge. He sidled up to her and patted her bum in what he thought was a friendly fashion. "Where's the girl?" he asked, twisting his neck to look up into her eyes. Dorrie jerked her head to indicate the lump in her cot over in the far corner. "When I got up," she said, "I told her to go back to sleep for a bit. Where's Mrs.?"

"She's making up for her lost sleep as well," Mr. Riley said. "I thought I'd take the opportunity for a word with you, Dorrie."

Dorrie went on stirring the porridge. Gladdie went on pretending she was asleep, which she had been until Mr. Riley came down, and very grateful she was to dear Dorrie who couldn't help being kind even though she disapproved of her.

"Won't you sit down a minute?" Mr. Riley asked Dorrie, and put his hand on her arm to still the stirring.

"And have Her Highness come in and kick the stool out from under me?"

"Ah now, sit a minute, for God's sake."

She followed him to the table and sat opposite him and folded her arms over her big stomach.

"Dorrie, Dorrie," Mr. Riley said.

"Oh Dorrie yourself," she said, not caring if she made no sense.

"Have you made any plans at all?" he asked. And when she didn't answer he said, "If there was a thing I could do..." Then he saw the tears spill down her cheeks and in a panic he went on quickly to the next thing. "And about this girl, now, this Gladdie, what in the name of heaven's going on? Do you know?"

"She's a little slut," Dorrie said, sniffing back her tears.

"No," he said. "She's a child. She can't be more than six or seven."

"She's nine and going on nineteen," Dorrie said, her voice rising so Gladdie could hear her clearly even from across the room. "Do you know what she's been doing? Crawling into bed with Mr. Shamata. Poor man. That's why he give notice. And last night – she tried it on with that new lady."

"Miss Avis, do you mean?"

"Yes. Why else do you think she made such a fuss?"

"But the child must have been too cold here on the floor, that's all. It wasn't right of us not to find her a bed."

"There's more to it than that," Dorrie said. "She's depraved."

"She's too young to be depraved," Mr. Riley said.

"Humph," Dorrie said.

"Don't you like her?" Mr. Riley asked.

"She knows things she shouldn't know." Then Dorrie bent to his ear and told him what Gladdie had done to her. Mr. Riley sat back in his chair as that information rolled over him. "And didn't you see how sick Mr. Shamata looked those last days?" Dorrie went on. "Lord knows what she did with him."

"Dorrie," Mr. Riley said. "I'm shocked."

"I should hope so."

"A little child."

"I'll tell you one thing. Mrs. Riley can talk all she wants about her respectability. She'll be running a house of scandal if this girl stays. For all that she's 'such a good worker.'"

"Jesus," was all Mr. Riley had time to say before Mrs. Riley herself interrupted the conference. Being tired, she descended to the main floor in dreary stages, giving Dorrie time to get up off the stool and go back to the porridge. Mrs. Riley was too tired to speak till she'd had her tea, so she plunked herself down and waited for it to be brought to her, rubbing her eyes and her head and scratching under her arms while it steeped.

"I'll tell you one thing," she said after she'd taken half a cup. "We don't let rooms to screamers."

Dorrie gave Mr. Riley a look. She was one for fairness, and it was a that's-not-fair look. Mr. Riley put his head down and stirred sugar into his own tea pretty thoroughly. "Georgina," he said, "maybe give the old lady a chance."

"I beg your pardon?" Mrs. Riley said.

"It's not uncommon to be unsettled. Is it now? On your first night in a place?"

"Did she slip you a fiver?"

"No, no."

"Then what on earth are you talking about?"

"Just – give her another few nights. She's paid in advance, hasn't she?"

"A week in advance."

"And she looks a respectable lady."

"Well, Laddie, since when did you start sticking up for the lodgers?"

"Aw, she looked so frightened last night, and sad. She's a sad case, Georgina," Mr. Riley said softly.

"In good company, I'd opine," Mrs. Riley said. With the return to her more usual good humour, she settled to work on her left tit, which was always absentmindedly itchy. And later, after breakfast had been taken in the dining room, she called to Miss Avis just when that poor lady thought she'd almost made her escape. "Oh Miss Avis," she said. The old lady stopped on her way through the parlour. Her hand went up to her mouth. "Yes, Mrs. Riley?"

"We don't take to screaming here. Not even in the daylight hours and certainly not in the night. A nightmare, was it?" she went on since Miss Avis didn't respond.

"It must have been," Miss Avis said. "I really never dream, Mrs. Riley. I'm sure it won't happen again."

Mrs. Riley said nothing, and in a few moments Miss Avis surmised thankfully that she'd been dismissed, and she wobbled up to the dubious safety of her room, where she unconsciously hid her mouth for the next hour.

the stick people

A storm came up when Gladdie was on her way home from visiting Orillia at the hospital. The first big drops hit, raising the scent of dust as she turned into the yard, thinking what a nice house Hilda had, with dozens of geraniums in the verandah windows. It was a plain frame house, exactly like the houses on either side of it, the three of them stranded at the end of the otherwise empty block. Like pioneer sisters, she thought, and Hilda's was the prettiest. She ran up the steps with the rain pelting down on her and opened the door to a homey smell of roast chicken and a henhouse flutter: three women in a panic because they couldn't find Susan. Besides Hilda there was a handsome woman with her hair falling out of its bun who turned out to be Mrs. Best, the wife of Hilda's day lodger, and Lettie Pringle, an elderly woman who wore a curdled look and a cardigan the colour of her own old flesh. They'd looked everywhere, they said, and when Gladdie walked in she guessed it must be true because they were hauling the lamps and ornaments off the piano in the dining room as if the child might have hidden there. The storm had cracked into the city by then. Thunder shook the house and Hilda wrung her hands. Then Lettie Pringle stopped with a pair of grape-strewn silver candlesticks in her hands and said for heaven's sake did they think the child had crawled in and the ornaments had put themselves back in place. When the lights went out they all shrieked and Hilda started crying. Then the other two wrung their hands.

Gladdie went upstairs in the dark, thinking the child's own room was the most likely place for her to hide. The others said they'd looked there as well as everywhere else, and Hilda was ready to put on her coat and go outside, but Gladdie couldn't see Susan leaving the house in the storm.

The third floor was just the attic, and as it was small the stairs came up into Susan's room, and Gladdie had to walk through it to get to and from hers. It was a snug space at any time. As soon as you were up there you could forget the rest of the house existed. With rain hammering on the roof it was like opening a book and walking right inside. Green ivy patterned the paper on the walls and slanted ceiling.

Her own room, papered in yellow flowers, looked empty when she walked in, and it sounded empty except for the rain drumming away. Yellow is a colour that's cheery in sunlight and a bit sad when the sun's gone, she thought. She went straight to the closet although she hadn't thought of the valise. She opened it as soon as she didn't see Susan hiding under her dresses. She'd unpacked the bag on arrival and put it away. No one had thought to look into it and no wonder; it really looked too small to hold the child. But she was knees to chin inside it, trembling and faint with the lack of air. Gladdie felt faint herself at the sight of her. She sat on the floor and pulled Susan out and into her lap.

"Mary Mother of Jesus," she said, just as Mr. Riley might have done. She sat for a long time with Susan in her lap, rocking her and stroking her hair until they both stopped shaking.

Such a small body the child had, fitting comfortably in her arms, with hardly any weight at all. She reached up and patted Gladdie's cheek with her little hand, and Gladdie felt something move inside her. She wondered if it could be her womb, if it was stirring at the nearness of the child. Something like peace rose within her. She would have been this age herself, once, she thought, looking at the little bony arms and legs. A shock went through her at the recognition that she'd been just like this, so small and alone in the world. Shaking all over again, she stood the child up. "Just a minute, Susan," she said. She got up slowly from the floor and so awkwardly the little girl put her hands out to steady her. "It's all right," she told the child. "We're fine now, aren't we, Susan?"

A storm can upset people in different ways. Hilda got angry with Gladdie because she hadn't hollered to her immediately that Susan was found. She didn't say anything about it, but it preyed on her mind. It wasn't right of Gladdie, she felt, to let her suffer even one more minute of anxiety. And Lettie Pringle had yelled at her, accusing Hilda of jangling her nerves. Hilda said Lettie had more nerves than were good for her. Gladdie heard all about that, at least, over tea once Susan was sleeping, safe in her bed. The good thing that came of it all was that Lettie Pringle left the next morning, and a room was free for Orillia.

One evening on her way home from the hospital, Gladdie noticed the corner store on Hamilton Street was open and she went in looking for something to bring Susan. Crayons and a scribbler were what she decided on.

"For her alphabet," Hilda said.

"You get her another for that sort of thing," Gladdie said. "This one's for whatever she wants to put in it."

As soon as Susan came down to breakfast the next morning, she saw the notebook and crayons waiting for her on the kitchen table, at her place, where her bowl of oatmeal waited, and as soon as she'd climbed up on her chair she looked up with a question on her face.

"Yes, they're for you," Gladdie said.

"After breakfast," Hilda said, because Susan had already opened the book to the first page and picked up the little flat box of crayons. She put the box down and ate up all her oatmeal porridge.

"First time she's ever finished it," Hilda said, and she'd tried everything she could think of to induce the child to eat more, thinking she was too thin.

Susan drew out the black crayon, put her head down and worked hard while Gladdie and Hilda washed up the dishes. Every once in a while the little girl grunted softly with the effort she was making. She drew three figures.

The stick people weren't recognizable. Hilda said afterwards they might just as easily be the Father, Son and the Holy Ghost, but Gladdie and Hilda knew who they were. She'd placed a little one you'd take to be herself in the middle and had her two big-fingered hands meshed with the others'. All the fingers were drawn about as long as the arms and legs and sprang from them like spokes.

"I bet that's you," Hilda said, pointing to the little one, and Susan nodded agreeably, as if it seemed a good guess.

"And who's that?" Hilda asked gently, pointing to one of the big figures. "And that?" she asked, pointing to the other. Susan shrugged her little shoulders and looked at her stick people as if they were holding her words, as if they owned them. Tears ran down behind Hilda's glasses. You could see how much she loved the child already and how she was torn, wanting her to have her parents and hoping they'd never come.

The scribblers were cheaper if you bought six. Gladdie went back to the store for more, and Susan had filled four by the week's end. Every page with the three figures.

learning

Mr. Riley said he'd take Gladdie for a walk. She waited for him at the street corner where he'd said to meet him, down the street from the house. It was one of those hoarfrost days that a little sunlight turns magical, and white glittery flakes danced in the air between Gladdie and the tops of the frosted trees. She had a wet foot. In spite of her thick stockings, it had come right out of Sarah Tupper's boot as she'd walked to the corner, but she wasn't as cold as she might have been. Dorrie had seen her at the back door before she left and called her. At first Gladdie thought Dorrie was going to make her do more work, or tell her she couldn't leave the house, but that wasn't it at all. She lent her a sweater to wear under Mrs. Tupper's shawl. She didn't ask where Gladdie was going, which was as well since Gladdie didn't know. While she waited for Mr. Riley, she pulled the shawl about her, snugging the big sweater closer, and she thought: Dorrie wouldn't give it to me if I wasn't coming back.

She could still see Mrs. Riley's house. From where she stood she could even see the smudge she'd made on the front window to look out. She was only across the street and down by the grocer's where Mr. Riley had said he'd meet her, but she wished he'd come soon. She didn't like being outside where anyone might see her. She was forgetting not to think the name she didn't want to think again. In fact she could think of nothing but that best-forgotten family. She had no idea how far she was from the Tuppers' house; she'd got so turned around the night she'd followed Mr. Riley home. Once she started worrying about how close they might be, it seemed more than likely Mr. Tupper would stride up to this very store this very day for a tin of Stag. It seemed probable he'd have told his friends to look out for her. When people went in and out of the grocer's, Gladdie put her head down so they couldn't see her face, and she kicked at the lamppost if they looked at her, to be doing something. She saw a woman coming from a long way down the street, and she turned hopeful and teased herself for a while that it could be Margaret. Then a man came out of the grocer's with a sack of flour and didn't see her, and she stepped back and her feet nearly slid out from under her. She looked right up at two Jews, into their dark brown eyes, but then Mr. Riley came along, looking jaunty with his jacket done up and his bowler hat on toward the back of his head and his ginger moustache and sideburns combed down. "Well, Gladdie," he said, speaking loudly because Dorrie had warned him he'd need to shout. "Let's be off." He stopped just the two or three seconds it took to speak to her, and then crossed the street and headed south with her hustling beside him.

She had to walk fast to keep up to him. She had to watch out so she didn't run into other people or their bags or canes. Before she remembered she should be reading street signs and paying attention to buildings, to find her way back if he left her, they'd turned two corners. She couldn't recall the name of Mrs. Riley's street. She figured she'd have to stick to Mr. Riley like his shadow because there wasn't a thing along the way you could pick as a landmark. It was only small, dark shops and restaurants, and they all looked the same, or if each one was not exactly like the others beside it, it was repeated down the street. She tried to look inside them, and all she saw was herself in their glass, hurrying past. Outside a big hotel a doorman in a tight uniform nodded to Mr. Riley.

Of course she knew Mr. Riley might take her wherever he'd decided and, before he left her, demand the return of Dorrie's sweater. It was no guarantee he'd escort her back.

The further they went, the more traffic there was on the streets, and the frozen ruts, under the influence of all the wheels, started to thaw into churned mud. Carriages flew by close to the sidewalk, passing the slower streetcars, and threw up the slush and, if you were unlucky, horse manure. The sidewalks were crowded here, too. All the men were in a hurry. All the women carried things: reticules and string bags and packages. The buildings got bigger and higher, but Gladdie recognized none of them. This wasn't the same part of downtown where she'd first spied Mr. Riley, where the newsboys had called her names. It was a more exciting part of the city, with the signs of businesses on all floors and criss-crossed wires overhead. Mr. Riley grabbed her by the collar at one point and hauled her out of the way of a power pole.

At Front Street they stopped for traffic, and that's when she saw J. W. Venn Confectionary. It was about the fanciest shop she'd ever seen and had curlicues on all the gold letters, and when they got to it and had to wait before crossing the other way, she could hardly believe her eyes. She stared into that window full of candies of all kinds laid out in categories, and she forgot to worry about where she was and how she'd return if Mr. Riley left her. Barley sugar and toffees and chocolates and fruit drops like coloured lights – pineapple and raspberry and lime – and crystallized fruits with sugar coating and peppermints and humbugs and jujubes (sounding just like they would taste) were all divided up like a complicated rainbow. Each one had its own section, and the sections were arranged in spokes. Then a big girl came to the inside of the window and put her hand into a white glove. She held her hand over the toffees and plucked out six, putting them into a little sack. Gladdie had never in all her life imagined that anything could be done with such respectability and order, and in a white glove. "Oh Mr. Riley," she said, and then she stopped – for she'd turned to speak to him and he wasn't there.

The first thing she thought was she still had the sweater. But at the same time fear went shaking through her like a pain. She knew she must look a fright because the girl in the candy shop halted and didn't serve her customer, seeing her so stricken. She looked right at Gladdie with her hand stopped over the little paper bag. Then she did a wonderful thing. Just by looking at her through the window, she sent Gladdie courage. Gladdie watched her do it, and it made her so grateful she stopped being sick with fear. Some of her thoughts got detoured toward the big girl. If only she could *be* her, or be just like her, have a job in a shop, do everything just so, she'd send courage to poor children through the window too. She didn't think about going in there. She knew it wasn't a place for her, but she quit being so scared. She looked about her, as was only practical, and there was Mr. Riley across the intersection, reading a notice painted on a wall. He turned just as she spotted him and waved at her. When she looked into the confectionary again the girl was back to waiting on her customer, so Gladdic went to the street corner and stood with the others. Then she saw the building behind Mr. Riley that you'd think she'd never have missed, a huge building in the shape of an octagon with a cupola and a spire and a wide, sagging banner. On the side of the building in letters a foot or more high, it said *Cyclorama, Jerusalem on the Day of the Crucifixion.* People were lined up waiting to go in the door. And there was Mr. Riley, coming for her. He crossed the street and brought her to see it for herself. "Gazing on this Masterpiece of Human Art, one is Magically Transported from the scenes of the busy Nineteenth Century back Eighteen Hundred Years," the poster said. Mr. Riley said he'd been inside; he'd seen it with Mrs. Riley, and without her saying a thing, he promised he'd take her in sometime. "But not today," he said. Some of the people waiting in line smiled on them, and Gladdie knew Mr. Riley had spoken so they could hear him and think him a good man.

They went along to Union Station, to see how the construction was proceeding. Workmen were hanging by ropes from the centre tower. Gladdie and Mr. Riley stood side by side at the edge of the tracks and watched them.

"They'll be putting the clocks in soon," Mr. Riley said. "Four of them facing all directions so's you can tell the time from anywhere."

"I can tell time," she said, in case he thought she couldn't. The earth began to vibrate and rumble, or she thought it was the earth. It was a sound like thunder but coming from below. She grabbed onto Mr. Riley's arm. "It's a train," he said, pointing down the track. The locomotive barrelled toward them, steam gushing up from its stack, then its wheels started screeching.

"Now," Mr. Riley shouted, bending to her ear. "You and me can have a talk." He glanced about him to be sure no one was near. "On a delicate subject. Can you hear me?" She nodded. But then the train screamed to a stop, and its whistle shrieked even louder, and people came running from nowhere, and Mr. Riley couldn't hear himself think let alone make her understand what he needed to say.

"Come along," he said. "We'll try further on."

Down at a pier they walked among the carriages and carts. A man holding the halter of his team gave her a piece of turnip to feed his horse. She'd never fed a horse before, and the thick feel of its lips set her shuddering. As soon as it had picked up the turnip, she yanked her hand away.

Mr. Riley and Gladdie walked as close as they could to the big boats docked there. She read "St. Catherines Niagara Falls" on one, and Mr. Riley said they were two places, and he'd never been to either, nor expected he ever would, but Niagara Falls was said to be a marvel. Gladdie was starting to worry what it might be he wanted to tell her, and pretended she wasn't hearing him. They walked past warehouses and lumberyards and machinery depots. It was all very noisy, but Mr. Riley couldn't seem to find the right place to talk to her – there were so many people around for one thing – and she kept on acting as if she couldn't hear a word. Then he got the idea of writing down what he had to say. But he had neither pen nor paper on him.

Off they went, zigzagging diagonally across downtown to the lobby of the Bay Horse Hotel where Mr. Riley was known to Mr. Cleland, the proprietor. It being still morning, Mr. Cleland was not to be seen in the lobby. A bellhop came along and quietly asked Mr. Riley if he required assistance. Mr. Riley said, "Me and my daughter require a place and the means to write a letter."

"Are you guests, sir?" the bellhop asked.

"Not at the moment," Mr. Riley said.

"Then I'm afraid you can't use our lounge, sir. But if you'd like to partake of tea or a lemonade or some such refreshment, our restaurant is open, and I could bring you pen and paper there." Mr. Riley couldn't countenance taking Gladdie to the restaurant. For one thing, it went against the grain to pay money for a non-alcoholic beverage, and for another, it would be a hideous affront to Mrs. Riley, one that would surely draw her like hellfire across the city to the Yonge Street window to witness his disrespect.

"Not today," he told the bellhop.

"I'm sorry we can't oblige you, sir," the soft-spoken man said. He managed to seem a little sorry, which added to the melancholy exit of Mr. Riley and Gladdie from the Bay Horse. But just outside the door, as they were descending to the street, Mr. Riley met a friend who was on his way to the bar and was able to ask him if he could think where he'd get pen and paper. "Well, come in with me, my man," said Pat Maguire, but Mr. Riley said no, he couldn't at this time, and Pat Maguire noticed Gladdie.

"You could go to the library," Pat Maguire said. "Over on Church Street."

For the second time in a day, young Gladdie could not believe her eyes. She stood blocking the entrance, in awe of the vision before her. Candies were one thing; this was books. Shelves and shelves of books, hundreds, thousands of volumes, and people were sitting doing nothing with their time but reading. Mr. Riley tugged her out of the path of others who were trying to enter. He waited until several of them coursed past the front desk, and then, hauling her with him, he struck out as if the two of them were members of the crowd. Gladdie felt sure one of the gentlemen or ladies behind the desks would stop them, but they reached the inside without any trouble. They marched along with the rest, trying to look as if they meant business, which, as Gladdie knew, always helped. It took them a while to adjust to the atmosphere. It was altogether quiet in that place, and full of a bookish smell. They had to slow down to fit in, but nobody said a word to them.

Near the filing cabinets they discovered small squares of paper and pencils in little boxes and saw that people used them without asking. They took a pencil each and Mr. Riley filched about a dozen of the small sheets of paper. He headed over to the windows where there were some tables and chairs, and found them a spot to themselves. Two ladies sitting by the window stared at them, but Mr. Riley and Gladdie just cleared their throats and tried to look as if they were thinking. Mr. Riley sat for some time with his pencil lead balanced on the tip of his tongue. Gladdie guessed he really was trying to think and didn't know what to put down. Then with a flourish he set to and in nearly unreadable handwriting, he wrote, "Whyd yu run away from hom?"

She took the bit of paper and frowned over it. She couldn't think of a way to answer. Mr. Riley saw she was trying. He took the piece of paper back and crumpled it into a ball and put it into his pocket.

He took a new sheet and wrote something else, but he seemed to think it a stupid question, and he balled that up too and put it with the other. Next he wrote one he liked better and passed that over.

"Wat du yu want to du?"

She knew the answer to that, and quick as a wink she printed her reply. It was pride in her that wanted him to see how fast and clearly she could form her letters. She wrote: "Stay with you."

Mr. Riley sat for a long time staring at that piece of paper. She figured he was thinking: What would he get in exchange? He'd take her in and feed her and the bit of work she'd do for Mrs. Riley wouldn't be anything to him. You don't get something for nothing, Mr. T. and Uncle Tiny had told her often enough, so she leaned forward to reassure him. "I don't mind giving pleasure, Mr. Riley," she said, whispering so the ladies at the table next to them couldn't hear.

Mr. Riley sat back again and stared at the piece of paper some more. He cleared his throat, took out his handkerchief and cleared it again more thoroughly into the hanky, and then he folded the hanky and returned it to his pocket. Then he took a fresh sheet and wrote on it, "It was a bad hous yu come from." He started to hand it to her but retrieved it before she had time to read it. He added, "In a bad hous yu lern bad things."

She thought about that for a while. Then she wrote: "Is it bad to give pleasure?"

Mr. Riley nodded. "You're too young," he said, loud enough for her to hear him. The women at the next table smiled at him, as if it was a good thing to say whatever the circumstances.

She wrote, "They think you're my Dad."

Mr. Riley nodded and pulled out his handkerchief again, and this time blew his nose hard into it. In a ball, it went back into his pocket, which was getting full.

Then she wrote: "How will I get on if I don't please people?"

Mr. Riley took the pencil, and this is what he said: "Werk hard and be cherful and yull kepe a job."

She bent her head over that one to decipher it, and he said, "Gladdie, I'm no good at explaining. Just make it a rule to..." He took the paper back again and wrote: "Touch no one til yore–" He thought about that a while, then wrote "16."

You'd think she'd be happy. Mr. Riley was taking her back to their place. He wasn't trying to lose her like she'd thought he would. But she couldn't be happy.

Mr. Riley, on the way back to the house, could feel her brooding at his side. He didn't know what was wrong, but he wanted to fix it. His own mood bounced when he hit upon the thing. "Now," he said. "We've just time for the Cyclorama."

She said she didn't want to go to the Cyclorama.

"What? What?"

Nothing he could say would change her mind. After a few blocks and many glances in her direction, Mr. Riley got an inkling of the problem. Even he some days would get so low he couldn't get back up, not at least without the aid of drink. "They don't call it spirits for nothing," Mr. Riley often said. He really couldn't stand the long trudge home with her miserable beside him. He kept telling her they'd have another outing another day, wouldn't they? And: "The first spot on our itinerary will be you-know-where."

Dorrie couldn't wait for the moment she could catch Mr. Riley alone and ask him what he'd said to Gladdie. She asked him right out, in front of the girl, as they were sitting at the kitchen table.

"I only said she must not touch people anymore," he said. They both looked at Gladdie, and she nodded to corroborate Mr. Riley's statement.

Dorrie said, "I think she's taken it to heart." Then she turned forlorn and tears came to her eyes. "You've good advice for others," she muttered.

Mr. Riley sighed. He said, "Ah Jesus, I'm a gomless shite."

Dorrie nodded, and their conversation fell into a big pause. Other days, Mr. Riley would have jostled her about agreeing with him – he was a great one for nudging a person to his point of view – but this time after a while he only said, "I know you're down."

What could she say to that? She'd given up the first baby the year before and it nearly did her in. And what else could she do? Nobody would hire a servant with an infant, and if she could find a job in a factory, who'd care for the child? As for Mr. Riley, he didn't seem to know what a man could do in the circumstances other than leave these things to nature.

As a diversion Mr. Riley tried to get Gladdie to eat a piece of meat pie. But she couldn't. "I'm having some," he said, but she only shook her head. Mrs. Riley was taking her nap. Dorrie was cleaning the black off the kettle. "We have to do quiet things while Her Highness sleeps," she reminded Gladdie. She gave her a saucepan to scour. The three of them sat at the table saying nothing for a while, then Mr. Riley slapped his thighs and got up, grabbed his bowler off Mrs. Riley's chair and jammed it on. "I'm off," he said and went out the back way, pulling on his jacket.

Soon Mrs. Riley came downstairs and got her girls working harder, so the afternoon passed quickly enough. It was nearly supper hour, the potatoes were ready to mash, when Mr. Riley returned and his friend Mr. Shannon with him. Mrs. Riley sniffed when her husband said, "Mr. Shannon's just helped me home with this."

"This" was a large, square object that would have been awkward for Mr. Riley to have carried alone, a large, square object that Mr. Riley, with Mr. Shannon's help, unfolded in the corner of the kitchen nearest the dining room. In their hats and jackets, the two men puffed, red-faced and hot with the bit of exercise, and then stood back grinning. Dorrie and Gladdie and Mrs. Riley looked at it too.

"*What* is that?" Mrs. Riley asked, although it was evident it was a cot with a mattress.

"Georgina," Mr. Riley said. "I know it's been troubling your conscience, letting the little girl sleep on the floor. I said to Mr. Shannon, it's more than it's worth to have Georgina fretting over the child."

"You'll not get your money from me," Mrs. Riley informed Mr. Shannon.

"No, no," Mr. Shannon said, his red face alarmed. He was a new friend of Mr. Riley's. From inside his jacket, he extracted a folded blanket made of good thick wool and placed it on the cot. "I'll be off now," he said. "Pleased to have met you, Mrs. Riley." Mr. Riley walked him the few steps to the back door.

"It's your bed, Gladdie," he said when he returned, and then he went into the parlour where some of the lodgers had gathered hoping for a sign of supper. Mrs. Riley followed him, since there was really nothing more to be said.

In her new bed that night, Gladdie thought about Mr. Riley's kindness to her. She'd liked Mr. Riley when she'd first seen him. It was because of him she was there, at Mrs. Riley's. She thought about Dorrie. She'd said she could keep the wool sweater. She tried not to think about what Mr. Riley wrote and said at the library. She dreaded letting herself know what he'd meant. She wanted it never to have happened. How could it have happened that she hadn't known better? That he'd thought she had to be told? He'd thought she was just like the Tuppers. Bad because she came from a bad house. All along she'd assured herself she knew better than the Tuppers. Well, she knew better now. She tried to keep it out of her mind, all the knowing involved in the day, all the knowing between herself and Mr. Riley and Dorrie, but it flared in her. Oh, yes, she was full to the top and red hot with knowing now.

When she woke in the morning, swaddled in her very own blanket, with Mr. Riley's coat on top of that, as near to warm as she was likely to get in that house at that time of year, the dread about herself had eased a bit. It had been elbowed aside to some extent by her happiness at waking in a bed that was hers. And after the morning chores and dinner were over, and Mrs. Riley had gone for her nap, Dorrie said to her, "I'm going to get you a bath." She put the copper boiler on the range because it was to be a real bath and there wasn't enough hot water in the cistern on the side of the stove. She got out the big round washtub and set it by the oven door. She pulled two chairs out from the table and hung a tablecloth over them "in case anyone comes into the room, you'll be hid." All these things she did while Gladdie watched in a daze, feeling she was being hypnotized, tracking Dorrie's capable movements, all of them for her.

"Don't know why I didn't think of it last night, with you getting a new bed," Dorrie grumbled. Then very nicely, when she'd filled the tub, she said, "I'll leave you now." She closed the kitchen door, then immediately tapped on it and stuck her head in. "Don't forget to wash your hair," she said. "And leave your clothes there on the floor." The door closed again, and this time Gladdie was left alone.

The soap was handmade by the next-door neighbour, Mrs. Halladay. A big rectangle of soft, slippery jellied lye soap, the smell of clean. The water was warm, to start at least, and over the tin tub side Dorrie had draped a square of flannel to use as a cloth. Gladdie scrubbed herself all over and washed her hair. The soap stung her eyes, but the towel was right there handy. Dorrie had hung it over the oven door for her and it warmed even her bones when she dried herself. Dorrie returned when she was done and sitting on the stool wrapped in the towel. She replaced Gladdie's pile of dirty clothes with clean underwear and a housedress of her own that Gladdie could hike up with its belt and, like a dear sister, she said, "There you are now – spotless."

at mrs. wutherspoon's house

Side by side, Gladdie and Hilda waited on the verandah steps. As there were no houses across the street, they faced the mapped-out neighbourhood, a long stretch of woolly prairie and the western sky. The sun was halfway along its path, and the verandah roof still offered a rim of shade.

"It's a good thing she's arriving while Susan's having her nap," Hilda said. "Less fuss." She'd noticed Gladdie was picking at her fingernails, and that was a thing she did when she was tense. "I hope she'll like the room," she said. "I know it's small. The poor girl. When you think what can happen to a person. Out of the blue. And here, a few blocks away, we didn't even know there was a cyclone. We only got the rain."

So they stood waiting, looking out into the blue, whence anything could come.

Gladdie said Orillia looked like a bed of pansies. And she did. From her toes to the top of her head she was multihued, like the yellow pansies that have dark at their edges. Today her lips were pinched, as she had, in choosing to leave the hospital, been taken off morphine.

She wore a white blouse and a black skirt on this first day out in the world. She'd decided since the cyclone she'd always wear only black and white, and Gladdie had bought her what she wanted. They were a stylish blouse and skirt. Dr. Kitely liked them. He'd come to the ward to release her officially, and on this slightly sentimental occasion he'd gone so far as to say her outfit was smart.

Nurse Macklin and an orderly were to accompany Orillia to Mrs. Wutherspoon's house. The orderly sat at the front of the buggy, with the driver, and Nurse Macklin sat with Orillia in the rear seat where her legs, encased in casts up to the knees, took up much of the space. It was a sunny day with light bouncing off every wall and fence and twig. It was the first time in weeks Orillia had been outside. Her feet were healing faster than anyone would have predicted. She was leaving the hospital sooner than anyone had expected. She was going to spend the rest of the summer with Gladdie McConnell. She sat up straight in a fit of anticipation.

"Take us by the devastation," she called to the driver as soon as they started off. The driver turned to Nurse Macklin for consent, and the nurse, in a mood to indulge her patient, nodded.

"A lot's cleaned up," the driver said. But there was plenty to see. As they approached Lorne Street, the damaged library and the nearly demolished YWCA beside it came into view.

"First the telephone exchange," Orillia said, leaning forward.

Ropes marked off the site of the exchange. They wouldn't have stopped anyone who wanted to search the area; they were there to indicate that people were supposed to stay back, that it might be dangerous to go further. Much of the rubble had been cleared away. It wasn't as breathtaking a sight as it must have been right after the cyclone struck, though only a corner piece of wall was still standing. From the buggy Orillia could see partway into the basement where she'd landed after falling with the switchboard through the building.

"Can you stop a minute, please?" she asked, and the driver pulled his horse to the side of the street, and they all looked into the gaping hole. "I don't remember it," Orillia said, "but one of the girls said the bricks flew about like crazed birds." She pictured herself in the row of girls at the switchboard, up on the third floor, then the walls swayed, the floors caved, the bricks flew and she fell through. "The girls said the noise of it was as frightening as the force and the things flying through the air," she said. She was wearing a white dress when she fell – in the picture of her falling –

and black birds flapped around her in a romantic depiction of distress.

"There's the house where I boarded, what's left of it," Orillia said when they came to her block, on Smith Street. The house still stood, unlike many others that had been hit and had to be torn down, but its roof was missing. "They found the roof across the street, on the neighbour's lawn," Orillia said. "My room was on the second floor, and they said the entire contents blew out. They never retrieved a single one of my possessions, not one. Quite a coincidence, when you think about it, isn't it? Both the place where I lived and the place where I worked were struck. The wind must have had to change directions to destroy them both," she said, perhaps a bit too brightly. Nurse Macklin heard a note she thought Orillia hadn't meant to sound when she spoke, an undertone the nurse interpreted as hysteria. She took the girl's hand and squeezed it in her capable grip. As they pulled away, a woman standing in the glassless window of a tilted house waved at them.

The nurse clasped Orillia's hand the whole way to Mrs. Wutherspoon's house. It wasn't a long journey; it only seemed long after that. They crossed the creek, passed the legislative building, turned two corners and finally pulled up at the very western edge of the city. Nurse Macklin sprang down from the buggy and Orillia sat up straight again, taking in her new lodgings while she waited for the orderly to come round to let her out. It was just as Gladdie had described: the three narrow frame houses stood shoulder to shoulder surrounded by empty lots and facing miles of prairie. The houses were brand new and nearly identical, having been built by the same contractor the summer before from kits out of Eaton's catalogue. Orillia was pleased that her destination was the one in the middle; she wasn't sure why.

And there was Gladdie with a woman who must be Mrs. Wutherspoon, standing on the verandah steps. An unmatched pair, those two. Mrs. Wutherspoon stood head and shoulders over Gladdie and was twice her width. She was a downy, white and pink, freshly-scrubbed-looking woman, and her spectacles misted at the sight of Orillia. Both of the women had started down the steps to greet her but halted before they reached the bottom, seeing that the orderly had scooped her into his arms. So she was carried into the house like a bride across a threshold, as her new landlady pointed out.

They were quite a procession. The orderly and Orillia went first, Nurse Macklin followed, then Hilda Wutherspoon. Gladdie, scowling, brought up the rear. Orillia watched her over the orderly's shoulder as they marched, silent but for the sound of their boots, up the stairs. "See you don't knock her feet against the wall," Gladdie said finally, when they'd almost reached the landing. She'd wanted to warn him from the first step.

White lace curtains blew over the bed as the orderly carried Orillia into her room. The nurse forged by them and pulled back the white Marcella bedspread and the bright white sheet.

"I'm afraid it's small." Mrs. Wutherspoon said just as the orderly plunked Orillia down and yanked his arms out from under her. Maybe he was frightened by the sight of the open sheets and the thought that he was laying a young woman down on a bed. It certainly occurred to Orillia, watching his naked Adam's apple convulse above her face. She meant to thank him with a touch of acerbity, in case he had any lascivious ideas, but before she could speak he'd fled the room. His footsteps rattled down the stairs, through the hall and out the door, and nothing was left of him but the lingering sinewy odour of overheated worsted and male sweat. Nurse Macklin adjusted the pillows and wiped Orillia's face and neck. Gladdie offered her a glass of water, but she couldn't take any yet.

"The room *is* small..." Mrs. Wutherspoon said again.

"Perfect for me," Orillia said, and was rewarded with a grin from Gladdie.

"I hope so, Miss Cooper," Mrs. Wutherspoon said. "I hope it will be just right for you." She looked as if she might cry.

"I'm sure it will be," Orillia said. Sweat broke out on her brow. "I'm very fond of lilac." It would have been bad if she hadn't liked the shade, since all the walls were papered in it, and the ceiling, the door, the mouldings, and even the bedstead, all but the shining brass top rail and knobs, had been painted that colour. "It's very pretty," Orillia said. Then her own eyes filled with tears. She didn't dare blink or say another word. It was lucky for her Nurse Macklin decided to clear the room. Orillia had thought her obnoxious on the way to Mrs. Wutherspoon's house – with her hand-holding – but now the woman settled her. She had a deft way of smoothing the sheets that made Orillia feel cooler in spite of the hot breeze that continued to blow the curtains out from the window and over the bed. "What a pretty view," the nurse said before she left, and it was true you could see the legislative building across Albert Street and the little lake and what was left of the wind-ravaged park.

Orillia lay back against the two pillows in her white nightgown. The red silk Chinese bed jacket Gladdie had bought her was folded at the end of the bed, ready to be pulled on if anyone should come to her door and ask to enter. Red. But she didn't need to wear it outside the room.

Gladdie brought the supper tray up to Orillia's room. Hilda had made it very dainty with a doily under the plate and a tiny fluted dish of her tomato relish on the side and chocolate cake, because young people like chocolate, they'd decided. Orillia couldn't face it. "I'm sorry," she said. She looked as if she might vomit.

"That's all right," Gladdie said. "Do you want me to stay or go?"

"Stay for a bit," Orillia said.

In the upstairs hall afterwards, before she returned to the kitchen, Gladdie leaned against the wall and forked down some of the supper on the tray. Then she wiped her mouth on the embroidered napkin, and went downstairs to eat her own.

"She couldn't finish her meal?" Hilda asked, and Gladdie said the doctor had mentioned Orillia's appetite would be small for a couple of days. Good thing she'd passed that on. The next day she ate the better part of two breakfasts and two lunches.

"She's very pretty, isn't she?" Hilda said. "But so thin. We'll have to fatten her up."

Mrs. Wutherspoon came up with a cup of tea in her hand. An oatmeal cookie rested on the saucer. Orillia dunked an edge in the tea and ate it like a child while Mrs. Wutherspoon watched her with her hand on her heaving bosom. Then she crossed the room to the window. "Look," she said, and Orillia looked – not that there was much to see, just a little girl running about in the vegetable garden below them, chasing a butterfly. It was only a white cabbage butterfly, only a skinny little girl in a summer dress.

"Susan," Mrs. Wutherspoon said.

"Oh, yes," Orillia said. "Gladdie told me about her."

"Nothing to her, is there?" Mrs. Wutherspoon said as she peered down at her garden and the child hopping about, first in one direction, then in another, after the butterfly. Floating over the plants like a piece of fluff. "And she's so *careful.* I don't think she's stepped on a single leaf. She never gets dirty, you know, Miss Cooper. She could wear the same clothes a week."

"She should have a dog," Orillia said.

"I never had children," Mrs. Wutherspoon said. She tilted her prematurely white head while she watched the little girl skipping over her peas and carrots.

Orillia watched, too, with her lips pinched, and nothing happened, but the sun went on glaring, and the butterfly went on flicking its white wings and bobbing up and down over the dusty vegetables, and the little girl bobbed up and down, too, with her hands out to catch what she was never going to get.

"There's Gladdie," Mrs. Wutherspoon said, and Gladdie appeared below them, carrying a basin. She took it out to the garden and dribbled grey dishwater along a row of carrots. As soon as she saw her, the little girl stopped chasing the butterfly and picked her way over the cabbages to lean into Gladdie. And Gladdie's arm dropped over her.

"Don't they look small from here," Mrs. Wutherspoon said, and it was just what Orillia was thinking, how small, how vulnerable they looked as the sun glared down. And everything looked so temporary. The wilted vegetables hovering over the cracked ground, the scattered houses, the spindly bits of broken shrubbery in the park by the lake seemed hardly fastened to the earth. Even the looming legislative building, resplendently clad in sturdy Tyndall stone, looked as if it had just landed to rest in the sunlight, ready at any moment to sail off, as a butterfly might do. But Gladdie and the little girl were going nowhere. Small they were, but they were stalwart. Gladdie's doing. Her arm instinctively protected.

She was a little woman – that was part of the poignancy of the picture – but she was little in a strange, large-boned way, as if nature had meant her to be taller and she hadn't been given the nutrition her body needed. Her hair had come partly undone, and some of it had slipped down her neck above that tender, almost widow's hump. The rest of the escaped coppery strands flew straight out from her head as if electrified. The air was so dry. Her white muslin apron looped the back of her shoulders, scooped up her tidy hips. The pale yellow housedress came to the tops of her oxfords. The fabric of her dress was flowered; from a distance it looked speckled. It was greyed and softened by many launderings. The dishpan, held in her left hand, leaned against her leg. The little girl stood on her right.

Susan Smith. Mrs. Wutherspoon called her that after her own grandmother, and how appropriate the sibilance, in regard to her. Silent little thing. She was found after the cyclone, after the commotion died down, sitting on the roof of a new Ford automobile just across the bridge from Mrs. Wutherspoon's house, sitting with her legs out in front of her, like a doll who'd been set there, her ringlets still curled, her dress untouched. She must have had parents, or caretakers of some kind, but they hadn't been found. Susie Q was what Gladdie and Mrs. Wutherspoon liked to call her, verbally chucking her chin, hoping for a smile to reassure them that she wasn't afraid, that she ate enough and wasn't too thin.

Susan wore a short dress, light blue with white polka dots. It had been donated, along with some other clothes, by an Anglican family who'd learned of her plight. The ruffles on the yoke weren't enough to perk Susan up. She was a delicate child, everything about her a little too frail. Her hair was light brown, streaked by the sun, and very fine and straggly. For minutes now she hadn't moved, her head fitted into Gladdie's waist, her tiny shoulders under Gladdie's arm.

Small they were, but they were stalwart.

"It's very hot, isn't it?" Mrs. Wutherspoon said, as if the heat had suddenly, utterly, got her down.

"Yes," Orillia said. She could barely summon a whisper.

Mrs. Wutherspoon pulled a handkerchief out of her sleeve and mopped her face. Her pale blue eyes started to water and her spectacles fogged up. She said, "I think I'll lie down for a bit." And she left, gently closing the door behind her.

a mouth to feed

Mrs. Riley wasn't given to hitting her servants. She preferred to inflict a more dainty kind of misery on them. It was really only Mr. Riley who roused her to lambasting and, as she pointed out, that was only to keep herself from becoming bitter, which was what happened to women who held themselves in. As for her girls, she mostly yelled at them and threatened them with being turned out of the house. They mostly ignored her warnings, and used their own defenses. Dorrie took a dogged approach, gritting her teeth, sometimes snarling. As for Gladdie, though her ear infections cleared up over time and most of her hearing returned, she never did quite give up pretending to be deaf. At the same time, she kept in mind and adhered to Mr. Riley's advice: "Werk hard and be cherful." Whenever she recalled Mr. Riley sitting across the library table from her, she replaced just about everything they'd said to one another with that piece of advice of his. She could see all over again those scrunched-up words on the thin scrap of library paper, and above it Mr. Riley's hopeful face.

Gladdie had learned her duties at Mrs. Riley's quickly, and she performed them quickly too, which meant that once in a while she was able to sit down and ponder things. That's what she was doing one afternoon during her first summer at Mrs. Riley's – sitting on the back porch steps taking a break from pulling the great tall weeds that had taken over the garden since they were all too lazy to put in anything but potatoes and didn't give much care even to them. She'd nearly stepped on a dead mouse and right after that a fat toad jumped in her face, so she decided it was time to take a break. She was sweating, and the skin of her forearms and face was smarting with sunburn, but still she sat watching a snail creep along a strip of light, thinking it was the most beautiful day she'd ever seen and hoping Dorrie's baby would be born. And then into her mind in a flash came a room. It was a dark room with one thing in it shining: a locket that lay on the dresser on top of a cutwork scarf. In the dimness she could see her own fingers pick that locket up and open it. She knew she was opening it in secret, and she knew a photograph would be inside. She could see the face and hair. She was leaning forward, trying to see who it was in the picture, then it vanished and she saw just that snail creeping its slow way across the board they'd laid down over the mud in the spring, and hesitating because it had come to the edge. It was Margaret's room, she was sure of that, though she hadn't seen anything to prove it. She only remembered the rocking chair, and she hadn't seen that until she'd thought of it, and then she could almost feel the crocheted seat cover, it came to her so clearly. But now she wondered if she'd invented it all. There was no way to be sure. She couldn't even be sure which of the things she knew Margaret had taught her. She knew Margaret would have approved of Mr. Riley's advice. You weren't supposed to let yourself be sad. One of the best things, after wisdom, was a merry heart.

The question that had come to Gladdie when she first arrived at Mrs. Riley's popped into her head then. Why did Margaret have Gladdie call her by her first name? And the answer could only be that she was a servant. Margaret was a servant, just like she was and like Dorrie was. Dorrie. She jumped to her feet.

In the kitchen Mrs. Riley sat on her chair fanning herself with Mr. Riley's bowler. "Uh-uh!" she yelled, seeing Gladdie about to step in. "You've mud on those shoes." They'd had no rain for days and there was no mud anywhere, but Gladdie stopped in the doorway as she'd been told.

"Mrs. Riley," she said. "Can you just tell me what day it is?"

"You're very close to becoming a nuisance," Mrs. Riley said. "Why do you need to know?"

"In case Dorrie has her baby."

"In case Dorrie has her baby." Mrs. Riley shook her big sweaty head. "Lord love us, she can't help having it. The sooner the better, too."

"Please," Gladdie said. "I can't see it from here." And since the calendar hung close enough that Mrs. Riley could read it without rising from her chair, by only turning her head, she bothered to do so. "July 16th," she said. "The year of our Lord eighteen hundred seventy-seven."

"Thank you," Gladdie said, and turned to go.

"Thank you is as thank you does," Mrs. Riley muttered. She had a dark view always of Gladdie's politeness. In Mrs. Riley's opinion it was only part of Gladdie's fondness for thinking herself above her lot in life. She tried to encourage herself into a state of irritation, but it was too hot.

The snail had found some shade and drawn himself inside his pearly shell, so Gladdie went back to pulling weeds. They were warm in her hands. They'd started to be cooked, and stained her fingers a blackish green. A breeze came up, enough to keep her happy, thinking about Margaret again after a long time. July 16th, she thought, must be the best possible day for a birthday, for she'd never known one so beautiful. And whether or not Dorrie's baby was born, it was too good a day to waste, so she took it for her own. The rest of the day she hummed a little tune under her breath whenever she remembered she was now ten years old.

It was the next day Dorrie went into labour and the weather changed. Rain threatened all morning; about noon it began to drizzle, but by then Mrs. Riley and Gladdie and poor Dorrie were too occupied to look out the windows. As for Mr. Riley and the lodgers, they stayed as far from the kitchen as the layout of the house would allow, and most of them found something pressing to do off the premises, in spite of the rain. It was not a long labour, according to Mrs. Riley, but it was long enough to wear Dorrie out and make her cry a few times. The baby, when it finally came about eleven o'clock that night, was a boy. As a reward for Gladdie – because she'd stayed steady throughout the whole business and fetched and carried everything Mrs. Riley had called for and didn't add to the fuss – once the cord had been tied and cut and the baby had been wrapped in a flannel square into an oblong package, she got to hold him. Mrs. Riley advised Dorrie not to take him in her arms or even look at him. "Or I'll be telling you I told you so," she said.

He was not a handsome baby, in Gladdie's opinion. His skin was scaly and looked too loose on his forehead and cheeks, as if he'd been given too much for the size of his face. Nor was he much entertainment. He only wanted to sleep. Following Mrs. Riley's earlier instructions, Gladdie had pulled a drawer out of the china cupboard, emptied it and lined it with folded sheeting. The drawer sat waiting at the back of the table. Before Mrs. Riley went up to her own bed, she said to her, "You put him there for the night and don't be troubling yourself if he cries. Let him bawl all night if he's a mind to. You and Dorrie need your sleep."

When Mrs. Riley had gone, Dorrie, in a weary voice, said, "Give him here, Gladdie." Though she was afraid to go against Mrs. Riley's orders, not knowing what might come of it, Gladdie put the bundle into Dorrie's arms. For a good long time Dorrie held him and cried and cried.

"You'll ruin your voice, Dorrie," Gladdie said; however, Dorrie ignored her.

Finally Gladdie asked, "Will I put him in the drawer now?" She was falling asleep sitting up on her own cot.

"Bring it over here by me," Dorrie said through her tears. So Gladdie took the drawer over by Dorrie, and then went to bed.

"Good night, Dorrie," she said, but Dorrie didn't answer.

In the morning Mrs. Riley took the baby away. Dorrie cried all day. The next day was worse; her milk came down, and she rocked back and forth all day with her breasts bound and aching. No one but Gladdie went near her. On the fourth day Mrs. Riley stood over the cot where Dorrie lay with her face to the wall and said enough was enough, and Gladdie wasn't Dorrie's personal servant, and there would be mutiny in the dining room if the child cooked any more suppers, so it was up now, if you please, Missy.

Mrs. Riley guarded herself against maternity in any and all its forms. She prided herself on having no feelings in regard to children of any age and that included Gladdie. Nor did Gladdie ever, even once, wish she could be Mrs. Riley's child, but she knew one thing. A mother would be an advantage to a person. In fact, having parents of any kind would be a grand thing. It was the other end of the equation, she could see – it was bringing into the world another mouth to feed – that caused the problems.

Gladdie came up from the cellar where she'd been sent to scout for dirty dishes Mr. Mainwaring might have left in his pitiful room. She'd found a sticky plate and two cups growing frothy mould in the dank, low-ceilinged space. While she climbed up the rickety narrow stairs she heard Mr. Riley saying, "We'll just give him a bite, Georgina. The lad looks like he could use a bite." Dorrie was out, having taken the afternoon off, so it was Gladdie who was sent to the pantry to fetch the gravy from the night before and some bread for a boy who was sitting on the stool by the table.

"There's a bone there, too," Mr. Riley said.

"That's for soup," Mrs. Riley said.

"Well, it was," he said. "But this being a special occasion, Georgina." He got up himself from the kitchen table and went to the pantry for the remains of yesterday's roast.

"Mr. Riley's a generous man," Mrs. Riley said to the boy. "And if he had more of his own, we'd all be fortunate."

Gladdie stirred the gravy while it heated, and tried to flatten the lumps with the back of the wooden spoon. It was the middle of the afternoon. She had no idea who the boy was and waited to find out. He didn't seem at all curious about her, or in fact about anything, but sat hunched over on the stool gnawing on the chunk of bone Mr. Riley had given him until she set the gravy and a wedge of bread in a bowl before him. He didn't look up once, nor did anyone speak from that moment till he'd eaten the meal and scraped every lick from the bowl with his fingers and sucked the flavour from them.

Mrs. Riley said, "Now Harry, why is it you've done us the honour of this visit?" He glanced up then to Mrs. Riley. His eyes had the shining, guarded look of someone who's been hurt. You know, when you see that look, the desperation that came before it, the no help for it, not then, not now. In that instant he looked up, Gladdie saw everything she needed to know about the boy, and she knew that the boy understood as well as she did that Mrs. Riley would do nothing and Mr. Riley could do nothing to change a thing. No one was paying any attention to her, so she took herself off to the backyard and swung on the gate. It creaked and wailed while she rode it, the sound putting thoughts out of her head while the motion numbed her brain and soothed her.

When she heard them at the door, and Mr. Riley saying he'd see the boy part of the way home, she ran to the outhouse and barred herself in. Wouldn't you know it, she heard his voice for the first time, saying he needed to use it. Mr. Riley knocked on the door. "Gladdie? You in there?"

She slipped out and passed them as fast as she could. The kitchen was deserted. She sat down on Mrs. Riley's chair, and his voice came back to her, a deep voice for a boy and full of hope. Nothing in the words but the request to use the biffy, but she knew the sound of that self-deception and the reason for it – because Mr. Riley had been good to him. He knew better than to hope, anyone would, but he couldn't help himself. The pain of it hit Gladdie. She wished he'd run off without saying a word, or he'd thumbed his nose at them all. Mr. Riley didn't understand how awful it was to be half kind to a person if you weren't going to be kind all the way. And the boy would never say, he'd never tell, he couldn't, what it meant to him, neither the kind behaviour nor the mean. Gladdie set her head down on the tabletop, cool on her cheek, and let her throat ache.

Mr. Riley caught hell when he got home. It was suppertime by then, and Gladdie was in the dining room clearing the plates away from the lodgers and not letting herself think about the boy anymore. They all heard Mr. Riley enter by the back door and go upstairs. They all looked up at the ceiling to help them hear what would happen. Mrs. Riley had been in her room long-suffering for hours and she'd boycotted supper.

"Kindly stop interfering in my affairs," was the first clear statement from above. Then: "You're a goddam meddler." Then: "You've no Christly pity for me!" This last ended in a wail that reminded Gladdie of the gate.

They had a full house that summer. The lodgers included, besides Mr. Mainwaring, who'd lived in the cellar so long Mrs. Riley had started calling him Mushroom Mainwaring, and slimy Mr. O'Connor, and old Miss Avis, a Mrs. Friel who'd taken the back room off the kitchen, and an odd young man, by anyone's standards, named Mr. Twigg. Mr. Twigg looked like a smaller, younger version of someone else. Seeing him, you'd imagine his father, a man not quite so wee, married to a bossy big woman. Young Mr. Twigg wasn't attracted to females who were large and overbearing and was, maybe in consequence, single. He had round wire spectacles and a shiny face and was blessed or cursed with bristling hair that began low on his forehead and bristled from there up and over his head and far down the back of his neck. He was a journalist and wrote for anyone who'd print him. The lodgers and Gladdie thought he must be a failure at his occupation or he'd never have been rooming at Mrs. Riley's. On this occasion he rose from the table smirking, pointed to the floor above, where Mrs. Riley's voice had disappeared out of hearing range, and went out of the room on tiptoe. Mrs. Friel gave a shake of her head in Miss Avis's direction and Miss Avis blushed. She often got on the receiving end of Mrs. Friel's gestures and she never had any idea what the other woman meant.

Mr. O'Connor grabbed Gladdie as she was clearing the table and clutched her arm while she held her breath against his pomade. "How's about another helping of pudding?" he said, making the word pudding sound obscene. He knew very well Gladdie didn't have the power to grant such a request, if there had been any pudding left, but he'd also noticed that Mrs. Friel, a tall scrawny blonde woman with little appetite, hadn't eaten hers.

"You may have mine, if you wish," Mrs. Friel said. "I've not touched it."

"Thank you, dear lady," Mr. O'Connor said, in his crafty manner – for experience had inexplicably led him to believe women liked a bit of the wolf in a man – and before Mrs. Friel could lift her pudding toward him, if she was inclined to do so, he demonstrated his boarding-house reach.

Mr. Twigg had told everyone on arrival at Mrs. Riley's that he was an amateur thespian, and he was always keen to use his talents. So it was, when he returned after supper to the parlour, that he lowered his voice and, delivering looks in all directions, gave them the gist of the upstairs discussion, the parts that had been too subdued for them to hear. That conversation was ending, as he spoke, with another couple of wails and a burst of tears and the thump thump of Mrs. Riley's back being patted.

The story was that Mrs. Riley had, late in her child-bearing years, delivered herself of a son. But rather than drop him off in secret at an orphanage, which is what she'd done with Dorrie's babies, she'd put him with a woman who'd raise your child for a fee. She'd paid all along for his upkeep. He was eleven years old this summer and the worst thing was she'd let him know her. She'd visited him and even brought him, a few times, to the house. She'd been weak. He wasn't Mr. Riley's son, and she couldn't expect Mr. Riley to take him in, nor did she wish to have him with her in her matrimonial home. He was the child of a previous common-law arrangement. And now the boy, named Harry Doney, had shown up at her door, having made his own way to see her. He was bound to be a nuisance, reminding her of her past.

two in the hand

She's very ladylike, isn't she?" Hilda said. "Just as you said. Such a little thing. Those poor thin cheeks. Oh, Gladdie, it must be awful for her, to be crippled and so young. I wonder if she's bottling up her feelings. Do you think she's bottling up her feelings? I confess I'm a little puzzled by her. You know, never a complaint, and she must sometimes feel badly about her fate. She's a little cool toward me. I think I talk too much and it irritates her."

"Oh, no," Gladdie said. "She told me just this morning how happy she is here."

"Here's Miss Cooper I was telling you about," Gladdie said.

"Hello Susan."

Gladdie didn't push the little girl forward but waited with her in the doorway until the child's curiosity got the better of her fears and she raised her face to Orillia's.

"How do you do?" Orillia said. Then Susan went over with her hand out and in it a few tiny flowers, weeds were all they were, with lacy yellowish heads. When she reached the bed she opened her hand, and the delicate stems, all bent in the direction her fingers had held them, clung to her skin. She had to brush them off onto the coverlet. Orillia scooped them up and reformed the bouquet, clumsily, since the stems were limp from the heat of Susan's hand.

Gladdie liked the way Orillia studied the little girl's mild face for the few seconds before Susan ducked her head and stepped back to Gladdie's side. It was a careful face. Orillia would understand.

Gladdie and Hilda brought their sewing to Orillia's room in the evening, after Susan had gone to bed. Hilda asked if Orillia would like some handiwork to occupy her, and Orillia declined. She thought she'd entertain them while they worked.

"Did you hear the story about the baby?" Orillia asked. "They say the cyclone plucked a baby right out of its mother's arms and hurled it into the vortex." She liked the word vortex. The nurse who'd told her the story had used it, and Orillia had been impressed. The word, even the shape her mouth had to take to say it, was remarkably like her idea of the cyclone. It whirled sound in and spit it out.

"It ended up in the oven of a cookstove a block away. Not a bit hurt." A small smile played about Orillia's lips and then vanished. "I don't know if it can be believed," she said. "There's that saying, 'a bun in the oven,' that makes it doubtful, since it's so satisfying."

Gladdie and Hilda laughed a little, to encourage her even if they didn't understand her.

"I'll adopt Susan if I can," Hilda said suddenly. "If her parents aren't found. My only fear is my age. They might say I'm too old to adopt a child."

"Pshaw," Gladdie said.

Hilda went on, "I've heard it's hard for a single woman to adopt, but if a husband's all that's needed..."

"You could snare a husband like that," Gladdie said, snapping her fingers in Hilda's face.

"I don't want children," Orillia said. "I've seen enough of other people's."

Gladdie and Hilda may have been accustomed to young women saying such things. They accepted her remark quite placidly. "It would be different if they were your own," was all that Hilda said.

"I have so many things I want to do," Orillia said.

Gladdie and Hilda were quick to agree, too quick for Orillia's liking. They went back to their darning and embroidery and she looked up and down the lilac walls and took another tack. "And who is Mr. Best?" she asked.

Oh, well. They were eager to tell her that. Mr. Best rented the big room next to Orillia's and used it in the daytime, as an office.

"What kind of work does he do?"

"Very Important Work," Gladdie said, grinning with her wide ripply grin so the crows' feet at the outside corners of her eyes fanned in that attractive way, reminding you how likeable she was.

"Yes, indeed," Hilda said. She glanced at Gladdie over her glasses for permission to be naughty. "He pays full board, which means all meals. But I have to bring them upstairs. I have to leave the tray on the dresser in the hall. He's *not* to be disturbed."

"Oh my."

"Oh my is right. Sometimes his food gets cold before he thinks to open his door and take it."

"But Hilda says she isn't to knock except if there's a fire."

"How Very, Very Important his work must be," Orillia said. "I heard his footsteps and his door opening and closing today, and I heard him typewriting now and then," she said. "But I didn't see him."

"Mr. Best doesn't think much of my having Susan here," Hilda said. "I didn't consult him before bringing her into the house, and when he saw her, his face went so red I thought he might be having a fit. 'A child, Mrs. Wutherspoon?' he said. 'She's visiting, I presume.' And when I told him she was lodging, he said, 'I can't tolerate a child, Mrs. Wutherspoon. I can't work with a child in the house. I rent a room to escape my own children. This will not do.' So I asked him if he'd accomplished anything the week before, and he had. He'd got quite a lot done. I let him know Susan had been in residence all the previous week – with him not aware of her presence. 'But it's up to you,' I said. 'There's no problem letting rooms at this time if you decide you have to leave because of the child.' 'Well, well,' he said. 'We'll see.' And he's never raised it again. That's how quiet Susan is."

"Susan's wise," Gladdie said. "She's learning what's expected of her here."

Dr. Kitely arrived without his nurse. His nurse was indisposed. Would Mrs. Wutherspoon accompany him to Miss Cooper's room?

Orillia heard the murmurs in the hallway. She recognized her doctor's calm, diffident intonation and could tell by the delight in Hilda's voice that he was already a great success with her. No doubt by the time they reached the landing, she'd have decided to send him home with cookies, his only fault his being too thin.

It was different, seeing him in her bedroom, in his nice summer suit. His black hair slanted over his forehead when he bent over her, accentuating his angular face. A twitch of his cheek showed he was aware of more than he would acknowledge. Only by accident would he ever reveal any feelings. She found herself responding to him in two ways at once: on the deeper level she respected him, but she wanted to mock him, too, for his rectitude, and the way he hid behind his role. Or did she want to punish him? After all, he'd offered her his devotion. She'd seen it in his eyes. He knew she'd seen it or he wouldn't have blinked the way he did. And ever since that day, he'd denied it.

Mrs. Wutherspoon stood back, at the end of the bed, in case she should actually be needed.

Bedside chat pained Dr. Kitely; there would be no idle talk. Orillia answered his terse questions with a masklike face and a matter-of-factness bordering on mimicry. She really couldn't stop herself, when he was being so brusque. He tapped the casts and peered at them and took hold of her toes. She flinched.

"I'm not hurting you, am I?"

"You tickle," she said.

"I'm sorry," he said gravely.

Mrs. Wutherspoon was beginning to look bewildered.

"Oh, it's better than hurting," Orillia said in her best spritely manner. The good doctor didn't blink, but Mrs. Wutherspoon did.

"When can I get up?" Orillia asked when he headed for the door.

"Two weeks, if all goes well."

"Two weeks?"

He was kind enough to give her a rueful grin.

"Doctors are too cautious," Orillia said.

After Hilda had shown him to the door, she'd come back up with Gladdie, who wanted to hear the verdict, and Susan, who only wanted to be with Gladdie.

"Two weeks!" Orillia said. "Why did he put casts on if I have to stay in bed another two weeks?"

"He's the doctor," Hilda said. "He's very good-looking, isn't he?"

"You should hear the nurses gossip about him," Orillia said.

"I think he should get married," Hilda said. "I'm sure all his patients imagine they're in love with him."

"Do you think so? But he is married," Orillia said.

"Oh, I didn't get that impression. I'm not sure why. He was certainly professional in his attitude. He's very wise, anyway, to have a woman in the room on house calls. His nurse couldn't come today, so he asked me," she told Gladdie.

"I don't like that nurse," Orillia said. "She was the one who came here with me. She sat beside me all the way from the hospital, ordering the driver to avoid potholes after he'd hit them and grabbing my hand when we lurched. She kept hold of my hand the whole way. It hurt. My hands are still bruised. I see no reason why I should have put up with it. A man wouldn't have. A man doesn't have to put up with touching he doesn't want."

Orillia sounded really angry, but Hilda was watching Gladdie. How concerned she looked – as if the obnoxious nurse had walked into the room and taken *her* hand and squeezed it till it hurt.

"A letter, from San Francisco," Hilda sang from the bottom of the stairs. She'd just come from the post office where she checked every day for Orillia's mail as well as her own and Gladdie's. Four loud clacks from the typewriter in Mr. Best's room, followed by the ripping sound of paper being torn from the platen, and then an ominous silence, answered her. She tiptoed up the stairs and whispered, "From your mother," as she handed it over. "Mrs. Cooper Hagan, I see she calls herself."

Mr. Best's door flung open, and he strode across the hall and pounded down the stairs and out of the house. It was the first Orillia had seen of him, and he was only a blur behind Hilda.

"Oh dear," Hilda said and sat down. "He complained yesterday after the doctor was here that we shouldn't have come up to your room. Not during working hours."

"It's bad luck for him, isn't it? Having an invalid next door. He must have expected someone who'd go out to work all day and leave the upstairs to him."

"You might complain yourself, Miss Cooper, with him clattering and banging on that machine for hours."

"I think he naps more than he typewrites," Orillia said. "And please – Orillia."

"Orillia. And you must call me Hilda."

Just then they heard the front door open and close. "Gladdie!" Hilda called, and Gladdie came up with Susan behind her.

"Did you see Mr. Best go out?"

"Face like a thundercloud," Gladdie said.

"We've annoyed him – again."

Susan went to the window. She bent to see a spiderweb in the corner of the frame. She blew on it till it wobbled and swayed. A tiny black speck on it was some kind of bug. Dead.

"Miss Cooper – I mean Orillia – had a letter from her mother today."

Susan actually looked at Orillia.

"Yes, Susan, from her mother," Hilda said. "Who doesn't know she's here, injured."

"Who doesn't want to know," Orillia said. "She's on her honeymoon, after all, Mrs. Wutherspoon."

"She'd come if she knew, honeymoon or not."

"Well, I don't need her, do I? I have you. I have you two. Two in the hand are worth one in the bush. Isn't that what they say?"

Later, she told them about her letter. "Almost impossible to read," she said. "Mother writes on the front and back of every page and across in both directions to save paper, and half the time the ink bleeds and kills whatever she meant to say. It's all advice, anyway. She managed to write two pages saying almost nothing about San Francisco." Florence had also written saying almost nothing about her new husband, but Orillia didn't mention that. She said, "For two cents I'd write and tell her what a very nice life I have here in Regina."

It was a very nice life. She knew that when she said it. Every evening Gladdie came to sit with her just as she had the weeks she was in the hospital. Every evening, between washing the dishes and putting Susan to bed (because she was the only one who could calm the child so she slept), she came upstairs to sit in the back room with Orillia and do absolutely nothing, or so she said, trying to make it seem as if Orillia was doing her a favour, giving her a chance to rest. In the meantime, Hilda read to Susan from *Hurlbut's Story of the Bible.* They'd established quite a routine, Gladdie and Hilda. They tried to keep Susan from drifting away from reality, and Orillia from getting bored or sad. To repay them, Susan obeyed them and Orillia acted happy. And she ate, she ate a little from every tray, because it pleased them.

It was a joy to Gladdie to have Orillia in the house, to see her improving every day. They were almost a family, except for Mr. Best. Gladdie could have done without Mr. Best, but you couldn't have a perfect world. As Mrs. Riley was wont to say, "If the world was meant to be perfect, they'd have had to leave you out."

Hilda liked Orillia. She'd said so. And she'd told Gladdie she was amazed how well the girl withstood the pain. "You can see by her face how hard it is sometimes," Hilda said. "But she never mentions it; she never complains."

The story about Dr. Kitely's nurse had come at Gladdie out of nowhere. "I see no reason why I should have put up with it," Orillia said. "A man wouldn't have. A man doesn't have to put up with touching he doesn't want." It felt like a slap. It made her remember Dorrie's arm flung against her, and her outraged face. It made her remember, like a child again, that she'd come from a bad house. She knew one thing for sure: Orillia Cooper had been raised better than she'd been, even if Mrs. Cooper wasn't her idea of a good mother. Orillia would be horrified to know half of Gladdie's past. There was a big difference between their lives, and a summer of helping the girl over a rough spot wasn't going to change that.

The letter from Mrs. Cooper was another mote in her eye, a reminder for Gladdie that she was on a dishonest course. She'd lied to keep the woman from her daughter. Hilda would think it a crime to do that to a mother. But Orillia had made herself clear. "I don't need her, do I? I have you two." She'd come right out and said that. And it was true. She was better off here. This house was better for her, this little made-up family was better than her own, with Florence Cooper and the Captain, could ever be. She was happy here, she was eating more, she was improving every day.

Susan was improving too. She had more life in her, and even sparks of fun. You just need to be with people who care about you; that's all you need to turn your life around, Gladdie thought.

blood

Since he'd first appeared, Harry Doney hadn't come back to the house often, but every few months he'd turned up. As he seemed to like them, Mr. Riley had suggested they take the boy in. Mrs. Riley said she wouldn't. There was no reason given, or needed; Mrs. Riley wanted people in their places. It was common during that time to find Harry in the kitchen gulping down whatever food could be scrounged, hardly saying a word unless Mr. Riley happened to be home. His visits resulted in Mrs. Riley spending an extravagant length of time in her room, and if she came down at all afterwards, it was in an altered state, either chippy or weepy. Harry and Gladdie had tended to keep away from one another.

Of all the times Harry Doney visited at Mrs. Riley's, the one Gladdie always remembered best was the last. It seemed that day was designed from the beginning to have just the ending it did. In the morning a cat got into the house, a wild scrawny tabby from the back alleys. Mrs. Riley shrieked at the sight of it and yelled to Dorrie to get the broom. They chased it, the two of them, squealing while it raced from room to room, desperate for a way out. Miss Avis quaked in the parlour. She nearly uttered a cry as it leapt over her feet, and she dropped a stitch in her knitting.

"Hold the door open," Mrs. Riley shouted to Gladdie as they ran through the kitchen on the animal's second whirl through the house. "Dorrie," she screeched. "Make it go back there now."

Dorrie swacked the broom on the floor and against the door frames, and together they so boosted the cat's panic that it shat as it streaked through the kitchen to the open day beyond. What a stink. You couldn't just wipe it up. The floor had to be scrubbed. "You might as well do the entire thing," Mrs. Riley said to Dorrie. "Gladdie, you help, for it's a hot day for heavy work." This was how it came about that Mrs. Riley got to experience the scene she'd pictured several years before, wherein side by side her two servants washed her floor. She did appear to derive a little mild satisfaction from the sight.

Mr. Riley, earlier in the season, had rigged up a shower out back in the corner between the porch and the house. He'd found a section of a high fence leaning against the rubble of a demolished cottage where a glass factory was going up. "It was there for the taking," he said, not knowing at the time what use he'd have for it. Once he'd dragged it home, he was so hot the idea of the shower came to him. Since building it, he'd had himself a sprinkling every warm day. When they'd done the scrubbing, Dorrie declared she was going to try Mr. Riley's contraption; she couldn't bear her own smell.

"You should try it," she said afterwards to Gladdie. She looked considerably fresher and five years younger with her wet hair plastered to her head. They'd passed the two milestone days of summer – Gladdie's secret birthday and the next day that no one mentioned for fear of upsetting Dorrie, and Gladdie was thirteen, or she thought she was. She felt shy at the thought of being outside naked, however much the fence shielded a person from view, but her skin prickled with sweat and heat, and the thought of clean hair made her scalp itch. Her armpits smelled tinny, a new smell she liked and often sniffed. The shower lured her, though, and she took a bar of Mrs. Halladay's soap and a towel outside along with her change of clothes.

Gladdie'd had a good acquaintance, by the time she was nine, with the various discharges of the human body. Of them all, what she hated most were the yellow brown slippery globs of phlegm that had to be dumped and cleansed from Mr. Tupper's spittoon daily, and she was relieved – no, more than relieved – she was the happiest she'd been in a long time the day she heard Mrs. Riley say she wouldn't, no matter who asked for it, have a spittoon in the house. Of course she knew about monthlies, but she hadn't considered them in regard to herself, so she came back into the house that day feeling she was a different person. Dorrie was humming at the sink. If she wasn't the happiest she'd been in years, she had, at least for now, stepped outside the shadow of her grief. Gladdie went to her cot and lay down on it, thinking it was her turn now. It was her Dark Hour.

"I wouldn't like to be you if Her Ladyship comes in and catches you napping," Dorrie said. When Gladdie didn't answer, Dorrie dried her hands on her apron and came over to the cot. She said, "What's wrong?"

"Nothing."

"In that case, I'd like some help with the dishes."

"Dorrie," Gladdie said. "I'm dying." She didn't know why she said such a false thing, but it was what she wanted to say in spite of not really feeling it.

"You're young to die," Dorrie said. She sat down then, plop, on the bed beside Gladdie and put her head in her hands. "I sounded just like Mrs. Riley," she said.

Poor Dorrie. Right when she was happiest, a moment of misery smote her like that. Out of nowhere, she started telling Gladdie about one day she'd gone to the park at Allan Gardens and sat on a bench all afternoon and evening and what she'd seen. A mother and her daughter passed by the bench, the mother in front. Something was wrong with her. She was stout and knock-kneed, maybe that was all that caused it, but she walked in an odd staggering way, and she was followed by her girl, a child of five or six, who was made perfectly normally, as far as eyes could see, but she'd lurched just like her mother. Dorrie lost herself in ruminating about how awful it was that in spite of her not liking Mrs. Riley at all and never wanting to be anything like her, in fact wishing to be very unlike her, and in spite of efforts she'd made to set herself against the woman and keep her influence at bay, it was all too probable that, just by living with her, she'd become like Mrs. Riley in some of her ways. "Next thing you know I'll be scratching my left tit while I'm talking, Gladdie," she said, trying to laugh about it. But she felt, as she put it, a shudder in her soul, remembering the park that day, and how she'd sat on that bench wondering what would happen to her if she never went back to Mrs.

Riley's. She hadn't been able to think of a single place in all the world that would take her in. She'd sat there until the sky grew dark and she realized the people in the park had changed. A poorer class of people had slipped by her to their accustomed posts under the black trees. They'd offer her no alternative to Mrs. Riley's that Dorrie would want to take.

Dorrie came back to the present after a bit and remembered Gladdie and felt her brow. "What's wrong?" she asked. She looked at Gladdie as if she hadn't seen her in a while, and then she said she thought Gladdie was almost pretty these days though her hair was as red as ever.

Gladdie whispered something very foolish to Dorrie. "The Lifeblood's flowing out of me."

"Well," said Dorrie. "If it's flowing out where I suspect it is, you'd better get used to it." She'd always been very private about her body's functions and had not spoken ever to anyone, even to Gladdie, of her time of month. "It's the curse," she said. "It's blood on your drawers, isn't it? You're a woman now, that's all."

Gladdie let Dorrie tell her what to do.

Mr. Riley came home too late for dinner that afternoon and found silence rolling through the house. Mrs. Riley was napping and Dorrie was nowhere about. Mr. Riley went to the pantry to see what he could scrounge and heard a sneeze in the bedroom next door. Mrs. Friel must have stayed home from work, he thought. She must have come down with something. She might appreciate a show of affection, Mr. Riley thought.

Not wanting to risk even a quiet rap, he opened Mrs. Friel's door, expecting to find her conveniently in bed. But it was Gladdie he found, deep into the perils of someone noble, in the corner chair. She had her legs up, her skirt wrapped around them, her chin resting on her knees and the book in front of them. Mr. Riley whispered that she looked paler than usual. She had a sudden wish that he was dead.

Whenever Gladdie had a few minutes to herself, she'd sneak into Mrs. Friel's bedroom off the kitchen. That was during the daylight hours when Mrs. Friel had gone to work in what she called the salt mine, which was actually a dressmaking establishment.

Gladdie curled up in Mrs. Friel's wicker chair and read Mrs. Friel's cheap novels.

"Did you go to school, Gladdie, before you come here?" Mr. Riley asked her, still whispering.

"No," she said.

"But you're quite the reader."

"I was privately taught," she said.

"Privately?"

"By a person, privately."

He could tell she didn't want to speak of it, or to talk to him at all just then, but for some reason known only to himself he couldn't seem to leave. "Where you lived before?" he asked. "Why did you leave?"

"I had to leave."

Mr. Riley sat down on Lizzy Friel's bed and nodded several times as if he knew something wise about leaving. Then he got up finally and took himself off, and Gladdie went back to reading about the dangers of being young and beautiful and soft in a hard world.

That evening Mr. and Mrs. Riley went out to a church function. The lodgers sat in the parlour after supper discussing this unusual turn of affairs, and luckily Mr. Twigg was able to enlighten them as to its cause. In the afternoon Mrs. Riley had got the idea into her head that Mrs. Friel had stayed home from work. She'd thought she'd heard voices in Mrs. Friel's bedroom. Luckily for Mr. Twigg's story, and in seeming support of it, Mrs. Friel had retired to bed early with a headache. The others leaned forward in anticipation. Mr. Twigg, in an astonishing way, always came up with the goods. "I heard her say to him," was a phrase common to the amateur thespian, and he used it now. "I heard her say to him," he looked over one shoulder, then the other, then leaned to meet them, "'don't think I don't know you've been tucking into that Friel.'"

Mr. Twigg chuckled. He'd scandalized them again.

Harry Doney came to the back door while the lodgers were in the parlour. Gladdie was clearing the dining-room table and listening to Mr. Twigg's account, and didn't hear him knock. Harry opened the door and entered the kitchen. He could hear them all in the parlour. He went upstairs and searched the two floors and found no one, and when he returned to the kitchen, only Gladdie was there, clearing the plates into the slop pail. "Where's my mother?" he asked. She jumped a foot.

"Gone out," she said. "Where did you come from?"

"Where's Dorrie?"

"Gone out."

Maybe Harry had been changing all along and she hadn't noticed, or maybe it was a sudden thing, as it seemed. Anyway, she saw a difference in him. His face was sharper, his shoulders were wider than before and he was taller. He'd become all angles, and sinewy. He'd replaced the hurt look in his eyes with an amused expression, and instead of slipping from one place to another, he'd developed a bit of a swagger. Talking to him was like dancing would be with somebody faster than you and greased.

She was holding a dripping plate in one hand and a spatula in the other, and her nose got itchy. She rubbed it on her sleeve, and that made it itchier than ever. She set the plate on the pile of dishes, the spatula on the counter and pulled up her apron to use as a hanky. She chafed her nose hard with both hands.

Harry sat on the stool, tipping it and leaning his back against the wall. It made her nervous, having to deal with him alone. She offered to feed him what she could scare up, though there were no leftovers from supper. The lodgers, as they often did, had eaten everything in sight. She went to the pantry and got him bread, with sugar and milk because the bread was stale. "Baby food," he said, but he ate it. She brought him an apple and set it on the table. She watched him eat and tried to pretend she wasn't because he held the apple in an awkward way, cradling it in the palm of his hand instead of using his fingers. After he'd done, he said, "Where'd they all go?"

Dorrie had a man friend and had gone out to meet him. She hadn't had permission for the afternoon and evening off. It was a secret, and a worrisome one – Dorrie was so wrapped up in the fellow she didn't have much time for anyone else anymore – so Gladdie said they'd gone to church and let it seem she meant that all of them had gone.

"You go to church?" he asked.

He hadn't ever before asked her a question about herself. The mocking tone in his voice flustered her. "No," she said.

"You have to work while the others go?"

"No."

"Why don't you go?"

"I don't know."

She sniffed. Her nose was itchy again but she didn't like to scratch it.

He grinned. "What kind of thing is that to say? You have to know."

She wasn't going to tell him she'd never been inside a church. To get out of saying it, she thought to turn the question around, and asked him if he went.

"I'm an unbeliever," he said. Proud. She sat down in Mrs. Riley's chair across the table from him. She made her sitting neat and small and let it take up some time.

"Shocked, ain't you?" he said, pleased with himself. She *was* shocked, but not by what he'd said. It was the new way she felt about him. Instead of wanting him to leave, like she usually did, she wanted him to stay. She wanted him to talk more in that personal way to her, but at the same time she was nervous of him. In Mrs. Friel's novels, young women started to *palpitate* when with young men. It was such a silly word thinking about it made her laugh. Then she got the giggles when she tried to stop.

Harry had no idea why she was laughing. He tried to counter it with as much scorn as he could muster. He said, "Bet you say your prayers every night."

She did of course say her prayers every night. She had since before she could remember, as Margaret had taught her. She knelt and prayed to God to make her a better girl. In the past year, especially, she'd given hours and hours of thought to God and Jesus and Mary, and especially Mary, as she thought she could help her get into heaven. But Mary, whenever Gladdie pictured her in her pretty clean blue and white robes, had no comfort in her face. Most of the time she wouldn't so much as look in Gladdie's direction. Thinking about that helped her to get her laughing under control. Harry's face was fierce, and she understood how much it meant to him to disbelieve, how he needed that as a certainty. She had a vision of flames surrounding him. Then a beautiful, thrilling picture came to her of the two of them walking hand in hand into the flames down a long corridor where pitchforks were poised above them.

Mr. and Mrs. Riley came in the front door. They went directly to the parlour and joined the lodgers, distributing unusual good cheer. "Go get her," Harry said.

"Leave her be," Gladdie said. "What do you want with her?"

"I've slivers in my fingers," he said. He held up his hands. A fine pain flipped through Gladdie, up her spine, at the sight of his shiny, swollen fingertips. The slivers were in deep and had become infected.

"I'll take them out," she said. But he shook his head.

"Mrs. Riley, could you come here?" she asked, stopping at the French doors between the dining room and the parlour. They were all listening to Mr. Riley's account of the meeting to raise money for the missionary fund. By slightly changing the stress of a few words earlier uttered by some of the good ladies of the parish, Mr. Riley had the lodgers gasping for air, and even Mrs. Riley was laughing. Mrs. Riley had stuffed herself into a wine red dress with old-fashioned leg-of-mutton sleeves for her evening out. When she turned in her chair to glare at Gladdie, her entire body had to revolve, and the sleeves took up all the space in the room. She didn't answer, so Gladdie repeated the question and then said, "It's someone to see you."

"In the kitchen?"

"Yes."

"If it's Harry." She put her hand out for Mr. Riley to help her to her feet, and followed Gladdie to the kitchen.

Gladdie couldn't understand why Harry insisted on having Mrs. Riley called to help him and then when she came, he cowered from her. And Mrs. Riley was in a state. You could hear it in her voice, the alarm. Harry brought that out in Mrs. Riley, a high degree of alertness. The way Mrs. Riley acted around Harry made Gladdie want to lie down on the floor, just lie right down flat out on the floor and let everyone in the house step over her.

"Get me a basin and a jug of cold water, Gladdie," Mrs. Riley said. "You soak your hands," she told Harry. "I'll find me tweezers." Off she went, leaving a space of relief in the room. Gladdie filled the jug and brought it to the table, fussing with the way she poured the water into the basin. She couldn't think what to say to Harry. She couldn't say, "Someday we'll walk into Hell together." But that was what she wanted to tell him, even though she knew it was the most froward thing she'd ever contemplated.

That night she lay in bed thinking about the worst thing. Being froward wasn't the worst thing. Being foolish wasn't the worst thing either. At the time, she'd thought getting the slivers out might be the worst thing she'd ever witnessed, worse even than a woman giving birth, and she'd seen two of those since Dorrie. Harry ground his teeth to keep from making any sound while Mrs. Riley dug with a needle into the pads of his fingers. "There's an end," she'd say. "See it sticking up there?" And she'd go after it with the tweezers. She placed each sliver on his other palm, remarking on the size and difficulty of each. He winced and gasped throughout, but never cried. Mr. Riley came to the kitchen after the lodgers retired to their rooms, but he left again right away.

The worst thing was when Mrs. Riley was finished and she stood over Harry and asked, "How'd you get into such a mess? What were you up to?" And he didn't say anything for a while, and then he said, "I won't come here anymore." It was as if he'd hit them or even killed them. His voice so sullen and his eyes dull, blind to them. Gladdie didn't remember Mrs. Riley leaving the kitchen. She was just gone and there was silence and Gladdie was alone with him.

When he got up to go without saying a word to her, she followed him. Outside it was dark, a warm tender kind of darkness that she could feel on her skin. She'd have walked on, down the path with him, kept up with him. She imagined going with him, staying with him wherever he went. But he turned at the bottom of the porch steps and put his hand out and touched her cheek, and when she moved toward him, he set his hand on her shoulder and held her back.

She lay in bed and wished she'd told him she'd always be his friend. She wondered at all that had hurt him so and why Mrs. Riley had given him up, why she couldn't after all let him live with her, and how anyone could go on in the world with so much sadness. And then she wondered who was being hurt now, this very second while she lay safe in her bed, and she could hardly bear to be alive. No, she thought, I can't live in a world this bad. I'll have to change it.

In the morning, she was sitting up when Dorrie came in from the outhouse. "You've got blood on your cheek," Dorrie said in a perfect fit of disgust.

young love

Harry Doney didn't come back to Mrs. Riley's house again. Once or twice in the next few years he caught sight of his mother on the street and ducked into a doorway until she'd gone by on her business. Once Mr. Riley stopped him on the sidewalk and gave him a dollar. Soon after his last visit to the house, he turned fourteen and began to look for work. That was an endeavour made to order, it seemed, to show him that he was fit for nothing unless given a chance at the same time as he couldn't be given a chance till proven fit. Finally, because he was lucky enough to be a big lad for his age, he was taken on to deliver coal, doing the heavy work for a driver named Vernon Ormiston. Vernon was an Englishman of fifty trying hard to appear nimble, and that was an effort that left him little energy for comradeship and less for kindness. Harry found a room in a men's boarding house on Bathurst Street, where he was thought to be considerably older than his years, not so much because of his size but on account of his keeping his own counsel. He was no fool.

On his way to and from the coal yard every day, Harry passed two establishments that interested him. The first was Paragon Engravers Co., on King Street, who displayed their art in the ground-floor windows of their plant. The intricacy of the engravings fascinated him, and sometimes, even if he was tired after work, he'd stop to look if they had something new. Without thinking about it, he judged their compositions. The owner came out after office hours one day and saw Harry with a scowl on his face, regarding a new piece that demonstrated their work in livestock portraiture. The owner must have thought it odd to see a begrimed young working man interested in his window display.

"Do you find it lifelike?" he asked, pointing at the prize bull.

"No," Harry said. "It's a picture."

"It is a picture. It represents a bull," the owner said.

"It makes a bull look a fine thing," said Harry. "But the words are wrong."

"That's the animal's name and specifications," the man said.

"I mean the way of them. The letters. They ain't firm enough."

"Well," the owner said. "I believe you're right. And he asked Harry if he'd ever considered learning engraving as a trade.

"No," Harry said. He wasn't sure what engraving was, but if it was a kind of drawing he wanted to do it.

"Can you read?"

"No," was the answer.

"That's a pity," the man said. "Good day to you, young man."

The other interesting place Harry passed on his route, without ever venturing inside, was the Cyclorama on Front Street, where Mr. Riley had promised Gladdie he'd take her. But that hadn't ever come up again.

Some changes had taken place at Mrs. Riley's during those years, the best of them being that Mr. O'Connor had given notice. Mr. Parchman, a new lodger, had taken Mr. O'Connor's old garret but was waiting for Mr. Twigg to move out so he could take over his superior chamber. He didn't want the ground-floor room. To Mr. Parchman, ground-floor rooms, when off the kitchen to boot, were for common folk. Mrs. Friel had left suddenly. Even Mr. Twigg hadn't been able to discover her reasons for departing, though he was cheery in speculation. "I went to her," he told the others, "and begged her to be frank. For the good of the rest of us. She knew what I meant. Oh, she knew exactly what I meant." The lodgers all sat with their elbows on the table, forgetting to eat their breakfast gruel. But Mrs. Friel, if she had known exactly what Mr. Twigg meant, had decided not to speak up, so there was never confirmation of his suspicions. Most of the lodgers didn't really think Mrs.

Riley would have gone to such lengths. She'd have warned Mrs. Friel, threatened her too, but poisoning the woman's food they thought was beyond her. "She was wasting away those last days," Mr. Twigg said. Pale Mr. Mainwaring, who usually didn't utter a word, snickered then and said it was her other appetite that had suffered during that time, for Mr. Riley had been called off and hadn't they all observed him mooching about with his tail between his legs. So to speak. Mr. O'Connor had snorted, and Miss Avis had covered her mouth with her knitting.

Mr. O'Connor was the lucky one. A promotion to supervisor at the brewery where he worked came about through his own initiative. He bought himself a suit although he didn't need one, kneaded extra pomade into his hair and found himself better rooms. No one mentioned it, but they were all at Mrs. Riley's glad to see him go. It wasn't until she saw the others' relief, when the door closed on Mr. O'Connor's back, that Gladdie realized the rest of them had liked him no better than she had. For years she'd ignored his smirks and suggestions and evaded his fat fingers. He was a big, rude man and his pomade stunk.

Vernon slipped and it was Harry's fault. He'd spilt a shovelful of coal right by the cart and left it there to slide out from under Vernon's feet when the driver hopped down, nimble as ever, from the seat. Vernon's back seized up. He couldn't move, not even to stand up and get back into the cart to be driven home, nor could Harry lift him by himself and haul him up. They waited until a fellow came along, and in that time Harry was cursed so thoroughly he was reminded of his childhood. The result of it was that Harry as well as the driver was off work without pay until the back rectified itself, or perhaps forever if it didn't. There were no other vacancies at the company.

Harry walked downtown one day to the Cyclorama. He had no intention of paying money to see the show, but the afternoon was dull, with a miserable, fitful wind, so he strolled down to Front Street to see if he might be able to sneak in as a way to pass the time. Right away he could see by the lineup and what looked to be practically armed guards at the ticket office, that he would have to give up that notion. For a bit of free entertainment, he stood watching the real customers. Religious people, he guessed, for he'd been told what the Cyclorama was about and how famous painters had travelled to the city of Jerusalem to see for themselves what they should paint.

The same day that Harry went to hang about the Cyclorama, Gladdie was making biscuits. She rubbed her nose with the back of her hand and left a dab of flour there that made her cross-eyed when she looked at it. She wiped her hand on her apron, rid her nose of its dusting and looked straight again. There, in front of her, was Mary, for the first time ever, pretty with her blue veil over her yellow hair. She was looking right at Gladdie. She smiled before she faded.

Gladdie went on with the biscuits, kneading them and rolling them and cutting them and setting them on the pans. When the oven was roaring hot she put them in. She cleaned off the table and washed up the dishes. "Werk hard and be cherful" was her motto still, and she was so successful that now she worked alone. Dorrie had gone off with her man. They'd married in secret, and without any but the one day's notice she'd moved to the country, to a town named Milton where her husband had bought into a grocery. Gladdie still couldn't believe Dorrie had done such a radical thing, and she still couldn't believe how empty her life was now, without the big girl to talk to and rely on almost like a sister. Gladdie didn't even know where Milton was, but it was a train journey away, far beyond her means, and Dorrie hadn't said she'd ever come back to visit, though Mrs. Riley had asked her to, at the last minute. Gladdie tried to imagine Dorrie working in a grocery, behind a counter, with a butcher's apron on like the clerks wore at the store at the end of Mrs. Riley's block. She pictured her whipping string around brown paper parcels packed with meat or sugar and being grumpy and kind at the same time to customers. It didn't help to make her less lonely.

Mrs. Riley didn't replace Dorrie. "I'm back to one, I see," she said gloomily, the day Dorrie left them with a new hat on her head and an altogether different look about her, as if in getting married she'd already turned into a stranger. "But you're a good worker, Gladdie," Mrs. Riley said, not ready to hang her big head just because a servant quit. "I know you won't let me down."

She didn't let Mrs. Riley down. She did the work of two girls, though her cooking was nothing to brag about. She didn't have Dorrie's hand, for example, with biscuits. She had no one to talk to, that was the thing. She and Dorrie had nattered all the time they worked, and Gladdie saw now how happy she'd been. Her whole life had changed with the loss of Dorrie, and not just in the kitchen where they'd spent most of their time. Every room of the house was empty without her and even the city had nothing much to offer, since Dorrie wasn't there either. If Gladdie ever took an afternoon off, she had nowhere to go. Being out made her miss Dorrie more, thinking how grand it would have been if her man had bought into a grocery in Toronto so you could take a streetcar to visit her and see her behind the counter in her apron. Gladdie felt a special despondency when streetcars passed her by. She seldom went out anymore. But this day, having imagined Mary, she removed her apron when her baking was done, and went to kneel at the bottom shelf in the pantry. She reached to the back and brought out an old pot, lifted the lid and removed some coins and bills. She put the pot back, the money into her purse, and off she went without a word to anyone.

She saw Harry right away when she got to the intersection on Front Street. It seemed she didn't even see the Cyclorama with its dome and its flag or the lineup of people waiting to get in. She did see all that, but it stayed in the background because her eyes went to him. He was leaning against the wall of J. W. Venn Confectionary, his long-legged body like fabric in a store window carelessly draped. She didn't even look into Venn's window to see the candy all arranged. Just as she walked up to him, it started to rain.

"Oh Harry," she said.

"I don't understand," Mrs. Riley said. She and Mr. Riley were sitting in the parlour, just the two of them. Gladdie had slipped into the house by the back door, as usual, and they didn't hear her come in. She snuck into the dining room and peeked at them. She had a feeling they were talking about her.

In spite of the mild weather within the parlour and without, Mr. Riley shivered and Gladdie knew why. For Georgina Riley to say she didn't understand a thing was tantamount to saying she didn't like it.

"Her mind's not here at all. And a good deal of the time her body's not here either."

"What do you say to figs?" Mr. Riley asked.

"What do I say to *figs?*"

"She don't care a fig?"

"Are you completely insane?"

"I hanker for figs," Mr. Riley said. He thought he'd distracted her, you could tell, even if it was only to bring down her wrath on his head.

"It's a man," Mrs. Riley said. "She's sixteen."

"No."

"What do you mean, no? She says she is."

"She can't be. Little slip of a thing."

"She's as tall as she's likely to grow. What's the matter with you?"

"I'm flabbergasted," Mr. Riley said. "Time went so fast."

"You needn't sit there rubbing your head free of the little hair you've left," Mrs. Riley said. "Or I'll make you speak to her. And don't give me that what-for look. We pay her for her work. Your idea, if you recall."

They sighed together, though about different thoughts. Mr. Riley wouldn't have told Mrs. Riley for anything that years ago sixteen was put down in writing as the age for touching.

Neither Harry nor Gladdie ever got inside the Cyclorama of Jerusalem. Harry never saw how realistically the panoramas had been painted. Gladdie never saw the artists' rendering of Mary. "Someday we'll go in," they said.

They had so much to talk about – the three years that had passed since they'd seen one another, for a start, though not why that had been. The unsaid mingled with the said. Somehow, they knew each other well. Every day the weather was fine, and they walked all over the city, talking about how things needed changing and about the way they'd do it. When you added them up, together they had hundreds of ideas for improving the world. They didn't have quite so many opinions on how to set about these improvements, but they agreed on one thing: the first step was to see. And not how other people saw. "Look anywhere," Harry said, "and you'll see how people are deceived." Gladdie could certify that.

"And people lie," Harry said.

"But you can tell by their eyes," she said.

"That's right. That's what I mean. It's simple really. If you look, you'll see. People look at the wrong things," said Harry. "Say, at someone's clothes rather than at them. That's a simple example." They were looking, at the time, at a down-and-out sort of fellow who was begging on the street corner. They crossed the intersection and said hello to the man.

"Hello," he said. He held out his cap.

"I think begging is wrong," Harry said.

"So I do too, young fella," the man said. "And good for you for speaking your mind. But you see I've a wife's got a falling-down disease and six kids to feed and I've lost me job. I was on at Bricks but me back went."

Having some experience with backs going, Harry gave him most of his coins and Gladdie gave hers, too. When they walked away, Harry said, "No way to tell if it was true. You couldn't tell, could you Gladdie?"

"It doesn't matter," she said.

"You're right," he said. "He had a need, didn't he, to get money from us. Whether it was for his wife and kids or a bottle."

"Or just a need to get money from us."

Harry stopped walking. "Gladdie," he said. "You are *right*."

"A word," Mrs. Riley said, stopping her on her way out. "I know, I know, it's the summer of your life. Me and Mr. Riley have discussed it. Don't think you're sneaking out of here every evening without us remarking on it. But you come here a starveling, didn't you, Dearie, and we took you in."

"Yes, Mrs. Riley."

"You're a good worker, Gladdie."

"Yes, Mrs. Riley."

"Don't get yourself compromised. Do you take my meaning? Pregnant. Do not get yourself pregnant."

"No, Mrs. Riley."

"Do you know how it happens? You're looking at me vaguely like you did when you couldn't hear. He kisses you. He touches you. You're fine so far. Got me drift?

"Oh. I think so."

"It's after that you're in trouble. Hands will do you no harm. But you look out for another appendage. Ha! Remember that."

"Yes I will, Mrs. Riley," she said.

"I never could stand talking to a person with her hand on the doorknob," Mrs. Riley said. "Don't come crying to me next year, Missy. That's my last word."

They walked and walked till they were out of the jumble of streets and pedestrians and vehicles and on a path down by the lake. It was almost like country down there except for the railway tracks and factories. They were friends, like a lost brother and sister who'd found each other by accident, but now as they walked she thought about him kissing her. She couldn't think of anything but him kissing her. And it was that way she thought of it, not her kissing him. It was something he would have to do because he was beautiful and she wasn't. She felt him beside her, his body sending its force inside her.

"You're quiet," he said.

"So are you," she said as smartly as ever, not wanting to be like the silly girls in Mrs. Friel's books who swooned at a word from a young man.

"I'm thinking," Harry said, his voice low and intimate. "Do you know what I'm thinking about?"

She did know, then, but she said, "No."

"This," he said, and stooped and turned her face up to his. They were both still walking and stumbled, then they stopped, cobbled together, and he kissed her. There was no give to him, he was as hard as hard could be, his chest so bony she felt her own softness against him.

"What's wrong? Are you afraid?" he asked.

"No. Nothing's wrong."

"You pulled away."

"I'm not afraid."

"I'd never hurt you."

"No, of course not." She was surprised. Of course he wouldn't hurt her. She'd never have thought to be afraid of that. It was herself she'd feared, but it was only for a minute. I'm sixteen, she reminded herself.

One day they set fire to a field. It happened so fast they didn't think to run away. They did it together; Gladdie lit the match and Harry dropped it. She always picked up anything she found that might be useful and put it in her purse or tucked it up her sleeve. The matches were in the gravel by the railway tracks.

"Let's sit down," he said. Gladdie sat on a big rock, and he sat beside her and put his arm around her. She lit a match, and they watched it burn and sniffed up the strong sulphur. Then they turned toward one another and kissed. It became a game: with every match the kisses went deeper. Then she lit another and said, "This time I won't let go." The flame ate its way down the stick, leaving behind a glowing that died into black. The match head shrivelled and bent, but a breeze blew out the dwindling flame half an inch before her fingertips. She lit another. Harry took it from her and sheltered it, and together they looked into the cup of his hands, but then his fingers fumbled and he dropped the match. One second they were looking for it, the next it flared. Whoosh. In front of their eyes the fire grew inches every second, alive and greedy, and soon it crackled and flowed into the knee-high grass of the field, and shrubs lit up and flames and billows of black smoke climbed into the sky.

That was in June. By July they found a new place to walk, in the wooded ravine to the north of downtown. They didn't talk as much anymore, and when they did talk it was more planning – how to use their time, how to spend the fewest of their precious pennies and minutes on transportation and locomotion and the most in one another's arms. It was as if they held their breaths until they could descend into the ravine on one soft path or another, the spongy decay springing underfoot.

One evening they were tangled together in a hollow half undressed, and Gladdie had her hand on Harry's appendage, as she always called it in her mind, with a nod to Mrs. Riley. Stroking the suedy skin over the hardness, she was thinking it was only in her hand and reassuring herself that this time that's where it would stay. Then they saw a man watching them.

He looked as ordinary as anyone on the street. There were hundreds of men like him on the street corners any day, wide-whiskered, top-hatted or bowler-hatted, smoking a cigar or a pipe. If you'd never seen him before, you'd never remark upon him if you sat across the aisle from him on the streetcar or if he bumped your shoulder as you crossed an intersection. When they looked into his eyes he just looked back. They couldn't move, either of them. He finished what he was doing, squatting in the bushes not far from their feet. When he'd done, he crooned quietly to himself and rocked back and forth on his heels, petting himself. After a minute he stood up, rearranged his clothing and walked off.

For some time, and neither of them could have said how long it was, Harry and Gladdie stayed still, hardly breathing. The light came through the leaves in lacy patches, a full golden early evening light. They heard a rustle and sat up, alert, but it must have been some small animal. Without speaking, they tugged on and buttoned up their clothes and hiked up out of the ravine.

In the streetcar afterward they spoke of it in whispers, but there wasn't much to say. Harry wanted to ignore the episode, and Gladdie had her own reasons for silence. By the time they'd left the ravine she was sure she'd recognized that ordinary face, the wide whiskers that could have hid buck teeth. She thought she had an old acquaintance with that crooning. If he was the man she thought he was, it meant he'd seen her with Harry and he'd followed them down to the ravine. She couldn't tell Harry about him. She didn't want to say the name.

Harry went to visit Vernon Ormiston. He'd been unable to find other work except for occasional day labour. He didn't expect much from Vernon, who'd blamed him for his fall and who'd never seemed anyway to like him much. Mrs. Ormiston said he must call her Mary Ann, and he must stay to dinner, didn't he like roast beef? Mrs. Ormiston's father was a butcher; however hard up they might be, they would always have meat. "I'll be back at work on Monday, son." Vernon said. The enforced holiday seemed to have done him good, but the thought of going back to that job turned Harry's outlook as black as the soot that would begrime his clothes and hair and skin.

It was August by then, and Gladdie and Harry argued. She didn't want to go to the ravine anymore, and she couldn't tell Harry the reason. She couldn't make herself explain. In the days since the incident in the ravine, the old shame had returned along with the fear. If she went to the ravine again, she was sure Mr. Tupper would be there. He'd be watching for her, and once he saw her again, he'd follow her home.

All she could say to Harry was that she didn't want to go there anymore, that she felt ashamed. Harry said he understood, but he seemed angry. The weather was getting colder, he was working ten hours a day, and by the time he met her at the streetcar stop nearest Mrs. Riley's he didn't have the energy to stand shivering, talking.

"Maybe tomorrow night," she said.

"No."

"No?"

"I need to get to bed early."

"When will I see you then?"

He shrugged.

"You won't come to Mrs. Riley's?"

"No."

"Will I come to your place? If you give me the address, I could come there and meet you."

"I'm in a room with two other men. It's useless. We shouldn't have been doing that anyway."

"But Harry. That's all right. We don't have to do that anymore. Remember how we used to walk up and down the streets and talk?"

"Christ, Gladdie, you don't see do you?"

"You're tired."

He walked away.

loss

Miss Avis laid her knitting down momentarily when the men came into the parlour, and one hand fluttered at her mouth while the other tapped her chest to communicate to them that she couldn't speak, her throat was so sore. Since none of them was in the habit of consulting her, whatever the conversation, the information was neither here nor there, but they nodded to show they'd received it. Mr. Parchman snapped open his *Globe.* Mr. Mainwaring, pale as ever from his life in the cellar, did his unwitting imitation of a mushroom. Mr. Twigg hadn't returned from work, though it was nearly suppertime, which was why quiet reigned in the parlour but for the clicking of number ten needles and the occasional crackle of the paper.

Mr. Riley had fled for the afternoon and thought it worthwhile to order supper at the Bay Horse, since Mrs. Riley had taken to her sickbed and required only Gladdie's constant attendance. Luckily for Mrs. Riley, Gladdie was spending her evenings at home these days. She hadn't seen a thing of Harry for a couple of weeks. He hadn't contacted her, and she'd got more and more afraid to go out in case Mr. Tupper should see her and follow her back to the house.

She should have been making supper, but she hadn't started it. She had orders to bring Mrs. Riley soup and to make a new mustard plaster for her chest. All she needed in her life, she thought, was to get sick herself. The back door was open, as was usual in the summer months, and a chilly breeze was coming in as if to warn them fall was coming. She sat in the draft and thought about laying her head down on the kitchen table and stretching her arms out full length along the cool wood. Then the kitchen floor looked the coolest thing she'd ever seen. She bent over, still sitting on the chair, and felt it with a thick hand. Then she put down the other hand. It was thick too and absorbed the coolness. When Mr. Riley came home later, after whistling his approval of his own behaviour through the back alleys, he found her as good as unconscious on the floor.

"No trace of him," Mr. Riley said. "I've searched high and low."

"Will we go to the police?" she asked.

"Ah," Mr. Riley said. "That I don't know." He patted her hand, so she knew she looked pathetic. She got up and went to the hall mirror after he left her, and saw that her hair was matted and stuck to her skull. You'd hardly know it was her in the mirror. For the first time ever, she had cheekbones you'd notice. In her pallor, the freckles floated over her skin.

Mr. Riley had gone everywhere he could think Harry might possibly be found. He'd gone to Rogers' before dawn that morning, fired by Gladdie's panic when she realized she'd been delirious and had lost several days. He'd interviewed Vernon Ormiston, who'd given him an earful. "Took him back, I did," Vernon said. "After he'd as good as caused me accident. Then he leaves me in the lurch." Mr. Riley described the encounter in brief, and then again, when Gladdie asked him, in fuller detail.

"Some harm must have come to him, Mr. Riley," she said. "Did you ask at hospitals?" He had not.

"I will then," he said.

The day before she'd fallen ill, she'd relinquished her pride and overcome her fear. She still thought Harry was punishing her for not giving in to him, but she missed him so grievously she couldn't let that matter. She'd covered her hair in case Mr. Tupper was lurking, and she'd traipsed from one boarding house to another on Bathurst Street. It had been a humbling thing. Men and women, whoever opened the door to her, stared her up and down, insinuating. A few of them wouldn't give her any information, thinking she was trying to trap a young man. At the place where Harry had boarded, though, Mrs. Clark, his landlady, invited her right into the house. Mrs. Clark hadn't seen Harry for two weeks. "He was a close one," she said, swivelling her neck to watch Gladdie while she let her into the small room with nothing in it but three beds, and beside his a few clothes hanging on pegs, and a dresser with wash things on it, a cloth he'd used, a grey scrap of towel, his hairbrush. "Delivered coal. I expect you know that," Mrs. Clark said, lifting a shirt that exhibited signs of that. Gladdie looked about the room, at the narrow, unmade beds with their rough blankets, at the low window, for it was a ground-floor room in a sinking house. On the wall by the window was a poster advertising an exhibition of artwork, a picture on it of a horse in a winter scene. They'd stopped and looked at it somewhere once, and he'd been taken by it. There was nothing else in the room, but she looked and looked, trying not to cry. Mrs. Clark pulled open the one drawer of the dresser and riffled through the contents: his underwear and a few papers. She held the papers up for Gladdie to read. They were only wage stubs and a note she'd written him before she knew he couldn't read. "Are you in trouble, dear?" Mrs. Clark asked.

Gladdie said she was afraid for Harry as she didn't know what could have happened to him.

"Now, now, dear."

"If nothing was wrong, he'd have come back for his things."

"They don't sometimes. You see, dear, they sometimes don't want to be found. Can't face the responsibility, if you take my meaning."

"What do you do with his things?"

"Depends, don't it? Your Harry'd paid up to the end of this week, and as I'm an honest woman I've left his bed. Once it's not being paid for, it'll be let. That's only business. I'll bundle up his things, though it's unlikely he'll be back for them."

"Could I leave a note?"

"Sure, Dearie. You do that."

On the back of her old note, she wrote: "Please come. We are friends forever. Gladdie."

"Put it in the drawer," Mrs. Clark said. "That way it'll be with his things."

Gladdie went to the shirt hanging on the peg after she'd put the note into the drawer. "You'd have to read it to him," she said. She buried her nose in the shirt.

"What's your name, dear?"

"Gladdie." Her voice was muffled by the shirt.

"Ah well, I'll remember that. And it's really all he needs to know, isn't it?" Mrs. Clark said, taking up the hem of her apron to wipe the smudge of coal soot off the tip of Gladdie's nose.

That night Gladdie worried so much about Harry and what could have happened to him, she nearly burst. She knew she had to find something good to think about and sent her mind searching. Her thoughts spun out in a panic, flying into walls until at last she spied a window. Behind the window the girl with the white glove on her hand carefully picked out candies to put into a small paper bag. Gladdie fastened on the glove. How white it was, how clean. Her mind's eye opened wider, and she saw a neat stack of gloves on a gleaming counter. Then she saw a pile of limp, soiled, finger-bloated gloves tossed in a corner. It would be someone's job to scrub them every day or so, probably boil them, too, to get rid of stains. She had a picture then of the gloves pegged to a clothesline, dozens of them, and as it was winter for some reason in the picture, they were frozen stiff. All the hard fingers pointed down, the thumbs any which way. What a satisfaction it would be to have been the one to pin them there, she thought, showing people you'd cared enough to launder them properly. She drifted into sleep with the long row of them dangling, as bright as the snow on the ground beneath them, and it wasn't trampled dirty slush either because she amended that. Before she nodded off she got snow falling steadily, and then she made it nighttime so the white shone in the dark.

It was Mr. Twigg who took her to the Provincial Asylum. Mr. Riley had meant to go there, and to the other hospitals, but what with one thing or another, as he said, he hadn't got around to it. Once she recovered, Gladdie visited Victoria Hospital and even the Hospital for Sick Children in case a boy of seventeen might be called a child for medical purposes, and she travelled out to the General, all with the same result: he was not an admitted patient. Gladdie was sitting with her head in her hands, rocking with the motion of the streetcar taking her back downtown after that last attempt, when the familiar voice of the amateur thespian urged her to sit up and be surprised.

"It's me," he said. He expected her to be as pleased with the announcement as he was. He hadn't ever paid much attention to her all the time he'd lived at Mrs. Riley's, but now he plunked himself down on the seat next to her and chattered at her, asking a dozen questions in a row and furnishing his own answers before she could open her mouth. Finally he gave his opinion that she was looking low, and that made her cry. Once she started, the tears fell down faster than she could wipe them off, and all the other passengers were perturbed just as much as Mr. Twigg was. They soon came to the stop at Elizabeth Street, and Mr. Twigg got off with her, gallantly edging past her in order to be able to reach up and hand her down. Being unused to such treatment and in a hurry to get it over with, she stumbled in his path and gripped his hand with both of hers. Mr. Twigg took that for a meaningful gesture, unfortunately, and was smitten.

The Asylum was a grand structure with a dome like Union Station's though even more imposing. Mr. Twigg skipped up the steps with Gladdie in tow, and thoughtfully did all the asking. She was silenced by the seriousness and hollowness of the entrance of the institution with its huge circular staircase that spiralled so forcefully upwards she feared, as she gazed at it with her head back, it would pull her with it if she went too close. It would take her to the crazy place, as it could take anyone who entered here. When the answer to Mr. Twigg's questions was no, he told her it was the best news she could get. Then he took her to the police.

It was well known that the city police were Ulstermen, or many of them were Ulstermen, and although Gladdie was nothing in religious denomination since she didn't attend services, nor did she know anything about her parentage, she had, through living with the Rileys, inherited a dread of the Orange Order, the military and the police. Her personal knowledge of policemen included the information that they wore high helmets with peaks that shaded their eyes from your view. They rode tall horses through the parks and blew whistles at intersections. They could, if they wanted, shut you up for years in the Girls' House of Industry, where you'd have to wear a mean uniform and be a hundred times worse off than a girl was at Mrs. Riley's. This last piece of wisdom came from Mrs. Riley herself.

Mr. Twigg, who now insisted on being called Wib, short for Wilbur, knew the constable on the desk since he often visited the station to gather information for his pieces. Mr. Twigg was a specialist in the social conditions of the poor and criminal classes, but Gladdie and the others at Mrs. Riley's didn't know that yet. They'd never read anything he'd written.

Gladdie followed Mr. Twigg through the fancy arch into the station and listened while he discussed the weather and football with the constable in a style that was just as relaxed and chatty as that he employed when relating Mrs. Riley's antics to the lodgers. When he'd told the constable the problem, Gladdie had to describe Harry. It made her blush to do it. Trying to say what he looked like brought him like a real person not just to her mind but almost to her body. At the same time, his not being there became clear to her. He was gone from her life. She knew that then, even as she talked about him to the constable.

When they left the station, she didn't say a word. She had no energy in her to consider Mr. Twigg's feelings, but after they'd walked a bit she started to feel him brooding beside her, and she understood what was wrong. Harry was a big, good-looking fellow, and Mr. Twigg knew himself to be a small man, a man whose hair would not stay down but stuck up to put him on the edge of ridiculous at all times. He tried to make up for it by being energetic. He knew his mimicking and gossiping weren't always appreciated. It was hard on him to have stood by listening to her talk about Harry. But Harry was the link between them, and after a bit he said, "We'll find him, Gladdie." He said it very nicely and she thanked him.

"We'll go back to the station every day to see what they've discovered."

"Won't they think we're a nuisance?"

"What of it? It's nuisances get what they want." Before they reached Mrs. Riley's, for it wouldn't do to be seen associating with the servant, he parted from her in good cheer, which he kindly tried to hide.

From the porch steps she could hear them talking in the kitchen.

"Her head's too big for her body," Mrs. Riley said. "She's no cheekbones. She's splotched with freckles. And that mop of red hair. We're in no danger of losing her, I'd say. A man will want her for the one thing." Mr. Riley declining comment, she went on, "But you'd have no opinion on that topic yourself?"

Naturally Gladdie waited to hear what he might say.

Mr. Riley had an opinion, she was sure, but he kept it to himself.

In spite of Mr. Twigg's optimism, Gladdie retained the feeling that Harry was gone. She went out with Wib Twigg for something to do, not bothering about being seen by Mr. Tupper. She didn't care anymore what happened to her. Harry's absence was the only thing that mattered and it couldn't be cured. She was destined to look for him always, whenever her eyes moved to the distance. Like she still looked for Margaret, not being able to stop herself, after all those years.

Then she started to hope she was pregnant. You'd think I'd know better than make that wish, she told herself. But she wanted something of Harry. The more she thought about it, the more she wanted his child to be growing inside her. She wouldn't be like Dorrie either; she'd never give it up. Not that she blamed Dorrie. It wasn't the same for Dorrie as it was for her. Mr. Riley wasn't the love of Dorrie's life, the person who'd grown right into her.

Mrs. Riley wouldn't let a baby stay on at her house; Gladdie knew that well enough, but she didn't worry. She'd find someone who'd take them in. She'd talk her way in somewhere. Day and night she hugged herself around the middle whenever she got some time alone, to reassure the baby she'd never let it go. She hoped it wouldn't have red hair and a big head. Best if it looked like Harry, whether it was a boy or a girl.

It was in December that the postcard came with a picture on it of a giant tree and tiny people standing by it, a couple and a young man. She couldn't tell if it was Harry, in a nice suit. An educated hand had written her name and address, another the message. A careful, right-handed slant, the writing of someone new to the ability, said, "I am fine. I am an artist now. Harry." Underneath was an afterthought: "How are you?"

Mrs. Riley saw the postcard before Gladdie had the opportunity to read it, but she didn't mention it. Nor did Gladdie, but she kept it – the only thing she had from Harry. The small printed words at the top corner said, "Giant Sequoia, California." She didn't intend to answer, but on the other hand she didn't think it entirely impossible one day she'd go there, and she wanted to take no chances on forgetting the address.

One day some months later she did write to him. The name, Giant Sequoia, sounded Indian to her, so she wrote, "Do you have wild Indians there? Your friend, Gladdie." Later she learned the sequoia was a kind of tree. It wasn't a town or any sort of address, so he'd never have heard from her. She guessed it must have given some postal worker a laugh.

When time had separated them more firmly, Gladdie was happy for Harry that he'd become an artist. She told herself he'd known somehow he had to go. But it was years before she stopped wondering why he couldn't have taken her.

Mr. Twigg was no substitute for Harry, poor fellow. Some weeks before the postcard from Harry came, Mr. Twigg found his infatuation had dwindled. Mr. Twigg found Gladdie's behaviour stiff, he said, and that was after he'd spent several days attending to her and demonstrating his detective abilities along with his less definitive worth. To one of Wib Twigg's nature, sadness in a young woman was appealing only so long as he imagined he could cure it. As for Gladdie, if she hadn't always heeded what was said to and about her, still the teachings and misteachings of the adults around her stayed with her, and she was conscious that she didn't want to be wanted for the one thing.

She wasn't with child. She learned that pretty soon after she gave up on seeing Harry again. At the time she told herself that's that, but looking on it in later life she knew how disappointed she'd been, and for a reason she wouldn't have understood then or maybe wouldn't have let herself know. You think a little child won't leave you.

a hiding place

"Oh," Orillia said when she saw the Aquadell return address. She fanned her face with the envelope. "Aquadell," she said.

Gladdie sat down by the bed. "I always liked that name," she said. "From the first time I heard it. Aqua means water. Well, I guess you know that. Em Knelson told me your mother was the one who came up with the name. I'm glad she thought of it." Gladdie figured it was only fair to mention Mrs. Cooper now and then. "Makes you think of a cool, clear pond on a summer day, in a little green valley."

"Not quite the reality."

"In a way it is. If you have friends there, good people like Em and Halvor Knelson, then the town seems like that."

To which Orillia replied, "Oh, it's a regular oasis, then."

They both looked out the window for a long minute. Then Orillia, in an odd, flat voice, asked if the letter was from Percy.

"It is. And I didn't tell him to write to you. It will have been his own idea."

"It's not that I don't like him, Gladdie."

"Anyone would like Percy Gowan," Gladdie said.

"You always say that," Orillia said. "You could find goodness in anyone."

"You don't have to look hard to find it in Percy," Gladdie said. "Well, I'd better get downstairs. Hilda and me are canning the last of the spinach this morning. You ought to see how it cooks down.

An armful" – she opened her arms wide enough to hug a horse – "ends up in a pint jar."

After she was gone Orillia held the envelope for some minutes, staring at her name. She wondered what she would have been like if she'd been raised by someone like Gladdie. Or indeed by Gladdie. Her whole life would have been different. She was sure she would have been a better person.

"Remember when Susan hid on me," Hilda said one evening after the little girl had been put to bed. "It was only a thunderstorm, but she must have thought another cyclone was coming. It was while you were still at the hospital, Orillia. We searched everywhere for that little girl. Mrs. Best was here and helped us look. She could see how worried I was."

Orillia had been only half listening until she heard Hilda say "Mrs. Best." "Mrs. Best was here?" she asked.

"Yes," Hilda said. "She came here looking for him. I'd never met her before. And it was a day he hadn't arrived. You know how unusual that is. In a bit of a tizzy, wasn't she, Gladdie? Wanted to see his room, wait for him in his room. What could I do?"

"Did you let her into his room?"

"Yes. She waited there half an hour or so until she heard me calling Susan over and over. Then she came downstairs and offered to help me search."

"What's she like?"

"Well. What's she like, Gladdie?"

"Sweaty," Gladdie said.

"Sweaty?"

"Like a gospel preacher you'd hear in a park."

"Passionate, do you mean? Mr. Best's wife?"

"I'd say so."

"Gladdie's right," Hilda said.

"And did Mr. Best arrive?"

"No, and we never did learn where he'd been or what he'd been up to. But I expect *she* did. Jealous. Oh yes. You could see it clear as day, in her eyes. Well, no doubt we put her suspicions to rest, once she saw who lived here – me and Lettie Pringle, the old maid who used to have your room, Orillia."

"You're the one of us snared a husband along the way," Gladdie said. "Maybe she *should* be on the lookout with you around her man."

"Oh pshaw," Hilda said, looking very pleased. "Anyway, you'll never guess where we finally found Susan. I should say where Gladdie found her, for I'd never have looked there. I'd never have thought it possible she could fit."

Again, Orillia wasn't really listening. She was thinking of Mr. Best in the light of his wife.

"In my valise," Gladdie said.

"You wouldn't believe it to see it," Hilda said. "Just a minute. I'll go fetch it. You've got to see it, the most unlikely thing." And off she went up the stairs to Gladdie's room and came back with a small leather suitcase to demonstrate.

It *was* odd to think the child had crawled into that bag and then closed it over her head. She could only barely have fit.

"Look at it," Hilda said. "Whatever could have possessed the wee thing?"

"She was frightened," Gladdie said. "A storm's frightening if you think it can hurt you."

"But *she* wasn't hurt," Orillia said. She didn't even say "in the cyclone," but they knew immediately what she meant.

Gladdie said. "She's lost her parents."

"She can't *speak,*" Hilda said.

Orillia knew all that. She'd known as soon as she'd opened her mouth that it was a stupid thing to say. "Well," she said. "It certainly is a wonder she fit in that bag."

Hilda snapped the valise shut. The initials on the silver clasp weren't Gladdie's, Orillia noticed. Someone must have given it to her, someone she'd once worked for, perhaps. It appeared to be an expensive bag. Hilda got up to return it, but Gladdie told her not to bother. She'd take it up herself when she went to her room. She seized the valise from Hilda and held it on her lap. Why, she loved the old thing. She cradled it as if it was something she needed to defend.

Orillia hardly heard their good nights when they left her, and she didn't go to sleep for ages. She kept remembering what she'd thought when Hilda had come back to the bedroom and set the valise beside her on the bed. She'd thought: I'm too big to fit in there. Really, even to herself she'd rather not have admitted such a revelation.

a young woman with grave brown eyes

Gladdie understood that lodgers came and went; that was only natural, but then Dorrie left, and then Harry took off, and she decided she had better get used to people walking out of her life. She decided she was tough and not the least bit sentimental. But when Mr. Riley quit the premises, she was the one who missed him most. Mrs. Riley didn't lament his loss. Mrs. Riley answered with asperity and spite whenever reminded of him, though even she once admitted she had some fondness for him still. She told Gladdie that his voice, if she'd let him talk to her through a crack in the wall, could have transformed her yet from the waist to the knees to jelly. But he'd eaten more than he'd earned, and he'd messed more than he'd fixed, and he'd done a few other things she didn't want to speak about, so he'd had to go. They were all often reminded of him.

"Gladdie, the tablecloth's getting wet," Mrs. Riley hollered, one night, from the dining-room table.

It was a miserable night in early October, and the year, as Gladdie was never to forget, was 1891, and the tablecloth was indeed getting wet. The ceiling, two floors above them, was leaking. The rain was invading the house. Gladdie brought a bucket to the table and plunked it down beside the potatoes.

"Really," Mr. Parchman said.

The drips pinged into the pail. Nobody else said a word while they listened to that sound. They were all eating as fast as was humanly possible so they could leave the table and crawl into their beds where they might be able to conserve a little of their bodies' warmth. Gladdie stood back with her arms folded and watched them. She'd pulled a cardigan over a sweater over her housedress, but it didn't do much good. The lodgers were similarly clad, and still the damp went through all their bones. The rain was getting on everyone's nerves. Bad enough it pinged into sundry basins and buckets and pounded on the roof; more alarming was the sound of water running through the walls.

"You need a man, Mrs. Riley," Mr. Parchman said. He was a great one for this kind of authoritative statement, made as if he was accustomed to giving sage advice and bossing others around, when the truth was he scalded bottles in a brewery for a living.

"You recall Mr. Riley's acrobatic acts on our behalf, do you, Mr. Parchman?" Mrs. Riley said. "He'd be up there with a ladder, you'd remember, when the ceiling leaked?"

Mr. Parchman declined further comment.

Mr. Twigg had left them too. He'd moved to a seedier boarding house than Mrs. Riley's, which had got them all talking. They didn't know yet that he was doing research for a series of articles that would expose poverty and degradation in the city, beginning with them. That autumn, except for his leaving, they had mostly the same lodgers they'd had for a long time. Mushroom Mainwaring still lived in the cellar. Mr. Parchman (Perchance Parchman to Mrs. Riley, for what she called a literary reason) was, of course, still with them. Miss Avis had lived with Mrs. Riley almost as long as Mr. Mainwaring. She was well into her seventies and still knitting for a living. Across from her at the table was Pearl Fink, the newest by far of the bunch. Pearl was about twenty and not nearly as green as she looked. She worked nights at the General Hospital and cleaned the operating rooms. When Mr. Parchman said he'd never have thought he'd sit at a table with a bucket on it, Pearl darkly said, "I've seen worse things in buckets."

"Please," Mrs. Riley said.

"They throw what's not wanted in them after surgery."

"Please," Mrs. Riley said, more faintly.

"You don't need nearly the length of gut you have inside you. Did you know that? Miles of gut you have inside you. And you should see what's inside *it*. Just last week Dr. Peterson threw a gallbladder away by mistake in a bucket of gut and I had to look for it. They wanted to cut it open to see the stones. Have you ever seen gallstones? They have greenish stuff like mould growing on them."

A knock at the door interrupted Pearl. Ping, ping went the drips into the pails set at various locations around the main floor – as loud as gallstones might have sounded if they'd volleyed down – and the rain drummed on the roof and ran through the house. Mrs. Riley and the lodgers and Gladdie waited in case they hadn't really heard a knock.

At the second rap, Mrs. Riley said, "Who can *that* be?"

It was so unusual that anyone visited – and in such a storm – that the lodgers and even Mrs. Riley rose from the table and followed Gladdie to the hall to see who it was.

The door opened on a glittering night and a dark form under a wet umbrella. The young woman raised the handle and tipped the umbrella back and let herself be seen.

The lodgers and Mrs. Riley, gathered at the parlour door, peered overtop of Gladdie, and saw the young woman with her umbrella held high and tilted back so that ribbons of rain coursed off it in a horseshoe shape around her. Like a liquid wedding veil, it seemed to Gladdie. "Like a cabana," Mrs. Riley said later, remembering her beach days. "Like a little hut to hide your nakedness from the world."

Mrs. Riley had a fanciful streak that went two ways. One was to make a drama out of somebody else's life, the other, and her favourite, was to make a drama of her own. She made no mention of cabanas when asked several weeks afterward about Mrs. Dole's arrival, but she said the instant she heard the name a shiver went up her spine. She stepped forward and elbowed Gladdie aside and attempted to close the door in the young woman's face. "She had the appearance of a nuisance," she said in a statement, later, to the papers. "It's the ones who look well cared for that expect soft treatment. Give me a girl who looks peaked any day. She'll have resigned herself to life."

This girl popped her umbrella down and stuck it half unfurled between the closing door and the frame. "Wet as a dog she was, in seconds," Mrs. Riley described it. "She soon looked miserable enough."

Two rooms were empty, the small one in the attic and the other larger, airier room on the ground floor next to the kitchen. One thing Gladdie knew – and it showed the difference in people – with enough money to last a lifetime she'd have taken the first because it would be cheaper and you never know. With no more than would do her two months, young Mrs. Dole took the bigger room.

"Staying for a short while, Dearie?" Mrs. Riley asked her. No need for the girl to remove that tight jacket. Mrs. Riley had seen her like before. "Very private she was," Mrs. Riley told the various agencies. "Took the room for two months. Paid the rent in advance. No one visited the poor soul the entire time, though Gladdie tried to befriend her."

It was true Gladdie did try to be a friend to her, or at least some use. She'd seen what the world did to gentle people and knew Jessie Dole to be one for all that she was quite the little lady and carried herself with pride. Jessie Dole was not by any means the first single girl to take a room after tacking a Mrs. to the front of a phony name. Gladdie had seen them come and go. She'd befriended a few of them that she'd considered less fortunate, temporarily, than herself. She'd also discreetly befriended a few of the young men who'd boarded with Mrs. Riley. She was twenty-four, by her own reckoning, on the October evening Mrs. Dole arrived, and still looking for love in anyone who liked her, still wishing to be wanted for more than the one thing. She had her occasional dreams of a better life, but she'd learned it was best not to burden anybody with them.

Mrs. Dole raised her arms and brought her tidy green felt hat down off her head, and Gladdie thought how she'd witnessed this same thing countless times, this same motion and the sigh that went with it marking the surrender. Jessie Dole had lovely grave brown eyes.

Though supper was over, Mrs. Riley let Gladdie fry an egg and warm up a dollop of potatoes for Mrs. Dole while she changed out of her wet dress.

"I'll say this for her," Mrs. Riley said later, "though she was used to better than most of the lodgers, she took no better treatment than the rest of them, and it did them all good to have her sitting at the table with them. They didn't whine so much with her example. I do not think she had a valise," Mrs. Riley said when questioned closely by the police.

On that first night Jessie Dole ate her egg and potatoes alone in the dining room. She sat to her meal saying thank you to Gladdie. She didn't comment on the bucket on the table. Gladdie brought her a pot of tea and left the milk and sugar with her so she could take as much as she wanted. In the meantime, Mrs. Riley went through her valise. "Not much in it, but it will do to defray the costs of keeping her if she skips out owing us," Mrs. Riley whispered to Gladdie before she went to bed. It was a good leather case with a silver initialed clasp and buckle. The initials were J.L.D. "Not that I believe for a minute her name is Dole," Mrs. Riley said. "Name like that. It means charity. It would have come to her mind naturally in the circumstances."

Gusts of rain slapped the windowpanes, giving Mrs. Riley's dining room more of an atmosphere of refuge than it usually had. Gladdie watched Jessie Dole from the kitchen doorway while she ate her supper. The smooth, dark hair, parted in the middle and put up in elegant fashion, the white skin, the black ruffles at her neck, all bespoke a class of young woman not seen before in Mrs. Riley's house. Not that she looked rich, like the ladies you'd see driving up to department stores in carriages. But she was a cut above a shopgirl and a treat to watch, and Gladdie stood back in the doorway feeling as if she was in a dream. The drugging rhythm of the rain was like the muffled sounds she'd lived with the years of her ear infections, that had put the world at a remove. A dot of egg yolk stuck to Jessie Dole's chin. Gladdie grinned, watching it move as she chewed. Somehow it added to the girl's young dignity. But she hoped Mrs. Dole wouldn't see it; she hoped it would fall off before she reached her room and her dresser mirror.

By the time Gladdie climbed into her cot in the kitchen, the stove had been out some time, and she was frozen all through. She tucked her covers in at her back and neck and drew her knees up almost to her chin and shivered. The rain still beat down and ran through the house, and she could hear all the buckets she'd emptied ringing out the new drops on their bottoms. In her mind she heard the knock at the door again. Then the second knock. In the few moments between the two, the old wish for Margaret had come to her. She hadn't moved. She hadn't straightened and folded her hands as she had as a child during those old breath-held wishes, but she'd felt the shadow of that straightening and folding of hands within her. And then she opened the door and saw Jessie Dole. She saw her again, as she was in her room, removing her hat and her sodden jacket; she saw her serious brown eyes. She thought: she can never arrive again. This beginning is already ended.

Jessie Dole wasn't with them the full two months she paid for. It was just over six weeks, and of that time there was little to report, even to the reporters who would have been content with gossip, even to Wilbur Twigg, who made his name as a journalist with his front-page story about her. She was quiet, polite, said nothing about herself and seldom went out. All the lodgers loved her. Once she came back from a walk with a ruby maple leaf stuck in her lapel, and all their hearts leapt.

Little scenes like that were what Gladdie remembered forever. Jessie Dole with that leaf in her lapel and her cheeks red from the wind and her jacket open because she couldn't do it up. The night she arrived, of course, in the rain. And the day she came in to find Gladdie in her room. Gladdie just wagged her finger at her. "I saw you scratching," she said. She had the bed taken completely apart and was sitting flat out in the middle of the slats and sides brushing them with varnish. She grinned up at young Mrs. Dole and the girl blushed, so Gladdie knew she'd been right.

"First you go over the entire thing with turpentine, then you varnish, but you must get every crack and corner," she told her. The others had bedbugs from time to time, too, but they were well advised to follow the procedure themselves as she had enough to do with the general cleaning and cooking. They'd be bitten something fierce if they waited for her to get to *them*.

Not you, though, she thought, watching Jessie Dole yanking at the window to raise it. She set her brush over the pot and went to help. "You shouldn't be straining like that," she said. "It's not good for you now." She lifted the window right open; her arms looked strong and scrawny next to young Mrs. Dole's. They got a blast of fresh air in their faces, and Jessie Dole smiled.

She had the parlour carpet over the clothesline and was taking runs at it with the broom raised, giving it such whacks that sand streamed from it and dust rose from it, and each place she hit the worn pile the pattern shone so you could see it was rusts and reds, not browns and maroons as it looked in the parlour. The morning wasn't warm, but the backyard drew some sun and Gladdie had her sleeves rolled up. It came to her she was being watched, and she turned her head to see who'd come out on the step. It was Jessie Dole, with her gloved hands folded over the knob of her stomach where her jacket pulled open. Gladdie put the broom down and looked at its bristles splayed on the ground at her feet. She didn't know why, but it was an embarrassment to her that she'd been seen. Not that Mrs. Dole had seen her working; she wasn't ashamed of working. But enjoying herself doing it, as if it was what she was good at and good for. Mrs. Dole passed her by with a quiet good morning and went out the back gate. Why not the front way, Gladdie wondered, once she'd composed herself and reminded herself it was nothing for the likes of her to look foolish in front of someone superior.

Worried by the back-door exit and what it implied, Gladdie took to following Jessie Dole if she could, whenever the young woman went out. And every time, Jessie Dole brought her to the same place, a place she would never have come to on her own. The first time Gladdie followed her it was new to her, and she wondered why the girl would take that route along York Street, if she didn't see what a bad street it was, full of pawnshops and gambling houses and worse places. Even Mr. Riley had avoided York Street, but that was partly because he owed people money. Gladdie, when she had to go downtown, always crossed over to Bay, where the businesses were respectable. She thought maybe Jessie Dole was in a hurry, meaning to take one of the trains waiting behind Union Station, until she saw she was trekking down to the lake. In a tearing wind, Gladdie stood back while young Mrs. Dole walked down to the wharf, where boats and machines and rough men came together and she had no business being. She walked along until she came to a string of boathouses that shuffled side to side on the water. Only girls with no reputations went down to the boathouses, even if it was the afternoon. Gladdie knew that much. There Jessie Dole stood, looking out to the island, with her hands stuck into her sleeves. Gladdie put her collar up and wished she had a scarf. It came to her mind, while she waited to see what Jessie Dole would do, how eerie gulls could sound, how out of place in a busy daylight world where important people worked in banks and insurance companies and grand hotels, and even unimportant people bustled through the streets. The gulls' brief screeches cut the shapes of tipping basins in the sky, just as their bodies did, swooping. On and on they went, crying those little half screeches and stopping so quickly you'd think their own sound had frightened them.

A young man came striding along the wharf in Mrs. Dole's and Gladdie's direction, his coat flapping in the wind. Tall and good-looking, with determined eyes and the air of the future owner of the world about him. With a metropolis full of places to choose from, he knew where he was going. Gladdie watched him from a ways back and thought how different he was from anyone she'd ever known. You could see by his walk as much as his fine clothes that he'd been raised to treat himself well. He caught sight of her, and their eyes locked across the distance as he walked toward her. His eyes were as black as could be, and she thought for a second recognition flickered in them. But he couldn't know her. It was likely only pride she saw there, disdain for the woman he took her to be. He didn't turn into the wharf where Mrs. Dole stood with her back to him, though he glanced her way and slowed a bit, looking at her. Then he hurried by. He'd noticed her, Gladdie figured, and was scandalized by her pathetic condition; that was the cause of the change in him. Because he did look changed. He passed her like a different person from what he'd been before, a person with more on his mind than himself.

Jessie Dole stood for a while on the wharf, not looking around her at all, just gazing out to the island. Gladdie wondered if the young man who'd passed them could have been the one she'd come here to meet. She thought maybe she should have followed him rather than letting him go. Jessie Dole had too much self-respect to follow him herself. She'd put herself where she could be seen, but she'd faced the lake, not the wharf. She wouldn't stand there searching for him, wouldn't even turn around when she heard someone passing. If she was disappointed nothing had happened, she didn't let on. After a while she turned and walked back up to York Street with her head down and her own thoughts on her mind.

Before Gladdie left she went onto the wharf herself and walked out to its edge and stood there. The lake heaved under her feet, and the gulls cried in their queer voices. The island looked far away.

Then came the day she was cleaning the range in her oldest clothes with her paisley kerchief on to keep her hair out of her eyes, and she was all over the stove with her rags, and it was all over her, soot and black grease. Jessie Dole opened her bedroom door dressed in her hat and jacket.

"Oh, it's too cold for a walk, Mrs. Dole," Gladdie said.

Out Mrs. Dole went with a thin smile as if to say she pitied her. Gladdie dropped her rags and looked down at herself. She couldn't afford to take the time to change. She grabbed her jacket and was out the back door before Jessie Dole made it to the corner of the block.

It was the same route as the other times, but this time she caught up to the girl across the street from Union Station. She walked right up behind her and took her by the elbow. Jessie Dole pulled back. Of course she was surprised. People hurrying by them turned and stared. No doubt they made a striking picture, Mrs. Dole with her belly so big she couldn't do her jacket up and had to hold it together with one hand, and Gladdie with her face streaked with grime and giving off a powerful scent of stove blacking into the wind. Once she'd stopped the girl she didn't know what to say, so she just tugged at her jacket sleeve and led her across the intersection into the station.

They sat at one end of a long bench and soaked up the warmth from the dark varnished wood. The air smelled of cigars, voices bounced off the walls, people walked right by them and the sound of their footsteps came from far away. Everyone was going somewhere, criss-crossing in front of them, whole groups of people in a hurry, trailing old folks and children. It was hard to know what to say. It was Gladdie's first time inside Union Station, and her mind was boggled by the sight of so many people being so businesslike about setting off on their way somewhere else.

She said, "I've a bit of money saved." She said it staring out at all the people passing by, and Jessie Dole was watching them too and didn't turn her head Gladdie's way or say anything, so it almost seemed the words had been said to those strangers neither of them knew. "Enough for a year maybe, for rent," Gladdie went on. "I was thinking of an arrangement that might work for the two of us. If I was to take a small house or a part of a house. I'd go out to work, so I'd not be around in the daytime. Or I could work nights if it suited you to work. Then there'd always be one of us to look after the baby. There's nice jobs in shops," she said, so Mrs. Dole would know Gladdie didn't mean she thought she should be doing any sort of rough work.

Jessie Dole didn't speak at all. She just sat looking at a tiny man who was scraping a trunk over the floor, walking backwards. The trunk was as big as he was, but besides that he had on a long brown muffler that he'd wound about his neck, and it hung down behind him almost to the floor, and every time he took a step backwards his heel nearly pinned the scarf down.

"I've given it a good deal of consideration," Gladdie told her, not wanting her to think she was being impulsive and would by the next day regret it.

"You're kind," Jessie Dole said.

Gladdie said, "I'm just being practical. It would do I think for both of us."

"I'm hoping," Jessie Dole said. "I'm still hoping."

"I see," Gladdie said. What she saw, though she didn't say it to Jessie Dole, of course, was how young she was. Quite a bit younger than Gladdie. And how useless a thing hope could be. She didn't say that either. They stood up and pulled their jackets around them, and when they were outside Mrs. Dole walked her way and Gladdie walked her way, and they weren't the same, though they both ended up at Mrs. Riley's house.

part two family

the authorities

The newborn baby woke squalling, her arms and legs thrashing like windmills under her covers. She was mad against the world, fighting the air until she could find a warm body. Gladdie held her over her own heart so she'd feel it beat. She was more sure of herself after a day of looking after the infant's needs, and could hang onto her with one arm while she set the bottle into a pot of water to heat.

The baby wasn't happy. Even the milk didn't soothe her. She didn't want to take it. "Little Fighter," Gladdie whispered to her, looking into her eyes until the baby started making cooing sounds instead of crying. That made Gladdie certain Jessie Dole must have thought she was dead before she walked out on her. Even so, she got mad thinking about Jessie Dole drowning herself. She got angry with Jessie Dole, and at the same time she got angry with Margaret. She'd never blamed Margaret before for leaving her. She'd always wanted to imitate her, to be as good as Margaret had wanted her to be, but what she thought, looking into the baby's black eyes, was that she *wouldn't* be like Margaret. She'd made a promise to the child that she wouldn't let her go, and she was going to keep it. She wouldn't even let herself die, no matter what accident or illness came swinging for her. Fierce was how she felt about it, and competent.

"Everyone will let you down," she whispered, watching the baby taking her bottle finally, gulping the milk down. "You'd better be ready for that. There's nobody in this world that won't let you down – but me. I won't."

In the morning they would go someplace where she could say the child was her own. She would wrap the baby in an oblong package in the bit of old sheeting Mrs. Riley had given her, then wrap her again in her own blanket against the cold outside. She'd make a sling out of Mrs. Tupper's old brown plaid shawl. She'd tuck in a couple of rags Mrs. Riley would hardly miss to use for nappies. She'd fill the bottles they'd borrowed with milk. She still had her savings in a pot on the bottom shelf of the pantry. She'd fill her purse before she did anything else. It would be enough to live on for a few months, she figured, while she looked for work in a place where she could keep the baby.

First thing in the morning, before Gladdie could carry out her plan or start to worry if it was selfish even to consider doing it, the Children's Aid Society came to the house and took Mrs. Dole's infant. The suddenness of the attack stunned her. Mrs. Riley said that was what Children's Aid always did in the absence of the mother, and Gladdie said she wished Mrs. Riley had told her that, if she knew it all the time. Mrs. Riley scratched herself thoroughly then, under both armpits and all over the left tit, and said it was a relief to the entire household to have the child gone. When Gladdie didn't answer, Mrs. Riley looked at her funny. "What are you doing?" she said in a sharp voice. Gladdie was picking at the dry skin around her fingernails. She was nipping with her teeth at the bits her nails had loosened. Maybe it was a way to avoid talking, at first, but before she knew it, it got to be a habit, and at the end of a week she had her fingers in bad shape.

"Let me tell you, Miss Gladdie," Mrs. Riley said. "A child could not do any worse than be raised by a single, I mean unmarried, servant, even if it was her own mother, which in this case it isn't." She said Miss Gladdie or Missy whenever she wanted to put Gladdie in her place only there was some embarrassment on her side, as for example when they'd together observed Mr. Riley grabbing a feel of one of the women and Mrs. Riley had caught Gladdie's knowing of it out of the corner of her eye.

Since the baby's birth they'd had the police visit twice, the priest had come from Mrs. Riley's church, the Anglican church had sent a woman, another lady had descended from the Women's Christian Temperance Union, and they'd been pestered nearly non-stop by reporters from more papers than they'd ever realized were printed in Toronto, until Mr. Twigg advised Mrs. Riley to send them packing and give him her exclusive, deeply insightful interview. But once the excitement was over, no one came. The house went quiet and the lodgers avoided looking at one another, as if someone had just made a rude noise. Then one dim afternoon Mrs. James Parker occupied the parlour with her cape and skirt and big bosom.

Mrs. Riley got the impression, somehow, that Mrs. Parker was Mrs. Dole's mother. Mrs. Parker didn't look like Jessie Dole. She was more like Mrs. Riley herself if the truth be told, or like Mrs. Riley might have been if she'd been rich and harped on hope instead of resignation. And P was not the last initial on Mrs. Dole's valise, but Mrs. Riley was never one to require evidence for her ideas. She tried to shoo Gladdie into the kitchen when Mrs. Parker arrived, in case she'd reveal anything pertaining to the things Jessie Dole had left behind. Gladdie pretended not to see her and retreated to a corner where she knew Mrs. Riley would forget about her. She picked at her fingers to occupy herself. They were raw by then down to the first knuckles, but there were dry horny bits clinging here and there on them and she couldn't let them alone.

Mrs. Parker said she was visiting on behalf of the Children's Aid Society and wished to obtain more information about Mrs. Dole. "More personal, you understand," she said, "than official." Mrs. Riley was having none of that. Mrs. Riley knew when a person's eyes looked over her shoulder that person was avoiding the truth. Mrs. James Parker wanted something, but not for the Children's Aid Society; she was after something for herself. Mrs. Riley figured she knew what Mrs. Parker wanted: Mrs. Dole's things – the jacket, the hat, the umbrella and of course the valise – so she didn't at first follow the conversation she was having with the woman. Mrs. Riley didn't need those things of Mrs. Dole's, but she'd kept hold of them, and it wasn't in her nature to give them up.

Mrs. Parker asked if Mrs. Dole had been healthy.

"She was pregnant," Mrs. Riley said. There was a bit of a silence between them while they took some time to reconsider one another, then Mrs. Parker went on questioning Mrs. Riley until finally Gladdie knew what it was the woman wanted. It was just to know that Jessie Dole wasn't peculiar or half blind or in the possession of too many toes, that kind of thing. She wanted to know about Mrs. Dole because she wanted the child. Gladdie could see that: she wanted to adopt the baby. She watched Mrs. Parker flouncing and heaving while she talked. She was a big woman, and it seemed she was determined to take up as much room as she could and make an impact on any space she was in. Gladdie tried to see Mrs. Parker sitting, in a rocker maybe, with the baby in the crook of her arm, holding the bottle for her, and she wondered how long Mrs. Parker would sit still and look at the baby and if she'd even notice if the baby tried to make her promise to stay with her and look after her for the rest of her life. Gladdie had come to believe that was likely a little trick all babies did, a thing they would do to anyone who held them, a knack they were born with in order to make a person think she owed them something. She had to conclude any baby would be better off with Mrs. Parker, anyway. She had a husband and a jet brooch at her collar that would be worth half a year's wages to someone like Gladdie. She stayed in the corner gnawing at her fingers until Mrs. Parker had satisfied her needs. Mrs. Riley, seeing the woman to the door with no demands having been made concerning the return of Jessie Dole's things, was so relieved she started babbling about resignation. She often did that anyway, before she headed up to her room for some private refreshment.

"It was God's will," she said, speaking of Mrs. Dole's demise.

Mrs. Parker turned to her, as she was at the door by this time, and said: "He gave us our wills; we choose our way." Mrs. Riley said afterward that was an altogether unfeminine thing to say and perhaps even unchristian. "It was an urge to comfort that led me into speaking of God's will," Mrs. Riley said. "For I still had half a thought the woman was Mrs. Dole's mother. It's hard for me to give up an idea once I've had it." She said from now on people could find their own solace. "As for me," she said, but she didn't finish. She started upstairs.

"Just one minute," Gladdie said. While Mrs. Riley had been expressing her thoughts, she'd been thinking a few of her own. "Have the goodness to hold on a minute, Mrs. Riley," she said. "For I've something to say."

And she gave notice.

It was all the high talk that had gone to her head. She started spouting off and even to herself she didn't sound like herself. "'We choose our way,' the lady said. Well I've not chosen mine. I've only fallen into it. If I'm to have my own life it's time I left this house and set my foot on a path to somewhere."

Mrs. Riley closed her eyes a moment and when she opened them she gave Gladdie a long look. Gladdie knew it was because she couldn't think of a thing to say. She turned her back on Gladdie, then, and went up the stairs as if she'd become a heavier woman.

Gladdie opened the cupboard in the pantry for her money and her things. It didn't take long to haul them out and see what was worth taking. By the time she'd done it she heard Mrs. Riley coming down the stairs again, then down the hall to the kitchen. Gladdie was on her knees at the cupboard and didn't have time to stand up, but she straightened her spine, remembering how often Mrs. Riley had said Mr. Riley did not possess a backbone. When she looked up, there was Mrs. Riley with Jessie Dole's valise. She set it down on the linoleum by Gladdie and stooped and started putting some of her things in it. Seeing the bag made Gladdie wonder, as she had before, about the initials on the clasp, and what Jessie Dole's real names might have been, and if maybe her first name really was Jessie. Maybe at least she'd told the truth about that. Then she started to think about herself taking that valise into another boarding house and saying her name was Mrs. Dole. Or Miss, she supposed it might as well be, since the Mrs. wasn't necessary. A little happiness flared in her at the thought, like a candle flame will when you blow on it, before it goes out.

Mrs. Riley did the buckle up and handed Gladdie the keys. She went and looked out the kitchen window over the sink. The way Gladdie's fingers were then, shiny and red with just a slick of skin to cover them, any touch sent thrills through them, not exactly pain but something too alive. She let the keys slip to the floor, and mostly using her knuckles, she opened the bag and unpacked it and put her things back into the cupboard.

"What's this?" Mrs. Riley said, but not until she'd seen that Gladdie was finished. "We'll have that stew for supper," she said before she left the kitchen.

Not having access to Gladdie's mind, Mrs. Riley thought her act of generosity had made Gladdie decide to stay. But Mrs. Riley also understood futility and its numbing effects, and she recognized resignation, since she was always looking for it. In this case she rewarded it: she never demanded the return of the valise.

As if he knew his effect would be more violent at a weak point in Gladdie's life, Mr. Tupper appeared again. They met on a busy sidewalk, or almost met. Gladdie had taken to wandering about the streets whenever she had time, thinking she might catch sight of the baby, or Mrs. Parker, who might have the baby. Mr. Tupper looked into her eyes when she passed him. He was standing outside a tobacco store sucking on his pipe. She kept on going until she reached the end of the block, where she stopped and waited in case he dared to follow her. Then she couldn't confront him. She couldn't bear to see again the interest on his face. A streetcar stopped at the corner and she climbed on. She went to the opposite row of seats and sat with her head turned to that side of the street.

"Something wrong, is there?" the conductor asked, standing over her. She hadn't realized she was biting her fingers something fierce.

weeds

Orillia lay in her hot bed thinking about Dr. Kitely's cool hands. But even the image of the six breasts – and she could feel all six of them tingle – couldn't bring those hands to life. And Mr. Best was pecking away, next door, on his typewriter, so she couldn't even sleep. Peck, peck. She could feel the reverberations through the wall, and when she concentrated, she could feel them in the breasts. Peck, peck. Each peck like a tweak. Moving from her chest down to her belly. Tweak, tweak.

Inspiration must have hit Mr. Best just then; he began composing at an unusually rapid rate. Then suddenly he stopped. Orillia smiled. The keys had jammed together. She pictured his big fingers pulling them apart. Then peck, peck. Clack, clack. Orillia's breathing began to copy the jagged rhythm. She lay back against her pillows and let the clatter vibrate inside her, as if he was writing his words up and down her bones. No, as if her whole body was his machine.

"Oh, Mr. Best," she whispered. His hands were not cool; they were hot, and meaty, and calloused at the fingertips.

The front door opened and closed authoritatively. It was earlier than his usual hour; the east sun at her window had only minutes earlier nudged her awake, but it had to be Mr. Best. Those could only be his firm footsteps crossing the downstairs hall. And her own door was ajar. She reached to the foot of the bed and quickly pulled her Chinese jacket on and decided she didn't care that it was red. The extra colour might be flattering. She was likely pale from being so long indoors.

She smoothed her hair and leaned forward and peered through the narrow gap left by the half-open door, and caught him as he crossed the landing. He was walking quickly, a man with a job to do. He was a big man but, oh dear, he was portly. And his hair was greying. He saw her obviously trying to see him and stopped. Full on, he was better looking than she'd thought. Impatience appeared to be his first response, but then he came to the door and said hello.

"Mr. Best, I presume?" she said, donning the light social manner that had got her through fowl suppers and wedding dances in Aquadell.

"Miss Cooper," he said as dourly as two words could be spoken.

He had stern features with heavy eyebrows that fell naturally to glowering, yet there was a hint of recklessness in the eyes, she thought, and a sort of in-spite-of-the-tedium-of-life interest in his manner. His size was his most formidable attribute. She was sure he was aware that he loomed.

Once he'd gone inside his room she listened for the tap, tap when he emptied his pipe and waited for the smell of his tobacco, and for the typewriter to start clacking. How brazen, she thought, with her hand to her mouth to suppress her grin, though there was no one in the room to see it.

"Don't forget he's married," Hilda said that evening when Orillia told them she'd seen him.

"Oh, it doesn't matter, does it?" Orillia said as nonchalantly as she could, knowing it would provoke.

"It would matter to his wife," Hilda said. "Wouldn't it, Gladdie?"

"Yes," Gladdie said.

"Marriage is an institution that was devised in the Dark Ages to ensure property didn't go astray," Orillia said. "It's an old, worn-out idea. It traps both men and women. Who are better off free."

"That's one way to look at it," Gladdie said.

"It certainly is one way to look at it," Hilda said, with a catch in her voice that made her look out Orillia's window. "For myself, I enjoyed marriage. My late husband, Mr. Wutherspoon, was a dear, generous man."

"He was good to you, Hilda," Gladdie said.

"In the four years we were married I had three miscarriages," Hilda said. "He was kindness itself."

Orillia looked out the window, too, and as it was getting dark she could see the faint reflections of Gladdie and Hilda on the glass, and herself.

Susan was crouched down like a pink and white toad by the raspberry canes at the side of the yard. She stayed utterly still, absorbed in watching something Orillia, from her bedroom window, couldn't see. Then Gladdie came out of the house, carrying garbage to the burning barrel, and the little girl jumped up and ran to her side. She stood beside her while Gladdie lit the match, then, with her nose level with the lip of the barrel, she watched the flames with Gladdie, leaning into her so that Gladdie, naturally, put her arm around her. She just loved Gladdie, that was plain.

Hilda carried a chair out from the kitchen and set it in the shade back of the house. She brought a pail full of pea pods and a basin to the chair and sat shelling peas while Gladdie worked nearby in the garden. Hilda wasn't used to remembering that Orillia was upstairs in the back bedroom, usually with her window open. "You know, Gladdie," she said, "you're right about Orillia. She is a complicated girl."

Gladdie was hoeing between the carrots and the beans. She tried to do a row every day to keep up to the weeds. She stopped hoeing and swiped her arm across her forehead to show she was listening. Hilda went on shelling the peas, stripping the pods with her thumb so they thundered into the basin. She looked up, afraid she'd said too much. "Like an African violet," she went on, trying to explain. "Usually they thrive and bloom, but sometimes they won't, and in either case you don't know what you did right or what you did wrong."

"She's happy here."

Hilda went back to her peas, and Gladdie knew what that meant. She was holding her tongue. On the clothesline, housedresses and bloomers and vests snapped and flew straight out for a second, filled with a stray gust, and the line bent in the same direction and looked about to break away. But the clothes flapped down, the line sagged, and Gladdie went back to hoeing the chickweed and dandelions and thistles out of the way of the carrots. The hoe rasped against the dry clay. You go looking for weeds in any garden, she thought, you'll find them.

Upstairs, Orillia thought about being an African violet. Then it occurred to her she might use this summer to become a better person. She was vague as to how that could come about, and hoped Gladdie would teach her, in some less than obnoxious way. Or perhaps it would just happen naturally, as a result of her misfortune.

Hilda brought Susan up to Orillia's room to be safe because they were ironing. "I'm nervous with her around the hot irons," Hilda said. She set the little girl on the chair by Orillia's bed and propped the Hurlbut's on Orillia's lap.

Hurlbut's Story of the Bible advertised itself "for Young and Old." Inside, the pictures glowed; gold and fire glinted from the pages. Men and women and children wore robes of rose red and indigo that contrasted with the subtler shades of sky and sand. The desert country portrayed was not unlike Saskatchewan, but exotic. The pictures were made to look obviously from another time and another place, recognizable yet unreal, the very settings for the stories. Orillia paged through the book until she came across an illustration she liked. A girl in a white shift, with soft hair curled about a soft face and with her hand on her heart, stood facing a sitting priest. The priest was reading from a scroll opened across his knee. There was an oil lamp suspended by his head, and other scrolls lay on the divan beside him. Then she saw that she had the illustration wrong. It wasn't a girl. The caption said Samuel had come to learn. Well, Orillia thought, the artist had misled readers. Samuel not only looked like a girl, but the picture showed him doing the talking. She thought for a moment about another Sam,

Captain Sam Hagan, her mother's new husband. Then she shook him out of her head.

"Look at this," she said, shifting the book toward Susan, who still hadn't spoken a word to anyone. "A girl who lived in a temple. See, she's talking to the priest. Isn't she wise? What do you think she's saying?"

It didn't work. Susan only shrugged and looked at her bony knees.

a young man with black eyes

Gladdie saw her from behind. She was a woman you'd notice on the street. Even if you hadn't met her before, your eyes would be drawn to the heft of her and that flounce she added to her walk as if to show there was a girl still inside that big lardy body. Gladdie had been watching for her so long it only seemed right to see her sailing through the crowd half a block ahead, the feathers bouncing over her hat. Christmas was near, and the sun had decided to shine for a good ten minutes, and others besides Mrs. Parker were stepping along jauntily. Gladdie wasn't up to it herself. She didn't feel remotely jaunty. She was only out in the city because she'd had a talk with herself in which she'd been firm. She'd told herself she wasn't at all sure it had been Mr. Tupper she'd seen outside that tobacco store. It might have been some other pair of leering eyes over some other whiskers. And if it was Mr. Tupper, she couldn't let him keep her a prisoner in Mrs. Riley's house. Not when that baby was out there somewhere.

Mrs. Parker went into a shop, and Gladdie couldn't follow. It was a pharmacy and it would have that hushed sound of pharmacies. You could be an anonymous person in a crowd on the sidewalk, but as soon as you walked in there you'd confront them with yourself. The sign over the window told her everything she needed to know. It said Jas. P. Parker Drugs. Mrs. Parker had said her husband was a druggist.

It was that odd time of day people can't get used to in early winter, when it's still afternoon, but it's twilight and the street lamps are just lit. While Mrs. Parker was inside, the sunlight dimmed, and it began to snow fat flakes that sank down faster and faster, and when Mrs. Parker came out the door, she did what everybody else on the street was doing. She looked up and got some on her face. Just then a cab came tooling along like Providence, and Mrs. Parker stepped forward and hailed it. At the same second a dashing young gentleman in a beaver coat emerged from the tailors' next door and waved it down with his hat. Gladdie couldn't tell if he'd run outside to help Mrs. Parker or if he'd wanted the cab for himself, but of course he gave it to her, hoisted her up with his hand on her elbow and Mrs. Parker put some spring into her knees and bounced into the seat and settled herself high above them all. The young man gave a nod to the driver, a pat on the horse's rump, and Mrs. Parker was off into the traffic and the swirling snow, the carriage lamps swinging.

The young gentleman turned and recognized Gladdie. If he hadn't, and if he hadn't shown it, startled, she might not have known who he was. She'd only seen him once, on the wharf, the first time she'd followed Jessie Dole down there. When he turned back from helping Mrs. Parker, and saw her watching him, fear as well as recognition flared in his eyes. That fear came from guilt; Gladdie knew it. He was the same young man who'd strode alongside the lake as if he thought he could run the world without looking. She remembered poor Jessie Dole saying she was still hoping. He'd been in touch with her, of course he had. He must have come to see her at Mrs. Riley's, meeting her outside those times she'd slipped out without Gladdie knowing. He'd be sure to have kept out of sight of anyone like Gladdie, who'd have held him to account. Before she could think what she was doing, as fierce as could be she leaned forward to him and said, "Do you have no concern at all for your own child?"

She almost pitied the young man, he went so pale.

She went on. "That woman you just give your cab to, she's got her."

He looked after the cab. Traffic being heavy, it was stopped at the intersection. "Give me some money and I'll go after her," Gladdie said. "I'll find out for you where she lives. You'll want to know that much."

Like a man in a dream, he pulled out a wallet and handed her three bills.

"You know where to find me," she said gruffly, and he didn't say a thing, so she was right; he'd followed Jessie Dole and met her outside Mrs. Riley's those last weeks of her life, and made her hope. The shock of what she was doing was beginning to hit Gladdie, but there was no time to lose in thinking. The young man still seemed stunned and ready to do whatever she said. She waved down a cab. The driver looked doubtful but saw she was with him so stopped. He gave her a lift on the elbow as he'd done for Mrs. Parker; it would be habitual with him, that kind of manners, Gladdie thought, and he told the driver he was to follow that cab at the intersection and then take the young lady home.

"Tomorrow. Come see me tomorrow," she called to him, leaning out. The carriage was already off, rocking. His black eyes followed her. His face was wet with snow and still so pale he looked sick. Served him right, Gladdie thought, sitting back against the leather seat. It was her first ride in a cab and, without needing warmth, she pulled the rug about her knees like she'd seen women do. God, she felt fine. She'd been down lately with everything going wrong – the baby taken away and herself not leaving Mrs. Riley's, not having the guts to go, and then thinking she'd seen her old haunter. But she'd taken this fellow on. The unfairness of his being alive had struck her the moment she recognized him. She was there like retribution in front of him; she knew it and had to act.

She couldn't know for sure if Mrs. Parker had been successful in adopting the baby, of course; she was just going on the strength of the woman's personality. She seemed to Gladdie someone who'd grown used to getting what she wanted.

Gladdie wasn't surprised to leave the business district and the little shops and houses of the inner-city wards behind and find herself, before she reached the Parkers' house, in better surroundings, almost like she imagined the countryside must be, with big oak and maple and chestnut trees shading stretches of snow-covered lawn. Driving by the solid brick house, with its bay windows and big fancy verandah, all Gladdie saw besides Mrs. Parker getting out of her cab was the faint figure of a young woman standing in one window watching the snow nestle into the gooseberry shrubs where the garden turned a corner toward the kitchen. Later she learned that was Milly Cooper, Mrs. Parker's niece; she came to know Milly and her sister Clara and their brother Ralph Cooper and his wife Florence and the whole family. That evening she had to be content to find out the address and to note it was set back from the road and surrounded by a wrought iron fence, and even if the young woman at the window did look bored or sad, for some reason or other down at the mouth, it was in Rosedale. It was the kind of neighbourhood and the kind of house you should be glad to live in.

Pearl Fink came to the kitchen in her kimono, her eyes bugged out with excitement. "Gladdie," she whispered, "there's a man to see you."

Cleaning the surgeries at night at the General Hospital, in Gladdie's opinion, wasn't a job you'd want if you gave it any thought. Men were high on Pearl's list of better things to think about. This one was good-looking, and Pearl didn't know he hadn't come to court Gladdie, though a glance at his beaver coat should have put her wise about that.

After she got rid of Pearl, Gladdie sat her visitor down at the kitchen table. He looked too big for Mrs. Riley's kitchen, and it made him seem a little awkward, all elbows and knees and knuckly hands sticking out of his sleeves. Still, Gladdie didn't feel comfortable enough with him to ask him to take off his coat, so he sat at the table holding his glossy hat on his lap and taking on a glossy look himself, as he heated up. Gladdie stood by the table instead of sitting, and crossed her arms. He cleared his throat. It was likely hard for him, she thought, being in the house where young Mrs. Dole had lived her last weeks. Then she remembered how he was that day at the wharfs, full of confidence then, with his black eyes flashing his own sense of himself. What good did it do poor Jessie Dole to have him looking at his feet now, as if the whole story was laid there on the linoleum? Jessie Dole might have lay there herself, her body lifeless and bloated as it would have been when they fished her from the lake. Boys oh boys, Gladdie said to herself, you are one sorry fellow. For all the world I wouldn't be you. Then she was glad she'd stoked the fire in the range just before he'd arrived and the kitchen was abnormally hot. The sweat was breaking out on his brow under his dark, well-cut hair.

John Dabb was his name. He gave it simply when she asked.

"My name's Gladdie McConnell," she said.

"I know," he said. "She talked about you." He looked up at Gladdie with a quizzical expression as if he'd like to know her better, as if he hadn't just referred to a dead girl, a girl who'd killed herself because of him.

"Why didn't you marry her?" Gladdie said. It came bursting out of her, and she was glad to see it set him back.

He said, "I couldn't."

"That's that, is it?"

"She knew I couldn't."

"No, she did not. She said she was hoping." Gladdie's voice rose on the last word and made it into an ugly sound that physically hurt her throat. He was wise enough not to attempt an answer. He stood up and Gladdie thought he was going to walk out before she'd finished.

"I suppose you're married already," she said. He shook his head. "Well, then," she said, at a disadvantage now that he towered over her. "What's your excuse?"

He set his hat on the table and removed his heavy coat and laid it over a chair back, then he sat down again as if he knew it would be better for him to be lower. "My family," he said quietly. He had a refined way of speaking that made her just about see his family when he spoke of them.

"She wasn't good enough for them?" She was getting harsher and louder as he grew quieter. "You didn't love her?"

He looked up, his dark eyes glittering and rimmed with red. He reminded her of Harry the last time she saw him, the way he couldn't seem to give her anything, as if to give her anything he'd have to subtract it from himself. "Men," she said. "You're all the same."

"No," he said. "There are better men than I am."

"That's a mouthful," she said.

He roused a bit then. "I tried to help her," he said. "I gave her money. And I told her I'd provide for the child. I still mean to."

"And how do you mean to do that, with no idea where she is? You haven't even asked me about Mrs. Parker, the lady I followed yesterday to her house. A fancy place in Rosedale."

"Yes," John Dabb said. "I don't understand why you think she has the child."

"She come here about Mrs. Dole, asking for information about Jessie Dole. I could see she wanted the child."

"Jessie Dole?" He seemed very interested, himself, in that bit of information. The quizzical expression came back to his face, and he fastened her with his black, curious eyes. "What do you have to do with all this?" he asked.

"I saw you one day on the wharf. You walked right by her." Gladdie pulled away from him and went to the window for an excuse to keep her back to him. "You must have followed her here. That's right, isn't it? So every time the poor girl took a step, either I was dogging her or you were, and neither one of us did a thing to help her. But I'll tell you, if I'd known that day you walked by her that you were the one, or if I'd seen you down there again or hanging around the house, I'd have made you behave like a man. You don't pay your way. Men." Her anger was dissipating, being replaced by exhaustion, and she hadn't yet got to the important matter. "You see what I mean?" she asked, turning back to find him watching her sympathetically. "Women pay. You don't pay." She crossed her arms again and glared at him.

"What do you want me to do, Gladdie?" he asked.

She stepped back at the sound of her name in his low, considerate-sounding voice. She bumped into the sink, and there she stood her ground. She had it all figured out what she wanted him to do.

They made the deal that day. He'd finance her to find the baby, whether she was with the Parkers or not, and make sure the child was well cared for. She'd report to him on her progress. The payment was necessary if Gladdie wasn't to use her savings on streetcar fare, but they both understood it was symbolical as well. John Dabb departed bemused and more satisfied than the situation warranted, but he hid that from his would-be Nemesis, and if Gladdie felt a little uneasy at his abrupt acquiescence, she ignored her feelings in favour of activity. She left the house soon after he did. She went back up to Rosedale to see if anything had happened yet at Mrs. Parker's house.

They were all sitting in the parlour when she returned.

"Who died?" she asked, deciding to be brazen with them, and after all, it was about the only time they all sat down together when it wasn't mealtime. Mrs. Riley blew her nose. She might have been bawling; if so it was for effect. She'd certainly been drinking.

"You've come back," Miss Avis said, lifting a pale green angora bootie on four thin needles to her mouth, and it struck Gladdie she'd lived at Mrs. Riley's even longer than the old lady had. Miss Avis went back right away to her knitting. She was always working every minute of the day to make what passed for a living. She'd seen more cardigans and baby sets go through her fingers than most people could dream of. You'd never see her without her needles unless she was holding her knife and fork. She'd stopped just that second when Gladdie came in, keeping the fine wool hooked over her thumb.

The fuss was all because a man had come to see Gladdie. And then she'd taken the afternoon off, which she'd started to do anyway once a week or so, almost daring Mrs. Riley to fire her. "We thought you eloped," Pearl Fink said, grinning all over her face.

"Oh for pity's sake," Gladdie said, and she went to the kitchen and started on the potatoes.

She went to the pharmacy and bought some dusting powder, lilac in scent, from Clara Cooper, as she later knew her to be. While Clara Cooper was ringing up the sale on her cash register, Gladdie saw behind the counter a man she thought was Clara's father but later learned was her uncle, the Jas. P. Parker of the sign over the window, and Mrs. Parker's husband. She saw him counting pills, five at a time, sliding them along a tray with a flat knife, filling a bottle. They seemed like decent people. Clara, an upright young woman with an unfortunate face, as plain as a pudding, said something kind about the lilac reminding a person of spring though it was the beginning of winter, and she wished Gladdie a happy Christmas. Then Gladdie took the streetcar to the city limits and walked the few blocks into Rosedale, to the Parkers' house.

John Dabb became Johnnie without Gladdie even noticing she'd made that leap. They started meeting at Union Station regularly in case she had something to report. They'd sit side by side on a bench, as Gladdie and Mrs. Dole had done, and he encouraged her to continue being vigilant by asserting his belief that her instincts were right.

When nothing came of three more visits to the Parkers' house and subsequent strolls about its perimeter, she suggested to Johnnie he might go to the Children's Aid Society and tell them he was the father. Then he could ask them what had become of the child. She knew of course he'd never do it. He'd never put himself and his family to shame. He understood she was trying to be cruel and hung his head and didn't let her see that her sternness and her strangeness – she was unlike anyone he'd ever met – fascinated him.

Parts of a person's body could get to Gladdie, especially the tender parts you don't often see. The back of the neck was one such place, and when Johnnie was sitting beside her with his head down, and she saw that his hair at the nape of his neck grew in circles, one on each side, she knew she'd remember it afterwards, though she was on her guard against him.

"It takes a while to adopt, that's why they don't have her," she said. She was only bluffing. What did she know? She stopped looking at his neck, and her gaze fell to his knuckly hand that gripped the bench near her thigh, and she sighed so loudly he jumped up and said he must go.

They'd taken to meeting at Union Station because she couldn't have him coming to Mrs. Riley's, setting off alarms in them all, especially Mrs. Riley, who'd had a talk with her, after the first incident of his coming to the house, in which she warned her not to give herself without a business arrangement and money up front. Then one day Mrs. Riley called her into the parlour and showed Gladdie what she called her pessary and described where she put it and what it could do. For a couple of weeks that gave Gladdie a good laugh, Mrs. Riley looking so earnest over her welfare. "Oh you're on top of the world now," Mrs. Riley said, flexing the stained old rubber disk. "I can see it suits you and he suits you, but how long will you suit him? You're not to all men's tastes. And you'll be old before you know it."

It's true she was feeling fine. Her fingers got better right away. As soon as she took charge of Johnnie she was cured of that habit. She just knew him going along with her plan was a sign she'd find the baby.

She loved Union Station, all the people to-ing and fro-ing, sometimes shouting out greetings and sometimes crying at parting. If she had to wait for Johnnie she'd sit there and make up stories about them all. She'd think about the day she and Jessie Dole had sat there, and she'd given Jessie Dole a chance. It wasn't her fault Jessie Dole didn't take it. Then she'd get an eerie feeling, looking down at the marble floor, because it looked like water the way threads swirled through it. If you concentrated on it, the threads seemed to drift like the shadows of ripples in the lake. But it wasn't water, it was a solid floor. She thought how good it must feel to descend from a jerky, swaying train and find your footing on that floor.

"The Parkers will have her by Christmas," she told Johnnie. "The Society won't want extra babies on their hands over the holidays. You wait and see."

It was a week to go. Johnnie looked more at that marble floor than she did.

christmas

Christmas was the one day that week Gladdie didn't steal away for at least a bit to spy outside the Parkers' house. Every day up to then she'd watched them carting in presents. She'd looked through the window into their parlour and seen them decorating a big pine tree. She'd seen the youngsters in the family taking their sleighs down the street to a hill to play. There was a school-aged boy and a girl. The bored older girl about her age or a few years younger did most of the tree decorating. She looked quite a bit like the one who'd helped Gladdie in the drugstore, only she was more squat and even plainer. Mrs. James Parker played the piano, and Mr., the pharmacist, read a book with his feet up on a footstool. There was no sign of a baby. Then, the day before Christmas, she noted they had a toddler, a little thing not much over two, she'd guess, and that brought her down. Why would Mrs. Parker adopt an infant with a family like she had? Gladdie thought she must have imagined it in her, that want.

Christmas Day a nasty wind blustered up and down the street, whining around the corners, and gave even Mrs. Riley's drafty house a coziness it didn't deserve. They had a turkey, and Mrs. Riley herself made the dressing, and they had a steamed carrot pudding Gladdie had done up a few weeks before, and a brown-sugar sauce. Mr. Parchman put a bottle of Irish whiskey on the table, a piece of generosity that in itself made for an unusual day.

They all but Gladdie had a drink, and some of them had several. The cellar lodger, Mr. Mainwaring, had more than his share. At Mrs. Riley's insistence Gladdie sat at the table with them. She didn't take part in the conversation, so she was the first to notice the effects of Mr. Parchman's whiskey on Mr. Mainwaring before he turned green and vomited at Mrs. Riley's feet, then passed out, pulling the tablecloth with him to the floor. Mrs. Riley grabbed the Irish; the rest rained down on Mr. Mainwaring – the cutlery, the glasses, the turkey carcass and all the plates piled with their picked-clean bones and cold gravy. Mrs. Riley stood up with a cranberry on her collar and made her way to the parlour, and the lodgers fled behind her. Gladdie closed the glass French doors on them all, rescued the carcass, took it to the kitchen sink and pumped water over it to dislodge the fluff balls and dust. That kind of fluff that hovers above the floor, they call that Irish lace, she thought as she watched it clog up the sink hole and she thought it was, taken all together, quite an Irish Christmas. She stirred up the embers in the stove and put the beast on to boil for soup.

When she came back to the dining room and started pitching the cutlery into the potato bowl, Mr. Mainwaring groaned. A lot of the knives and forks had fallen on him. He wasn't pierced but it made her think of *Gulliver's Travels*, the picture of Gulliver tied down and tiny spears sticking out of him like pins in a cushion, and that made her think of Mr. Shamata and wonder where he was now, if he was still alive and what kind of Christmas he would be having. She cleaned up the dishes and utensils and swept up the broken glass and swabbed the carpet and floorboards with the tablecloth, then went to the back door and threw the cloth into a snowbank. It would be easier to shake the crud loose when frozen.

Miss Avis glanced up from her chair by the parlour fire and saw Gladdie brushing off the dining-room chairs, and immediately looked back to her knitting. Gladdie cleaned up everything, but she left Mr. Mainwaring on the floor. She figured he was Mr. Parchman's responsibility. Then she went out on the back step again for a breath of fresh air. The neighbours were partying and singing; boys were throwing snowballs in the alley. She looked up and imagined the stars winking out, and that made her wonder what John Dabb was doing for his Christmas. The neighbours' back door opened. Before she could be hailed, she retreated into the porch. She took a last look at the snow before she closed the door and noticed how dark it was, especially in the hollows, the closest thing to black white. Then she went and started her dishes.

John Dabb, at that same time, was taking pleasure in a glass of superior port and a cigar, both courtesy of his sister's husband's uncle. He was sitting back in a leather easy chair at Maretta and James Parker's house, with his long legs stretched toward a coruscating fire. He was listening to a piano duet being played by two spinster sisters of whom he was fond, in a wary way that was exceeded by their attitude toward him. While Clara and Milly entertained, he was thinking about Gladdie McConnell, that fascinatingly forceful young woman who had stepped up to him and rescued him from what had threatened to be a depressing time. He knew something that was going to make Gladdie McConnell happy, and because that something was going to make her happy, he didn't consider at all the possibility that his role in her life was a betrayal.

In his mid-twenties, John Dabb was already adept at the kinds of rationalization that let him off the hook whenever his enjoyment of life – and he did enjoy his life – resulted in unwanted consequences. He wasn't hard-hearted. In fact, in his dealings with women he believed he was too soft, too easily intrigued by their difference from himself, their winning earnestness or innocence or spirit. When faced with fate, he tended to go in its direction, but he'd found he was often spared. Only a few months earlier his destiny had seemed to be marriage to an admittedly unsuitable girl. Jessie Dole, she'd called herself after she'd fled from her home. He thought it endearing – and like her – that she'd used his initials. He'd informed his sister he was going to have to marry the girl, and Florence had told him he couldn't throw his future away.

"Give her money," Florence said. "And do it quickly, firmly, once and for all. Don't be drawn into any further relationship with her."

Florence was four years older than John and had always indulged him, but when she had his best interests at heart she could be stern. If he'd been able to be as resolute, he might have saved a life. This was a thought that nagged at him now and then when he sensed Florence's anger. She was angry with him, and had called him stupid for seeing the girl during her pregnancy and letting her hope he could possibly waver. Johnnie didn't really understand hope, having so seldom in his life experienced disappointment.

The motherless child had to be taken into account. Self-sacrifice wasn't part of Florence's character, and she didn't offer to accept her niece and raise her as her own, even though her husband, Ralph, had broached the subject of adoption when it seemed they weren't going to have children. "I think I could interest Maretta," she said. "She will have read of the incident in the papers." Maretta Parker was Ralph's aunt, wife of Jim, the pharmacist. Maretta was mother to several young Parkers, but she was a stalwart worker for the board of the Children's Aid Society, and could be counted on to rise to the challenge of saving a child. Maretta had been spoken to, her generous nature had been praised, the plight of the infant born under such inauspicious circumstances had been discussed, and Maretta had responded well. Much was made of the romantic death of the mother in the case. No mention was made of the father. It was enough to say the woman had been unmarried to imply the father couldn't be named or found, and no one suspected it was Johnnie. No one guessed there was any connection between that infant and Johnnie or Florence. Before long, Maretta had thought adopting the infant had been her own idea – her youngest, Louise, was two, after all, it was time for another baby – and she set herself and her community connections to work. So it happened that, as John Dabb exhaled a series of soft smoke rings that drifted through the parlour (mingling momentarily, he thought, fancifully, with the notes of the sisters' duet) and dissipated near the stairwell, and as he drained his glass of port and accepted another, the infant none of them knew was his daughter lay in a crib two floors above him, though he hadn't seen her yet.

Gladdie had nearly decided she wasn't going to go back to the Parkers', she'd felt so glum after seeing that toddler. She was having second thoughts about the whole enterprise and not just because she was afraid she'd invented Mrs. Parker's intentions. She didn't approve of herself being drawn to Johnnie Dabb. She didn't want to think about him when he wasn't there. She didn't want her power of refusal tested. It was a business arrangement – she knew what kind of man he was. But she and Johnnie had a meeting set for between Christmas and New Year's, so she thought she'd go to the Parkers' one more time and at least she'd have that to report.

It was one of those clean afternoons when a light blanket of snow had freshened everything, and a little bit of sunshine peeking through the clouds brightened everything, and in spite of herself and her troubles Gladdie felt her spirits rising as the streetcar took her into the better neighbourhoods where even the roadside snow looked purer and shone with an expensive glitter. A small dilemma faced her when she reached the house because no footsteps led from the road up the path to the verandah. No one had come to the house recently. Although she'd crept up to the windows several times before, by walking up the path as if she planned to go round to the back door, Gladdie couldn't do it across the fresh snow. The thought of leaving her footprints visible for anyone to see alarmed her. She passed in front of the house and found a passageway between the hedges of the Parkers' property and their neighbour's. The snow lay over her boot tops there, and her ankles were soon stinging, but she was able to keep half hidden in the shrubs at the side of the house until she got to the parlour window.

And wouldn't you know, right in the window, by the Christmas tree, large as life, Mrs. James Parker sat rocking a cradle with her foot. Gladdie stared so long at the baby in that cradle, Mrs. Parker looked up and must have seen her, but if so she looked right through her. She'd think it was someone going round to the back, anyway, selling or begging, Gladdie was sure. She wouldn't recognize her as the servant she'd seen at Mrs. Riley's. She likely hadn't even seen her back in the corner of Mrs. Riley's parlour, the day she'd visited, and if she had, she'd have known she was just the help, nobody to remember.

Gladdie ran for the streetcar and caught it, but even so she was late for their meeting, and Johnnie was there before her. She saw him from the moment she stepped into the station. He was standing apart from other people, looking out the door she usually came in. She stopped and watched him watching for her. She thought about Jessie Dole, how sometimes she must have come on him like this, with excitement spilling out of her that quieted when she set eyes on him, the urgency replaced by awe. That would be the only way to describe it, the wonder of someone waiting for you.

She pulled her face to its normal look as she walked up to him so she wouldn't give away the news at once, but he saw something was up. "What is it?" he asked. She took his arm and told him.

"I saw her. The baby. Oh Johnnie, she's plump and beautiful. And she has your dark eyes. I could see them through the glass, like coal, shining."

They sank down on the bench together and sighed the same sigh.

He went with her that day on the streetcar to the Parkers' house. She told him he must in case she died accidentally. He'd need to know where the baby was. He rode beside her, smiling down at her over and over again. Just pleased as punch. When they reached the house, he got anxious in case they'd be caught, but Gladdie reassured him. It was the family's supper hour; they'd be in the dining room. It was the best time. The rocking chair was empty in the window by the Christmas tree when they snuck up, but the cradle was still there. And the baby was there, sleeping in the cradle. Gladdie knew she'd be in trouble when she got back home, the lodgers and Mrs. Riley all in a state from not knowing when she'd return and no supper on the table for them, but she didn't care, there was such joy in seeing the baby again and showing her to him.

boredom

"Look who's come to see you," Hilda said. "The girls from the telephone exchange."

Maud and Harriet and Isabel. Well, they were going to congratulate themselves afterwards. Orillia was so glad to see them, she had quite a time keeping the smile off her face. And they brought so much life into the room. They were not dressed exactly alike this time, but they were in sprigged cotton, all of them. "You look as fresh as flowers," she told them.

"Three chairs for us!" cried Isabel. There were three chairs crowding the little room, for Gladdie, Hilda and Susan. The way Isabel said it, it sounded like "three cheers." And the visit went on like that, through tea and cake, with the girls chattering among themselves and Orillia their appreciative audience. Only very soon she began to feel older than they would ever be and wiser. She saw how they reinforced their friendship by telling her about their loves and hates. It was happy talk, among them, that built like children's blocks, one bit of scandal topping another until a tower of it was ready to tumble and nearly did when they accidentally revealed that Harriet was married. The others had gone to her wedding.

"You must tell me all about it," Orillia said manfully.

When the excitement of describing the marvellous event had died down Harriet looked concerned. She'd have to leave her job if it were known.

"Have no fear on my account," Orillia said. "I never expect to see Miss B. again and would certainly not mention it if I did. I'm not in favour of marriage, as an institution, you know. Especially since a rather interesting married man has the room next door."

The girls gaped. Maud, who was sitting nearest the door, glanced over to Mr. Best's room.

"Orillia!" Harriet said. "You don't mean it."

Orillia raised her eyebrows, and remembered Miss Harmon, and said nothing.

"Gosh," Isabel said. "What's he like?"

Orillia put her hands up and raised her eyebrows again, and they smiled at her, delighted.

"Propinquity," Orillia whispered, "accounts for many an illicit affair, I shouldn't wonder."

That pretty much stopped conversation. The girls glanced at one another, and stood up and hovered awkwardly. Like three big moths afraid of battering themselves against the walls, they didn't know how to depart.

"You're well looked after here," Harriet said.

"Mrs. Wutherspoon and Miss McConnell are awfully nice," Maud said.

"You're looking much better," Isabel said timidly, in the doorway. She was the one dressed in lilac, who almost blended into the wall.

After the girls left, Orillia decided what she meant about being a better person was that people would like her more. She didn't seem to have the knack of making friends. She didn't know why. She meant well, and she tried to be entertaining. But she seemed out of step. And why had she mentioned Mr. Best? What if they came again, and saw him? They'd pronounce him ancient. They'd never imagine him in their beds. Really, it was impossible to think of them – any one of them – lying in a hot bed, yearning over anyone, let alone a fat old guy banging his fingers down on a little machine. He'd typed only a little, sporadically, that day, and it hadn't aroused her. He'd been tentative, unsure. It was the rough, commanding rattle that got to her. The word manhandle came to her mind, and it was so silly she snorted out loud, but the thought of it set her skin tingling, and Mr. Best – in the phantom form she knew best – entered her room and climbed like a lumberjack onto her bed. When that wasn't authentic enough, she succumbed to an old trick and pulled a pillow into his place and rolled over onto it. This was awkward because of the casts, but it was wonderful. "Oh Mr. Best," she whispered into the mattress because even in the midst of such serious business, she thought it was funny.

In the kitchen Hilda was watching Susan make one and one add up to two. Gladdie was peeling potatoes for their supper. All was cozy and companionable, the way only kitchens can be at the end of a sociable afternoon, until a barely perceptible tapping or rhythmic rocking from above gradually invaded their consciousnesses. Susan looked up.

"What's that?" Hilda asked. She stood, ready to go upstairs and investigate, but Gladdie put a hand on her arm to stay her. A look passed between them (the sound went on) and a vivid pink infused Hilda's face, and her scalp under her white hair lit up like a sunset. Without a word she plucked Susan from her chair and carried her out to the garden. Gladdie wiped her hands on the kitchen towel and followed. They all went and stared at the snapdragons as if concentration would make them bloom.

background

From time to time, at Hilda's instigation, Susan brought a notebook to show Orillia. The book was in the gradual and somewhat painful – from the looks of it – process of being embossed with Susan's ABCs. A blind person could have read the little girl's letters on the reverse of each page, though it would have been a confused reading since she printed on both sides.

She'll get a bump on her middle finger from pressing her pencil so hard, Orillia thought. Her mother would have told Susan that. Not that Florence wouldn't have understood the satisfaction of a perfectly rounded *a*, but she wouldn't have appreciated the control that was required to achieve it.

Whenever the notebook appeared, Orillia admired it with the sort of dutiful praise the child saw through. Susan bowed her head until it was over. This time Orillia was prepared to do the same and have the same result. She really didn't care. If it pleased Hilda, she and Susan would both perform as expected. But this time when Susan passed her work over, it was different. As soon as Orillia opened the scribbler, Hilda said, "That's the wrong one." It looked, from the cover, like the other, but this book was filled on both sides of nearly every page with crayoned people, every one of them drawn in black except for the last pages and for them she'd used brown. Orillia flipped through the notebook. When she'd reached the end she didn't know what to say. Hilda didn't say anything either. Even Susan seemed to regard her drawings with awe. She stared at the pages she'd created as if someone else must have made them.

They were all the same. The brown stick people on the last page looked just like those on every preceding page. The width of every page was taken up with three figures; two tall figures flanked a smaller. Their arms and legs protruded from their stick trunks at unanatomical angles. In every picture, the girl's long stick fingers meshed with those of the others like the spokes of dark suns.

Finally Orillia said, "I see you've used up all of your black crayon."

"Yes," Hilda said. "I told her that would happen. And now she'll use up all her brown, so what will she do if she wants to draw dogs or fences or trees?"

"It appears unlikely," Orillia said. She ran her finger down a waxy limb.

"I tell her there's a whole world to picture," Hilda went on. "There's a whole world *behind* people. *Around* people. Look at photographs, for example. You'll never see a person without some sort of background. Clouds or the sun or trees. At the very least, if indoors, you'll see a wall. There's never a blank space behind people," Hilda said. She sounded as if she might cry.

Why fuss about the background, Orillia wondered. Surely it was the figures that disturbed her.

"Picks at her food," Gladdie said. "Picky eater, Susie Q."

Susan nodded, serious. Gladdie placed her hand at the back of the small head, cupping the straggly ringlets, then Susan smiled. Too vulnerable, Orillia noted, those smiles. Susan had better learn not to wear her emotions on her face.

The day was cool and dull, and only in the past hour had the sun come slanting from the south to warm the bedroom. Orillia was wearing her red Chinese jacket that had once moved Susan to reach out a forefinger, to touch its silkiness. Orillia had touched it herself, earlier, imagining Mr. Best, envisioning his big clumsy finger stroking the silk and at the same time feeling it as if she were him. Mr. Best, unknown, unloved but for his jagged male exterior, was a daily diversion for Orillia now, and nightly too.

Half of Susan's cookie remained in her saucer long after her milky tea had grown cold. Today they couldn't induce her to believe she was one of them. Maybe it was because Gladdie was unusually cranky. She'd pulled weeds last evening, ironed all morning. She said her back was sore. And Orillia, all the time, was looking past them, looking for something that existed beyond the bodies on the chairs, something beyond herself and them. It was Hilda Wutherspoon's fault: saying everyone had a background, no one existed alone in an empty space. If she hadn't pointed out the emptiness behind Susan's drawings, those pictures wouldn't have kept recurring, making Orillia feel restless.

"A letter from your mother," Hilda said, MOTHER with capital letters, then she vanished. Orillia opened the envelope with her thumb and took out the cross-hatched page. It was one sheet only, to say they were coming, bound straight for Regina. Someone had sent Florence a clipping from the local newspaper, an article that had been for the most part invented, since Orillia had declined to give an interview. "Miss Cooper is recovering at her new home," the article said. And the headline: "Plucky Girl Vows to Walk Again."

The letter was full of concern, and under the concern Orillia read anger. Well, of course, Florence realized she'd deliberately misled her. She was humiliated because someone knew she hadn't known Orillia had been hurt. For the first time Orillia tinkled the bell they'd given her to summon help. She forgot she'd promised herself not to touch the thing – it made such an invalid of her. Hilda came running up the stairs. Naturally, she thought there must be something wrong.

"I'm sorry," Orillia said. "The bell sounds so urgent. I didn't mean to make you hurry."

Hilda took a chair, fanned her face, then leaned back with her hand on her breast, which was rising and falling rapidly.

Until she spoke, Orillia didn't realize she was angry. "Mrs. Wutherspoon," she said. "I wanted to keep my injuries from my mother. But someone has informed her."

Hilda's mouth opened. Perspiration rolled down her cheeks and she drew her handkerchief from her sleeve and patted her face. "You hoped to spare her," she said.

"Yes."

"Well," she said. "A mother would want to know, Orillia."

"But who would have done it? Who would have sent her that clipping?"

Hilda looked out the door and said she didn't know.

Gladdie, when asked, said, "I've lived too long in other people's houses not to know to mind my own business."

solomon

Gladdie didn't approve of some of the stories in the Hurlbut's, and she always read them to herself before she would read them aloud to Susan. The story of Solomon was a good example. God had come to Solomon when he was young and asked him what he wanted; whatever it was he'd give it to him. Solomon asked for wisdom, so that's what he got, with honour and riches thrown in, since he'd made such a good choice. Soon after this, two women came to him with two babies, one living, one dead, and both said the living child was theirs. One woman (the haughty-looking one in the illustration) told Solomon they'd been sleeping in the same bed with their infants and the other woman had rolled over on top of her baby and it had died. She said the other woman had traded the babies in the quiet of the night. And that the living child was hers. The other woman said just the opposite had happened and the live baby belonged to her. Solomon said, "Bring me a sword." He told his men to cut the child in two and give each woman half. One of the women cried out not to do it, let the other woman have it as long as the child could live. The other woman, the haughty-looking one, was willing to let him go ahead with it. So Solomon gave the baby to the first woman, who must have been its mother since she'd spoken out of love.

Gladdie wouldn't read it to Susan, not like that. She didn't believe it. What did they take women for, in those days? There wasn't a woman alive who'd say to cut the baby in two, whether she was or wasn't its mother. The haughty one already had a dead child. Half another dead child wasn't going to satisfy her, if you could imagine her evil enough to agree to it. Gladdie figured God might have come through on the honours and riches, but if that was his idea of wisdom, he didn't know women.

She remembered the story, though, when she found out Florence Cooper was coming. The phrase she recalled was "in the quiet of the night." She didn't know why those words stuck in her memory, unless it was because she was lying in bed at the time, having woken up at a bad hour. She did not want to ponder the meaning, in her own life, of the story of Solomon's wisdom. Instead, she thought about the illustrations in the Hurlbut's, and wondered if the paintings in the Cyclorama had been similar. She tried to imagine bigger-than-life scenes with wells in the desert and figures in flowing robes, but once she had them painted on the walls of her mind, she was not pleased to see the way the noble, halo-lit heads cast their eyes downward in her direction. They all had those earnest, soulful gazes that were surely designed to make a person's heart stoop.

Orillia wrote her mother back. She told her she could save herself the bother of coming to Regina. Orillia didn't need her, thank you very much, because Gladdie McConnell was looking after her. Sealing the envelope, her hands shook. Her fingers fumbled. Before she could change her mind, she called Hilda, who, as luck would have it, was on her way downstairs, still adjusting her hat in the hallway.

"Going to the post office?" Orillia asked her.

She didn't tell anyone what she'd written.

mirror, mirror

Orillia kept thinking she was catching Hilda and Gladdie studying her. Then when she noticed, they looked away.

"Hilda, can I have a mirror?" she asked. From the bed she couldn't see into the dressing table mirror along the side wall. She hadn't asked to see herself in the hospital or anytime since, and no one had suggested she should.

"What do you want with a mirror?" Gladdie asked.

"I have an unusual purpose in mind," Orillia said. "I want to see myself."

The look on Gladdie's face reminded Orillia of the African violet conversation, but she soon forgot about that. Hilda went to her room and got the silver-backed mirror from her dresser set. Gladdie watched silently, with her hand on the top rail at the foot of the bed, as if she might need to hold it down.

Well, it wasn't so bad. She had raccoon rings around her eyes, but they were already fading. Her face was gaunt; she'd lost her looks, but wasn't disfigured. Her right cheek seemed swollen and blurred. She moved the mirror, thinking the glass might be flawed just there. She leaned closer. Nothing. She held the mirror out again, and she thought she saw a cross-hatching of scars there, dimpling the skin.

"You're nearly yourself again," Gladdie said.

"Is my cheek scarred?"

"Where?"

"Here." She ran her fingers over the skin. It felt perfectly smooth.

"There's no scars on your face," Gladdie said.

Orillia handed the mirror back to Hilda. "Thank you," she said and at the same moment fell backwards through time. At least, that was how it felt. She saw her small self. It wasn't a memory, more like one of those dreams in which she was present, watching her own little body, lost to her in growing up, yet existing still in that other time.

She was walking up the path to her great-uncle James Parker's house. Clara and Milly and several of her cousins were there. They were taking her to the house to live with them.

"You remember the house, Orillia," her aunt Clara said when she hesitated outside the pillars of the front verandah. They all stopped and waited for her, turning their bonnets and hats toward her.

She wouldn't follow them inside. She stood firm in the doorway, her sturdy knees locked, until they left her. She hid in the cloakroom, where she fell asleep on the floor, and when she finally joined the others, the pattern of the Italian tiles was imprinted on her cheek. "Look in the mirror," they said when she found them, and after she looked they told her what had made the marks on her cheek.

Now she was as happy as could be just because she knew she'd been that little girl.

family

If you have to lie to someone, simplest is best, so Gladdie borrowed Miss Avis's knitting needle roll. Miss Avis had needles of every size in there, and when you unrolled it they were displayed in order from long to short and of every thickness. Luckily for Gladdie, Miss Avis was involved in a patterned sleeve for a lady's sweater that would take her a day at least with the needles she was using. Gladdie was pretty sure she could slip the roll back in her bag that same evening, and Miss Avis would never know it had gone for a trip across town in a smart-looking valise with the initials J.L.D. The needles had numbers imprinted on them. You didn't have to know a thing about them to sell them, and if it should happen she did sell some, she knew from buying them for Miss Avis the address of the wool shop where she could purchase replacements.

She went to the back door, dressed respectably and with cowed demeanour, neither of which she needed to have bothered putting on, as it happened, since the door was opened by a youngster with frizzy hair popping out of its pins and a look on her face of having had her wits scattered so badly she'd never know where to look to collect them. Gladdie soon learned her name was Annie and she was new at her job. She'd replaced a woman who'd worked for the household ten years and knew the ropes. Poor Annie, you could fill a tome with what that girl didn't know, and here she was the cook and cleaner, the only servant in that big house. "They can't get nobody else," she told Gladdie. "Girls don't want to work in houses."

That gave Gladdie an idea. She could easily get a job right in their house, then she'd be able to watch over the baby every day. The very thought set her shaking. She could hardly question Annie as she'd planned to do, she was so caught up in thinking about herself working in that kitchen and carrying meals to their dining room and cleaning their bedrooms and peeping over the side of the baby's cradle and whispering to her. In her imagination she watched the child grow up to school age while she tried to remember what she was there for.

That poor Annie didn't have time to look at knitting needles, let alone to knit, but she was a soft girl, and once Gladdie got talking to her she didn't know how to make her stop and go away. She kept looking about her for something that would rescue her, and nothing did, so Gladdie easily found out that yes indeed they had a baby in the house, though Annie couldn't say whether or not anyone in the family would be wanting to knit booties and bonnets for her. Annie told her the baby was called Orillia, a fancy name, they both thought. Just then, with Annie looking for all the world a gossip, in walked Milly Cooper, into the kitchen. She looked like her sister, Clara, but with the same weight she stood a head shorter, and from the same features she'd deducted a chin.

At first Gladdie thought, what a sourpuss, but then the girl acted embarrassed and said, "Oh excuse me." And blushed, in her own house. Annie didn't have the presence of mind to make any excuses, so Gladdie said she was there to sell knitting needles, and Milly Cooper said, "Oh, I don't knit" – as if it was a flaw in her character.

If she'd had more presence of mind that day, Gladdie lectured herself later, she could have got Milly Cooper to hire her on the spot. Afterwards she was angry with herself. She didn't know why she'd been so slow and let that chance slip through her fingers. But when she told Johnnie about her idea, he didn't like it.

"I could be with her a lot of the time," she told him. "I could make sure she was happy."

"I don't know if even you could make sure of that," Johnnie said, in his serious mode. He wouldn't say what he had against her living in the Parkers' house.

"That Annie they've got's no better trained than I am, if you ask me," Gladdie said, thinking Johnnie must feel she would be asking for a rise above her station in applying for the job.

"You have more independence where you are," he said, and that was the closest he came to explaining his aversion to the idea. In the end it was just as well she didn't do it. She'd have been stuck there when the baby left, and though with Mrs. Riley her wages were lower than they might have been at the Parkers', she had less work with less fuss, and Johnnie was right: it left her more independent – if that was what she wanted.

"Orillia," she told him. "Big name for a wee mite."

She wondered sometimes why she didn't walk into that house and scoop that baby out of her cradle and carry her off where none of them could find her. But she knew the answer. She wanted what was best for her.

Gladdie didn't know Mrs. Parker was sick or that there was anything the matter with her, though when she and Johnnie talked about it later she realized she hadn't seen her in a week or two. It was near the end of January. It was wet and windy, and Gladdie hadn't thought of making the trip that day since she'd been to the house earlier in the week, but she got uneasy. It had been some time since Johnnie had left a note for her. They had a drop-off place for notes under the eaves of a shed down the alley from Mrs. Riley's, and she'd check it daily and he'd check it once in a while.

She got to Rosedale in the late afternoon, just after the funeral. People were pulling up to the house, carriages full of people with black armbands on their coats. Gladdie had to figure out who had died by seeing who was absent. She hid behind a shed between the Parkers' and their neighbour's house, mentally checking off the family members as they came into view. It was lucky for her it happened to be winter and the Parkers had the lamps on so she could see them all lit up clearly from outside. She knew them by that time quite well, or at least she did in her mind. She was glad it wasn't Mr. Parker; she'd developed a fondness for him. All he ever did when he was home was read books. She was glad it wasn't Clara and gladdest of all it wasn't Milly. But it seemed it must have been Mrs. Parker who'd died, and that was the worst thing that could happen. It was the worst thing for the baby.

Just as she was slipping away along the leafless hedge between the two properties, Johnnie came striding along the wrought iron fence and turned in at the gate. He caught sight of her and stopped in his tracks. He motioned to her to stay where she was and turned back himself to go around the hedge and join her.

"What are you doing here?" she asked.

"Same as you," he whispered, bending over her like the co-conspirator he liked to be. "I came to see what was up."

"I think Mrs. Parker died."

Johnnie acted as if it was news to him. They didn't say any more then, but they hung about behind the shed for some time in the light, silvery darkness while the snow gleamed up at them and a little ashen moon rose over the treetops. Gladdie would have been happy to stop the clock and stay there, the two of them standing close, watching the family in the bright house, but the wind shifted and blew colder, and people started drifting out to go home. Johnnie said he was afraid they'd notice them and take them for thieves looking to rob the house.

Gladdie worried so much about what would happen now, she didn't want to put her thoughts into words. She didn't think Milly or Clara could keep the baby legally because they were spinsters, and she didn't know if Mr. Parker could hold onto her or if he'd want to, having several of his own.

"I'll keep watch," she told Johnnie. "And I think you should, too." They were waiting at the streetcar stop, going in different directions. A couple of other people were standing about, so they faced one another, close, to talk, and their breaths met in the frigid air and rose together. Then Johnnie said he had to go away; he'd be gone a couple of weeks. Gladdie bit her tongue on asking him where he was going. She could tell when someone didn't want to give out information. He gave her extra money for the streetcar fare and her time, and she took it without comment. It's as well to keep things businesslike, she thought.

Ralph's aunt's death was an unwelcome complication for Johnnie and for Florence. Maretta had been such a good answer to the problem of what to do with Orillia. For a few days Florence dithered over the possibilities, then Ralph came up with the only logical solution to the child's existence, and he did it without knowing or guessing who Orillia was. He and Florence must adopt her themselves. In their three years of marriage, no pregnancy had occurred. He knew better than to allude to that little problem, so he put forward a strong case for Orillia's welfare, and for some months afterwards believed himself to have more influence with his wife than he'd ever had before.

"She even looks like you, Florence, with those great dark eyes," he said.

"You'll pay for this in the long run," Florence told Johnnie. He turned unnaturally grave and let her know he was relieved.

"I should think so. Your responsibility's over."

"Ralph will make a better father than I'd ever be," John said truthfully. Already he was cheering up.

Florence hired a nursemaid.

While Johnnie was away Gladdie lost the baby, or she lost sight of her – she figured the Parkers had given her up. She was considering visiting Annie again with Miss Avis's needles as if she'd forgotten nobody in their house knitted, but she didn't have to do that. Milly came out of the house one day carting a shopping bag, and poking over the top was a teddy bear. It was the easiest thing in the world to outrun her once Gladdie knew she was headed to the streetcar stop. She hastened to the stop ahead of Milly's and got on before her and sat near the back. When Milly boarded, Gladdie looked down, and when she stepped off, Gladdie followed.

Milly took her right to the baby, to the couple they'd given her to, on Clinton Street. It was a small house but neat and in a respectable enough neighbourhood, in Gladdie's opinion, with trees and pram-sized front gardens. And the couple was part of the Parker clan. Gladdie had seen them at the Parker house after the funeral.

Johnnie was gone three weeks, and when he came back Gladdie insisted on taking him to see where the baby was living now. She felt excited, with that strange kind of sick excitement you feel when you know bad news is coming. As for Johnnie, he stayed tense, and he seemed almost angry with her until they'd got the viewing of the new place over with.

He was going for good, he said, to a job he'd taken in Buffalo, New York.

After Johnnie left, they kept up the arrangement. Gladdie wrote to him about the baby every month, and he often sent a bit of money and sometimes a note that Gladdie read with a wry eye to counter his tendency to be sentimental. He was a great one for putting deep thoughts into easy words. And so it went for years. The child was a cute little thing, like they all are with their baby fat, though Gladdie thought she was prettier than most. They kept her nicely, her shoes always polished, and they dressed her in little pinafores and put her hair in curls and ribbons. The woman was strict with her; she often looked stern. The husband, when Gladdie had seen him at the big house after Mrs. Parker's funeral, she'd known was Milly and Clara's brother. You'd need no introduction to determine that. They were a homely crew, those Coopers. None of them had a chin to speak of, their skin was pasty, their hair was sparse, and their eyes didn't seem to have lashes, but they were good-hearted. She watched them laughing sometimes, the kind of laughter you know you'd join in if you could hear what they were saying.

candy

I guess Florence Cooper should be here any day," Gladdie said to Hilda. She knew it was Hilda who'd written to Mrs. Cooper, but she couldn't hold it against her.

"It's for the best," Hilda said.

Gloomy as she could be about her own prospects, Hilda was apt to be confident that she knew what was best for others. Even if she knew Florence Cooper, she'd say it was for the best. She wasn't nearly so concerned that Susan should have her mother, Gladdie might have pointed out. It wasn't that Hilda was happy Susan's parents hadn't been located, but she was torn between wanting what was best for the child and wishing to keep her. She'd stopped attending church services, and Gladdie knew why: out of sight, out of mind. Susan was a ward of the church, but if he never saw her the minister might forget about her. Gladdie would never comment on it. It was none of her business. She'd listened to Hilda reasoning it out, and her concerns made sense. What kind of parents wouldn't know their daughter was missing? Wouldn't be searching night and day to find her? If it was Hilda, if she had a little girl lost to her, she'd be knocking on every door in Regina. They didn't deserve a nice little girl like Susan. It was Hilda's firm belief Susan was better off where she was – at least it was her firm belief when the notebook with the stick figures wasn't in evidence – and Gladdie had to agree.

"You'll stay on here, won't you, when Orillia leaves?" Hilda asked one day, and in the second after the question, Gladdie knew Hilda wanted her to go. She wanted Susan to herself once Orillia was gone. It wasn't hard to understand. Gladdie had felt uncomfortable often under Hilda's gaze, the times Susan was clinging to her and seeming to prefer her. She tried to make sure the child spent at least half her time with Hilda.

Susan climbed up onto the velour-upholstered couch to watch Gladdie water the plants in the window. The velour was cut into the pattern of leaves. You could trace your fingers along the furrows. She laughed when Gladdie tipped the spout too far and water cascaded over the pot of Hilda's hoya. It was a certain sound from above that had jolted Gladdie's arm. Sighing, she went to the kitchen for a rag.

Dirty water the colour of tobacco spit was running out the bottom of the pot and overflowing the saucer when Gladdie returned. In a counter-rhythm to the rocking above, it dripped onto the floor. Gladdie was thankful Hilda was out of the house. And that Mr. Best had already left. She should talk to Orillia. Especially because of him. But she couldn't imagine doing it. What could you say that wouldn't embarrass you both?

It was only part of the problem, anyway, only a symptom of a more worrying illness that was showing no signs of lessening. Orillia was turning inward. Gladdie remembered her looking at herself the day she'd asked for a mirror. At first she'd peered into it critically as if she needed to know what it could tell her, but then she'd got a look on her face that reminded Gladdie of the heroines in Mrs. Friel's books. It was a false expression, dreamy and cheeky at the same time. Then it had changed, and she'd looked into the mirror as if into the eyes of someone she loved.

Orillia was a complicated girl. Maybe it was a good thing Mrs. Cooper would be here soon. Unconscious of the wet rag in her hand, Gladdie sat down on the sofa and stared into space.

Susan all this time had been sitting as quiet as a little wraith beside her, but now she started rocking back and forth, banging the back of her head over and over again against the sofa. The rocking still went on above. Gladdie dropped the rag and clapped her hands over her ears and to her own astonishment wished they were both, right this minute, back with their mothers.

"About two hours a day," Dr. Kitely said, standing at the foot of the bed, "you can be up and about on your crutches. But don't attempt the stairs yet."

"Finally." Orillia meant it to sound impudent and was quite sure it did.

"I'll put a chair in the hall for you," Hilda said. "Or you can come into my room. Perhaps in the evenings."

"No," said Dr. Kitely. "Miss Cooper can rest in the evenings. In the mornings she requires stimulation." He spoke as seriously as ever. Orillia had to consider she might have completely imagined he'd ever looked into her eyes and blinked, letting her see inside him.

"Perhaps she could teach the little girl," he said.

Hilda said she didn't know about the other lodger, Mr. Best, how he would feel about conversation on this floor in the morning. Of course, she knew all too well how he would feel.

"Perhaps," Orillia said, "there's something I could do for Mr. Best. Some secretarial work." She could hardly believe she was saying such a thing, but it gave her a lift. It was *so* cheeky to consider sitting taking dictation from Mr. Best. It would serve him right, she figured. Arrogantly, since they'd met, he'd ignored her.

Hilda acted doubtful about the suggestion, but Orillia hooked Dr. Kitely's evasive coffee brown eyes.

"Yes," he said.

"We haven't met, you know, Mr. Best and I, except for one short hello as he walked by my door," Orillia told Dr. Kitely. She felt a surge of energy, almost of the old euphoria from her hospital days; she could feel the heat rising. "Mr. Best is a mystery to me," she said. "Every bit as much as Susan is to all of us."

"He's working here," Hilda said, catching some of the vibrations Orillia had set going in the air. "He uses his room as an office. He wants to work undisturbed."

Hilda was behaving just like the nurses had, putting herself between them. She said, "Miss Cooper's mother will be arriving soon, Dr. Kitely. We expect her any day."

It was true they expected her any day, Orillia as much as Hilda and Gladdie. Not for a minute did she think the letter she'd sent would stop her mother, not once Florence had decided to come. Anyway, Florence would have left for Regina before the letter could possibly travel all the way to San Francisco. She would be here any day.

Dr. Kitely said she was to take care to use the crutches, and put her weight on her left foot for now to save the right the strain. How gravely he spoke.

Afterwards Hilda said, "He's very dark, isn't he? The folds of his skin, especially around the eyes, are blackish."

"Yes," Orillia said. "He makes me think of licorice. Well. Look at Susan. She knows that word. Don't you, Susan? Next time you shop, Gladdie, would you please pick up some twists? What do you say, Susan?"

Without looking up, the little girl grinned to herself.

"Do you want some too? No? No licorice for you? Or yes? Yes, licorice for you."

Susan nodded her head.

"Yes! Licorice for us all!" Oh dear. Her words were so exuberant. And then their faces swam in her gaze. Wasn't she being childish. Tears. Worse than childish. You didn't see Susan crying.

She was much harder later, reminding herself she was only putting in time here until she was ready to leave, and it was only a game she was playing with Dr. Kitely, and she was quite sophisticated enough to enjoy it. What was it Hilda had said to her the other day? "Oh, Orillia, you're such a modern girl."

"Goodness, six sticks each," she said when Gladdie and Susan brought the candy from the corner store. "That will do us a week, won't it, Susan?"

A cloudy smear across Susan's lips and some sticky black at the corners of her mouth indicated she'd already begun to enjoy the candy, but she didn't respond to Orillia's question. She reached up to Gladdie and took her hand.

As soon as Orillia was alone, she ate three of the twists immediately, secretly, and the sweet black taste of them was so like Dr. Kitely, after every bite she slid her tongue over her teeth, into the molars after every morsel. How startled he'd look, how he'd blink those sooty lids of his, if he knew.

the baby moses

A dozen pint sealers rattled in boiling water in Hilda's canner while the chokecherry syrup bubbled at the front of the stove. Gladdie squeezed out a purple cheesecloth bag over a basin in the sink.

"Thank goodness that's the last of those berries," Hilda said. A neighbour had picked them and brought them as a gift, so they'd had to use them. Hilda held up her hands and Gladdie held up hers. They were stained to the wrists. "And I told Susan not to get that licorice all over herself," Hilda said.

"She'll shake her finger at us," Gladdie said.

It was something Susan had started doing, teasing them by acting as if she were the adult. It was such a hopeful sign, the thought of it made Hilda want to find the child and wrap her arms around her. But it also made her think about someone she'd like to shake her finger at. And there was nothing she could say. She didn't want to tell Gladdie about Orillia's silly behaviour with Dr. Kitely, not when Gladdie thought so highly of the girl. Never mind, she thought. Her mother will be here soon.

Susan had been deposited in Orillia's room to be safe while Gladdie and Hilda filled the jars with the hot chokecherry concoction. At least it was a diversion, Orillia thought as she opened the Hurlbut's, and she needed diversions. As usual, Mr. Best was rattling away next door.

Susan wanted the story of the baby Moses. She wouldn't say that's what she wanted, but she turned the pages to show Orillia.

Rat-a-tat-tat. Orillia wished he'd go home.

The Egyptians were killing the baby boys of the Israelites. Oh yes, that was the story. One mother wanted to save her little boy, and she fashioned a small box into a little ark.

Rat-a-tat-tat.

The baby's mother waited until the Pharaoh's daughter came to the river to bathe. Then, knowing the princess would love the child as soon as she saw him, she put him into the ark and set it on the water. She sent her daughter, Miriam, to follow the little boat as it floated down the river until the Pharaoh's daughter should see it bobbing in the reeds.

Silence. What was he thinking? Susan poked her to make her read on. Oh yes, the little girl, Miriam, had a trick up her sleeve. Of course the Pharaoh's daughter loved the baby at first sight, but Miriam knew her mother didn't want to be parted from him. She ran up as soon as the princess lifted the child from the ark – as if she'd come upon them by accident. She asked the princess if she would like a woman to nurse the child for her and take care of it. "Yes," the princess said, and Miriam brought her own mother to the palace, so her mother could watch over her baby.

"What a wise and thoughtful little girl," Orillia said.

How big Susan's eyes were, although she'd heard the story dozens of times.

"Susan should have a doll," Orillia said that afternoon.

"Mention it to Hilda," Gladdie said, pleased. She liked Orillia to show an interest in Susan. Not that she would ever say so, but you could see it in her eyes.

Hilda, later, said, "She has a teddy bear and pays it no attention."

"A doll's different, a baby doll."

"It is different. That's true. I'll buy one tomorrow," Hilda said. "What makes you think of it?"

"She's been thinking of herself as a baby," Orillia said, her voice quite hard for someone in the middle of doing a good deed. "It's time for her to start growing up."

"That's wise of you," Hilda said.

"It's getting dark," Gladdie said.

She was so quiet, Orillia hadn't heard her come upstairs, and she hadn't realized she was sitting in darkness by herself, staring into space. "It was reading the story of Moses in the bulrushes to Susan that gave me the idea for the doll," she said.

"That's the story she likes," Gladdie said.

"A fairy-tale kind of story. I guess everyone likes a happy ending."

"It's a comfort," Gladdie said.

Orillia sighed. "Oh, I'm getting so restless, Gladdie," she said.

Her mother was packing her bag. That's what Orillia saw in her mind's eye when Gladdie left her, her mother bending over the bed in Orillia's own bedroom, in their house in Toronto, packing her suitcase. Orillia was five or six years old. She sat on her bed, watching. It was so early only a grey light seeped through the curtains, giving the morning the look of a time of adventure. Orillia was barely awake. She could feel the sleep gritty in her eyes. The house and the whole city outside were quiet; she and her mother might be the only ones in the world awake.

"Where are we going?" she asked.

"You're going to Uncle Jim Parker's, as you know very well," Florence said.

"But you're coming too."

"Why on earth would you say such a thing?" Florence asked. She went on folding Orillia's things and placing them in the right spot in the bag. "You know your father's ill. I told you last night: I'm taking him to a hospital. It's nothing you need concern yourself about," Florence told her. She went on packing the bag.

"I thought I'd come with you," Orillia said.

"I'm afraid you can't," Florence said.

"I want to," Orillia said.

"I know you do," Florence said. "But that's not to be."

She took up Orillia's doll and smoothed its dress before putting it on top of the clothes in her bag. Her hands were womanly, with big capable knuckles. There was sadness in the way they stroked the dress.

"To be or not to be," Orillia said, thinking out loud. "To sleep, perchance to dream."

"That's pretty," Gladdie said.

Orillia was so bored she'd volunteered to do some embroidery with them, and was stitching knots and curlicues onto a pillow slip. "It's Hamlet," she said. "Contemplating suicide. He decides against it, in case after death his dreams are as awful as his life."

"I knew a man once somebody called Perchance," Gladdie said.

"Perchance Partridge. At Mrs. Riley's," Hilda said. "In Toronto," Hilda told Orillia.

"Parchman," Gladdie corrected.

"Are you from Toronto?" Orillia asked. "You never said."

"Of course we are, the both of us," Hilda said. "Oh we could tell you some stories about our time at Mrs. Riley's, couldn't we, Gladdie?"

"We could," Gladdie said, getting to her feet. "But it's late now."

Hilda jumped up, too. "Goodness," she said, glancing over at Gladdie. "It is late."

After they left her, Orillia could feel her heart thump in her chest; she really could.

under the willow tree

At the Parkers' house Orillia could stand very still under the weeping willow tree in the front yard, and no one would know she was there. She liked being hidden. She liked being a secret no one knew. Under the tree the light shivered. The branches whooshed when the wind blew, and the tips wrote scrolls like bits of letters in the fine dirt, like writing only she could read.

Across the yard, she heard voices and she heard her name. I'm just like Father, she thought. I can hear voices too. But it was only her aunts, sitting on the verandah, talking about her, and when she concentrated she caught bits of the conversation.

"Such an odd little girl."

"She misses her parents."

"No wonder she feels sad."

I don't mind, she thought. I like being sad. And I like it here under the tree, where they can't see me. If only she could stay forever under the tree. But she knew she couldn't. Sooner or later she had to come out. And it was just that, knowing she couldn't stay, that made the suspense unbearable.

She heard her name again. All this time, they were talking about her. Her mother had warned her not to let her aunts spoil her. Her mother was packing her bag while Orillia sat on the edge of her bed in her own room at home. Her mother took up Orillia's doll and smoothed its dress before laying it on top of the folded clothes.

Under the tree Orillia smoothed her own dress. It was all right, being sad. It made her feel she knew who she was.

When she finally parted the branches and stepped out from under the willow tree, she saw a woman standing by the gate. She'd seen her a few times before, this red-haired woman, but this time the woman was looking right at her. She must have known where Orillia was hiding. She must have been waiting for her to step out from under the tree. Yes, Orillia thought: Here she is, to show me she's watching over me.

"Who's that?" her aunt Clara said. "Down by the gate, that woman."

Milly sat up, startled by the sight of the woman.

"Do you know her?" Clara asked.

"No," Milly said slowly. "I don't know who she is."

"I'll ask her what her business is," Clara said. But she hadn't got down the verandah steps before the woman had walked away.

"Was she looking at Orillia?" Clara asked. They had just noticed Orillia standing by the willow tree.

"Looking for work," Milly said. "If anything."

"I doubt that. Nobody wants to do housework anymore," Clara said. "Including me."

"Here she is," Milly cried, opening her arms as Orillia walked up the path toward them.

"We were wondering where you'd got to," Clara said.

"I was in the garden."

They nodded. "I'm hot," Orillia said, and laid her head against Milly's arm.

"Me too," Milly said.

Clara reached out her hand and said, "Why don't we all go upstairs and put something cooler on?"

Up the stairs Orillia went with them, smiling her secret smile that no one could see.

part three

at the gate

at the gate

Where the time had gone Gladdie didn't know. Just nowhere. She was the same place she'd been when it all started, when Jessie Dole came to Mrs. Riley's. The only difference was that Mrs. Riley had been giving her years of I-told-you-so looks, not realizing she still heard from Johnnie because she had a post office box to prevent everyone knowing her business. She checked on Jessie and Johnnie's little girl about once a month. It wasn't necessary to go more often than that. The child was well looked after.

Then one day the blinds were all pulled at the house on Clinton Street. Gladdie went again the next day and the day after that, and she didn't see a soul come or go in the hours she hung about. The third day she went over to the Parkers' to see what was up there. It was hot, and by noon ladies on the streetcar were fanning themselves with swollen fingers. Fat men wiped their foreheads and necks with their handkerchiefs. It was only June, but the heat and humidity were settling in. By the end of the day they'd be wading through thick air.

When she arrived at the Parkers', Clara and Milly were sitting out on the pillared porch. Between their fence and the porch was a fair stretch of lawn, but it was a low wrought iron fence. They'd see her if she stopped, so she strolled by, thinking she'd come back later, for all the good it would do her. She figured she'd have to haul out the knitting needles again to find out what was going on.

Poor old Miss Avis was still at it, her bumpy old arthritic fingers creaking at a rate fast for anyone, and she was eighty-two or three. Mr. Mainwaring sometimes used to tease her, break her concentration so she'd drop a stitch and forget herself and swear at him, but even he wouldn't do it to her now. She was knitting every hour of the day, and maybe night too, in fear of the day she couldn't, trying to save up some of her income, knowing Mrs. Riley didn't fancy herself a philanthropist.

Gladdie slowed down before the gate, by a couple of lilac bushes. She couldn't dawdle for long in full view of the sisters on the porch, and anyway she couldn't hear a word they were saying. There was no information to be gained from it. Just as she began to walk on, the little girl, Orillia, stepped out from under the big weeping willow tree on the far side of their front yard. Gladdie had to take hold of the gate. The child had been hiding in there, under the tree. She'd parted the branches, then walked out. There she was, looking Gladdie full in the face.

The moment the child stepped out from under the tree and looked at Gladdie, she became herself. Before that she was the baby. After that she was Orillia. The baby was a pretty little thing with a heart-shaped face, big dark thoughtful eyes and curly hair tied back with a bow, a sturdy little girl – more in spirit than in body, for she was tiny. She was a happy child, happy enough. Orillia – who she was Gladdie didn't know. But she knew she'd been hiding. She'd been hiding under that tree, from the others. It was all over her face: her aloneness. She was looking for something when she walked out from under the tree, and though she was way across the lawn, her big eyes fastened on Gladdie. If she'd walked right up to Gladdie and asked her to take her away, in that moment Gladdie wouldn't have been surprised. You could tell they loved her. They were good family people. But she wasn't like them, she wasn't one of them, and she knew it. And they didn't. They couldn't see what Gladdie could see in her eyes.

After that, what could she do but let the child see her? Just once in a while, so when she searched the distance like that with her need in her eyes she'd see a person with comfort in her face.

home

"Where's her mother?" Hilda asked. She was rinsing and wringing out the clothes Gladdie had washed on the board. Her face was all creased with concern. "I'd have thought she'd be here by now."

Gladdie put her head down and scrubbed the life out of a pillowcase until her knuckles hurt. It was meanness in her that made her feel jubilant. Here was Hilda with only kind thoughts about Orillia, and in her own heart this mean response, this gladness that Florence Cooper was showing her true self.

Hilda whispered, "I'm afraid she isn't coming."

"Oh, she'll get here sooner or later," Gladdie said.

"And Orillia will go back to Aquadell with them?"

"I guess she will," Gladdie said. That was the instant she knew she wouldn't go back, herself. No matter whether she stayed here with Hilda or not, she couldn't go back and pick up where she'd left off. She'd visit sometimes. She missed Em. She could stay with her and Halvor any time she liked, but she couldn't live in Aquadell again.

"About Toronto, Hilda, and Mrs. Riley's house," Gladdie said. "It's not that I'm ashamed."

"No, no. I understand," Hilda said quickly. "There's no need for Orillia to know all that." The perspiration started up at her hairline. She could feel it prickle as her face got hot, and she reached into her rolled-up sleeve for her hankie. There was a good deal of her own past she didn't want Orillia or anyone else to know. There were years she could hardly believe she'd lived through; her circumstances were so different now. She wiped her face and sighed as if to say the heat was getting to her, but she didn't need to worry. Gladdie was uncharacteristically preoccupied with her own concerns.

"Orillia isn't interested, you know, in those old days," she went on. "They lived in Toronto when she was growing up. That was the only reason she perked up the other evening when she heard about it. She hasn't mentioned it again."

"I'm sure there's nothing about our lives she'd find very fascinating," Hilda said, still mopping her face. "She's a modern girl."

Once she'd got Hilda's agreement on the Toronto question, Gladdie still had the other thing to fret about. What she was privately calling The Problem. She was worried they'd have to talk about it. Or that Orillia would find out they knew. It hadn't been as bad since Orillia could get out of bed for part of the day, but she'd heard it again this morning, and Mr. Best was in his room at the time. Gladdie tried to imagine having a talk with the girl about privacy and the way sound travelled through a house.

"Hello Susan," Orillia said. She'd been practicing walking with her crutches up and down the hall, quietly because of Mr. Best, and she caught the little girl coming down from the third floor after her nap. Susan had ridges from her pillow on one flushed cheek, and was clutching her new doll.

"Hello?" Orillia said again, and put out a crutch to stop her when the child tried to sidle past. "How are you?" Orillia whispered. She would have reached her hand out and raised that little chin if she'd hadn't needed her crutches for balance, and Susan must have known she wasn't going to be let off the hook easily. In place of an answer, she slowly raised the doll until its plaster face blocked her own. That stopped Orillia for a moment. Then she had to laugh, seeing she'd been bested. "Oh, hello Betsy," she whispered, and was rewarded with a smile she could just discern by the dip of the head that always went with it.

Dr. Kitely brought his wife to see Orillia. Mrs. Kitely had been a nurse before her marriage, and she was interested in Orillia's case. In fact, she'd become so interested in all the doctor's cases she'd taken over as his home visiting nurse. She was a petite, pretty, very fair woman with the pink-nosed look of a rabbit. She had an annoying – to Orillia – habit of staring up at her husband as if he towered two feet above her instead of one. Twice, while they were there, Dr. Kitely had blinking spells under the influence of that gaze.

Mrs. Kitely was almost as mute as her husband and, without Gladdie or Hilda to help her out, Orillia had to make conversation and ask the woman questions as if she was her mother at a tea party. Mrs. Kitely stood by the bedside, waiting to take things out of her husband's hands while he, with a saw that did not look special, only smaller than a regular saw, opened the cast on Orillia's left calf. When it was split to the bottom, it fell apart. A scrawny, scaly, hairy leg lay revealed and threatened to float away, it felt so light. Mrs. Kitely looked at the lilac wall after seeing the foot.

"Let's see if you can put your weight on it," the doctor said.

Orillia swung her legs over the side of the bed. "Ouch," she said before her feet touched the floor. He asked what had hurt. "Nothing," she said. "I just thought it was going to hurt."

"And it doesn't?"

She was standing now, lopsided because the right foot was still encased in its cast. He was close beside her; she could have grazed her cheek along the nubby material of his tweed jacket. "It doesn't hurt a bit," she said. Mrs. Kitely gave the doctor one of her rabbity upwards glances.

Dr. Kitely cleared his throat and hazarded a smile. "I've asked Mr. Forster to visit you tomorrow to measure you for a boot," he said.

Why not two boots? It was on the tip of Orillia's tongue to ask, but she answered her own question. She'd have to be measured again for the second boot. When the right foot healed it would be a different size and shape.

"Did you want to speak to Mrs. Wutherspoon now?" Mrs. Kitely asked her husband, with a more level look this time. "I'll tidy the bed."

Dr. Kitely nodded and went downstairs without meeting Orillia's eyes.

"He's a very talented surgeon," Mrs. Kitely said, her hands lying idle on the counterpane.

"Yes," Orillia said.

"I think he has a brilliant career ahead of him," Mrs. Kitely said. Above her pink nose her round blue eyes stayed so wide open they might have been painted on, just like the blank eyes on Susan's new doll.

"Did you see his wife?" Hilda asked.

Gladdie hadn't seen her. She'd heard a woman talking in Orillia's room and thought it was the nurse who'd held Orillia's hand on the way here, her first day out of the hospital.

"I think he brought her to show Orillia he's happily married," Hilda said. "You know, Orillia's very pretty. She doesn't need to flirt, let alone with a man who can have no interest in her, in that way. I thought one of us would have to say something to her. Dr. Kitely has been quite distressed. She didn't seem to see it, how her teasing upset him. Well, he's solved it himself, I expect. Or his wife has. There, I shouldn't have mentioned it. I've worried you."

"That's all right."

"You know what she needs? She needs a nice young man." Hilda had heard about Percy Gowan and his letters. Gladdie hadn't been able to resist telling her about him.

"You're right, Hilda," Gladdie said. "That's just what she needs."

They smiled at one another. "Now if only we can decide what to do about Susan, we'll have everything settled," Hilda said.

Gladdie told Orillia about the conversation Dr. Kitely'd had with Hilda. He'd become Susan's doctor, too, and was concerned with her progress, or lack of progress. The question was whether or not to send Susan to school, since fall was fast approaching.

"Hilda says she knows her alphabet and numbers, even if she can't talk," Orillia said.

"She thinks maybe she should go," Gladdie said. "She says she's a bright child."

"You're worried about her," Orillia said, and as if she hadn't really understood that before, the statement aroused the same anxiety in her, the same anticipation of pain she'd felt that afternoon before she'd stepped down on her naked foot. "Do you know what she did the other day? I tried to get her to say hello to me, and she held her doll up in front of her face. She really is a smart little thing, isn't she? To come up with such a convenient device. Whenever she wants to hide, she only has to put that plaster face in front of her own." She stopped. "That reminds me of Mrs. Kitely. I feel sorry for Dr. Kitely, with that woman for a wife. She bullies him."

Gladdie waited, saying nothing. She did that often, with a kind of instinctive patience, as if waiting for your better self to come through and say something kinder, as if she trusted you had a better self lurking behind the one that had just spoken. And it worked. Orillia stumbled, but she had to go on. "You know, I used to like to tease him, and make him blink. And I realized something today, because of her, and the way she treated him. He doesn't like to blink."

Gladdie nodded, and Orillia's spirits soared. She was quite thrilled with herself for seeing Dr. Kitely's distress, and for understanding that teasing him was a heartless thing to do. "But you were telling me about Susan," she said, happily aware she was changing the subject back to one that mattered more to Gladdie.

"The doctor will decide what to do about Susan," Gladdie said. "But she can't be ready. She can't go to school when she doesn't speak."

Gladdie looked so troubled, Orillia said, "Well then, we'll have to keep her at home."

Afterwards she reflected on how easily the word home had tripped off her tongue.

The boot, when it came, was worse than the foot.

"It's so ugly," Orillia said, holding her foot up for Gladdie's inspection. "And skirts are getting shorter!"

Gladdie just grinned at her. She wasn't one to point out the benefits of being able to walk, indoors and out, at a time like this.

Sometimes the woman had grinned at her, just like that, in an encouraging way. From the gate or from across a street. That was why she'd been drawn to Gladdie. Gladdie was like the woman.

She had that calming effect, making you feel everything would be fine. It didn't mean she was that woman, even if she had red hair. Even if she had come from Toronto. Everyone has to come from somewhere.

The woman, that's what she'd called her, just that. She'd caught sight of her sometimes passing by her uncle's place or their own little house on Clinton Street. But she didn't even know if it had been one woman or if she'd just been attracted to any red-haired woman who chanced to be passing, who happened to smile in her direction. She'd told Clara about her, and Clara said she'd invented her because she was lonely. She'd talked to Milly about her, too, a year or two later, and Milly, looking stricken, had said maybe the woman was real after all, maybe she was watching over her, just as she'd thought. But Milly was so obviously trying to console her, she'd made Orillia feel sure it wasn't true.

It was ridiculous – and embarrassing, at her age – to wish that the woman had followed her all the way across the continent from Toronto. It wasn't as if she'd recognized Gladdie when she'd first moved to Aquadell. Or ever thought about the woman in connection with her. Until this summer she'd never wondered who Gladdie McConnell was. And Gladdie had never said or done a single thing to hint that they'd ever met.

caught

Clara Cooper opened the door of her brother's house on Clinton Street and looked at Gladdie, and Gladdie knew why. Clara had seen her go by; once too often she'd seen her go by. It had been nearly a year Gladdie had been letting Orillia catch sight of her, just once in a while. Clara tripped down the steps of the little house, pulling her coat on. She had her face set stern; no smiles this time. This wasn't the drugstore; there'd be no talcum powder niceties. Gladdie had been caught where she didn't belong, on the outskirts of their lives. The family had seen her about one house, then the other.

Orillia had been moved back at the end of the summer to Ralph and Florence Cooper's house. Gladdie hadn't seen them take her, but it made sense since with September she'd started school. Her father walked her to the schoolyard every morning, then took the streetcar to work in his office downtown. Her mother met her after school and walked her home. There was one word that popped into Gladdie's head every time she saw them together: careful. Whatever had happened to them, they didn't want it to happen again. Then one Saturday in the springtime she went down their alley, and she heard Orillia's young voice raised a bit and giving orders. A black and white spaniel-type puppy was running circles around her ankles, and that seemed a good thing.

Gladdie waited on the sidewalk for Clara Cooper, feeling like her own limp dress hanging on a line. Clara looked ready for combat. There wouldn't be any use in Gladdie pretending she didn't know what was going on. An explanation was going to be required. There's no law against watching people, she thought, but she didn't know if there was or wasn't.

Clara didn't speak until they were face to face. "A word," she said, out of breath, so much so she didn't say anything more. Neither did Gladdie say anything at all. She was afraid Clara might be thinking she was crazy, someone to be frightened of. She wanted to tell her she'd never meant any harm, but she couldn't think how to go about it without alarming her more.

"We'd better go somewhere we can talk," Clara said finally. There wasn't anyone to hear them if they'd stayed where they were; the neighbourhood was deserted. Gladdie couldn't imagine they had more than six things to say to one another. That would be the most – six questions on Clara's part, six answers on Gladdie's. She'd have been surprised if she could have come up with that many.

"Will you come downtown with me for a cup of tea?" Clara asked.

If Gladdie had thought it through, she would have said no. She'd have seen how in a café she'd be trapped. But Clara took her by surprise, and she went along with her to the streetcar stop and stood waiting with her, though she thought it was odd to be doing it. She put it down to class. One of those things the better classes don't do, she decided, is discuss their affairs on sidewalks. And it was borne upon her that the better classes have a way with them that carries the rest along.

They rode downtown without speaking, sitting side by side, lurching along, both of them anxious. Gladdie didn't try to figure out what she was going to say. Just being in Clara's presence made her aware she was going to tell her what she wanted to know. Clara Cooper was a person who could make you feel the necessity of the truth. They went to an establishment called Betterbey's, where the lady in black waiting inside the door seemed to know Clara and took them right away to a booth. For a café, it was a solemn place, dark and marbled, with a dull shine on all its surfaces. You'd have to be really crazy to act up in such a place. No doubt Clara was counting on that. Well, she needn't fear. Gladdie meant to be sensible and businesslike. She was going to stress the fact that she'd been hired to keep an eye on the little girl (not of course letting on that the hiring had been her own idea), so Clara would see she'd never intended any harm.

Clara ordered tea and a plate of sandwiches. Gladdie flushed at that, for did the woman think she needed feeding? Nothing was said until the tray came, the tea was poured, the rest ignored, and they'd each sipped a polite few drops. If Clara had lit into her then, high and mighty, Gladdie could have come out of it feeling fine. In fact, she was trying, as she sat there, to work herself up to some indignation of her own. But Clara set her cup into her saucer and it clattered. Milky tea slopped right over the saucer and ran across the table, and Clara dabbed at it with her napkin. Just like Gladdie, she was trying to think what a person said in a situation such as this, and she was too nice to know how to start. Just a plain-as-bread-and-butter, nice woman – girl, really, even if she was older than Gladdie. There was no haughtiness to her, and that meant you couldn't treat her saucily in response. You'd be earnest with her without thinking; she made you be.

It was Gladdie who had to begin. "Best if I tell you all about this," she said, grinning at Clara a little to let her know it wouldn't be too bad, what she had to say. She didn't know what Clara had been told about the child and her origins, and maybe what Gladdie knew would shock her.

She said, "I guess you seen me about your house and the one on Clinton Street."

Clara nodded.

"I was paid to watch over the little girl."

That statement had an effect. It was obviously not anything Clara had expected to hear. It seemed it was entirely beyond the scope of her imagining, and she had to look right at Gladdie for a minute to take it in. "I don't understand," she said.

"Her father paid me."

"No. Ralph?"

"Not your brother. Her real father."

Clara turned pink. First the colour sprang up in her face, then it flushed down her neck. "I've been watching over her since she was born," Gladdie said, thinking she'd better get this over with quickly. "She was born at Mrs. Riley's. It's the boarding house where I work."

Clara sat there for a minute staring at the table. Finally she said: "You're mistaken."

"Your aunt, Mrs. Parker, adopted her."

"My aunt's been dead for years."

"Just before she passed away. Then they gave her to your brother and his wife to raise. Johnnie and me – Johnnie's her real father – we saw what happened." Gladdie was talking faster now, trying to explain.

"Johnnie?" Clara said, and for a moment Gladdie thought something was wrong with her, the way she stared. Her small pale eyes, which protruded naturally, bulged now to the extent that Gladdie would have been worried about her if she hadn't been so intent on saying what she felt she had to say to pardon Johnnie. "Johnnie had to leave the country," she said. "I don't mean he had to. He emigrated. It was business. He's of very good family."

Clara sat back and looked at her, puzzlement now in her eyes. For a minute she looked almost sick, then she put her head in her hands. "Mrs. Riley's," Clara said, not looking up from the tent she'd made of her hands. "Do you mean the Boarding House Infant?"

"The papers called her that."

"The child that was born, or left – abandoned – in the *privy*?"

"That's not true. That's gossip. The papers picked it up. Them good-for-nothing reporters. She was born in a bed. In the bedroom off the kitchen. And her poor mother – just a girl herself – thought she was dead. And herself to blame." Gladdie was getting a bit hot in her attempts to explain as quickly as she could in order to have the truth straight as soon as possible, and maybe it looked as if she might cry.

"I'm sorry," Clara said. She sounded as if she was genuinely sorry and might say more, but she took up her cup instead.

They both lifted their cups and drained them. Clara poured again and passed Gladdie her hankie.

"No, thank you. I'm done. The time is past for those tears."

Clara called for hot water, then she said: "Maretta tried to adopt that baby."

Gladdie said: "I know that. And I saw her in your house, that baby, in a cradle. I saw her right there by the tree you put up for Christmas. And your aunt rocking that cradle with her foot. In your house. And there she stayed till your aunt died and she was shipped off to your brother's."

After a few moments Clara said: "That wasn't the baby from your boarding house you saw in the cradle. You saw my brother's baby girl. She was staying with us for a while." She sighed and gave Gladdie the look of an old friend. "My brother's sick sometimes," she said. "Mentally. When the child was born, he fell into one of his episodes. It was the first he'd experienced since his marriage and Florence – his wife – was frightened. Naturally. She sent the baby to us and concentrated all her care and attention on him. On Ralph. Well, he came out of it, eventually. He always has. It's a matter of two or three months and he seems normal again." She looked kindly on Gladdie again. "Maretta's death was just a coincidence. Once Ralph was better, they took Orillia back to their own home."

"She doesn't look like your brother. Nor any of you."

"No, she's a pretty little girl, isn't she?" Clara said gently. "Were you close to the other baby's mother?"

"Oh no. No, she was a boarder – just for her time, you know. She only came to the house a few weeks before."

"But you felt a tie? An obligation? I forgot – you said the father hired you."

"That was my idea. I told him you – Mrs. Parker – had the baby."

"He actually paid you to watch over her?"

"He had to take some responsibility. He could see that. It was his baby."

Clara sighed. She picked up her spoon and clattered it around her cup. In a shaky voice that sounded as if she might cry, she said, "That baby died."

"How do you know that?" Gladdie barked right back. "Who told you that?"

"The Children's Aid told Maretta. The child she wanted to adopt died." Clara's voice still shook, and she picked up a little sandwich made without any crusts and took it to pieces with her fingers. They got minced shrimp all over them and she had to fuss with her napkin to get it off.

"What was wrong with her?"

"I don't believe we were told. I'm sorry," Clara said.

"Well, that's enough," Gladdie said. "Thank you very much." She opened her purse and rooted around in it for change, which she never could lay a hand on when she was in a hurry to be gone.

"No," Clara said. "It was my invitation." Now she really looked as if she would cry.

"I'll pay for my tea," Gladdie said. She put some coins on the table. She neither knew nor cared how much, whether it would have paid for half a cup or ten pots. She wasn't going to sit there any longer and hear any more.

She stepped out onto the busy sidewalk, buttoning her jacket while she walked away. She moved into the crowd of people, keeping to the right, near the storefronts where she could walk faster. She wasn't seeing anything around her. She was seeing Clara's head in her hands, then her fingers shredding her sandwich, and her hand shaking when she stirred her spoon in her cup. Gladdie knew what all that agitation added up to. If you were used to it but not good at it, you looked over the other person's shoulder. If you'd had no practice at all and you didn't even know enough to keep it simple, you'd give yourself away ten times over. The truth was as clear as a glass of water. Clara was lying. It was nothing but a story, saying that baby had died. That baby? That little fighter? After surviving such a birth, *she* up and died? Looking the picture of health? Clean and well-fed and wanted by a society lady? She didn't die. Not her. Clara had made it up. Why would she? To stop Gladdie hanging around, that's why. To keep her from watching over Orillia – to get rid of her. It made sense. They wouldn't want the girl to discover the truth of her origins. Imagine being told your birth was written up in all the papers as a scandal. Imagine finding out they said your mother had given birth to you in an outhouse and left you there to die. The Parkers and the Coopers would have seen the risk Gladdie posed. What if she spoke to Orillia someday and told her who her real parents were? They couldn't know Gladdie agreed with them it was better she shouldn't find out.

She strode through the streets, her feet keeping time with her fast thoughts, until something that had been nagging at the corner of her mind caught up to her and stopped her dead. It was that Clara knew Johnnie. She'd sat right up at the mention of his name and her eyes had nearly popped out. She must have known Johnnie pretty well – but she hadn't known he was Orillia's father. That had been news to her.

Now Gladdie wandered through the streets not paying any attention to where she was going, thinking about what she knew and what she could piece together. She thought about the easy way Johnnie had approached the Parkers' house the day of Maretta Parker's funeral. She remembered how anxious he'd always been that none of the family should see him with her and how sure he'd been that the baby would turn up at their house, saying he believed in her intuition.

People on the sidewalks got annoyed with Gladdie; she was slowing them down, getting in their way. A couple of times they bumped into her. She found herself down on Front Street, where the Cyclorama used to be. She'd never gone inside the Cyclorama. When she could have afforded the admission, she hadn't wanted to see it without Harry. Now she wished she'd gone. She looked down the street toward Union Station and turned away from it and began walking north again, uphill. She wondered if she'd always known Johnnie was playing with her. She couldn't imagine why he'd done it, what there had been for him in the arrangement. And his letters, since he'd moved to Buffalo, had been almost tender, telling her he thought of her and thought highly. She remembered the puzzlement in Clara's eyes and understood. She must have been flabbergasted, hearing Johnnie had paid her to watch over the child.

She wrote to him that night after the lodgers and Mrs. Riley had gone to bed, sitting with the lamp beside her on the kitchen table, and when she finished the letter she read it out loud, whispering the words to herself and hearing them sounding like a sorry tale. The kitchen was gloomier than Betterbey's, and the more she thought about what she'd written, the better she could imagine Johnnie reading it, and she didn't want to send it. She folded up the letter and slid it under her pillow. For a couple of days she fussed over the problem, and finally she wrote a different letter. She told him her circumstances had changed – just that, because it's always easiest to keep a lie simple – and she'd be leaving Mrs. Riley's employment and her house. She told him she couldn't keep up the watch over the little girl, but he need have no fear for her. She was well cared for in that big, wealthy family, and they all doted on her, not just her parents but all of them. It was the truth; you could see that. She didn't need a servant from a low house watching over her.

Johnnie replied right away to Gladdie's letter, asking her to send her new address when she could, as he'd like to continue their correspondence. She didn't answer.

a visitor

"You have a visitor," Hilda sang before she'd even entered the room. Orillia was sitting at her dressing table and half turned to look at her. "Oh good," Hilda whispered. "You're wearing that nice blouse with the ribbon, makes you look so smart. I'll say you'll be down in a minute, will I? Give you time to fix your hair." She bustled off downstairs again.

Well, she was very happy. So, at last. Orillia turned back to her mirror and caught herself smiling. But there was no need to look pleased, after all this time. She picked up her brush and swept her hair up. With a few quick, strategic jabs, she pinned it.

Hilda waited at the bottom of the stairs while Orillia descended. Both Hilda and Gladdie were still nervous about this manoeuvre, and one or the other of them would rush to the hall if they heard her on the stairs. There was no need for it, and if she fell, she'd flatten them, but they couldn't help themselves. Hilda came up a few steps to meet her. "You look very pretty for your company. Waiting for you in the parlour," she whispered.

"Well, there's no hurry, is there?" Orillia murmured as she passed her. "She's had time to go around the world by now."

Behind her, Hilda cried, "Oh, Orillia, wait..."

But she was at the parlour door, she was inside the room, and Percy Gowan was standing up to greet her. He looked surprised, as if he'd been expecting someone else. Maybe he was reflecting the expression on Orillia's face.

"You didn't answer my letter," he said. "But I decided to come anyway. I thought I'd take a chance."

"Oh. Of course," she said. His letter was still unopened in the dresser drawer upstairs in her room. "Please, sit down," she said, as they were standing awkwardly gawking at one another. He took her arm and helped her settle on a chair before resuming his seat on the sofa. She was still feeling dazzled by the fact that she was talking to him and not to her mother. He must have wondered, she thought, if she'd been hit on the head as well as the feet.

"Last time we met, it was just the opposite," he said, grinning at her with the whole of his good-natured face. All she had to do was focus on him, and this really stupid feeling that she was going to cry would pass. He was taller than she'd remembered, bigger all round. His large freckled hands rested on his knees. She had no idea what he was talking about.

"You were down and I had to help you up," he said.

"Oh," she said.

"The day you went in the ditch in the Captain's auto and I pushed you out?" He grinned at her again.

Then she remembered it *had* been just the opposite, in another way as well. Today he was wearing his clothes. That day he'd been in his running gear. He was very nattily dressed today, in a good suit and a white shirt that made his eyes look like pieces of sky. And then she remembered: "Oh. I never returned your handkerchief." She'd borrowed it after a fit of sneezing. And that was at least twice she'd said oh as if she was in a state of perpetual surprise.

"I came out to the farm, but you weren't home."

"I left right away after that. I came to Regina."

"So I heard. Luckily I have other handkerchiefs."

"I didn't forget about it. But I – well, I don't know what happened, Percy. With the moving and all." The tears that had been threatening stung her eyes, and she thought: I have to make some light remark, that's all. Turn the conversation. She was being too earnest. She knew the danger in that. "The first time we met, do you remember, at the fowl supper? You gave me your napkin. You'll be thinking I'll always want something from you." Goodness, what was she thinking, babbling on, and saying such a stupid thing.

"I was wondering what it'd be today," he said. He leaned toward her, sitting forward with his elbows, now, on his knees and his head tilted to look at her. His face was tanned as well as generously sun-freckled, and his blue eyes looked so much brighter indoors than they did outside. He really seemed to hope she would need something from him. There was an awful pause then as neither of them could think what to say. Orillia was about to resort to the weather when he said, "Could you use a pair of suspenders?" He hooked his thumbs in his and stretched them out to show her.

Her first thought was: Oh God, how lame. (And how apt that word, was an under-thought.) But they'd created this clumsiness together. They were both as shy as wood. "Suspenders," she said. "Well, if they'd keep me up." And they laughed together, a little.

He relaxed then, and soon enough Hilda brought in a tray. Both Percy and Orillia insisted she and Gladdie and Susan join them. So they all had tea and butter tarts and the lemon cake Hilda had fortunately baked after breakfast, and even Susan giggled a few times at Percy's comments and expressions. He knew how to speak to the child. Instinctively, it seemed, he understood how to set her at ease. Why, he's being droll, Orillia thought. So he was, and he was good at it.

The visit being such a success, when he made as if to leave and the others vanished from the room, it was difficult to say he shouldn't come again. He'd said he would. "I know it seems odd to you," Orillia said. "And ungrateful. But I think it's best."

She remained seated, looking at Hilda's ferns and violets gathered in the window and beyond them the pots of geraniums in the verandah. He stood looking down at her.

"What's this?" he asked in a soft way, almost whispering, so she felt his voice on her skin.

But she was adamant. His visit today had confirmed what she'd always thought of him: he was chivalrous and thoughtful and healthy and wholesome. He was a runner, for heaven's sake. She hadn't known such a sport existed, as a serious pursuit, before she'd met him, and he was good at it. He won medals in races all over the country. He was good morally, too. Everyone in Aquadell respected him, and what you had to be and do to get respect in Aquadell Orillia couldn't even imagine. But she knew one thing: he deserved a good woman, someone who went to church and loved children and wasn't crippled or the least bit odd. And, of course, he'd want to live his whole life on his farm near Aquadell, and she was never returning there. "Mr. Gowan," she said. "You wouldn't like me once you got to know me better."

"Well if that isn't a dumb thing to say," he said. "And two minutes ago you were calling me Percy."

They were at an impasse again. She wouldn't speak, and he didn't seem to know what else to say. He stood over her, shaking his head. Then he started to remove his jacket. Orillia wondered if he had some notion of staying on until she relented, so she refused to look at him. There wasn't any point to their friendship. While she beamed that information to the hoya plant, Percy set his jacket on the chair by the door. She soon knew what he was up to.

"Really," she said. He unbuttoned his suspenders and pulled them off over his shirt sleeves. With elaborate, deliberate slowness he folded the suspenders and gently laid them in her lap. Then, gripping his jacket under his arm and holding up his pants as he walked (who could help looking then, or smiling?) he left the room and the house. And there she sat as still as she'd ever sat in her life, with the weight of those darn things like something alive in her lap.

Hilda didn't mention Orillia's mistake. She couldn't tell Gladdie that Orillia had thought her visitor was her mother, and had been happy at the thought. It was too sad a thing for Hilda to say out loud. And she wasn't one to crow that she'd been right, when she could see it wouldn't give Gladdie any pleasure.

"Didn't that work well?" Hilda said, instead. "You know, she was pleased as punch to hear she had a visitor. Poor girl. It's quiet for her here. You think quiet's what an invalid needs, but they need diversion, too."

Gladdie grinned. "Him and his suspenders," she said.

word

It was on the downstairs hall table with the other letters, the only one for Orillia, postmarked San Francisco. She carried it up to her room and tossed it on the bed. She tidied the top of her bureau, trickled some loose change into her purse and clicked the clasp shut. She picked a hair off the dresser scarf and let it float to the floor, shifted the vase of snapdragons then shifted it back. The water was cloudy. It should be changed. And the colours clashed against the lilac wall – too much pink. As much as anything, she wondered why Hilda hadn't brought the letter to her, or told her it had come. Either she must have been preoccupied with something else, or she had a presentiment that the letter would be less than welcome.

She came downstairs to find Susan sitting on a chair in the middle of the kitchen while Gladdie tried to comb through the tangles in her matted hair. Gladdie was patient, taking one knot at a time, and Susan was being patient, too, and trying not to wince.

"Let me," Hilda said, and Gladdie passed over the comb.

"A letter from your mother?" Hilda asked, looking up from the little girl's head, and Orillia felt obscurely relieved that she was asking.

"Just to let me know they're not coming," she said. "Some business matter came up, I believe."

"Your mother's not coming? Not at all?" Hilda said.

The three of them, Hilda, Gladdie and even Susan, looked at her in horror. She wished she'd told them she'd written to

Florence and let her know she wasn't needed. Even more, she wished she hadn't revealed herself to Hilda on the stairway that day, thinking it was Florence who'd showed up at last. Hilda would have told Gladdie all about it by now. Her cheeks burned. "Never mind," she said. "Goodness. At my age, I don't need my mother, you know."

Susan started and grabbed the side of her head.

"I'm sorry, dear," Hilda said. "I forgot what I was doing."

Orillia said, "Susan, why don't we cut your hair? It would be so much easier and cooler, too, in this weather."

"Just what I've been saying," Hilda said.

Susan put her head down and picked at her doll's dress. The doll went everywhere with her now.

"I'd like my hair shorter," Gladdie said. "I'll cut mine if you'll cut yours, Susie. How about that? And what's more, I'll go first."

Before the morning was over, they'd all had their hair cut. Curls lay strewn about the kitchen linoleum: copper, white, near-black and tawny brown. Hilda gathered a lock of each into a ribbon as a souvenir of the morning and pinned them to a cushion on the back of the sofa where they looked like pin-the-tails-on-the-donkey. Then Gladdie fetched rainwater and they washed each other's heads. Gladdie did Orillia's, her strong fingers massaging Orillia's scalp, and then Susan, with inept pats, finished the rinsing. Odd how her hands felt – so small.

It was just as well they'd decided not to send her to school in the fall. "You can't send her when she doesn't talk," Orillia had said, and Hilda and Gladdie had both looked relieved, though they'd already come to that conclusion.

They did each other up in pincurls and wrapped their heads in turbans made from Hilda's scarves, and after that they didn't venture out the door. They felt silly enough to be going about like that in broad daylight in the house. Although the weather was warm, their hair took hours to dry. They were impatient and unbound it a little early in all cases, so the results were uneven. Still, once Orillia had pinned their limper curls in place and put the backs up, Gladdie and Hilda professed delight at their new and fuller styles. They agreed they looked as if they had more hair than when they'd begun and were all so much more à la mode. Hilda got the catalogue out and showed Susan the children, and how she, too, was now right in style as a modern young miss. Then Gladdie and Hilda compared pictures of models with Orillia's head, turning her this way and that by the chin and muttering to one another. "Too flat still. Needs to be higher in back. A bow, she needs a bow there to cover the pins, like it shows here." They poked and tugged at Orillia's hair, not in the least consulting her. They were, in fact, talking literally over her head. Really, she might be a child again, sitting between Milly and Clara, or any two maiden aunts who have so much time on their hands they make you the centre of their attention.

Gladdie took Susan upstairs to put her to bed. Hand in hand they trudged up the two flights to the little vine-covered room. Gladdie sat on the small bed while Susan stepped out of her clothes and pulled her nightie on over her skinny, flat, little girl's body. They dropped to the floor together, kneeling with their elbows propped on the bed and their hands steepled, as Gladdie thought children should do, as she'd been taught by Margaret, long ago, to pray. Afterwards, looking down on Susan's newly shorn head, she thought about herself and Hilda fussing over Orillia's hair, half-conscious that they were trying to mother her as much as they were mothering Susan.

"No more tangles," Gladdie said to Susan, smoothing her round bob. She tucked her into her covers and kissed her forehead, then the little arms went round her neck and Gladdie received the firmly pressed smack on the cheek she got every night, which lasted nearly a full minute because it was the end of the routine and time for sleep.

"You mustn't worry about Mother not rushing to my side," Orillia had said. "She has her own life, you know, and that gives me the freedom to have mine."

Gladdie had her own opinion on that, but she'd kept it to herself. She drew away from Susan, and the child dutifully closed her eyes tight. "One October evening, in a hard rain, a young woman of good family..." Why not tell her? Why be afraid? Orillia was old enough to understand. She didn't need to know Jessie Dole had drowned herself, only that her mother had died when she was a baby. She didn't need to find out anything about the old Boarding

House Infant scandal. That was far in the past and no one would remember it now. She'd been raised without the taint. It would do her good to know about Jessie Dole. And with Florence acting the way she was, there wasn't any reason at all why Orillia shouldn't be told she wasn't her real mother.

She would tell her. Before the end of the summer. As soon as the time was right. Put the truth against Florence Cooper's betrayal of everything a mother should be.

Hilda pried off her shoes and lay down on top of her bedspread. Her west-facing room wasn't darkened much by the pulled blinds, this early in the evening, but she didn't intend to sleep. She had to think. She wanted to stand back, as she had that afternoon while she and Gladdie were doing Orillia's hair. She'd stopped just after they'd slid the pins out, to wipe Susan's nose, and she'd looked up to see Gladdie holding Orillia's hair aloft while she plied the brush. Such a simple picture. Gladdie's intent face, her blunt fingers, the shining hair tenderly drawn out. And Orillia calm. There's what a mother should be, Hilda had thought. Then she peered closer.

"What is it?" Orillia had asked, and Hilda said it was nothing. Because the truth had been revealed to her. What she should have known all along.

It was plain as day once you saw it. Orillia was Gladdie's natural daughter. They didn't look much alike. Hilda supposed that was why she'd been so slow to see the relationship, when all along it was staring her in the face. And as soon as the idea came to her, she saw that Orillia had faint freckles spattered over her nose and the tops of her cheeks. The bruises had likely hidden them until now. But they were clear enough, though under the surface of the skin, so you had to be close to notice them. And if you looked at her hair sideways in the sunlight, it wasn't the least bit far-fetched to say it had an auburn cast. It had glittered that afternoon with auburn highlights. In the fall of light, pulled into a shining rope by the brush, it had flared almost red.

Hilda sat up and tugged her shoes on over her swollen feet. She would have to come up with something to make things right. It would be delicate, of course. She'd have to think it through. But it wouldn't be meddling; it would be a duty. Her responsibility. After all, it was her house.

suspension

"Your hair," Mr. Best said, and out came his hand and touched it. They'd all coincidentally met in the downstairs hall. It was the morning after they'd invented their new hairstyles. Mr. Best had just arrived and started to mount the stairs as Orillia was descending the last steps. When his hand came out like that and he touched her hair, Gladdie and Hilda stopped in their tracks. They couldn't have stiffened with more alarm or alacrity if lightning had struck them. Mr. Best's hand dropped sometime or other, and they all resumed their more normal postures and pretended nothing had happened. Orillia smiled, enigmatically she thought, and more at the wall than at Mr. Best.

Orillia was sitting with Gladdie and Susan in the verandah with the screened windows open to catch a bit of a breeze when Hilda came back from the post office. "A letter for Miss Orillia Cooper!" she cried as she ascended the steps. Although the morning was already warm, it was cloudy and the mosquitoes were still out. Hilda's ankles were a mess of red bumps, but the pleasure of conveying the letter outweighed the irritation of the bites, and she handed it over smartly.

"Percy Gowan," Orillia said. She really couldn't keep the smile off her face.

"Wants his suspenders back, I'll bet," Hilda said.

She shouldn't have told them about the suspenders, but Gladdie had walked into the room while she was still sitting with them in her lap.

"Wants to visit again," Gladdie said, her pleasure as evident in her voice as on her face. In fact, pleasure was too weak a word; relief was more like it. And Orillia caught the glance Hilda threw her old friend. As if Percy Gowan was the answer to all their prayers, the whole solution to the problem of What To Do With Orillia.

She left the envelope lying across her knee. Hilda pretended to be reading a dispatch from Mr. Wutherspoon's old sisters, and Gladdie poked about in the geraniums with a pair of scissors. Only Susan looked right at Orillia, frankly curious.

Orillia rose and retreated to her room with her letter. She intended to read it when she got there, but for some reason she couldn't bring herself to open it. She put the letter into her dresser drawer beside the other one he'd sent before he'd visited.

"What do you think?" Hilda asked later, when she got Gladdie alone.

"I think he likes her."

"And anyone would like him."

"That's right. So I guess we wait and see."

"It's a relief, isn't it? That he's written. And she looked pleased. It would be so suitable." They both looked up toward the room where Mr. Best was rattling away on his typewriting machine. Hilda reached across the table and patted Gladdie's hand.

"I see you write," Mr. Best said.

"Only to pass the time," Orillia said. She'd come upstairs to jot down the beginning of a poem and had forgotten to shut the door completely. She closed her notebook, which contained hundreds of poetic spurts and hundreds more entries informing herself of the tedium of her days. It occurred to her that one good thing about men was they helped time to pass more quickly.

Mr. Best leaned against the door frame in the casual manner of a younger man. "Miss Cooper," he said, "I pride myself on my penetration. You do more than pass the time. I have some familiarity, you know, with the art form. And an appreciation of those who pursue it."

"I assure you, I don't pursue it. Not at all," she said, more aware than ever of the insipid lines in her notebook.

"Don't worry, little girl," Mr. Best said, looking down on her. "Your secret is safe with me."

"I don't know what you're talking about," she said, and felt her face flush as crimson as her bed jacket.

"Everyone's hiding something," he said. "You know that, Miss Cooper. Unless there's nothing at all behind that oh so charmingly blank mask you wear, nothing at all in your cubbyhole of a heart."

With that enigmatic, vaguely flattering and ultimately disturbing pronouncement, he left her, knowing she'd continue to converse with him in her mind and be unsatisfied with the result.

"Gladdie," Hilda said, not looking up from her darning, "All my life I've wanted a child."

"I know."

"Even when I was a little girl, I longed for a sister or brother." She paused, but only for a second, and then went on. "I don't think I ever told you I had a pregnancy before I met you, before I went to Mrs. Riley's house."

"No," Gladdie said. And when Hilda didn't continue, or look up, she said, "No, you didn't ever tell me that."

Hilda sighed, grateful for the bridge Gladdie had created. "It ended in a miscarriage, like the later ones. But it was different than the later ones, because I didn't want the child. I wasn't married. Far from it." She cleared her throat. "I was far from married," she said.

"Don't fuss, Hilda, dear."

"I didn't want the child. I was glad at the time that it aborted."

"Anyone would understand that."

"I might have had a daughter." Hilda blew her nose. She removed her glasses and wiped her eyes with the back of her hand.

"I am sorry," Gladdie said.

Hilda remembered why she was telling Gladdie this old story, and pulled herself together. "If I'd had a daughter, I'd have had to give her up. I'd have had no choice."

"I know."

The tears welled up again. Gladdie handed over her hankie, as Hilda's was already sodden. "If I'd had a daughter," she went on, trying to stay on track, "I might have been able at least to keep an eye on her over the years. That's what I'd have tried to do. Not lose sight of her."

"Of course you would have."

"I'd have followed her anywhere."

"You would, I know."

"I'd have told her who I was – once she grew up. So she'd know I hadn't abandoned her." Now the tears had stopped and Hilda's drenched eyes sought Gladdie's.

"You'd do what was best for her," Gladdie said.

She did not seem to be taking the conversation as personally as Hilda had hoped she would. She could not be, or she'd be crying, too, instead of looking a bit mystified.

"Will I light the lamp?" Gladdie asked. "And we can sit and talk some more?"

But Hilda didn't think she could go on, not without speaking right out. She was no good at being indirect. She'd always known that, and now she wished she hadn't tried. If she didn't leave the kitchen, she'd have to take Gladdie by the shoulders and give her a good shake, and that would never do.

a morganatic wife

Gladdie McConnell," Mrs. Riley said. "There's a man to see you."

This was along the lines of *the sky is falling.* Mrs. Riley had to sit down after saying it and breathe a few times. Gladdie sat down too and took hold of the table to steady herself. Just for a second, because she hadn't been expecting anyone, the thought had flown into her mind that her old haunter had found her. He'd followed her one day when she was unaware and he'd come, finally, to ruin her life. Once that fear had settled, with the reflection that knocking on the door wouldn't be Mr. Tupper's method of approaching her, hope came lolloping along to take its place. It couldn't be Harry, could it? Even when Gladdie hadn't thought about Harry for weeks, the hope of seeing him again someday was always humming along inside her.

But Mrs. Riley would know her own son. And for all that she was sitting like a heavily breathing lump in her chair, she wasn't claiming the visitor as her own, or one she shared with Gladdie. "There's a man to see you." It couldn't be Mr. Twigg. Mrs. Riley would have said it was. Mr. Sprig was what she called him. She always knew how to take a name that was silly enough on its own and make it sillier.

Who could it be but Johnnie? It was more than three years since she'd heard from him, or him from her.

"I've left him in the parlour," Mrs. Riley said. "I didn't say you were here in case you didn't want it known. He asked for your current address."

"What did you tell him?"

"He's under the impression I'm searching for it at this moment. He said he'd been told you'd left us."

She gave Gladdie a look of accusation, but Gladdie pulled off her apron and pretended not to see her. She hung the apron on the hook by the door and tried to smooth her hair up toward the knot on top of her head.

"Useless," Mrs. Riley muttered.

He hadn't been in the boarding house before with the exception of the hall and the kitchen. As she hurried through the dining room, Gladdie saw the house, and especially the parlour that Mrs. Riley thought so genteel, as the shabby place it was, all water-stained wallpaper and dusty windows that let in little light. And what light did come in only showed up the photographs of people Johnnie Dabb would never want to meet and enhanced the brownness of the room, for Mrs. Riley had everything matching if she could, and brown was serviceable, and it was all pitifully browned with age as well as intention. It was early September, but the weather had been foul, and the house needed airing as well as cleaning; it smelled of damp. He looked so tall.

"Hello Gladdie," he said.

At first they were stiff with one another, as would be only natural, and she didn't ask him to sit. They couldn't talk in Mrs. Riley's house.

"I'm back," he said. "I arrived late last night."

She led him through the kitchen, and Mrs. Riley half rose, but Gladdie waved her down. She got her jacket from under the apron at the back door, and out she and Johnnie went, down the path that Jessie Dole took the last hour of her life, though she didn't mention that to him.

"Where will we go?" he asked.

She said she guessed they'd go to the station like they had before.

"Let's not go there," he said.

She suggested Betterbey's. She thought it would be fitting. It was an easy walk from Mrs. Riley's, and they set out briskly because a wet wind was blowing.

"You're looking well," she said.

He threw back his handsome head and laughed. "I'm very well, thank you," he said.

"Are you in the city for long?" she asked.

"Gladdie," he said, "you sound as if you've been to finishing school."

"Oh well, have a good laugh then," she said. The truth was, she'd been reading improving books ever since he'd left, having finally got up the nerve to join the public library.

When they reached Betterbey's, Johnnie asked her where she'd like to sit. She'd have asked for the same booth she and Clara Cooper had sat at – there was a kind of rounding-off-of-things idea in her head – but that booth was occupied by two fat men she took for twins. On closer inspection, as they passed them by, following the black-dressed lady, she saw they were only dressed alike in suits of the same dark shade, and both were shaved and polished to a similar gloss. As her eyes grew accustomed to the dim light, she noticed just about everyone in Betterbey's had that smooth look, and Johnnie had it too.

They ordered coffee. She thought it well-bred to wait until it came and get the fuss of pouring over with before starting in on the topic at hand, but Johnnie was eager to have her explain herself.

"I wrote to you at Mrs. Riley's," he said. "A couple of times. Hoping my letters would be forwarded, but they came back. Did you just decide not to answer?"

"I thought it best."

"You never left there?" When she didn't answer, he said, "Why did you tell me you'd moved, Gladdie?"

"To end the arrangement," she said, and stared back at him. He was sitting across from her, trying to see into her eyes. She didn't mean to say more – not that she was afraid to tell him what she thought of him, but she didn't intend to demean herself by letting on she'd had better expectations of him. Then he said, "Why?" in that sad, serious way he had that showed he'd never understand how his actions could harm anyone, since they hadn't been intended to harm.

She wasn't angry with him. She sighed as many another young woman had sighed, knowing what he was like. She said, "Orillia is growing up just fine. She has a nice big family to look after her. There was no point in us continuing the arrangement."

"Gladdie," he said, and he leaned forward until she almost thought he was going to take her hand in his, but he didn't. "Thinking of her growing up," he said, "being well-cared for and watched over by you – it did me a world of good."

That was such an old-fashioned way of putting it, it made her see all the reasons she'd always liked him in spite of herself, and she could see, too, how he got around people and softened them: he knew how to make you feel happy for doing him some good. "It's nice of you to say so," she told him.

"I'm not saying it to be nice. Gladdie, I'm on my way overseas. I'm being sent on business, to England. I expect I'll make my life there. I told them I needed time here before leaving. I thought I couldn't cross that ocean without seeing you again."

"Without seeing *me*? I should think you'd be concerned about seeing your little girl. Or have you seen her already?"

"No, I thought I'd wait, and we could go together and see if we can catch sight of her."

"You don't need me, Johnnie."

"Don't you want to go with me?"

"No."

"Did you stop watching her?"

"Not altogether. I check on her now and then. But our arrangement is over. You can go see her yourself. Go visit the Parkers or the Coopers. There's no need for you to sneak around and peek in windows, is there? Go knock on their door. They'll let you in." She hadn't meant to say so much. That was the trouble with keeping your feelings to yourself, she thought – if you ever start to let them out, they don't know how to stop. He didn't even have to ask her what had happened. Her indignation boiled to the surface, and the lie that Clara had told her came out, full of accusation. "Clara told me Orillia wasn't Jessie Dole's baby. She told me that baby died."

He knew in an instant what had happened. "You talked to Clara," he said, to gain time. "That was their story. Maretta's idea. She didn't want the child to grow up with that stigma."

"Of coming from Mrs. Riley's house."

"Of the whole scandal," he said.

"Oh it was quite a scandal, wasn't it?" she said bitterly.

They sat for a while in silence, sinking into the echoing feeling of the café where the thick carpets soaked up the sounds and the big mirrors on the walls only reflected the shadows, then Johnnie sat up straighter and looked decisive. "Gladdie," he said, "I have three months in Toronto before I go. I'm moving overseas. When I leave, I may never see you again. I don't think I will." He stopped for a breath. He rubbed his hands all over his head. His hair was short and stood up in tufts, and he looked more like he had in the old days and not so much like the others in the café. Gladdie had forgotten he used to do that when frustrated with trying to put something just the right way. He looked up at the ceiling, still rubbing his head and shaking it, and he asked: "Do you feel there's something between us?"

"No I do not," she said very quickly. "You may play with others. I don't like people playing with me." She crossed her arms and leaned back in the booth.

Johnnie gave her one of his quizzical looks. "It's not all playing," he said. "Didn't you read my letters? I meant what I said. I thought about you often. It made me happy thinking about you watching over Orillia."

"Just lessened your sense of responsibility, that's all that did. When I think of the times I thought I was showing her to you, and you could have seen her anytime, you could have visited her anytime, there with her family."

"I'm the black sheep of the family, Gladdie. I'm not really welcome among them. And Florence doesn't want Orillia to know me."

"Do you mean to tell me you're a member of the family, not just a friend?"

"Florence is my sister."

"Your sister."

"I gave up all rights to the child, Gladdie. Nobody but Florence knows she's mine. And I promised Florence if she took her after Maretta died, I wouldn't live in the city – where I'd be a bad influence."

"If you think I feel sorry for you, I don't," Gladdie said.

"Let me tell you something, Gladdie McConnell. When you came at me that day outside Jim's pharmacy and accosted me about Orillia, it was the best thing that ever happened to me. You gave me something to do besides feel guilty. And you were so damn intriguing. Such a firebrand. How could I have told you who I was? I wanted to be part of your arrangement, Gladdie. I was already on the outside, looking in at Orillia – Maretta and my sister had taken over – and you were my confidante, my companion. I didn't mean to be false with you."

She saw exactly how it was with him, how his dark eyebrows peaking over his smoky eyes and his good looks and his persuasive ways would always let him win affection too easily. So when he reached his hand across the table and laid his little finger on hers and stroked her fingers, one by one, and apologized for any pain he'd caused her, and asked if she'd consider living with him for the few months he'd be in Toronto, she just thought about how much she liked the sight of that hand, with its big, friendly looking knuckles, and said yes – and the loose sound of the word in her own ears nearly made her laugh.

She knew there'd be no need to give notice. Mrs. Riley could find a girl to clean that very afternoon just by opening the front door and hollering that she needed one. She'd often told Gladdie so.

On the way back to the boarding house to pick up her things Gladdie looked up at Johnnie walking beside her and saw the back of his neck, the way his hair curled there in circles, and she remembered how, when she'd first noticed that, she'd steeled herself against being tender. Now was so much better. She didn't feel the least bit tender toward him. It was adventure he was offering and a body to lie with and something else he probably hadn't thought about.

He said he'd wait in the hall while she packed her bag and told Mrs. Riley she was leaving. It was obvious Mrs. Riley had been spending some time in her room and had subsequently given in to drowsiness: her snores rumbled through the house. Minutes were all it took Gladdie to pack, then she carried her valise to the hall and left it by the door. She wondered if she should be afraid to mount the stairs since she'd never got this far toward leaving before, but she wasn't afraid. She banged on Mrs. Riley's door.

"Christ Almighty!" Mrs. Riley called. "Is it fire?"

"It's only me," Gladdie said, entering.

Mrs. Riley sat up in bed, clutching her flannel wrapper together over her fat breasts. Speechless, she stared at Gladdie. And there – if Gladdie didn't feel sorry for the old harpy.

"Mrs. Riley," she said. "It's time for me to be leaving."

"Oh you won't leave me, Gladdie."

"I am leaving," she said, like the heroine of one of Mrs. Friel's long-gone novels.

"It's that man!"

"It is," Gladdie said, feeling awfully silly to be so happy, saying it.

"A man come out of nowhere. Gladdie, Gladdie. Think what you're doing. Leaving your home. Your home. At your age. One last fling, is it? You'll be ruined. I suppose you ain't seen enough of the consequences in this house to make you think twice – and you've no gratitude. I've been a mother to you. All you ever had. And look how I'm repaid."

Gladdie sat on the side of the bed and looked very gently on Mrs. Riley. She said, "Come now, Mrs. Riley. I could hardly be worse off than I am."

"You'll be back," Mrs. Riley said, regaining some of her usual hauteur. "You'll be back, Gladdie McConnell. Begging for your old job. And it'll be too late. A new girl will be in your place. Then where will you be? And you've no business sense, Gladdie. At least make him pay you. Buy you some dresses. Though you've no clothes sense either, have you, poor dear?"

"I'll say goodbye now," Gladdie said, and she stood over Mrs. Riley's sleepy body and Mrs. Riley turned her face away.

Whole flights of thoughts came to Gladdie while she walked downstairs, looking at the valise waiting by the door. My head's too big for my body, she thought. And my hair's too red. And I've lived all these years as a servant in a low house. And I've packed somebody else's bag to go live with somebody else's lover. But when she saw Johnnie standing waiting, she thought: at least it's me walking out the door.

John Dabb recognized the valise and noticed the initials on it, which were his own, but he never said a word about that to Gladdie, and he carried it for her twice, on the way to and from his suite of rooms in one of the new downtown apartment blocks. Nor did Gladdie mention it. She was refreshingly uninterested in discussing the past. One thing they did talk about that first day was a stop at a pharmacy. He said he'd look after it if she liked.

"No," she said. "I want a child. Wait. Let me speak. I want a child and I'll have one if I can. And Johnnie – I'll not give up any child of mine. You've notice of that this instant. I'll keep it and raise it alone. But I'll count on your help. Oh I don't mean you, yourself. I'd not expect that much. But I'll hound you for money if it's money the child needs. And you'll give it your name so it's legal and different from mine.

"I can't marry you, Gladdie."

"You'd be a bigamist, I suppose. Well then, I'll be your morganatic wife. For this while. If I don't care for the niceties, the child won't either. But it'll have your name and know who you are if it cares to know. So now's your chance to back down. You'd never be able to run out on me, you know. There's no place on earth you could hide from me if I came after you."

"You're so fierce, Gladdie."

"Only if there's a child. And I hope there will be."

"Is that why you're agreeing to this?"

"I am fond of you, in spite of myself," she said. "And I don't suppose you're going to declare undying love."

"You're a loveable person, Gladdie McConnell. I'll tell you that."

"Let's leave it like that, then," she said.

The noise of the city distracted them as they walked along, their half thoughts diverging. They stopped to watch two men digging a hole for a fence post at a corner where a lumberyard had given way – surprisingly – to a park.

"This city's planning," Johnnie said. "It's thinking what it wants to be."

"Like you do."

"You know where you stand, at least. Gladdie, you know what draws me to you?" He took hold of her arm. "You're so sure of yourself. Aren't you? You get that puckish expression on your face and I want to know what's behind it."

"Oh, if that's all," she said.

She'd never seen such a place as Johnnie's apartment. She'd never imagined she could live like that, in so much space where the furniture sat just where you'd want it and was made to match. The carpets were so thick you left your footprints in them; the upholstery was so soft she could curl all day in the same chair. When she did get up, she could see herself walking by in the tables. One of Johnnie's rooms was a bathroom, the real thing, with a water closet, a sink and a big curled-edge bathtub you could sit in with your legs flat out. The water spurted from taps in the wall, no need to pump. Johnnie saw how taken she was with the bathroom, and once he'd shown her all around the apartment, he asked if she'd like to have a bath. He said he'd take one himself afterwards. So she had a little time to herself, and she didn't have to fuss about the poor condition of her drawers and vest. She didn't wear a corset, never having need for any pulling in, and that was a good thing as they were one garment – she'd observed – that could get terribly grubby.

There were big towels in an armoire in the bathroom and perfumed soap. The water came out warm. You could make it as warm as you pleased.

Gladdie didn't have much in the way of clothes in those days, and not a single thing with her that was clean. She couldn't countenance the idea of putting on her shift that she'd worn at Mrs. Riley's every night for a couple of weeks, not over her fresh skin, so she wrapped up in a dry towel. She didn't know what Johnnie would think seeing her leave the bathroom like that, but it had to be. He only said, "My turn." How nicely he said it, though, softly and with something in his voice that made her think he admired her. That was a good feeling to have just then, even if she understood he'd practiced instilling it.

She got into the bed and pulled up the clean sheets and the good-quality wool blankets. He didn't take very long, and when he came out, he had his pajamas on. He doesn't want to frighten me, she thought, grinning to herself, with his appendage sticking out. It was sticking out – she saw that anyway, and his hair was wet and sticking up. He sat on the bed, on his side, and rubbed at it with a towel. Some water trickled down his neck and made his pajama collar wet. She thought of reaching out an end of her towel to dry the back of his head but she didn't. He crawled into bed and took her in his arms. He stroked her head and shoulders as if she was someone beautiful.

She woke up in the night and lay thinking in the dark with him asleep beside her. After a while she noticed she was breathing louder than usual, and she tried to be more quiet. It took a few seconds before she realized it was Johnnie she was hearing; it was Johnnie's breathing, and she'd thought it was her own. She adjusted her breaths to his. Next thing she knew it was morning.

September 6, 1900, was the day he came for her, and she would never forget a minute of it. It was the closest she'd get to a wedding day.

They went to see Orillia. From a street corner, they watched her walking to school with her father, her head level with his chest. From behind a delivery wagon they watched her sitting with him in the park at the horticultural gardens. "Ralph won't notice anybody," Johnnie said, and he was right. All Ralph Cooper's attention was on Orillia, or else – and more often – on something that was happening in his own head. The little girl seemed old for her nine years, wise and sober compared to her schoolmates. Even feeding pigeons, she moved deliberately, sedately, observing the greedy birds with her head on one side as if she might be learning a lesson from their behaviour. Seeing Orillia now wasn't at all like the times they'd spied on her together when she was a baby, though they told each other she was strong and healthy and doing well for her age.

"How can you go away? Across the world?" Gladdie asked him.

"It's best for her," he said.

She didn't reproach him further, having used that argument herself, in staying away. She understood, too, how different Orillia's upbringing was from what her own child's would be, if she had one. The knowledge of illegitimacy would have upset everything in the foundation Orillia's parents had built her. It would have made her different from her schoolmates, stained her.

They didn't try to see Orillia when she walked home from school with her mother. "Florence would spot us in a minute," Johnnie said. He didn't want Florence to know he was in the city. It would only make her angry, he said, because he'd promised not to return. His sister had demanded he stay away from Orillia. He wasn't allowed to pretend to be her kind uncle, as he might have done in some families. Gladdie understood why that was. Orillia would have grown too fond of Johnnie, and then he would have let her down. It was all so predictable, Gladdie had to agree with

Florence it was better he should remain unknown. But she wouldn't have stayed away if she'd been him, not with a real, legal claim to the child.

"But you're in touch with your sister? You write back and forth?" Gladdie asked him, and he admitted they were in regular contact and she normally wrote to him every three or four months. So he'd surely had no need of Gladdie's reports, but neither of them mentioned that.

While Orillia's father sat nearby on the park bench – and what a poor fellow he was, thin and wan and weak chinned – the little girl went into a reverie. She lifted her arm, quite gracefully, and then gazed at her hand. It seemed she'd just noticed it, as a baby might, as it moved across her field of vision. She flexed it at the wrist, down, then up a few degrees, and extended the fingers until it looked pretty to her eyes. To Gladdie the gesture looked birdlike, the way a dancer might carry her hand. She understood the child's fascination. Out of the corner of her eye she saw Johnnie check his watch, and start to walk away. Orillia raised her eyes and looked right at Gladdie. The little hand stayed up in the air. The black eyes, so big in the small, pale face, widened.

They were lying on the bed on top of the covers, and the window across the room was open, letting in the light, and Johnnie said, "I love to watch the sun play on your skin."

She thought of Harry saying he could see by the pattern of her freckles where the sun had never been. It made her feel grateful, that connection between them. It helped her not to feel too jealous, for she knew, though it was never explicitly said, that Johnnie had a wife. He'd told her he was leaving at the end of the summer. Well, she had this time. She said to him, "Time is about the only thing once it's given can't be taken back." She wanted it said out loud – just in case he thought it could. Then she remembered one other thing he could give her that he couldn't take back, and she was sure she could feel it inside her.

Gladdie didn't go back to Mrs. Riley's to work when Johnnie left. He offered to give her money, but she said the real favour would be if he'd help her find a job. He got her a place in Shaunessey Hall, a fancy hotel for ladies just off Bloor Street, where she never would have gone to look for employment on her own.

He gave her the address and a time to be there to make her application. It looked too grand an establishment for her, but he'd said they expected her. She was to ask for a lady, Mrs. Forbes.

The young man behind the desk went to a room off his own little cubbyhole, and out came Mrs. Forbes, a woman in her forties wearing rectitude and spectacles. "Miss McConnell?" she said in a brisk way that made all the consonants stand up and be accounted for, and at Gladdie's nod she raised the hatch of the counter and let her through into the back room. "Have a chair," Mrs. Forbes said. Then she went to the door and spoke to the desk clerk who went off, and after a minute, during which Mrs. Forbes made tick marks on sheets of paper and Gladdie watched her, he returned with a very combed and brushed gentleman. "This is Miss McConnell," Mrs. Forbes said to him, rising. He introduced himself as Mr. Hayden, and sat down in the chair near Gladdie's while Mrs. Forbes sat down again behind her little table with her papers on it. She picked up a letter and passed it to Mr. Hayden, and he looked at it while she asked Gladdie questions about her experience, which of course was only cleaning and some cooking at Mrs. Riley's. "You're an educated girl, are you?" she asked.

"I'm a reader, Ma'am," Gladdie said.

"Ah," said Mr. Hayden.

"First name?"

"Gladdie."

"Gladys, it is then."

"No Ma'am. It's just Gladdie."

"Gladdie is a diminutive," Mrs. Forbes said. "I don't call my girls by diminutives. It will be Gladys on your birth certificate, if you have one."

They sat there for a bit until Gladdie said, "I'm sorry for I've wasted your time."

The gentleman spoke up then. "Do you mean to say you'll turn down the job over this?"

Gladdie said, "I can't change my name."

Mr. Hayden stood up. "Well, Mrs. Forbes," he said. "The young woman comes highly recommended, but you're in charge here. It's up to you to decide whether you can get around the impediment of calling her Gladdie." He put out his hand to shake Gladdie's, so she stood up. They shook hands and off he went. Then she turned to Mrs. Forbes, who was smiling to herself, looking not at all as Gladdie had imagined she would at that moment. "Gladdie," she said. "Do you want the job?"

"I think so, Ma'am," she said. "Not knowing that much about it."

"I'd rather be called Mrs. Forbes than Ma'am," Mrs. Forbes said. "Come with me. We'll see if we have a uniform that will fit you. You won't object to wearing a uniform? They're not too ugly and they save your own clothes."

"That'll be fine, Mrs. Forbes," she said, and Mrs. Forbes smiled again, to herself, but in a way that made Gladdie think if she didn't have to supervise her, she might have smiled at her.

The management at Shaunessey's was good to Gladdie, though the ladies were often a trial. The pay was decent, and they gave her a good room and a day off each week. It was her own room that she loved. She walked into it that first afternoon, following Mrs. Forbes, and she put her valise on the little bed, and everywhere she looked she said to herself: my window, my cupboard, my chair, my hook on the back of my door where I can hang my coat. There was no child, not even a time when she could fool herself into thinking she might be pregnant. But she thought she was better off than she had a right to be.

"You proved me wrong," Mrs. Riley said. Her left breast evidently itched from the shock.

"I'm better off than I ever thought I'd be," Gladdie said.

"You're lucky, Gladdie McConnell, believe you me."

"I am."

"You take my meaning? At your age. You could have been saddled with an outcome. Out come. Ha! You remember Harry and the trouble he caused me."

"You never heard from him, did you, Mrs. Riley?"

"That once. Well, it was you, wasn't it, got that postcard? So he's fine." Even the right tit started acting up and Mrs. Riley's face got red. "Some women get sentimental over children," Mrs. Riley said. "I'm glad to know – for your sake – you're not one of them."

mischief

Teasing, Hilda said, "One of these days he'll have to come back, since he left his suspenders."

Orillia still hadn't read the letter, and now she was glad she'd ignored it. She wrapped up a parcel for Percy Gowan, returning his suspenders. She wrote that she'd been serious when she'd told him he wouldn't like her once he got to know her. The letter, meant to scare him off, implied that she would taint him, ruin his life. It made her smile. She sounded like a dangerous woman. Well, Mrs. Kitely had been worried about her, hadn't she? Worried that she'd spoil the doctor's chances of an illustrious career. Mrs. Kitely had known Dr. Kitely was interested in her, in spite of his attempts to hide it.

The simple fact was Percy wasn't romantic enough for her. He was, as she'd first intuited, old-fashioned, and too much like everyone else. She was crippled – unusual – and would appeal to the romantic in men, men who were unusual themselves.

Orillia opened her blouse and rubbed some talcum powder between her breasts. It left a chalky streak, but no one would see. The lilac scent rose to her nostrils. Gladdie had bought the powder for her when she'd come from the hospital. Lilac, probably because the box matched the room.

She opened her face powder next and powdered her nose. She was looking well, she thought. Hilda's cooking was working; she was putting on weight. She smiled at herself, a mischievous smile. She had a plan. The day before, after Mr. Best had left the house, she'd slipped over to his door and tried the knob and found it locked, just as she'd expected. She'd heard the key turn most days after he'd finished work. Now, with the others out of the house on an excursion to the park, she sat on the bench in front of her dressing table, listening for movement from his room. The typewriter had been quiet for most of the afternoon. He might have been napping, she thought. He might have been as bored all afternoon as she would have been if she hadn't been developing her plan. He might have been daydreaming about her. But she didn't want her thoughts to go that far.

When she heard the usual sounds that meant he was getting ready to depart for the day – the thump of pages being squared against the desk, the opening and closing of a drawer, the scraping back of his chair – she picked up her crutches. When he went to his door, she swung across the floor in step with him, toward her own door. At the moment his opened, she crumpled. Her crutches clattered down the wall, and she fell to the floor. Propped on one elbow, she looked up at the ceiling, where a tiny reddish spider ran on miniscule legs at incredible speed, as if to say there were other possibilities, better than this. Her mind went with it, skittering across the ceiling.

A knock on her door brought her back. "Miss Cooper?"

"Mr. Best. Oh," she said.

"Is everything all right?"

"I think – Mr. Best?"

"Yes?"

"Could you – ? Please?" She rearranged herself as gracefully as she could on the floor.

"Yes, Miss Cooper?"

That sounded impatient. She hurried on. "If you would come in and assist me –"

"Certainly," he said and opened the door. Unmoving, he stared down at her. She'd forgotten how unpredictable other people could be. She hadn't expected to feel foolish, and she hadn't envisioned him controlling the situation. She was fully dressed and decently covered, but she felt he was seeing more of her than she wanted him to see. But she had to go on now that she'd started.

"Mr. Best."

"Yes?"

"If you would give me your arm."

"Certainly."

He bent and briefly met her eyes with a piercing challenge she couldn't quite read. His hand enveloped hers in a tight grip. In a second, easily, he hoisted her to her feet, propped her up with one hand against her shoulder and scooped up the crutches.

"Thank you," she said, aware, now that she was standing in front of him, of his smoky, masculine, yet curiously stale smell. He was looking down at her with a half-smile, as if he knew all about her. She was finding that insulting and attractive at the same time, insulting because there was much more to her than had yet met his eye (or ever would!) and attractive because he cared to discover who she was. She remembered Gladdie didn't like him.

"All right now?" he asked.

"Yes, thank you."

"Good evening then," he said.

Without looking back, he descended the stairs and she heard him let himself out of the house. She leaned her forehead against her door frame. He was very sure of himself. Well. He didn't need to think he was so smart, did he? She'd waylaid him. He'd left the house without locking his door.

She was clumsy and slow in making her way to his room and in finding what she was seeking. He was neat, evidently, and had put his work away. The room looked peculiarly vacant, as if a person without personality inhabited it. A fat oak desk sat under the window with the typewriter on it, a stack of paper to the left, a pen set and inkstand to the right next to a framed family photograph. When she reached the desk she discovered evidence of occupation: the blotter was splotched with his dark blue ink. Here and there a word or half a word had bled through. She read "tar" and "ultry" and "thus" and "some." Not exactly enlightening, any of it. She laid her fingertips in the smooth hollows of the typewriter keys – and shuddered. In the bottom left-hand drawer of the desk, she found his manuscript. He was writing a novel, she saw at a glance. How daring of him, how presumptuous. What a conceited man. She plucked out the top pages.

She had barely scanned the first chapters when she heard Gladdie and Hilda and Susan at the front door. She dropped the pages into the open drawer and eased it shut. As stealthily as she could on crutches, she left his room and closed his door.

In her own room again, she took up her notebook and wrote down what she now knew about Mr. Best:

- His wife is pretty. She signed the photograph, "All my love, Kate."
- She is older than I am, but considerably younger than Mr. B.
- He has four children, unless there have been infants since the photograph on his desk was taken.
- He is writing a novel about a boarding house full of women.
- He does not like or admire me.

The beginning of Mr. Best's novel was quiet, just women reading books and drinking tea. In chapter three they were joined by a Miss Carter who was excessively prim and walked with the aid of crutches owing to some injury not yet explained. Orillia hadn't had time to read much further. She expected some time near the end of the first section a man would move into the house and then things would start to happen.

"Miss Cooper," Mr. Best said in his best peremptory manner. Really, he was insufferable. Who did he think he was, barking at her like that? She turned her head slowly to give him a cool look. She'd been heading across the landing to the stairs. She knew what must have caused his annoyance: he'd found what she'd written. She hadn't been able to resist leaving a clue that she'd been in his room, a few scribbled words. (After all, he had the nerve to write about her.) His typewritten manuscript was scattered with deletions, corrections and additions he'd made in ink. Goodness, he must read and reread the manuscript, she'd thought, just pore over the thing. She didn't know if he would notice her one line, buried on page forty.

They'd walked out of their rooms at the same time, or he'd emerged just after she had. Perhaps it wasn't accidental. She had to play along now, though after the first thrill at that note in his voice it wasn't as much fun as she'd hoped it would be. She wished she hadn't written on his manuscript and let him know she was interested. On the other hand, he must see her differently now. She wasn't a quiet cripple, waiting in vain for a man to change her life; she was someone to contend with.

He was much bigger than she was and came up close to her where she'd stopped in the hall. He was trying to intimidate her, she knew, and it was working. She felt almost frightened of him, almost feared he'd strike her, and she would have turned time back if she could have, and erased the evidence that she'd been in his room. She turned a blank face to him.

"Could I show you something?"

"Of course."

"If you'll wait a moment."

He went into his room and returned carrying a page of manuscript. He handed it to her. Besides the lines of typing there was one sentence on the page, written in blue-black ink in a small, backward-slanting hand.

"Do you recognize this, Miss Cooper?"

"Recognize it, Mr. Best?"

"I wondered if it might be your handwriting."

"Mine?"

"Perhaps because of the content."

The sentence came at the end of a paragraph that called the character known as Miss Carter a young old maid with a tediously prudish manner. The addition read, "However, Miss C. turned out to be a fascinating young woman."

Orillia protested. "It's not my handwriting. Nothing like it."

"Would you be willing to show me a sample of your handwriting?"

With a hint of a mock bow, he gestured toward his open room and the desk in front of the window. She put on a haughty air, as if condescending to enter his room. At the desk, she took up his gold fountain pen and dipped it into his inkwell. She set the tip on the blotter to soak up the excess while she thought what to write. With a smile she wrote a sentence on the new page he'd put before her.

When she pulled back he lifted the page from the desk, but he didn't immediately take his eyes from hers. While he watched her, his eyes darkened, until she dropped hers.

She'd written, in her right-slanted hand this time, "Mr. B. turns out to be a rather interesting man himself."

She waited for his response, proud of herself. She could play the game. She was no young old maid. "Do you see?" she said. "The two scripts aren't at all alike."

She expected – or hoped for – a similar arch response, but he became quite ominously serious. He said: "Miss Cooper, I won't have you coming into my room."

It made her angry to blush in front of him. He had no right to speak to her in that authoritarian way, no reason to get so angry when she'd only been teasing him – so she tried to tell herself, to keep standing tall. She turned from him as abruptly as she could manage given her crutches and two feet that seemed, at that moment particularly, to be made of clay. He didn't do anything to stop her progress, nor did he evince any interest in her reaction. As soon as she'd left his room, he shut the door.

She vowed she wouldn't speak to him again. Or think of him. But that very evening, in a fit of scorn and self-mortification, she took him – or at least his darkening eyes and sweetish smell (like old carrots, stored too long in the cellar), and his rough, impatient fingers – to her bed.

sentimental

It was a slow sinking that started the dream, a soft rocking with the weight of water under her giving way a bit at a time. Then she settled. She could feel the bottom under her, the sand. She'd touch it now and then but mostly float above it, drifting. She wasn't seeing anything but water, swirling. She touched the body before she saw it. Her side brushed up along it, then she pulled away and from a distance she could tell it was Jessie Dole. The water was tugging on Jessie Dole's skin; it started falling off, melting away into the shadows. You could see the bones. There wasn't a thing she could do because she was rising fast, up to the surface. She was leaving Jessie Dole behind, and she knew she'd break the surface soon, but what she didn't know was when she did there'd be a baby in her arms.

She pondered the dream. She felt different after it than she had before. She seemed to have gone down to the bottom of a question and back up, just as she'd descended and risen in the dream.

The dream made her see the baby again and those dark, scowling, stubborn eyes. In the dream she'd been afraid to look the baby in the face. She knew she'd let her down. She was holding her in her arms, the way she best fit, and felt the weight of her again, the fine smooth skin, the little fatty arms and hands, how warm she was. Just as she'd done when she'd had her those few hours, she laid her cheek in beside her little baby cheek and sniffed her neck where her smell was, and the baby turned and latched onto her chin, thinking it was a nipple, for she was crying with hunger.

The little girl, when she'd seen her in front of the Parkers' house, when she'd pushed aside the branches of that willow tree, weren't her eyes the same as the baby's looking up over the bottle? And again, when she'd looked up from watching her hand that day in the park, weren't her eyes asking for some kind of help? If ever a pair of eyes could claim a person, those eyes had. But Gladdie hadn't in any way acknowledged that she'd been watching her. She'd let her down. She'd walked away and left her comfortless.

She was standing on their front steps on Clinton Street, a pretty little thing, slim but sturdy, with fine brown hair in a braid down her back and curled in front above her black eyes. Gladdie tried to see if she looked like Jessie Dole or Johnnie, but she couldn't see a resemblance to anyone. Except for the black eyes she was just herself. She stood on the front steps waiting for her terrier puppy to bring her a ball. Gladdie remembered she'd had a spaniel years before, and she'd been glad because she was such a serious little girl. She had on a plaid skirt in green and blue colours and a navy blue sailor blouse with a big square collar that draped over the front, which was nice, Gladdie thought, because it filled her out a bit, covered her up, and girls that age could feel embarrassed if their chests could be seen. She'd be thirteen.

Orillia went inside the house just as Gladdie passed by, and she couldn't tell whether or not the girl had seen her. But there was lots of time, and it wouldn't hurt to watch for a bit before showing herself.

It was cold some days. In late March you never knew what the weather would be like. The streets were dirty, it was often windy and the tip of Orillia's nice little nose would get red, but you wouldn't see her hurry. Like her mother in that, like Florence Cooper, she had a refined way of walking. She went on a streetcar with her parents one Saturday, and that surprised Gladdie because she went and worked with them at a greenhouse.

They changed into overalls, not the mother but the girl and her father. The work looked hard, what Gladdie saw of it, a lot of bending and lugging of pails and big pots. Florence Cooper worked in the office with accounts, but Ralph Cooper just carted stuff about, looking dead tired. He'd worked down on King Street in a big office when Orillia was little, and then he'd gone to a warehouse, and this was another comedown, anyone could see. Gladdie watched Orillia lugging buckets of roses. She watched the girl cutting the stems off thorny roses inside pails of cold water. She knew the water was cold by her little blue hands.

It was a long streetcar ride to get to the greenhouse, so it was the next Saturday before Gladdie attempted it again, and she went straight there. They never did come, although the place was busy. The house on Clinton Street, when she got there, looked quiet and dark, with all the blinds pulled, and Gladdie figured Ralph Cooper must have fallen ill again. But in subsequent days there was no sign of Orillia at the Parkers' house either. The next week she discovered why. After all those years of living in that house as if they were there forever, they'd picked up and left. They went west, their neighbour said. Gladdie had seen the terrier puppy in the next door garden and leaned over the fence to pet it, and the lady was snipping the dead heads off her geraniums on her porch, so Gladdie was able to ask her. It turned out the puppy was the neighbours'. The Cooper girl had played with it. Their little house had been owned by an uncle, the neighbour said, and would be rented out to new people.

Gladdie fussed about it, about Orillia having worked in the greenhouse like that, about them leaving for the West. She kept seeing Orillia's face and those troubled eyes looking out as if they were searching for help. But there wasn't a thing she could do.

virginal

From the kitchen, Gladdie could hear the exchange when Orillia met Mr. Best in the hallway. A little flutter of You first. No, you. That's all it was. But she'd heard them talking upstairs the day before, and she was almost sure Orillia had gone briefly into his room. All through the meal, the thought of the man being near Orillia preyed on her mind.

After supper Orillia said she'd wash the dishes, and Gladdie told Hilda to go read to Susan; she'd dry. She took up the tea towel and wiped at a slower pace than usual so as not to annoy Orillia by taking the plates right out of her hands. All the while she fretted, until her thoughts burst out. "That Mr. Best," she said. "He thinks he's smarter than the rest of us. I don't like the way he looks at us."

Orillia didn't answer. Gladdie saw those lips pressed together. The stiff young back. Orillia didn't realize how little experience she had, how a man like Mr. Best could take advantage. He was one of those who thought he knew everything. A big man with a certain rude attraction for women. One of those who gave himself a nod while he gave you the once over. Married to a younger woman, which was helpful to a man who wanted to be looked up to. Gladdie'd seen him watching her, watching all of them, and adding up his two and two. He gave them tests; she'd seen him do it with Orillia, pass her on the stairs and hesitate on his step to see if she'd pause a second on hers. She'd seen him look smug when Orillia did stop and turn toward him. If Orillia just thought about it, she'd see he didn't have a thing in him that was true. "He's a crude man," she said.

Orillia passed the roaster over and began cleaning the sink. Gladdie dried the pan and put it away in the warming oven. She hung the tea towel on the bar on the back of the cellar door. You couldn't know what would happen with a man like Mr. Best in the house. "Don't have anything to do with him, Orillia," she said.

Orillia just stared at her with a look on her face that said she had no intention of obeying instructions now that Gladdie had suddenly started giving advice.

Hilda paused while rolling out the pie dough, and leaned against the rolling pin, watching Gladdie feed leftover roast beef into the food grinder. She'd hoped Gladdie would think over the conversation they'd had, and come to her and confess about Orillia. That hadn't happened, and short of asking her directly, Hilda didn't know what she could do. Give a hint to Orillia, maybe, but would Orillia want to know? That was the question that plagued her now. Or would she be ashamed of being illegitimate? And ashamed of Gladdie. In which case, Hilda would go to her grave without speaking.

Gladdie and Orillia were so alike, you could see that when you knew them, both of them so secretive. Hilda tried to picture the two of them sitting across from one another, having a real, direct conversation. Why, they were like those mountaineers who had to flash mirrors across great valleys. I'm here, was all they could say to one another. I'm here.

And in the meantime, poor Gladdie had to worry about Mr. Best. "Oh, I wish Percy Gowan would turn up at our door again," Hilda said. At least it was a topic that could be spoken out loud. "Right now. This minute. I'm sure he likes her very much, and she – well, she tries not to show it, but a fool could see... Her face all lit up. I remember sitting in the parlour the day he visited, looking from one to the other and thinking, Well, here's an end to the story. He'd be good for her. Steadying. You know she sent his suspenders back. I wonder what she said to him. You don't think she put him off, do you?"

"Why would she do that? It's harvest," Gladdie said. "He's busy with harvest still. He'll be helping out his neighbours, too."

"And Mr. Best. I wish I'd never agreed to let that room to him. He forgets he's a married man. If only there was some way to prompt Percy."

"No, you don't."

"What?"

"You can't. Hilda, you could tell him it would do her good to hear from him and he's a kind young man and maybe he'd write a few times and maybe he'd visit again, but it's no good if it's not his own idea."

"Hear, hear," came a voice from the pantry, and Orillia walked up to them.

Hilda said, "Oh."

"Oh indeed," said Orillia.

Gladdie said, "We didn't hear you come downstairs."

"I wasn't upstairs," she said. "I was in the pantry. Since you were talking about me, I thought it would be permissible to listen. You shouldn't worry so much about me, you know. I'm enjoying my little life. I don't require Mr. Gowan, for steadying or anything else. And as for Mr. Best, you can put down the heavy responsibility of upholding his virtue. If his marriage vows are important to him he'll maintain them."

Off she went, leaving Hilda mopping her brow.

"She hasn't got a clue," Hilda said, forgetting herself.

Gladdie had to agree.

Orillia remembered a couple of the words Mr. Best had used in his manuscript to describe Miss Carter: virginal, skittish. She hadn't had an opportunity to infiltrate his room again and read more. She'd ignored him after his boorish behaviour over her going into his sanctum, but lately he'd been so flirtatious with her, she felt sure she had the upper hand again.

A kind young man, that's exactly what Percy Gowan was. As Dr. Kitely was an honourable man. Both of them much too earnest, too serious, for her. You couldn't tease them; they couldn't stand up to it. Mr. Best was at least a worthy opponent. You could never hurt his feelings. With him, she had the delicious impression she was safely playing with fire.

westward

Gladdie recognized the familiar figure from a block away, and her breath caught in her throat. He looked up when she called his name, twisting his head on his stiff neck, and she wondered if he'd be disappointed seeing it was only her. But as soon as he laid eyes on her, his expression changed into one you'd have to call delight, and no one could have been more gratified than Gladdie to see it.

"Oh Mr. Riley," she said.

"Gladdie, by God," Mr. Riley said, and he wiped his eyes with the back of his hand. "When did I see you last? How old were you? Just a gal and look at you now. You left the boarding house, I heard."

"I go back to visit."

"You would do."

"What are you doing now, Mr. Riley?"

"This and that. This and that." He was beaming and looking right into her eyes, and she remembered the first time she saw him and noted how interested he was in what the other men with him were saying, his bright eyes following the conversation as if he'd never wanted to be anyplace else than where he was and never wanted those moments to end.

"Would you like tea, Mr. Riley?" she asked. "Or a coffee. I know a place."

"Ah, no. I've a – I've a meeting coming up shortly, Gladdie. A pal from the old days with a lead, you know. Another time we'll do it, won't we?"

"Let me give you my address and you can call for me some day. I've Tuesdays off."

"Surely, give me the address. There's a good gal. You're looking awfully smart, by the way, Gladdie."

"It's hand-me-downs from the ladies where I work. I'm at Shaunessey's Hotel. Did you know that, Mr. Riley?" She was scribbling the address onto the back of a card while she spoke, and it reminded her of the day they had gone to the library together and exchanged notes. "Ignore the printed side," she told him. "I save the ladies' visiting cards when they leave the hotel."

"To use when you meet old friends on the street, eh?" he said. His eyes were red around the rims, and he wiped them again with the back of his hand.

"I don't have many old friends, truly," she said. "But I'm glad to have seen you again, Mr. Riley. I missed you at the house."

"You've seen Georgina lately, have you?"

"A few weeks ago."

"As much herself as ever?"

"That's right."

"Say Gladdie, I often think of that day –" He looked up at her, full of story, but he stopped when he saw her face. "I'm getting old. Telling the same old stories over and over again. Never mind."

"That day in the library, do you mean?" she asked, feeling not very brave, for she didn't want it spoken of.

"Ah no. The library? I don't recall... No, I was speaking of the day I found you in the back porch. All blue and waxy looking from the cold, and I'd a terrible fear, I don't mind telling you now you're all grown up, that you could be my own, stepping up to my door to haunt me."

"You were saved from that terror, Mr. Riley."

"Well."

"Well."

"Me pal will be wondering where I've got to."

"You'd best be off," she said.

"It's done me a world of good to see you, Gladdie."

"Don't forget to keep the card. I could treat you to supper."

"Wait till I tell the fellows I've that sort of offer."

"Goodbye then," she said.

"If you're back at the house in the next while, you might say hello for me, if Georgina's in a mild temper."

"I will."

He seemed unable to leave her. She thought there must be something he felt he should say, but he didn't know what it was, or, knowing, he couldn't come out with it. "You're a good man, Mr. Riley," she said, to ease him, and it did perk him up.

"Did you hear the one about the good man, the bad man and the priest?" he asked.

"No, I didn't."

"Ah, well, I'll save it for next time."

"We'll have more time then."

"That's right."

"I should be going myself, if I'm to get my shopping done."

"Which way are you headed?" he asked.

She pointed east, knowing he'd say he was going the opposite direction, and he did. She started off then, and walked about twenty paces, then he called "Farewell." She turned to see him standing solid, with his bowler hat tipped back as if it would aid him in seeing to wear it like that, still in the same spot where she'd left him, with people passing by him, couples having to separate to get round him. He wasn't going to budge until she'd got clear out of his vision, so she waved and he waved and she let him watch her out of sight.

"It's Gladdie, isn't it?" Clara said. She put her head on one side and looked searchingly at Gladdie, as if she was trying to remember exactly what she'd decided to think about her. Then she gave her a toothy grin. God, she was a plain woman, not as homely as her sister but just plain. In the café the day they'd met she'd accepted Gladdie's remark that little Orillia didn't look like any of the Cooper clan, that unfortunately favoured family. She'd lied that day in Betterbey's, but Gladdie understood why she'd done it, and she didn't hold it against her.

They stopped there on the street, a block from Mr. Parker's pharmacy. Gladdie had been trying to catch her for a couple of days, trying to make the meeting look accidental, and now Clara chatted away as if she truly cared what Gladdie had been doing in the years since they'd had tea together at Betterbey's. She said how smart Gladdie looked, and Gladdie explained how ladies sometimes left her things when they'd stayed at Shaunessey's a while. It was partly gratitude and partly cheapness, leaving clothing as a tip, but she didn't explain that far. She and Clara had only one thing in common, that was Orillia Cooper, so it was natural they got to her pretty quickly. Clara didn't seem worried about letting Gladdie have the information. It was three years since Ralph and Florence Cooper and Orillia had left Toronto. She wouldn't think there was any danger in telling Gladdie where they'd finally settled.

"They were in Fenton, in the foothills of the Rockies. They were ranching there. But now they've moved to a place called Aquadell. Florence named the town. Isn't that something?"

"Aquadell. That's a pretty name for a town," Gladdie said, and Clara said aqua meant water, and Gladdie right then had a picture in her mind that was like the Garden of Eden, all viny and green, with a pool and a fountain, like the horticultural gardens, but more as they might have been painted on the wall of the Cyclorama. "And where's Aquadell?" she asked.

"In Saskatchewan. Near Regina, the capital city. Well, near is a relative term. We wouldn't call it near."

"Near is a relative term." Gladdie liked that. She grinned at Clara, thinking what a nice woman she was. They could have been friends if things were different. It seemed Clara must have decided to like Gladdie too, because she told her everything she knew. She couldn't imagine Gladdie would be heading west. And if she really knew me, Gladdie thought, she'd want me to go and find the girl again.

It had been on her mind, ever since the Coopers had left Toronto, that she would go west, but she'd never let herself think she'd do it. A daydream was what she called it, yet she'd saved her money. And then that meeting with Mr. Riley – seeing him had done her good, had put her back in touch with herself. She'd recognized Mr. Riley's trouble. He never could give himself to anyone. He was always wary in case the cost was too high. He was never going to call on her and take her up on that supper. Well, she wouldn't be like that. She was going to follow the person she cared about – not to put herself forward, not to make any claim or in any way upset the girl's life, but only to see her, to satisfy herself she was fine and enjoy the sight and the fact of her. And to be there – in case she was needed.

The very night after she met Clara in the street, Gladdie wrote to Johnnie – the first she'd written to him since he went overseas to England – at the address he'd given her for emergencies, and told him what she'd learned and what she'd decided. She had a response just before she left Toronto, from his wife, telling her John had died. No details were given, no comments and no comfort. And what comfort could there have been? He was just gone from the earth, Johnnie Dabb. She hadn't seen him for years and still there was a cold empty space where the thought of him had resided, a space she could feel the wind whistle through if she thought about it. If it was so for herself, it must be doubly hard for his wife. The poor woman, Gladdie thought, wishing she hadn't had to find out about Johnnie's past. She wrote to her and told her he'd been upright and responsible about the child, and she trusted the disclosure wouldn't in any way lessen her memory of him. She didn't receive any reply.

Now she only had Orillia left – and the name of a place to head for, a real place in the west: Aquadell.

part four

land of promise

land of promise

A big blonde girl on a street corner," Mrs. Riley said, describing how she'd found Gladdie's replacement. "Trying to sell hosiery from a box she'd hung over her neck. Putting out her hand" – here Mrs. Riley suited her action to her words – "to all and sundry with a feeble 'Excuse me' that was so timid you could easily pass her by, pretending you didn't hear." Mrs. Riley had gone up to her and said, "'What's a great big girl like you doing begging? For that's all this is.'" Fifteen minutes later Hilda Jensen was wearing Gladdie's old apron, and Mrs. Riley had the deal of a lifetime on hose.

Whenever Gladdie visited the boarding house she sympathized with Hilda, naturally, and over the years gave her advice, if she got her alone, on how to handle Mrs. Riley, so they got to be friends. Hilda was a soft thing, in the heart not the head, and sometimes Gladdie couldn't help being irritated with her. Mrs. Riley had taken terrible advantage. When Gladdie talked about her plans, whatever they were, Hilda would sigh. She'd never say a thing about what that sigh meant, but it was obvious she couldn't believe *she* was fated for wishes to come true. On her days off she went to the cemetery and talked to her mother and father in their graves. Hilda was about Gladdie's age but often seemed younger because she looked to others for advice. She relied on others to an extent that mystified Gladdie until she learned that the poor girl's glasses barely corrected her vision. Hilda had worn the same pair of spectacles since childhood, and it was only when she broke them one day and had to replace them that she understood, herself, how bad her eyesight had been. Mrs. Riley found her crying over the broken glasses and lent her money for new ones. She was no good to Mrs. Riley, cleaning what she couldn't see. "You're next to useless *with* your sight," Mrs. Riley told her and charged her interest on the loan, so that it had taken most of her wages, most of a year, to repay it.

Hilda hadn't belonged at Mrs. Riley's. She'd been to school until she was fifteen and should have had a better place. It wasn't shyness so much as awkwardness that plagued her, and she'd lost the few jobs she'd found. Who wouldn't be a bit clumsy with others, Gladdie figured, if they'd had Hilda's life. She always said she'd had a happy childhood, and it did sound as if that was true. She was the only child of gentle parents who'd doted on her. Gladdie guessed that was where the softness came from. Then they'd died young, leaving only unpaid bills. Two hospital visits for her mother, who'd suffered miscarriages, a couple of them dangerous, had put the family into debt, and all the bookkeeping on the part of Mr. Jensen and all the sewing on the part of Mrs. Jensen and Hilda, too, hadn't bailed them out. Hilda hadn't known it was miscarriages. A female problem was all her mother had told her until she talked to her about it the day before she bled to death in her bed. "My father died soon after," Hilda said, not saying how.

At fifteen Hilda had been a problem to someone, and the solution had been to pack her off to a little town outside Toronto to look after an old lady for the best years of her life. There she'd lived, in a big house where she did all the work and never received a salary but the roof over her head, the food she ate and some hand-me-down clothes, and she'd stayed ten years. Then one day, as if cold water had been thrown in her face, she'd realized the old lady could live another decade. The next time the woman's niece was visiting, Hilda sneaked upstairs, packed her few things and left by the back door. Gladdie got a kick out of picturing that. Between the day she'd run away and the day Mrs. Riley found her had been a bad time, however, since Hilda had had no more idea how to make a living or make her way than Gladdie'd had at the age of nine. It was a time she never wanted to speak about, and Gladdie knew why: a person had to do some shameful things, sometimes, just to survive.

Gladdie had arranged with Hilda to meet at the cemetery. It was lovely there in good weather, nicer than most parks with its raked gravel walks and huge trees where the light fell down in patches and you could have a private talk.

"I'll just say hello," Hilda said when they got to the parental graves. It was a long hello and a teary-eyed goodbye since she didn't get there often, and Gladdie had a few sad moments, too, staring at the mounds of fresh earth where the new bodies had recently been stored and thinking about Johnnie being buried underground across the sea, the other side of the world. She turned away and looked up through the leafy branches, not exactly considering heaven, but at least avoiding earth until Hilda finally got her visit done and she could broach the idea she'd been hatching. Would Hilda like to go west? To save Hilda's pride, she said it would be as her paid companion.

"Ladies do it all the time when they travel," Gladdie said. "So as not to be alone on the train or in towns they don't know." Hilda knew Gladdie was up on ladies and what they did, as she rubbed shoulders with them daily in her job.

"Everyone wants to go west," Hilda said.

"The Land of Promise," Gladdie said.

But Hilda gave a backward look at those graves. "When are you going?" she asked.

Gladdie said: "Today." She had a good laugh then, seeing Hilda's light-filled blue eyes water from growing so big, and her spectacles steam up. Gladdie had known how the idea would please her.

Hilda laughed too. "Today!" She started skipping up the path yelling: "Today! Today!"

So there they were, the two of them, like kids, splitting their sides laughing in the cemetery.

"Whatever will I say to Mrs. Riley?" Hilda asked on the ride back.

"Leave it to me," Gladdie said.

"I'll take only the clothes you've given me," Hilda said. She was plumper and taller than Gladdie, and Gladdie had given her the bigger dresses and things ladies had discarded.

"You pack," Gladdie said. "I'll talk." And that's how it went.

Mrs. Riley had got greyer over the years and fatter, but she'd kept her vigour and she could talk the best of them under the table.

You only had to walk through the door to set her off; there was no need to think of a topic. Before Hilda joined them, Gladdie wanted to tell Mrs. Riley about her encounter with Mr. Riley, but it was hard to get a word in edgewise. Now that Mrs. Riley was older, she seemed to doubt her listener was hearing her pronouncements, or maybe she just enjoyed them so much she said most of them twice. Finally Gladdie blurted her news. "I seen Mr. Riley the other day." She knew better than use "seen" for "saw." Her reading had taught her proper grammar, and she hated how in times of excitement she still sometimes got it wrong.

Mrs. Riley drew herself up into a parody of her younger self, at the mention of Mr. Riley, and she pulled her wrapper tighter from both sides over her breasts. The very thought of Mr. Riley roused her pride. She wouldn't ask how he was, but she allowed a pause in the conversation for Gladdie to tell her.

"I believe he misses you, Mrs. Riley," Gladdie said.

"That would only be natural," was the reply. "Did I not predict he'd be sorry? He thought he was young, Gladdie. 'False dreams are your affliction,' I told him. 'False dreams are your affliction.'"

Hilda appeared then – before more could be said about Mr. Riley's, or perhaps a universal, ailment – with her hat on her head and all her possessions in a woven straw bag.

Mrs. Riley gave Gladdie her baleful look, her mother-cat-when-you've-drowned-her-kittens look. She knew it would be Gladdie who'd brought this about. She'd always known Gladdie was ungrateful. When she didn't have the upper hand, Mrs. Riley was a great one for the well-expressed silence, and she adopted it now. Hilda stammered a bit about leaving, then burst into tears.

"You did your best for me, I know," she said to Mrs. Riley. She looked ready to kneel at the woman's feet. Gladdie handed her a hanky.

"So you're off to the west," Mrs. Riley said.

Gladdie said: "We are."

"I suppose you'll take up farming," Mrs. Riley said, snorting. "Or do I mean farmers?"

"Oh, Mrs. Riley," Hilda cried.

"I do not think men like headstrong women," Mrs. Riley said to Gladdie. "Even when they're *young*." She turned to Hilda and went on: "I suppose you think some desperate bachelor will have you. My advice if you're going, Hilda, is to rouge your cheeks and swear you're twenty-five." With that Mrs. Riley rose with some difficulty from her chair, declining assistance however, and walked past them out of the parlour and heavily ascended the stairs. For the last time ever, they heard the door to her room close.

A railway station, when you're leaving town, is a different place from when you're there just watching. The fuss and bustle that had felt calming when Gladdie wasn't involved got in her way when she had to line up at the right place and purchase the right fare to their destination. Hilda had never been to the station before, so she was no help. "Oh, Gladdie," she said, over and over. Then Gladdie lined up first at the wrong wicket. One thing she did wrong, and all Hilda's faith in her vanished. The whole enterprise nearly fell to pieces. Finally Gladdie asked her to sit down and let her see to it. She left her with the luggage, which luckily was only their two small bags and one tin box with a handle. She could see what trouble it would be travelling with trunks like some were.

They had only two hours to wait before their train went, if they went first class. Otherwise it would be a few days before they could get tickets – so they went first class. "You're lucky, at that," the ticket agent said. Gladdie knew it would be a hard time for Hilda, waiting, as it was, and she'd have to talk her out of second thoughts. She sat beside her, watching people, trying to keep Hilda interested in them by guessing what Mrs. Riley would have said about them if she'd been there to comment on each one, and thinking, in the spaces between likely candidates for discussion, about Jessie Dole, and the one day they'd sat in Union Station, and about all the times she'd met Johnnie there. She almost came to the point of telling Hilda her real reason for going west, but she didn't know what Hilda would think of her. She wasn't sure what she'd think of the whole thing herself, if the shoe was on the other foot and Hilda was travelling west to watch over a girl just because she'd said long ago that she would. But she squared her shoulders after thinking that. She wasn't going west because she was an old maid with no child of her own. She was answering a petition in a pair of eyes.

When it was finally time to board, they walked to the tracks in the lofty glass-roofed halls behind the waiting rooms, and found their train, with its locomotive all black and gleaming.

"It's huge," Hilda said. Shaky.

"Mr. Riley brought me here one time," Gladdie said. "I grabbed onto him, I can tell you, when the first train came into the yard, screeching and blowing steam and smoke."

"I never met Mr. Riley," Hilda said as if she'd have to go back and live her life again to have any satisfaction from it.

"You didn't miss a thing," Gladdie said to cheer her, though she wished right afterward she hadn't said it.

Hilda went ahead with her bag and the box to find their seats, but Gladdie felt such a thrill the moment she set her foot on that narrow metal step, she couldn't go on. She made it to the doorway and then turned around. She set her valise down and grinned out at the other trains on the tracks and the big station arches and all the people milling about. She'd seen another woman down the train do that, but the other woman was waving at someone. Gladdie had no one to wave to, but she didn't care. This was the life. This was her life that she was living.

"Gladdie, do you think we're too old to be having such fun?" Hilda asked. They were sitting in a plush booth in the dining car with their reflections beside them; they were eating roast beef and drinking red wine. "People are looking at us," Hilda said.

"They wish they were us."

"No."

"Yes."

"Really?"

"Yes, and you know why? Because we're having fun."

"What would Mrs. Riley say?"

"I don't know. But I'm glad she isn't here, for she'd drink all the wine."

Quite a lot of Gladdie's savings were going to the CPR, but she was thankful they were in the better class, especially after they'd strolled through the train and seen the colonists' cars. People were crowded on wooden benches or hunkered over the food they'd brought, trying to cook meals over a tiny stove.

"Do you think the colonists thought we were ladies in our Shaunessey dresses?" Hilda asked.

"Till we opened our mouths, maybe," Gladdie said. They'd gone back to their seats for the tin box Gladdie had packed with meat pies and good sandwiches and cherries, which were just in season. They'd carried the food through two of the colonists' cars, distributing it to anyone who put a hand out.

"Wasn't it strange, giving out that food?" Hilda said. Gladdie agreed. It had been strange.

"Charity," Hilda said. "I haven't been on this side of it before. I like it better being the giver, but I wish we could all travel the same."

Gladdie and Hilda agreed about everything, till along came the nuisance.

"May I sit with you?"

The question startled them both, and they looked up from examining their menus. Gladdie had been thinking her own thoughts, which centered on Orillia Cooper and what she must be like now. She'd be sixteen and a half, a little more than that, not as old as Jessie Dole was when she gave birth to her, but approaching that age, and it might be that now at last she'd look like her mother. It was an old man who'd spoken, with white hair in his nostrils and his hat in his hand.

"I'm afraid all the tables are full," he said. "But if I'm interrupting?"

"Do sit down, please," Hilda said.

Hilda sounded quite the lady, Gladdie thought, and she was happy to have the company, too, a lot happier than Gladdie was. As for him, he was as pleased as punch, you could tell, looking from one of them to the other while he told them about himself. He was a diversion, anyway, and the scenery had been getting boring. They'd stopped even looking out the window since there was nothing to see but rocks and trees. And maybe Gladdie wasn't always the best company. She was getting anxious as they approached the west, excited but worried, too, not knowing what she'd find.

After Hilda's enthusiastic reception, the old fellow came and sat with them for every meal. The country rolled by, slowly.

"You're stopping too soon," he told them. "You should stay on the train. There's nothing on the prairies. You couldn't find a poorer place in the nation than Saskatchewan."

"He has twenty-five years on us," Gladdie complained that night in the bunk over Hilda's. "And he keeps saying 'So you're going to be homesteaders' in a way that shows he thinks we aren't."

"But we aren't," Hilda said.

"I just don't want everybody and his aunt knowing our business," Gladdie said. "And Hilda, don't encourage him. He'll be embarrassing us both. He'll ask us both to marry him if we don't look out."

"Oh, Gladdie."

"Why else is he always on about Vancouver? 'You'd like Vancouver' – you've heard him, Hilda, then he peers from one to the other of us, trying to gauge which of us would like it best."

"You sound just like Mrs. Riley," Hilda said, ending that conversation.

Gladdie's plan, the part she'd told Hilda about, had been simple: they were going to set up a boarding house in Regina. It was what they both knew, and maybe – if it looked like the city could bear it – it would be a house for ladies only. "But only if there's moneyed ladies," Gladdie said, talking into the hotel mirror while she did her hair up and fastened her finery on. "Otherwise you're better off with men. They have better incomes and they aren't so fussy."

Hilda agreed. She was as keen as Gladdie was for the two of them to work together.

"Partners," Gladdie said. She was relieved they'd made it to Regina and left the old coot who'd latched onto them on the train, and there were just the two of them again.

"But I've nothing to contribute," Hilda said. "We can't be partners."

"Money's all you mean," Gladdie said. "And no wonder you haven't any, having received so pitiful little from Mrs. Riley." She pinned a maple leaf broach to her light summer jacket. Her maple leaf pins always reminded her of the day Mrs. Dole had come in with a ruby red leaf in the buttonhole of her lapel. That had been such an unexpected thing for her to do; it must have been a good day. Gladdie's jacket was yellow, her skirt was green. She grinned at herself in the mirror because now that they were in Saskatchewan she just knew everything was going to turn out well.

Hilda had already dressed. It hadn't taken her long since she had no jewellery to put on. She sat on the bed watching Gladdie with her arms folded and her head on one side. Gladdie could see her stillness behind her own quick movements as she jabbed and pinned herself together. Hilda wasn't a bit jealous, and that meant Gladdie was free to enjoy the bedecking. She picked up a little gold scarf pin with a horseshoe at the end. "This is for you," she said.

Hilda didn't want to take it, but Gladdie said, "I've had such good luck already, just getting here. Now we're to be partners, you need some too."

Hilda took the pin and traced the horseshoe with her fingertip, but she still looked serious.

"My savings amount to no more than would keep me a week, Gladdie."

"It's partners or nothing. There's more than money goes into a venture. There's your work and your support you're putting in."

Hilda threaded the pin through the material of her blouse, then she smiled at Gladdie, her nice soft smile that could take you by surprise, there was so much knowing in it. You'd almost think she knew their partnership was only one of Gladdie's plans. Gladdie hadn't said a word about the Coopers to Hilda, and she didn't intend to now, since she didn't know what she wanted to do about them. She thought she'd just place them before she settled, make sure they were living in Aquadell, and see the girl was fine. She had the feeling she should walk about with Hilda, get to know the city a little, stay until Hilda knew her way around, but having got so far she couldn't – she just couldn't – wait any longer. She kept thinking the Coopers might vanish. They were in the town called Aquadell this morning, but they might not be there tonight. Today might be the very day they were picking up and leaving for parts unknown, and she might never locate them again.

She turned back to the mirror to put her hat on. "Hilda," she said, "I have to leave you for a bit."

"What did you say?"

"There's something I have to do, on my own."

She tried to concentrate on her hatpin, getting it in just right, but she could see Hilda, behind her, sitting on the edge of the bed with her mouth open.

"Before I can go on with my plans," Gladdie said, "there's something I have to do. I'll have to be away overnight."

"But can't I come with you?"

They were talking to one another through the mirror. Gladdie knew it was craven of her, but she kept on pretending she couldn't get her hat just right. She caught sight of the enamel bird on the tip of her hatpin. She had to fly to them; she couldn't hold back; there wasn't a moment to lose. She clipped another maple leaf pin to her belt to add to her own good luck and turned and faced Hilda.

"No, you can't come with me," she said. "I'm sorry. This is private."

Hilda said, "Oh," as if Gladdie had hit her.

"I'll be right back. One night is all I'll stay away. The room and board's paid for the week."

"What if something happens to you?" Hilda said.

"For pity's sake. Look, Aquadell's the name of the town. And if anything happens to me, all I own is in my valise. You come claim it. Hilda, there's no need to worry."

She left the hotel feeling she had much to put up with. The morning was fresh as daisies; anybody would be fine on her own, exploring a new place on such a day, she told herself. And what would it be like to live the way Hilda did, expecting something bad to happen at every turn? But by the time she reached the station, she was sorry. It was all very well to be impatient, but Hilda had looked frightened.

"The train don't go to Aquadell," the agent said. He took his cigarette out of his mouth after he spoke and cleared the tobacco off his tongue.

"How will I get there?"

"Most folks take the train to Bragg's Butte and catch the mail-carrier's wagon."

"Can I reach Aquadell before evening?"

"Don't see how."

"How long does it take?"

It took two days, each way. She couldn't face Hilda and tell her she'd be away three nights at least. "I need to send a telegram," she said. Then she paced the platform outside while she waited for the train.

a key to the bedrooms

Orillia heard Hilda out in the hall and got up from her bed, using the crutch that lay waiting there. She was supposed to be learning to walk with an old lady cane, but there would be plenty of time for the cane later. Once she started using it, there would be the rest of her life. The right cast had come off, not as triumphantly as the left.

"I'm afraid this foot won't be as much of a success as the other," Dr. Kitely had said beforehand. He was obviously worried about how bad it might be, and it was a pitiful sight, even to Orillia who refused to be sentimental about such a vulgar thing as a foot. She had felt sorry for him, seeing him distressed, but Mrs. Kitely had blunted her sympathy with her own brand of blue-eyed realism, and just thinking about her afterwards revitalized Orillia.

"Hilda? Is there a key for my room?" she asked.

"A key for your room?" Hilda said. She took off her glasses and rubbed her eyes.

"Yes. There's a keyhole in the door. Mr. Best has a key. I thought I must have one too."

"Mr. Best doesn't want his work disturbed."

"I'm working too. I've started keeping a journal." Keeping a journal – if she had been doing so – didn't seem, even to Orillia, to be any great qualification for the possession of a key to lock her room, but after all it was her room. Even if they hadn't let her pay board yet, she should have the same privileges as any lodger.

Hilda went to the bureau in the hall, rummaged in a drawer and came up with a pretty little iron key. So it had been there all along, while she'd been trying to get up the nerve to ask for it, all those days she'd listened to Mr. Best typing and wondered what he was saying about her, all those afternoons he'd left the house and tightly locked his door. Hilda handed it over to Orillia cautiously, as if by doing so she was making some point, for of course she'd know, as Orillia had supposed, that one key would open all doors. But it didn't matter. That very afternoon she and Gladdie took Susan shopping.

All was neat in his room, as before, the bed unrumpled, the desk with the typewriter centred. To the left the stack of clean paper, to the right, on the blotter, the inkstand and the fountain pens waiting for his changes. The wastebasket was empty, and the photograph of his family was missing. She opened the top drawer of his desk and found it, neatly stashed away. Briefly she wondered why he'd wanted them out of his sight. She opened the deep drawer where she'd discovered his manuscript the last time, and it was there – and much augmented. "In Mrs. Wintergreen's House," it was called. She hadn't noticed a title page before; perhaps he'd only lately named the novel. She pulled the swollen manuscript out of the drawer. It was a huge stack of – she looked to the end – two hundred and ninety-one pages. Clutching it to her chest, she turned and faced the door, almost expecting to see him there, watching her with a sardonic, satisfied expression. For a moment she wavered, but she'd gone too far. It would be pathetic to back down now.

It will likely bore me to tears, she thought as she locked his door.

She set the manuscript at the head of her bed and plumped her pillows over it. She might have begun to read it. She was certainly curious to know what he'd written about her, but she wouldn't have progressed far; there wasn't time before the others would return. She preferred to settle with the tome after she'd retired for the night. She went down to the garden and picked some of Hilda's second set of lettuce and a cucumber to make a little salad for their supper, feeling domestic but stirred up, like a woman wearing an apron and no underclothes.

By the time the others came home, she'd made the salad dressing and set the table for supper. She had peeled potatoes and left them sitting in cold water. She didn't know what else she could do to hurry the meal.

Hilda slapped a brown paper package down on the counter. "Pork chops," she said.

"Do you want carrots with that? I could scrape them," Orillia offered. No wonder nothing happened in this house, she thought. So much time was spent getting meals and cleaning up after them, there was hardly time left over to live. She wondered if Hilda ever realized that, if she ever resented all the work she did to keep herself and others fed.

But Hilda was grateful. So maybe she had noticed. "And the potatoes already done," she said. She put them on to boil and got out the cast iron pan for the meat before she took off her hat.

Slowly, supper and the evening passed, and earlier than usual Orillia slipped up to her room and closed the door, to be alone for the night. There, under her pillows, the novel lay, waiting. Not that she cared one whit what Mr. Best thought about her. Still, she readied herself for bed quickly and quietly, and at last sat up against her pillows with the manuscript on her lap, and read.

Just as Mr. Best had taken her aback whenever they'd met, so his novel was not what she'd expected. How far it was from her expectations took some time to discover. It opened, as she knew from her earlier perusal of its first chapters, as innocuously as – well – as a young woman gathering salad ingredients in a garden. Tea trays formed a prominent motif. Gladdie and Hilda were immediately recognizable. A child, not recognizable as Susan or as any real child, but more like a small cipher, lived in the house. No man sat in a room writing. Only the women and the child lived in the house, walked through its rooms and the garden and spoke to one another about the weather and the temperature of their tea. Really, it was awfully boring and she read quickly, skipping whole paragraphs, until Miss Carter appeared, and then it was gratifying to see how the story changed. She settled back against her pillows, smiling. It wasn't just her imagination; the language now was much more charged, even portentous.

The story, and the language, changed again when, as she'd predicted, a man moved into the house, but this time she didn't smile. She set the manuscript down on her lap. She looked around her quiet, empty room, lit not quite to the corners by her bedside lamp. She'd never read such prose before, that mingled titillation and dread. It seemed unsafe to read on. She picked up the top page and held it gingerly and read to the bottom. The next, and the next, she read like that, turning them face down afterwards on the growing pile beside her on the bed. She was ready at any moment to stop. But something was going on in the house. She looked to the wall that separated her room from Mr. Best's. The child knew everything that was going on; the women knew. Only Miss Carter, who was young for her age, and innocent – how she hated the man – knew nothing.

She was depraved. She must be to read on, sick at her own fascination. She set a limit. She would stop as soon as the man had lured Miss Carter into his room. After that, she set a new limit. She would stop if Miss Carter returned to his room. She would stop if they did anything really dirty. Really ugly. Really monstrous.

She did stop before she finished the pages he'd added in the last days, the days he'd been greeting her in the hall with his knowing smile. She stopped when she reached a description of the man in the empty bedroom listening to Miss Carter, next door, who, now that she'd been inflamed by him, now that her sexual urges had been aroused by him, was practicing the art he'd taught her, practicing it alone and audibly.

"The bed rocking..." she read and dropped the pages she'd been holding.

Light was already seeping through her curtains, and she couldn't sit, immobile, unthinking, for more than a few indulgent minutes. She had to be grateful she had the presence of mind to take the manuscript back to its place in his room before he arrived.

Mr. Best came to the house at his usual hour and bounded up the stairs to his room. Full of energy this morning, he began typing almost at once. Orillia threw off her blankets. She hadn't slept since returning to her bed, and there was no hope of sleep now. She buttoned herself together and pinned up her hair. She didn't want to face Gladdie and Hilda – what would they see in her eyes? But before she knew it, she found herself downstairs. She found herself standing in the pantry, between the main hall and the kitchen, where Gladdie and Hilda were laughing. They were looking out the kitchen window, both of them, leaning with their elbows on the counter and their backsides toward her. They hadn't heard her coming downstairs because they were laughing so hard; they were laughing in spurts, first one, then the other, feeding one another's enjoyment. Were they laughing at her? Did they know? Because they'd heard her too? The bed rocking – they'd heard her throughout the house? Stop it, she told herself. They have nothing to do with this. And really, it seemed they lived in another world from the one she'd been inhabiting.

The back door opened and let in a swath of brilliant autumnal light, and Susan slipped into the kitchen, carrying her baby doll in the crook of her elbow. Orillia remembered a scene early in Mr. Best's novel in which the child walked downstairs in the morning with her baby doll dragging behind her, and the naive Miss Carter heard its limp body banging on each step and felt dread without knowing why. How asinine it seemed now, in the morning light.

Nothing like Mr. Best's child, but rather like one of the docile children in a Hurlbut's illustration (The Wise Child Questions her Elders), Susan put her head to the side, waiting for the women's attention.

"Well, Susie Q," Gladdie said, wiping the tears from her face.

"Dear Susie Q," Hilda said, and the hanky came out from her sleeve. Her whole face was wet with perspiration as well as tears.

Susan wagged her finger at them, so they reined themselves in and sobered their faces.

"Oh, Orillia," Hilda said, when she saw her watching them. "Susan was being so funny. She was chasing butterflies again and darting this way and that all over the garden like a butterfly herself."

"That's not what you said," Gladdie said.

"No, it's true," Hilda admitted. "What I said was, 'like a fart in the wind' – and she was so much like that, if you'll excuse us being vulgar, Orillia –" Hilda couldn't finish for laughing all over again.

"Ah, you can never explain a good laugh," Gladdie said, seeing Orillia's face.

Orillia tried to smile, but she made a poor job of it. "I didn't sleep well last night," she said. "I think I'll lie down on the sofa." But before she left, she said: "As for being vulgar, Hilda, you and Gladdie couldn't be that if you tried." From the looks on their faces, you might have thought that, of all the times she'd tried to unsettle them, this was her best attempt.

She lay down on the sofa in the parlour, though it wasn't much better than being in her room. She could hear the typewriter above her clacking. She was nearly vaporous with fatigue, but she knew she wouldn't go back to sleep. A shaky power coursed through her. She could kill someone, she thought, in this state – and she knew who it would be.

an excursion

Mr. Best said, "I wonder if Mrs. Wutherspoon would allow me to arrange an excursion. A treat for the little girl." He had in mind a picnic. He thought he'd hire a wagon to take them out to a pretty spot called White Butte. He asked if Orillia had been there.

"No," she said. She looked at her shoes so he couldn't tell she hated him.

"I think you would like it."

"Yes," she said. She put her blank face on and looked right up at him. She'd already figured out how to cook his goose.

"I'll ask Mrs. Wutherspoon, then?"

"Yes."

"What do you think?" Hilda said. "Mr. Best has invited us all on a picnic. A treat. For Susan." She beamed. All her umbrage against him was not forgotten, but she thought she might have exaggerated his misdemeanours. "Now, what will we take to eat?"

Sausage rolls, fried chicken, potato salad, celery sticks, cucumber pickles, bean pickles, cornbread, chocolate cupcakes, butter tarts and lemonade. There was so much to do to get ready you had to hope the picnic could be stretched to fill one-tenth of the preparation time. They all pitched in. Even Susan folded napkins and sliced pickles.

Gladdie said she wouldn't go with them, which didn't surprise Orillia. A minute was more than Gladdie wanted of Mr. Best's company. "Oh, Gladdie," Hilda said, looking stricken. "Susan will be disappointed."

"She won't mind," was all Gladdie would say. And when they left the next morning and Gladdie sent them off, Susan showed no signs of dimmed expectation. She was as complaisant as usual.

Mr. Best had arranged for the driver to take them out and wait for their return. It was a fine, clear day; even the weather fit in with the man's plans. As they trundled through the city, Mr. Best thought it incumbent on him to point out all the rebuilding that was going on as well as several other things they could see for themselves. The wagon creaked and swayed as accompaniment to his oration, the horses jostled one another, Susan grinned and Hilda beamed like the sun. Eventually they took a country road that turned into a trail through unbroken grassland. A mile or so on they came to a place where trees grew, and they clambered down from the wagon. Mr. Best said they'd walk as far as Orillia was able. Paths had been made through the trees and brush on that surprising bit of landscape where the prairie buckled, then sloped down to a pond.

As soon as they started, they were transported as if to another land. "Enchanting," Hilda called it, and even Orillia felt the setting's charm. Although they were well into September, tiny yellow daisies, with heads like clocks no bigger than fingernails, bloomed along the paths. The daisies had blue-green leaves almost as silvered as the sage that grew beside them in tufts higher than their knees. The beaded fronds waved in the breeze and broadcast their prairie smell. Almost all the plants and shrubs at White Butte had a silvered, ashy cast. Above them the aspen saplings shook their round, silvery leaves, and over the saplings the grown aspens, most of them half or fully denuded, reached their bare, crooked black and white arms to an intense blue sky. Mr. Best, an authority on everything, identified chokecherry bushes, wolf willow, goldenrod and delicate blue harebells on thin grass stems. Susan went first along the paths, swinging a lard pail like a little trooper. Hilda followed, carrying the other pail and a blanket, then came Orillia, carrying nothing because she was using her crutches. Mr. Best, bearing the picnic basket, brought up the rear.

As they strolled along the trail and the sun grew warmer, Mr. Best's presence behind Orillia grew more and more apparent. She knew his eyes were on her waist and hips while she walked in front of him – lurched in front of him. She kept her back straight.

On they walked, with the sun hot, now, on their backs, making them feel languid. The dirt thinned to dust under their feet, and the grass on either side of them parted in the light breeze and lay before them in stripes of many colours. A tan and buff swallowtail with chocolate spots that flashed like dark eyes accompanied them for a while. Orillia stopped at the sight of a dead frog. Luckily, Susan and Hilda had passed by without seeing the thing. Its skin had been stripped off, pulled right over its head by a passing boot or hoof. Its iridescent blue and red body glistened like the underside of a tongue. It's been degloved, Orillia thought and the technical term, her knowing it, helped her to overcome her first response, which was horror. Revulsion. A too-implicated pity.

"It's life," Mr. Best said pompously, looking down at her side.

"Oh yes," she said. "I know. One moment you're hopping down a pretty path, the next your skin's torn off." She did not look to see his reaction. The frog was dead, thank goodness; they didn't have any responsibility to end its misery. Mr. Best tried to take her elbow and guide her past it and on along the path, but she pulled away. Up and down, from then on, he stayed beside her, until they descended into dappled shade.

Ahead, Hilda had found the perfect spot and was spreading the blanket. They sat for their picnic as if they were all imperturbable, as if nothing more than a breeze would ever ruffle them. They had tins and packages and the bottle of lemonade to open; they had pickles and sausage rolls to pass to one another. They had pleases and thank yous to say. After they ate, Mr. Best lounged back with his elbows on the blanket and sighed while the women occupied themselves in wrapping up all the leftover food. Susan went exploring, never out of sight. The women watched the pink dress flit between the trunks of the aspens while the leaves whispered overhead – shush, shush – as if Susan had to be told.

The entire picnic played itself out quietly but for a background of crickets' constant shrill song, never varying and pitched a little too high for human comfort. Then they packed up the basket and picked up the blanket and went home.

Two people stood in the doorway when they pulled up to the house, Gladdie and someone else, a woman in a black dress. For a moment, from the distance, Orillia thought it was her mother. Then, of course, she knew who it was.

Mr. Best's face lost all its colour. He went quite bloodless.

Gladdie had been polishing Hilda's silverware that she'd inherited from Mr. Wutherspoon's mother. She'd been rubbing the tarnish off the knives and forks and spoons, getting her cloth black, and remembering that Orillia had commented once about her liking to clean things. It was true it was a satisfaction to her to hold up a shiny spoon that had been dull and dirty the minute before. "I bet you like doing laundry," Orillia had said. Gladdie did like doing laundry, but she hadn't just then wanted to admit it. "What do you like doing?" she'd asked instead, and poor Orillia, before she could turn her head away, had blushed right to the roots of her hair.

Gladdie was half through the silverware by the time Mrs. Best came to the door like Tragedy in her black dress, and insisted on coming in. Gladdie brought her into the parlour where she sat on the edge of the sofa, looking ready to explode. Gladdie didn't sit down. Whatever this was about, she figured they needed cups and saucers between them. "I'm going to put the kettle on," she said.

"Sit down," Mrs. Best said. "I don't want tea. Or leave if you want. I don't care."

Mrs. Best got up and started walking all around the room. How pretty she was, in the same shabby black dress, grayed at the seams, she'd worn before – that never was good and was only ever pathetic in its cheap attempt to be in style. "Is she here?" she said.

"Who?"

"I don't know her name."

"I'm here alone," Gladdie said.

"Is he with her? Now?"

Gladdie said, "It's just an excursion they've all gone on, with the little girl."

Mrs. Best said, "He has little girls of his own." She paced about the room. "I'll kill her," she said. She hadn't meant to say it, Gladdie could tell, but she put on defiance to cover up. She sat down on the sofa again and folded her hands in her lap. "I will," she said. "I'm going to. And then I'll kill him."

"Mrs. Best," Gladdie said.

The poor woman's cheeks were flushed red, as if they'd been set alight, and her breathing came so fast and shallow Gladdie feared she'd faint. Then the tears rained down. She didn't put her hands up or try to hide her crying. She sat there clutching her knees, her body shaking.

"My name's Gladdie," Gladdie said after a minute, when the sobs had lessened. "In all the fuss the other time when you were here, what with the little girl being lost, we didn't get introduced."

Mrs. Best started to giggle and cry at the same time. "Oh how *do* you do?" she said.

"What's your name?"

"Kate." Now she wiped at the tears with her fingers. "I'm quite in control again, thank you," she said. She had her hankie out and dabbed at her cheeks. She said, "I got a letter. From someone in this house. An anonymous letter. Maybe it was from you?"

"No," Gladdie said. "It wasn't from me."

Mrs. Best wasn't at all in control again, as far as Gladdie could see. She'd got more agitated, if anything. Her face was all transparent and red again.

They heard the wagon at the same time, as it drew up before the house. Mrs. Best jumped to her feet. "They're here," she said. "Good."

She went to the door, out through the verandah, and stood on the top step. Gladdie came up behind her and smelled the sharp smell of the woman's sweat. She seemed to make the steps shake, there was that much tension in her. Mr. Best had seen her from the street and was gaping at her, white-faced. He climbed down from the wagon to the sidewalk and helped Hilda and Susan down. Orillia stood alone in the wagon, waiting, leaning on her crutches. You could see the walk had tired her. The horse shuddered and stamped and the driver yelled. The whole cart rocked. Orillia jerked, but she didn't fall. She balanced herself quickly, gracefully, as if she'd learned to walk on moving wagons, with crutches. She kept her head high, waiting, but she looked thin to Gladdie, and all too breakable, standing there alone.

"Kate," Gladdie said. "Get your husband to take you home."

The driver helped Orillia down from the wagon.

Mrs. Best took her time going down the steps, down the path, and when she met her husband she took his arm and walked him back to the house.

"Don't come in," Gladdie said to the others. "We'll go for a walk in the park."

Orillia, with a sigh, set out immediately down the sidewalk, with Susan skipping beside her. Hilda dropped behind to walk with Gladdie. "I knew something like this would happen," she said. Hilda was provoked, and who could blame her? She was being kept from her own house in the heat of the afternoon.

As soon as they got to the park Susan drifted to the edge of the lake to watch a pair of ducks. Then Hilda said to Orillia, "This is what comes of your shenanigans. The way you've been behaving, you and Mr. Best. Now look what's happened. You've got his poor wife upset. And with reason. You've set yourself up as a home wrecker." The sweat rolled down the sides of Hilda's face, and she flushed so pink she seemed to give off heat.

Orillia didn't look at all offended, but she started walking away, along the path by the lake, back toward the house. Gladdie hurried after her. "You can't go home," she said. "Not right now. In case they're still talking."

"Oh, they'll be gone by now. I'm going home," she said. "I'm tired."

Off she went and Gladdie thought: You don't have a home. And that was the whole problem.

"You must be disappointed in that girl," Hilda said as they watched Orillia make her way back to the houses. She was far too angry to hold her tongue.

Disappointment wasn't a feeling about other people Gladdie had ever felt she had a right to, yet it wasn't far from what she felt just then about Hilda. "Why did you write to Mrs. Best?" she asked.

Hilda said, "I did no such thing."

"She said she had a letter telling her there was something going on between Mr. Best and someone in the house."

"But I didn't – I'd never have done that. Gladdie, how could you think I'd do such a thing?"

"It wasn't you? Then who was it?" A suspicion entered Gladdie's mind then that the letter might have been written by Orillia herself, but she couldn't see why in the world the girl would have done it.

Hilda said, "Do you know, I wonder if she didn't write it herself. Thinking if the truth was out he'd leave his wife and children. But really, she's very immature, isn't she? Just as likely she got afraid. Thought she was getting more than she bargained for."

"I don't know, Hilda. I don't understand at all why she'd do it."

The ducks had swum away from Susan, and she came over to Gladdie and Hilda, her eyes full of concern.

Gladdie said, "Sometimes people are unhappy. You know that, don't you, Susan?"

"I have to sit," Hilda said. She sank down on a bench by the path, and Gladdie sat with her, with Susan in between. For some time they stared at the Tyndall stone glory of the legislative building across the little lake.

In the morning, very early, Mr. Best arrived at the house with a man and a trunk. The man was to help him carry the trunk down the stairs and to drive him away. The trunk was to hold the personal contents of his room: his Underwood typewriter, a box of bond paper, a manuscript, his fourteen-carat gold-nibbed fountain pens, several bottles of ink, a package of blotters and his gilt-framed photograph of his wife and children. Orillia didn't witness Mr. Best's arrival or his departure. She kept to her own room.

They took almost no time packing Mr. Best's possessions, almost no time carting them down the stairs and away. No one went to bid him goodbye. Later, passing his open door, Orillia saw that he'd left a stained blotter on the desk pad, but it was a forgetting of little consequence since not a single word could be deciphered from the faint shadows of authorship that remained.

At the breakfast table Orillia expressed her doubts that he'd seek another writing place outside his home.

"All those children will disrupt him," Hilda said.

"So perhaps he'll write no more," Orillia said. "Yes, I expect he'll get himself more productively employed in an office downtown." She was pleased to envision Mr. Best, in a stouter, greyer form than the one she knew, miserably hunched over a littered desk. "Where he'll work at figures instead of words. And wear a green shield to keep the light from his eyes."

Having the choice of speaking to Gladdie or to Hilda's back, Orillia had chosen Gladdie, but even Gladdie ignored her. She got up from the table and started searching through the cupboards for a cake tin to store the gingerbread Hilda had already tucked into the oven. Clatter, clatter. Gladdie always busied herself when she didn't like what was being said.

"It's his wife I worry about," Hilda said.

"Oh, he'll make amends," Orillia said. "He'll tell his wife he loves her. And the Mrs. – she'll take his hand, won't she? Or make some other acquiescent gesture. What do wives do, Hilda, when they want to soothe men?"

Hilda would only shake her head.

"Thinking" – Orillia went on in her arch voice (and with the picture of Mrs. Best before her, perched on his despicable knee) – "although she wouldn't say so – a wife wouldn't, would she? – that she no longer knows what love is."

Gladdie stood up with the cake tin, pried open its lid and sniffed inside. She rinsed it out and dried it and left it on the counter to air, and all the while Orillia's words darted about the kitchen looking for a place to land. Nobody was going to take them up. Neither Gladdie nor Hilda was going to say a thing. Orillia almost hummed a little tune, but that would have shown them how very happy she was to have Mr. Best out of the house, and then they'd have wondered why that was. It was something they would never find out. They just wouldn't understand. Life to them was simple and good. Oh, she knew what they were thinking through that prolonged deliberate silence: that they knew who didn't know what love is.

Since she wasn't appreciated in the kitchen, Orillia returned to her room and sat down at her dressing table. She pushed her face powder and her hairbrush and comb out of her way. She picked up her pen and dipped it into her inkwell.

"Dear Percy," she wrote. "This morning very early Mr. Best arrived at the house with a trunk and packed his possessions and took them away."

But why was she telling Percy about Mr. Best? He'd never met the man. Yet she wanted to tell him, not about Mr. Best, really, only the important thing: this morning he'd left the house.

moral improvement

Orillia dressed carefully in her finest white blouse and her black skirt. She'd washed her hair the day before and curled it, and she thought it looked better than usual. She thought she looked competent and fey and ready for her future, like a governess about to be discovered by the squire at a garden party. And the others had gone downtown shopping, leaving her alone. And the sun was shining, and there was almost no wind. You could hardly find a leaf stirring. So this was the morning for the call.

Mr. Best lived in a good neighbourhood, with houses considerably grander than Hilda's, across the creek, but Orillia didn't take much notice of her surroundings on the way there. She didn't think about her mission either. She concentrated on viewing her cane as a stylish accessory and her limp as an exotic attribute, like paleness, for example. When she reached Mr. Best's corner, she loitered there, waiting for Mr. Best to appear. She'd come early, just before the time he'd usually arrived at Hilda's, and habit turned out to be a good predictor. He emerged from the house only a few minutes later. Really, he was quite fat. He lit his pipe on the doorstep, puffed on it a couple of times as an aid to deep thoughts, and then set off. Even his walk was arrogant, hateful, but at least he was walking away, toward downtown, not toward her.

Mrs. Best came to the door in an apron, with a little boy at her side. Orillia barely saw the child, who clung to his mother and popped his thumb into his mouth. She did note, just before it disappeared, that the thumb was the pinkest, most appealing and definitely cleanest part of him. Mrs. Best looked prettier this morning but tired and not at all happy.

"I've come to explain." Orillia said.

"Don't," the woman said.

"I wrote that note to you. It wasn't true."

Without so much as a change of expression, Mrs. Best closed the door in Orillia's face. Orillia hadn't expected such short shrift. She hesitated, wondering if she should knock again. Then she heard someone coming up the walk behind her and knew before she turned it would be him.

"Haven't you caused enough trouble?" he said. He looked enraged. And huge. He stepped right up to her, to the step below the one she was standing on, and loomed over her.

She said, "I wanted to tell your wife..."

"That you lied. To get me out of the house. I've already explained that to her."

"I didn't mean to upset her. I didn't think what it would mean to her."

"And you saw what it meant. Did I frighten you? You read my novel, didn't you? And – poor little girl, poor innocent little girl – it frightened you."

"It's disgusting. Depraved."

"What do you know about disgusting and depraved? You don't know anything about life. And you certainly know nothing about literature."

He didn't seem angry anymore. He'd pulled his superiority around him. His arrogance would save him, had saved him. It was useless talking to him, but she said, "I don't call what you wrote literature."

"Call it what you like," he said. "I don't call the way you live life. You're ignorant. You're afraid. You think anything you don't know about must be wrong. You're disgustingly, arrogantly *young*." With that he shouldered past her and went into his house.

She took her time going home. She noticed things along the way, the scent of petunias someone had planted in a bed beside their front path, the yellow leaves drifting down through the sunlight from a little elm that grew next to the street. She could walk as quickly as she ever had, now that she knew how to use the cane, and without too much of a limp. People stared at her, of course, but she didn't mind. After all, she was the victor. Mr. Best could say what he liked, she'd done exactly what she'd set out to do: she'd sent him packing.

And she'd tried to do the right thing by Mrs. Best, which showed she'd become a better person, for she certainly wouldn't have gone to that trouble in the past. She'd told Mrs. Best the truth, before she'd had the door shut in her face. Yes, she'd improved substantially in the past few weeks. She'd become quite ethical. She wondered, suddenly, if her mother had changed at all since she'd gone to San Francisco. She very much doubted it, and that was satisfying, too. Florence was likely as obtuse and defensive as ever. You wouldn't find her making any effort to apologize to anyone. But then, she hadn't had the benefit of a summer with Gladdie McConnell.

finding aquadell

Bragg's Butte was small, smaller than any place Gladdie had ever imagined before she came west, and its buildings were ramshackle and unpainted. "Wait till you see Aquadell," Mr. Welsh, the mail carrier said.

"Smaller than this?" she asked.

"Yup."

From living in the city all her life, Gladdie had a romantic idea of the country, and especially of the west. Smaller than Bragg's Butte was one thing. She sure hoped Aquadell wasn't any poorer.

Mr. Welsh didn't say much. He spoke mostly to his knees or his horses' brown rumps, and what he said was muffled by his handlebar mustache. He was a big, loose man, rough in his dress and his looks. He had sombre brown eyes in a bloodhound face that hung in folds from the bones. Gladdie thought he was sad about something, but it seemed that was only his manner. She was glad of that, and she was glad to have the time to think her own thoughts. She was on her way to Orillia Cooper. She could almost see the girl already, way ahead of the wagon, just out of real sight, the shape of her, all grown up, as if she was standing behind a window hung with a gauzy curtain. To the right of that window her own hand hovered, ready to pull the curtain back.

And no wonder she thought she could see all the way to Aquadell. The prairie put nothing but space in her way. She and Mr. Welsh rocked along side by side over the roughest stretches you could call roads, between miles of land spun out flatter than the roads, without a single tree, anywhere, and with only now and then specks of life, little farms you could see way in the pale distance that didn't get much bigger if you reached them. Whenever they came near to one of the farms, men stopped what they were doing in their fields and people ran out of their houses, if you could call them houses. Shacks were all most of them were, with a stovepipe sticking out of the roof and made of thin, unpainted lumber and tarpaper. It wasn't what Gladdie had expected of the west, where go-getters went to make their lives better.

The people all waved, friendly, and Gladdie turned around in her seat and watched them watching the wagon leaving them behind. Often it was both the farmer and his wife, and their children too, just watching as a preventative to loneliness because they might not see anybody else for days.

"You'll tire yourself out, craning your neck like that," Mr. Welsh said after a while.

They reached Aquadell in the late afternoon the next day. "Oh," Gladdie said when they drove in. It looked to her as if people had plunked down on that particular spot on the prairie without knowing why, unless it was just that they were tired of going on. Some of them didn't even have houses and were staying in tents. The only road was the one leading into town and away. The only sidewalks were single-file dirt paths in the grass where people walked between their tents or their shacks. A double trail worn in the grass from wagon wheels was the one poor excuse for a street. It meandered for about the length of a block between a row of shacks with false fronts. And that was Main Street. The population, Mr. Welsh said, was thirty-eight. The biggest building was the livery barn.

Mr. Welsh took Gladdie to a tiny house where she could get supper and a bed for the night.

"Are all of them wanting to stay, too?" she asked. Ten or twelve people were leaning against the walls of the little house or talking in front.

"Waiting for their mail. This is the post office." He helped her down from the wagon, then hauled out the sack of mail.

Everybody nodded or said hello to them as they passed on their way to the door with Gladdie scanning their faces, half fearful in case she should accidentally, unprepared, see the one she was seeking.

Mr. Welsh shepherded her inside, where another dozen people were sitting on every chair and stool and apple box. The room, which was kitchen and sitting room and post office combined, was so crowded everyone's elbows and knees touched. Of the bunch there were two young girls, one too blonde to be Orillia Cooper and the other too big.

"This is Mrs. Knelson," Mr. Welsh said when a pleasant-faced, fair-haired woman rose to greet them. "That's Nelson with a silent K in front," Mr. Welsh said.

"Em," Mrs. Knelson said, smiling at Gladdie. "That's M with a silent E in front."

Maybe it was an old joke between them, but Gladdie liked it and she took to Em Knelson right away.

"Miss Gladdie McConnell," Mr. Welsh announced to the others.

"You'll meet them one by one as I hand out the mail," Em said to Gladdie. She'd noticed how Gladdie was examining them all.

Gladdie thought everything about Em was nice. She had a once-willowy figure that was now, in her mid-forties, getting pear-shaped. That made her look comfortable in her clean housedress. She had pretty turquoise eyes and crow's feet at the corners that Gladdie admired because they made her look as if she laughed a lot. Em and her husband, Halvor, did laugh a lot, Gladdie discovered. They laughed so much they looked alike, both of them with attractive lines etched into their tans, and quick smiles that mirrored one another. It was as easy to talk to them as it was to sit up, later, to their homemade wooden table and share their baked beans.

The post office was the Knelsons' only income and it wasn't much, as Jim Welsh hauled the mail in only twice a week. The year before, Halvor had fallen from a grain elevator, and he couldn't work anymore, though he could still walk, after a fashion. They were pleased to have Gladdie's fifty cents for her bed and meals.

Em and Halvor were people who noticed things, and after supper they noticed Gladdie was restless. Halvor gave Em a nod as soon as the dishes were done, and she took Gladdie's arm and said they'd go for a stroll around the makeshift little town. Gladdie had told them she'd come to Aquadell because she liked the name, so Em said she'd show her how the town came by it. She took her to a dip in the prairie, a coulee, she called it, a five-minute walk from the house. A few low shrubs filled in the shape of it, which was like a comma. The sun was starting to go down behind it, lighting the clouds with colour.

"It's so quiet," Gladdie said. "Just a bird now and then."

"Wait till you hear the coyotes," Em said with pride. "Some nights they howl till you'd think you'd lose your mind. Where are you from, Gladdie?"

Gladdie didn't want to say she was from Toronto, in case Em knew the Coopers and might tell them. "I come from back east," she said. "A town called Milton." It was the only place she could think of to name.

Em said Aquadell had sprung up only that spring. There'd been rain right before the first bunch of townspeople arrived, so there'd been water in the coulee. "Mrs. Ralph Cooper – she and her husband and daughter were in that first bunch – thought it was a pond," Em said. "She was the one who named us Aquadell, thinking this was a watery place." She laughed at the idea, then said, "Why, there's Mrs. Cooper over there, with her daughter."

It wasn't such a coincidence, in a town the size of Aquadell, that people would appear just as they were spoken of, but the surprise unnerved Gladdie. In any of the times she'd thought about seeing the girl again, she'd never imagined anything like this happening. She'd never expected a town so small, and she surely hadn't pictured Florence Cooper and Orillia strolling like this out of the blue, arm in arm, toward her. This was no view between curtains. Yet they appeared so suddenly – and they were so real, there in front of her – it almost seemed this *had* happened before, not in her imagination but in reality. She'd seen it before, the mother and daughter, arm in arm, walking toward her. It was only natural that Orillia Cooper looked enough like Jessie Dole she could have been her, come to life again. It was what Gladdie had all along foreseen. The girl had grown taller and filled out a bit since they'd left Toronto. Her curly brown hair had darkened and that made her skin look whiter, her eyes even blacker. She was wearing a cream-coloured blouse with a high neck and big sleeves and a grey skirt with a belt around her tiny waist. She was shorter and a hundred times prettier than her scrawny, big-nosed mother.

Gladdie didn't have time to think what to do. She didn't know if she looked the same as she used to, when Orillia was little and she'd shown herself to her. She didn't know if either Orillia or Florence would remember her or if Florence had even ever known about her. For Gladdie McConnell, it was a cowardly day.

"Is the store open, Em?' she asked. She knew it was; she'd seen people going in and out the door when they'd walked past. The trail wound past the coulee and over to Main Street in a circle. The fastest way there was to continue in the direction they'd been heading, away from Mrs. Cooper and her daughter, and Gladdie started walking before Em answered. She saw Em looking at her, wondering, but she couldn't meet Orillia so unprepared. She didn't know what she might do – act like a fool maybe – face to face with the girl.

On the train a couple of days later, on her way back to Regina, Gladdie started to laugh. It was happiness and relief that set her off, for the great thing was she'd seen the girl, the grown girl that had once been the little baby she'd held and fed and promised to watch over. She'd seen she was fine. The other thing that made her laugh was a storm that was putting on a big show the other side of the train window. Thunder banged and lightning struck the earth in one fury after another. The flat land with the far horizon made the perfect stage. Time and again jagged bolts split the dark sky from the clouds to the earth, some of them close enough to light up the passenger car she was sitting in. So much energy was expended and all for nothing. It was like watching a kid have a tantrum from the safe side of its mother. It was like all big dramatic acting out of things – when you were safely out of it. It couldn't live up to its own billing. It was like her trip to Aquadell. Wasn't it over? Now that she knew Orillia Cooper was fine, a young lady, all grown up and fine, what was there for her to do but know? She would go back to Regina and make her own life, her new life, there. Once a year, maybe, she'd travel to Aquadell and check on Orillia Cooper. It would be enough.

It had been raining hard for hours in Regina when Gladdie got back from Aquadell, and she'd never seen mud like it. Gumbo they called it: a wet, yellowish clay slime, thick as paste. The conductor said you could bake the cake off the soles of your boots into bowls. In the entire city there wasn't one solid place to set your foot. They had wooden sidewalks near the hotel, and they slipped and slid under her as she tried to walk on them. Then she had to cross the unpaved street. The sky was still dark, rain was still falling, just steadily now, and the thunder had moved off and rumbled in the distance.

On the way back to Regina, Gladdie had tried to think how to make it up to Hilda for leaving her for three days in that poor excuse of a hotel, square as a box, built of skeletal lumber and with a false front that fooled nobody. "Imagine it in the winter," they'd said. Their room had been plain. They'd shared the one small bed. They'd got into it polite and had woken up even more so. They'd each turned away while the other washed.

She reached the hotel, filthy, wet and hungry and found a note in the room instead of Hilda. "Mr. Wutherspoon's asked me to marry him. We've gone on to Vancouver."

"The old coot," Gladdie said aloud, and sank onto the bed to read more.

"Oh Gladdie," the note said, and she could hear Hilda saying it. "Maybe it will be my only chance."

When she went to the dresser to take off her jewellery and her sodden things, there was the horseshoe pin.

the true problem of living

For weeks Percy's letters had lain at the back of Orillia's dresser drawer. Now she remembered things about him she'd forgotten. One warm April evening during a break at a dance at Robin Hood School, several of the young people had gone for a stroll in the moonlight. The road was so lit up they'd played at walking on each others' shadows. Percy had turned and walked backwards to keep in step with hers.

She remembered the day she had driven Sam's automobile into the ditch when Percy was running alongside her in his skimpy running gear, and he'd pushed her out. And she'd sneezed and sneezed. And went away with his handkerchief.

She would wait, she decided, and read the letters in the drawer after she got his answer to the one she'd sent him.

Gladdie staggered into the kitchen behind a huge load of laundry, and Hilda rushed to help her. They set the basket down on a chair, and each took an end of the table and started folding, and Hilda asked Gladdie straight out about the letter she'd received from Aquadell that morning.

"From Em Knelson," Gladdie said. And because they were folding together in such harmony, and because she knew what Hilda wanted, she went on. "I asked her a couple of things in my last letter, and she answered them. One was how was Percy Gowan doing.

Answer: fine. The other, how was harvest coming along. Answer: finished. They finished harvesting weeks ago around Aquadell."

Neither of them could think of much to say after that. There wasn't any use in speculating what Orillia might have said to Percy to put him off, or what might have occurred in his life since he'd visited. The neat piles of laundry grew. Gladdie thought about all the things she couldn't tell Hilda that would have helped her understand Orillia's behaviour, although she wasn't sure it was all that understandable even if you knew the facts.

Hilda, observing Gladdie's closed face, thought how hard it must be for her to have to stand by and watch and never say a thing. To have no right to intervene. Poor Gladdie, how she must wrestle, every day, with the burden of that secret. Hilda didn't think she could bear it, herself. If she was Susan's mother, and couldn't let on. Forced to pretend she was only a friend, just looking out for her welfare. The very thought made her want to kneel down before the child, and gather her into her arms and never let her go. And there was Gladdie, folding tea towels and pillow slips, all squared up so neatly into stacks without an edge overlapping, so they'd sit on a shelf in the linen closet like an advertisement for good housekeeping, while her heart was bursting.

Percy had received Orillia's letter and intended to answer it soon. But it had arrived on a busy day, the very day the well diggers struck flowing water on his property at four hundred feet. Then he'd had to haul hay for his neighbours and dig turnips and put in a new slide door in the barn. Then, at three o'clock in the afternoon a couple of days later, steel reached Aquadell. It was a grand sight with crowds of people watching, and Percy had to be there. The tracklayer was a wonderful machine.

The weather having been so glorious lately, he'd gotten in some long runs. The week before, he'd jogged to the Aquadell store and met the new teacher, Miss Marjory Gooding. She was a little thing to be in charge of twelve grades, and he told her if she had any trouble with the big boys she should call on him.

Orillia had written about her fellow lodger, Mr. Best, departing. Percy had never met him, but it seemed they might all be happier in the house without him. He hoped that would be true. He was glad to hear she was beginning to go out now, and meant to tell her that. He feared it would be some time before she recovered completely from the blow dealt her by the cyclone. He'd thought of her when he read something recently, in a little handmade book of quotations his mother had sent him, this by one J. R. Miller:

> "The true problem of living is to pass unhurt *in our real characters* through the greatest trials and to have our life softened, enriched and refined by great trouble "we endure." Therefore, we have not met grief aright if we come out of it with a loss of joyousness."

He didn't think he'd include the quotation when he wrote to Orillia, although that had been his first intention. There were so many things he thought of telling her, then thought better of. The dance, for instance. It wouldn't be fair to tell her how much good fun they'd all had, when she couldn't dance anymore. The evening after the railway came to town, he'd dressed up and driven to Union Jack School to a big shindig. He hadn't got home till five in the morning. Miss Marjory Gooding, the new teacher, was the belle of the ball and the only young lady there he could care about at all. She was so sweet-natured, so good-hearted and pretty and graceful, and she danced divinely.

return to aquadell

"Life is a long walk no matter where you're headed," Mrs. Riley liked to say. She'd often made this type of statement, which made no sense to Gladdie, accompanied by an air of profundity and followed by a sage nod of her big head. But life in Regina, alone, after her glimpse of the congenial hamlet, started to look to Gladdie like a long walk to nowhere, and it wasn't many days later that, from miles away, the little collection of buildings that was Aquadell came into view again, low against the sky. Gladdie sat up from a half nap and tried to stretch the kinks out of her back and return her body to the rhythm of the wagon. As they got nearer to the town, she gave her head a shake. She thought she must be seeing things. Jim Welsh was staring straight ahead, though, and he didn't say anything so she didn't either. She just kept on looking at Aquadell in the distance, and Aquadell kept on looking as if it was moving from left to right across the horizon. It was hard to believe, but at the bottom of the sky the little matchbox buildings were jerking eastward over the land. Gladdie shut her eyes for a bit and opened them again. The town, nearer now, was still jolting along, the whole town, swaying over the prairie. The houses, the store, even the livery barn.

Gladdie said, "Mr. Welsh. Is the whole town moving?"

"Looks like it, don't it?" he said, with not a glimmer of a smile on his mournful face, though she was sure by then he must be teasing her.

As they got closer, she could see that the buildings sat on top of long skids. Horses were hitched to the skids, six or eight to each, their muscles straining to pull the buildings in short bursts over the grass. You could see the trails they'd made so far. The long, pale grass lay down where they'd passed, silky and shining. Suddenly, it was a beautiful picture, full of the colours of people's clothes as they made their way, along with their homes, under the big blue sky.

"Surveyors," Jim Welsh said sorrowfully. "Laid out the town in the wrong location. They come last week and told us about it. Then they staked out the new townsite over there. That's where the railway's coming through."

"And the whole town's moving?"

"Had to move," Mr. Welsh said. "You gotta be by the tracks."

Cellars had been dug at the new townsite, black rectangles cut into the sod. The buildings were heading for them. It was like a holiday, Gladdie thought as they drew nearer. Men were hollering exaggerated, happy commands at the horses; kids were dancing around them, shoving one another, chasing one another; women were calling to one another, laughing as they trailed behind their houses. Everyone but the littlest children and the wildest of the boys was carrying something in their arms they thought was precious – best ornaments or china or lamps – as they trudged along through the knee-high grass that was dotted here and there with daisies and other flowers.

"Hey there, Miss McConnell," some of them called.

"Gladdie," Em Knelson said, in such a warm way Gladdie hopped down from the wagon right then and there and plucked a lamp from her to carry as if she was one of the family. They were at the end of the group since Halvor had to take his time, owing to the bad leg he'd had since his fall.

"We knew you'd come back," Halvor said.

"It's like going to a picnic," Gladdie said. She followed the trail of some who were walking ahead, a path the width of a footprint. The buff-coloured grass lay tufted and bent in all directions, as soft looking as the hair on a nice dog's back.

Up ahead and to the left, Orillia Cooper was walking beside her father. She was wearing the same grey skirt she'd had on the last time Gladdie saw her, but this time with a blue blouse a shade brighter than the sky. She was carrying a pink-edged wash basin with the pitcher standing up inside it, protected from mishap with some towels. The exercise and heat had put some colour in her cheeks. She looked every bit as pretty as Jessie Dole ever had. Ralph Cooper had aged. He looked greyer and smaller than Gladdie remembered, and a lot happier. He was talking the whole time to Orillia and not paying much attention to the safety of the dishes in the box he was lugging. Mrs. Cooper walked in front of them, and beside her, striding through the high grass on a path of his own, was a great tall looker of a man with a sewing machine, complete with cabinet, in his arms.

"Captain Hagan," Em said, noticing Gladdie watching him. "His wife died last year. He came here with the Coopers." The Captain looked younger than the Coopers, and about a hundred times more energetic than poor Ralph. He had fair skin, probably fair hair, though he was clean-shaven and wore a fedora, so Gladdie couldn't really tell. What she could see was that Orillia had her eyes on him.

"Just you wait," Em said when Gladdie said it was like a holiday, the way everyone was so cheerful, and once they'd got the tents of those who were tenting erected again and the houses jacked up off the skids and hoisted onto the cellars and the outhouses onto the privy holes, and everybody had hastened to put things back on shelves, they all gathered on the new main street that the surveyors, as part of their apology, had graded. Other than the grading, Main Street, and in fact the entire little town, was an exact duplicate of the old one.

The men set up sawhorses and put planks across them. The women brought out tiny roasted prairie chickens and baked beans and hard-boiled eggs and homemade bread along with salads and preserves and pies – a pie for every person, from the looks of it. People brought their own chairs or stools outside and put them in a circle. Everybody in town was there, in that ring of chairs, so Gladdie got a good look at them all. She didn't glance too often in Orillia Cooper's direction. She didn't want to be noticed watching the girl. She could look all she wanted at the handsome man with the Coopers because he was often the centre of attention. Captain Hagan had been a hero in South Africa, fighting the Boers. He had the lightest coloured eyes and they were often looking at Orillia.

Jim Welsh came and introduced his Tessie, who looked very hot and uncomfortable and near the end of her time. Gladdie had told Jim she'd birthed a few women's babies. He said they'd pay her to help out if she decided to stay in Aquadell. The doctor lived in Bragg's Butte, a half-day's wagon ride away, and often couldn't make it to women in time. Tessie took hold of Gladdie's arm like a child that had lost its mother.

"Is it your first?" Gladdie asked.

"Lord no," Tessie said. "It'll be my sixth. That's why I'm scared." The women around her laughed, as they were meant to do.

Then Florence Cooper and Orillia were standing in front of her and Em was introducing them. Gladdie was no better prepared this time than she'd been before. The girl stuck out her hand and Gladdie took it, a cool little hand, though the evening was warm, a soft, quick shake. That was all. She had no idea who Gladdie was. No recognition that she'd ever seen her shone in those dark eyes. Nothing, just the look she'd give anyone who was new and not very interesting.

Then Florence Cooper had her hand out, and it had to be taken. Mrs. Cooper was taller than the others, taller than Gladdie by far, and gaunt, with the kind of stringent boniness you'd think must have come from the enjoyment of denying all kinds of pleasures to herself as well as others.

"Gladdie's here because of the name you gave the town, Mrs. Cooper," Em said. "She likes it."

"I'm gratified, Em." Mrs. Cooper said and then she turned and spoke to the air over Gladdie's head. "I hope you'll like the town and stay on, Miss McConnell. We're anxious to expand." She had that better-than-you graciousness Gladdie had seen before in women of her class, but then, for reasons she didn't explore, or even acknowledge, Gladdie wasn't disposed to like Florence Cooper.

Ralph Cooper came up behind his wife while she was still talking into the space over Gladdie's head, so she didn't hear him. He had a twinkle in his eyes when he peeked over her shoulder at Gladdie, as if to say: Watch this. Then he put both his hands on Mrs. Cooper's waist and hoisted her into the air, right in front of them all. "Hey!" he said with a genial chuckle, and he held her up and dangled her like an overgrown puppet. You could hardly see how he was able to do it – she was taller than he was – unless her own energetic mortification helped to lift her. He set her down a foot to the side of where she'd been standing as if to say she'd been in his way, and held his hand out to Gladdie.

"Haven't we met?" he said. He pumped her hand up and down. "Haven't we met?" he asked again, smiling into her eyes with all the warmth of an old friend.

"Ralph," Mrs. Cooper said.

"Father," Orillia said.

"Aren't you the one?" Ralph asked and his finger darted out and jabbed Gladdie's breastbone hard.

"Ralph!" Mrs. Cooper said.

But Ralph wasn't going to be deterred. He had his eyes on Gladdie; he had her stunned. "Oh, I think you are, you are the one," he said. "I saw you from a ways back, hiding behind that red hair."

Orillia, her face calm and blank, tugged him toward her. She linked her arm in his and slick as you please turned him around and walked him to their tent. He talked and laughed all the way.

"I hope Ralph didn't frighten you," Florence Cooper said to the air quite close to Gladdie's face. "I assure you he means no harm. And now," she said, riding over Gladdie's attempts to say anything at all, "I'm afraid the mosquitoes are defeating me." Off she went, and ducked under the flap that served as doorway to their tent.

In the general tsk-tsking that followed, Em said, "Don't worry about poor Mr. Cooper, Gladdie. He thinks everyone's someone he knows from somewhere else, and we're all hiding something from him."

Now that the mosquitoes were out, there was a rush to clear the makeshift tables and haul the food and the dirty dishes away. They all went in to wash up and scratch their bites. Orillia Cooper and her mother would be in their tent doing their washing up, too, Gladdie knew. Mr. Cooper would be lying down, maybe, by now, or driving them crazy in those close quarters if he wasn't. He lived a step to the side of everyone else, you could tell. Gladdie's chest hurt where he'd poked her. Inside, there was another ache she was trying to ignore, from wanting to say yes. Yes, I am the one. You do remember me.

She was going to stay in Aquadell; she knew that. This was where she was meant to be. But she didn't feel content or sure of herself. While she dried dishes, looking out Em's little window at the store and the other buildings across Main Street, the idea came to her that it had been the other town she'd been heading for when she'd set out for Aquadell again, not this new place they'd moved to but the one she'd visited first. Then she plagued herself with thinking she'd missed some chance the first town had been offering, as if in that town, if she'd faced the girl, Orillia Cooper would have known her.

Whenever Gladdie saw Orillia Cooper in the store or at Em and Hal's waiting for the mail, there'd be enough going on with other people around, it was almost the same as seeing anybody. But Orillia on her own, that was different. She looked like a girl with a head full of thoughts far away from the wooden sidewalks and the poor roads of a little Saskatchewan town. Sometimes Gladdie couldn't help thinking Orillia should know she'd come from another family. The one she was with might have been genteel, but it wasn't what anyone would call satisfactory.

The Coopers built a little house at the edge of Aquadell. Captain Hagan lived with them while his big house was under construction on his farm just out of town. As soon as that house started going up, the talk began. It was the biggest house in the district, and you didn't have to cross the street to hear the opinion that a widower would have no need for such a residence if he weren't looking for someone to share. it. When the building was done, and he moved out there, Florence Cooper went daily to keep house for him, taking Orillia along. Mrs. Cooper gave the house a name. Everyone else called it Captain Hagan's place, but she called it Fairview. "We must get to Fairview," she'd say after stopping to chat to someone on Main Street, and the response was the same, whoever it was, a twitch of the lips that when their backs were turned would become a smile. Nobody else called a house a name. Every morning with the exception of Sunday, Mrs. Cooper and Orillia walked down their street to Main Street and up its length past the general store and the post office and the new town hall and then the mile up the little rise to Sam Hagan's farm. Good weather or bad, conditions were seldom forbidding enough to stop them. The Captain, at the end of the day, drove them home in his buggy and took his dinner with them. It was all very cozy.

Then Ralph Cooper had to go to the asylum in North Battleford. Mrs. Cooper looked more and more stern. Orillia, who had treated her father always with respect and a worried kindness, who had refused to look at others in his presence in case she'd see the same suppressed smiles her mother provoked, looked blander, blanker, no expression on her face and no communication with anyone in her black eyes. Except for Sam Hagan. She couldn't keep her eyes off him, and that was the source of the best of the town gossip. The consensus was that the Captain favoured Orillia too, and it was a more appropriate match, given that he was between the two women in age. Yet Mrs. Cooper acted as if she owned him. When they packed Ralph off to the asylum, the town settled back to see what would happen. Less than a year later Ralph died, never having come home. And it wasn't long after that Mrs. Cooper moved out to Fairview to keep house on a more continuous basis for the Captain. With Orillia as chaperone. Or with Mrs. Cooper as chaperone. No one knew which.

every good wish

Orillia read Percy's letters in the order in which he'd sent them. In the second he asked, "Do you remember the dance we attended at Robin Hood School last April when the weather turned so fine all the snow melted, and a bunch of us went for a walk in the moonlight, and played at stepping on each other's shadows?"

She found Gladdie sitting on the back steps. "Gladdie," she said, sitting down beside her, "Have you heard anything from Percy Gowan lately? I wrote to him and I haven't had an answer."

"No," Gladdie said.

"I suppose he doesn't feel any compunction to answer my letter since I never answered his. Do you think it would be foolish of me to write again?"

"No," Gladdie said.

Well over a week later, Gladdie went looking for Orillia and found her sitting on the back steps with her sweater snugged around her. It was already getting dark, though you could still see clouds like moody shadows in the sky.

"I had a letter yesterday from my aunt Clara," Orillia said when Gladdie sat down beside her. Gladdie knew that letter had come. She also knew it was the only mail Orillia had got, though she had written to Percy again.

"She wants me to come and stay with her and my aunt Milly, in Toronto."

Gladdie didn't say anything, the news being so sudden her brain stopped working.

Orillia said, "I think I will go. It seems like a good idea."

A tabby cat strolled into the yard and picked its dainty way down the path toward the dark bulk of the burning barrel. It walked the way Orillia had been talking: carefully, with an eye out for anything that moved anywhere either side of the path.

"If things don't work out you can always come back," Gladdie said.

"That's right," Orillia said.

With only her lamp for light, Gladdie sat on the edge of her bed in her yellow room, looking at the postcard from Harry, the picture of the huge sequoia tree with the little people standing at its base, two men and a woman. She still wasn't sure if it was Harry posed in the fork of the massive above-ground roots. The figures were small and the picture wasn't clear enough to tell.

"How are you?" Harry asked at the bottom of the card.

"Just fine," she said out loud. "I'm just fine."

The postcard would be the only souvenir of the past she'd have left, if she gave Johnnie's letters to Orillia. She'd kept the letters in the inside pocket of her valise for years – you'd think she'd known they could go like that to Orillia someday. She'd already decided to give her the bag. She'd thought of it as soon as Orillia said she was going back to Toronto, to that house with the big willow tree where she'd been lonely. She'd be lonely there again. She knew it herself, you could tell by the way she spoke about her plans, and the way she'd sat on the back step, smoothing down her sweater and her skirt, not realizing she was doing it. Gladdie ran her fingers over the polished silver clasp for the feel of the engraved initials. What was this summer for, anyway, if it wasn't to tell Orillia who she was?

"Every good wish," that's what he always wrote at the end of his letters. The envelopes were old and finger-tattered, tied in a stack with a narrow pink satin ribbon that had long since lost its freshness. She didn't open them and read them again. She knew what was in them. They were Johnnie at his best. He'd spoken often of his love and concern for his daughter. She'd put off telling Orillia about her real origins, waiting for the right time. Now she thought the letters would explain, better than she could, why she'd watched over Orillia since her childhood. Besides, they belonged to Orillia, just as the valise did. It was only right she should have something of her mother's and something of her father's when she set out on her own in the world.

fairview

Halvor opened the post office before Gladdie finished washing the floor, and Orillia was the first one in. She stood for a bit in a wedge of sunlight, blinking, while the door closed behind her. She was wearing a summer dress she must have made herself, as it was unusual somehow Gladdie couldn't have described. It had a dropped waist and seemed to float when she walked. It was a delicate blue-grey shade with a fine white pattern, and it made her look cool even though the morning was already hot. Her white stockings were dirty. And on the heel of one shoe were the marks of her fingers where she'd tried to wipe dust away. She undid the blue scarf from her hat while she waited for her mail.

She was standing on the sidewalk when Gladdie came out, her hat on the seat of Captain Hagan's automobile that she'd angle-parked in front of the post office.

"Can I have a word, Miss McConnell?" she asked in the polite, distant way she had with everyone.

"Gladdie," Gladdie said, as she did to anyone who addressed her as Miss.

They walked together the three doors down to Mrs. Pattison's, where Gladdie was due next. The sun was already high and glossing the town, making even the dandelions shine and look like flowers instead of weeds. Mrs. Pattison's young hedge was in bloom, yellow like the dandelions, and its heavy pea smell hung warm in the air. It was the twenty-fifth of May, Gladdie noted – she knew she'd want to remember this beautiful day – and summer was already here. They stopped at the gate, a prairie type of wire gate held up by two posts, and she waited to find out what Orillia wanted.

When the girl spoke, it was all in a rush. "Gladdie," she said, "I was wondering if you'd come out to the farm and help us with some cleaning. We're late this year and didn't get it all done in the spring." Fairview: Mrs. Cooper's name for Captain Hagan's house. You didn't hear Orillia using it.

They talked a bit more, about nothing. A breeze came up and blew both their hair about, and they put their hands up to pat it down at the same time, and laughed.

"I'll see you tomorrow morning, then," Orillia said, and she went off with a spring in her step.

Nothing had been said to suggest anything more than cleaning was being requested. It was as likely as not Gladdie's own imagination that had made her see questions in Orillia's eyes. But she looked so happy, walking away with that little spring in her step.

The next morning Gladdie took the road out of town to Fairview. When she got to the farm, she went round to the side door of the big house and knocked. Being asked to clean didn't mean anything special; she made sure she remembered that while she stood waiting for them to answer the door.

"Morning, Mrs. Cooper," she said. She thought the woman looked surprised to see her, but she said good morning civilly enough to the air above Gladdie's head, and asked her to come in. Gladdie was carrying an apron, and she put it on as soon as she stepped into the kitchen. It was a big farm kitchen with a fancy range decked out with chrome, and there was an icebox in the corner. It looked as clean as you could ever expect a kitchen to be.

"Would you like a cup of coffee?" Mrs. Cooper asked.

"Not just yet, thanks."

"Oh," Mrs. Cooper said. "Well, have a chair."

Gladdie sat down at the table and looked around the room. "Looks like you've got the kitchen shipshape," she said.

"Thank you," Florence Cooper said. "And what can I do for you?"

"I've come to clean."

"I beg your pardon?"

"Your daughter came into town yesterday and asked me to clean."

"She asked you to clean?" Mrs. Cooper jumped up and poured coffee into two cups, then brought them to the table. She pushed the cream and sugar over to Gladdie, so Gladdie took some and waited.

Mrs. Cooper stirred her coffee, then she fussed with her hair. "I sometimes worry about Orillia," she said.

Gladdie had nothing to say to that.

"Orillia's in bed today, Gladdie," Florence Cooper went on. "She hasn't gotten out of bed. She hasn't spoken to me. She refuses to speak. She didn't mention she'd asked you to come. This is embarrassing. I don't believe she's forgotten. She's completely perverse sometimes. I'm sorry to say it, but she's been behaving very badly lately. You've likely heard that Captain Hagan and I plan to marry."

Gladdie hadn't heard any such thing. She wasn't one to listen to gossip unless it was pressed on her, which all too often it was. She tried to think what this must mean to Orillia. Mrs. Cooper was still talking, oblivious to Gladdie's surprise, and Gladdie, after missing a bit, picked up on her saying, "Unfortunately, it seems to have put Orillia's nose out of joint. We told her a few days ago, and her behaviour ever since has been... I believe she may have thought..."

Here was a funny thing. Florence Cooper ran out of words and stopped not just talking but moving. Her face went blank. Everything about her stopped. It was the same thing Orillia did sometimes, a kind of freezing and glazing over. But the strangest thing was what Mrs. Cooper said then: "Sometimes Orillia reminds me of nothing so much as that china Dalmatian we use as a doorstop. Sitting at attention, overly alert and obtusely brave. When bravery isn't called for."

They both looked at the black and white china dog that sat by the kitchen door. It did have a stalwart pose, with its head high, its body tense and eager, as if it was more than ready to come to somebody's rescue. Gladdie thought it was the picture of Florence Cooper herself as she'd sat in front of her the minute before, looking more ceramic than alive, and heroic, too, in a way. There was a kind of misbegotten bravery in the woman. She obviously felt the need of defense. The years of living with Ralph had done that, no doubt, and the rumours that had flown around of the rivalry between herself and Orillia. She'd realize there'd be more talk, now, because of her marrying a man years younger than herself.

Mrs. Cooper came back to herself and said, "Well, Gladdie, be that as it may, I'm sorry you've been imposed on." She got up and went to the hall and got her purse out of a dresser. She took out a fifty-cent piece and brought it to Gladdie.

"No, thank you," Gladdie said, looking at the coin lying on the open palm as if she'd never seen such a thing. "I've done no work. But if you'll do me a favour, I'd be happy if you'd say hello to Orillia for me. I think her a fine young woman."

Mrs. Cooper remained standing, but Gladdie already knew it was time to leave. She stood up from the table and pushed her chair back. It scraped like a complaint across the floor and alerted her to a change in the atmosphere of the kitchen. The room felt bigger all of a sudden and the two of them stranded in it.

Then Florence Cooper, in a lofty voice to suit the enlarged kitchen, said, "I know who you are, Gladdie McConnell."

And hadn't Gladdie wanted to hear just those words a hundred times before, though not in that tone of voice?

"I've known who you were since the day you set foot in Aquadell. Clara pointed you out to me once in Toronto. She told us about her talk with you and how you were hanging around the child. And then you show up here. I think that very strange. I suppose you thought you'd become friends with my daughter." She was white with anger; her black eyes burned.

"She could use a friend," Gladdie said.

"I am not a wicked stepmother," Florence Cooper said. Standing over Gladdie she looked every inch of that, to the extent that Gladdie had a flash of wishing she could tell somebody about it later, as Mr. Riley in the old days would have done, sharing a laugh at Mrs. Cooper's expense. You could change experience that way, she knew. You could alter something pitiful that had made you want to cry or make a bitter pill palatable.

"It's true I'm not Orillia's real mother," Florence Cooper went on. "But she's my niece. I think you're aware of that. She's my brother's child." She gave Gladdie a fierce look, waiting for what she'd say.

Gladdie said, "Johnnie."

Florence's face softened at the sound of his name. "He died in England," she said. Then she straightened up. "Probably for the best. He was at his best young, as you might imagine. He was four years younger than I, and I'm afraid I doted on him. I got used to cleaning up after him, so he never quite grew up. He would have made an impossible father." She shifted thoughts and said, "Why he ever got involved with you..." The china dog look came over her for a few seconds, but she shook it off. "It was simply the sort of thing he did. A game. Intrigue. He was happiest when playing a double game. With us, with you." She took a breath. "But it's over," she said. "It's long over and you're still here and I don't see why."

Gladdie's eyes smarted from the light that shone up from the pale dirt road. She tipped her hat forward, but the heat hit her full in the face. She passed by the Captain's fence where a dozen or more bone-dry, bone-white tumbleweeds from the year before had tangled; then the silvery stones piled up at the corner of his field marked the end of his property. The skin on her arms and hands and thighs was as hot as a pressing cloth after you've ironed, and felt tight, as if she'd grown too big for it. She'd had no answer for Florence Cooper as to why she was still hanging around. She'd walked out on the question. She didn't have to answer Florence Cooper. But she did have to calm down a bit before she met up with anyone else, so it was a good thing it was a mile back to town, even if it was hot enough to send any creature with more brains than a grasshopper looking for shade. She stopped by the nearly dried-up slough halfway to town, and sat down under some stunted willows to rest. Blackbirds trilled to one another and swooped over the water while she sat there. Flies buzzed around the cattails. Even sitting, she could see for a long way. The land around Aquadell wasn't really flat; it swelled and dipped like a person's body, but it gave the impression of flatness overall, and it went so far before it met the sky you could almost see it tip at the edge. You could believe the earth was round and spinning, and if you let go you might fly off. Some people did let go. Jessie Dole was one of them, Johnnie another. Florence Cooper might be like that, too, one of those who let go when things get rough. Gladdie wasn't. She liked where she was. She was closer to dirt here than she'd ever been, and she'd never felt cleaner.

moses in the bulrushes

While Orillia pretended to look at the new winter catalogue, Susan sat at the other end of the table, etching her ABC's. Only the two of them were in the kitchen, silently involved in their own thoughts, with above and distant the sounds of Hilda and Gladdie mopping and dusting on the third floor. It was so quiet in the room Orillia could hear Susan's pencil whisper over the paper. The doll lay on the table beside her, dressed in its long white infant's dress that was grubby with handling and could have used a wash. It was one good thing she'd done this summer, Orillia thought, suggesting the doll for Susan. A companion, a comfort. You never saw her without it. Maybe, in silent words, she talked to it, told it her thoughts, her fears. At least she wasn't drawing so many of her too-scrutable stick figures that were so painful to look at and not just because of the dark colours she used. Something else made them disquieting. Maybe it was what Hilda had pointed out: that emptiness behind the three figures, the sense the pictures gave that the child had nothing in the world but the two adults that she clung to with both her hands.

Orillia sighed. She felt shaky and perceptive this morning, as if her self had been degloved and left to quiver in the air. In this state the child's quietness, which she'd interpreted previously as blandness, showed itself for what it was: a careful self-containment or perhaps a cautious, nearly hopeless kind of waiting. There she sat, placid as ever, mute as ever, working away at her letters to please Gladdie and Hilda. The only real clue they had to her mind was the drawings. They could guess, but they could never know what she was thinking.

Snap. Orillia closed the catalogue. Susan looked up from her printing.

Orillia said, "Susan. Let's play Moses in the bulrushes."

The child looked astonished and more than a little interested, and Orillia's spirits rose as she got to her feet. "Let's go outside. Bring your doll and the box Gladdie gave you."

The little girl climbed down from her chair and fetched the apple box, lined with old linen, from the pantry where it was kept. Fussily, as if to show she was willing to pretend it was a real baby, she laid the doll inside it.

So they went out into the garden together, into the warm fall day. Orillia took her crutches because the ground would be uneven. "I'll be the princess," she said to Susan as she walked ahead of her down the path. "And you can be Miriam."

They went straight to the end of the garden, to the tall grass that grew either side of the back lane. Susan carried the doll in the apple box and set it down carefully when Orillia stopped.

"We need a river or a creek," Orillia said. "I guess we'll have to make one. The grass will do for the rushes." She laid her crutches down by the box. She rolled her sleeves up and Susan rolled hers. Together, with Susan working as hard as Orillia, they pulled the grass from a centre strip, leaving two high edges. Before they were done, the palms of their hands had turned green. With the walking ends of the crutches, they scrubbed out a dry creek bed the width of the apple box and nearly half the length of Hilda's lot. By the time they'd done that, they were sweating, and dust stuck to the skin of their arms like brown lace, but they had their reward. The tall grass waved on either side of the path they both saw as the river.

"Would you like to launch the ark?" Orillia asked, and Susan took up the box and set it in place.

"Oh, look at the beautiful baby!" Orillia said after Susan had stealthily pushed the box toward her. She leaned over the rushes and picked the doll up and rocked it in her arms, surprised at its lightness. She barely had time to wonder if Susan would remember what came next before the little girl jumped up and tugged on her sleeve.

"Who's this?" Orillia asked. "Who are you, little girl? What's your name?"

Susan shrugged and pulled in her lips. She could speak, Orillia thought. She could speak if she wanted to. "Oh well, then, goodbye," she said, and began rocketing away on her crutches. She had the doll clamped between her left arm and her body. Right by my heart, she thought. Susan ran up beside her and grabbed the doll's arm.

"I'm the Pharaoh's daughter," Orillia said without even looking at the little girl. "And who are you?" She kept on walking down the alley as she talked, swinging along on her crutches while she held the doll imprisoned. Susan kept up to her by running alongside, and all the way she wouldn't let go of the doll's arm.

"If you can't tell me who you are, I'll simply have to take this baby home," Orillia said. She hiked along toward the end of the block, where there were no houses either side of the lane. She expected at any moment to hear the childish whisper, "I'm Miriam."

She stopped when they reached the end of the alley. She could see across the creek to the scattered houses of Mr. Best's neighbourhood and past the Albert Street bridge to downtown. She thought about the weeks she'd spent in her room, almost forgetting that all this world, and a good deal beyond it, existed. She wished she could keep on walking. She was ready to leave now, but she was out of breath, and she'd abused her feet. They were hurting. She had better finish what she'd started and get back to the house. She looked into Susan's upturned face. "I have to find a nurse for this baby," she said. "I'm looking for a girl named Miriam to help me. Do you know anyone named Miriam?"

Susan immediately pointed to herself, looking anxious.

"Oh it's you, Miriam. Do you know anyone who can look after this baby?"

Susan nodded. She swallowed. Her eyes were big.

"Who?"

She almost relented then. Susan was close to crying. But she'd come so far, she hated to give up. She looked right into Susan's eyes and tried to will the child to speak.

"Who can look after this baby, Susan?"

There was a dreadful, seemingly insurmountable impasse, then Susan broke it. She bent and with a fingertip began to trace letters in the fine dirt at the edge of the alley. She drew M and O quickly, then T, then she stood back, thinking. A feeling of sadness flew up and plastered itself on Orillia. It flew up from the child, from the sight of her thinking out the word, intent on the word as a puzzle to be worked out. Susan darted forward and wrote the rest of the letters. There it was. Perfectly spelled.

"You are a wise and thoughtful little girl, Susan," Orillia said. The sadness had been unexpected, and so was the longing to kneel and wrap the little girl in her arms. She let her crutches and the doll drop to the ground. She knelt and reached out, and Susan stepped into her arms. Her little bony body pressed into Orillia, her arms wrapped around Orillia's neck, and her warm cheek rested on Orillia's cheek.

Hilda called from the back step. "Susan!"

Orillia gave her a little extra squeeze, and then, drawing back, what she hoped was a motherly smile. Susan smiled too, as she knew she was supposed to do, but it was a naked smile. She had not really been comforted.

"Susan!" Hilda called again.

"Time to go back," Orillia said. She picked up the doll and brushed off its dingy white dress and gave it to Susan, who ran with it to the box they'd left behind in the grass.

purpose

With her watering can, Gladdie went from pot to pot along the verandah, telling herself everything was right in her world. The summer was nearly over, but Orillia wouldn't leave empty-handed.

"Susan, Susan." She could hear Hilda calling at the back door. Susan had taken her doll out to the alley with Orillia. That was another reason for happiness. If you needed reasons.

Gladdie had been punching down bread dough in Mrs. Faraday's kitchen across the street from the Aquadell General Store when Orillia Cooper walked in all white in the face and shaky. Mrs. Faraday had gone to visit her sister in Edmonton; that's why Gladdie was in her kitchen. She'd been hired to look after Mr. Faraday and their five children, and she was happy they were all out of the house at work and school when she saw the girl looking so upset. Standing marooned by the woodbox, in a smart travelling dress.

"I asked at the post office where you were this morning. I'm sorry you came out to the farm for nothing," Orillia said all at once, with one direct glance from those black eyes.

Gladdie wiped her floury hands on her apron and grinned as if it were any day. "That's all right," she said.

"Well, I am sorry," Orillia said. She seemed about to panic. "Mother and Captain Hagan are engaged, you know. They're going to San Francisco."

"You're not going with them?"

"Heavens, no," she said with a bright smile on her face. "Three's a crowd, isn't it? Especially on a honeymoon."

"That's a lovely dress you're wearing," Gladdie said. "The dark blue suits you."

"I'm going to Regina. We're taking the morning train," Orillia said. "Mother's going with me. She says they're hiring at the telephone exchange."

At least they weren't leaving the girl to the mercy of town gossip. "You'll come back and visit us, I hope," Gladdie said.

"I don't know. I don't think I will, really," she said, staring off in a way that reminded Gladdie of the black and white dog in Florence Cooper's kitchen, and what Florence Cooper labelled uncalled-for bravery.

"I wish you well," Gladdie said, seeing that any second the girl was going to flee. She held out her hand. Orillia took it in hers. Her hand was soft, and not as cool as it was the only other time Gladdie had held it, when they'd first met face to face. Shyly, she pulled it away and then didn't know what to do with herself.

"Goodbye, then," she said, and she was gone, and Gladdie was left alone in the kitchen, though it felt like being alone in a wider space, out in a field outside of town, right in the middle of a big wheat field, as Orillia might see her if she could be standing there when the train went past.

"There you are!" Orillia cried, bursting out of the house with her sleeves rolled up and her hair half down, her face all excited and so dirty you'd think she'd dug potatoes for the last six hours. Her hands were stained, too, as if she'd been pulling weeds, but seeing her so wound up Gladdie didn't ask her what she'd been doing. She went on watering the geraniums, waiting for whatever was to come.

Orillia paced the length of the verandah, her cane tapping on the wood floor. "Gladdie," she said. "I've been stupid. I've behaved badly and I don't know what to do about it." She stopped and stared out the glass veranda door as if the answer might be out there, in the front yard or beyond. "Mr. Best said I was afraid."

"Mr. Best. The man's a fool," Gladdie said.

"I might have been afraid. I was angry."

Gladdie nodded. It was easier being angry than afraid, anyone could tell you that. She went on with her watering. It didn't matter that Orillia wasn't entirely making sense; her words and thoughts had connections in her own mind. She just needed someone to hear her say them out loud.

"I didn't tell you what I did," Orillia said. She flushed and bit her lip and looked out the door again. "I wrote to Mother. When I got her letter saying she was coming to Regina. I wrote and told her I didn't need her here because I had you. That's why she didn't come. It wasn't because she didn't want to come."

She hesitated for a few seconds, and Gladdie knew she wanted her to respond, but she couldn't think what to say.

"She would have come if I'd let her. She wanted to."

"Of course she did," Gladdie said. "Of course she did."

"Do you think I should write to her and explain? I don't know if she'd understand. I suppose I should try."

She hesitated again, and then, answering herself, she said, "Well, of course, I have to at least do that." She looked at Gladdie just long enough to see her nod.

our little girl

"Now who's that?" Hilda said when someone knocked on the door. She was trying to get lunch ready and went to the verandah with a paring knife in her hand. Afterwards, she had to search all over the parlour for the thing. She'd set it down in a daze in the earth under the Boston fern.

She sent Susan out to play in the garden so she could tell Gladdie and Orillia what Reverend Hurst had said, starting with, "I've come to tell you myself, Mrs. Wutherspoon."

"They've found Susan's parents," Gladdie said.

Reverend Hurst was an older gentleman who'd never been married. He didn't have much understanding of others' love for children, but he'd seen Hilda was upset. "May I come in and tell you about it?" he'd asked.

"What you'll want to know first," Reverend Hurst had said, "is that the archdiocese and the authorities are satisfied that they are indeed Susan's parents."

That hadn't been what Hilda had wanted to know first. She'd wanted to know what they were like. But he didn't know what they were like; he hadn't met them.

"Where have they been all this time?" she'd asked him and was told they'd been travelling.

"Outside the country," she told Gladdie and Orillia. "Susan was left in the care of her aunt and uncle."

"But surely, Reverend Hurst, they'd have heard of the cyclone?" Hilda had asked. "They'd have tried to get in touch?"

Reverend Hurst had tried to explain that Susan's parents didn't know she was in Regina. They'd left her in Winnipeg, then they'd gone to Halifax where they'd boarded a boat for Europe. Hilda wasn't able to keep track of all the places Reverend Hurst mentioned. She was thinking: they'll come and take Susan away.

"I think they were going to the coast, the aunt and uncle," she said. Her glasses misted, and she took them off and cleaned them. "I'm sure he said they stopped in Regina, planning to attend the Dominion Day celebrations on Sunday before continuing on their journey to the coast."

"They didn't go on without her?" Orillia said.

"Oh, they were killed. They were killed outright when the cyclone hit. They were in the list of the dead, but no one realized they were travelling with a little girl." And then the police had lost track of Susan.

"Her parents were frantic, Mrs. Wutherspoon," Reverend Hurst had said.

"It was only when he visited the police station and reminded them the Anglican Church had taken the child as a ward that they could tell her parents where she was. But then for a week no one could find *them*. They were *here*, in Regina, walking the streets, looking for her."

"Here," Gladdie said.

"Yes, here," Hilda said. "I said, 'They'll want to see her.' It was all I was thinking of. And he said, 'Oh yes.' And they're on their way back."

"On their way back?" Orillia said.

"They should be arriving in a matter of hours. To take her."

"Just like that?" Orillia said.

"'The authorities are satisfied.' That's what he said. They're coming straight to the house to take her. I said, 'This afternoon? She might not want to go with them. She might be upset.' And Reverend Hurst said, 'I don't see that happening, do you, Mrs. Wutherspoon? It's her mother and father.'" The way Hilda said it, Gladdie and Orillia knew how Reverend Hurst had spoken: gently, understanding the words would hurt. They waited while Hilda struggled with her tears.

She went on: "If there's any problem, she can stay with us another day or two until she gets used to the idea."

"Where will they take Susan?" Gladdie asked.

"To Winnipeg," he said. "That's where they live. And it's Christine. Her name's Christine."

"I'll pack up her scribblers with her clothes and toys," Hilda said. "They'll want to know how she's progressed."

Gladdie got up from the kitchen table. She fetched the stack of scribblers from the cabinet where they were stored. She took them to the table and divided the pile into two, the school work and the artwork. "These we'll keep," she said, and neither of the others had to ask which ones they were keeping.

Hilda said, "That's right, Gladdie."

Hilda thought it best if she told Susan on her own about the change in store for her. She called the little girl in. Orillia went up to her room and Gladdie went out back to work in the garden. There were always weeds.

While she hoed in the garden that was almost dead now but for the weeds, Gladdie wondered what Susan must be thinking about this leaving. She tried to think what she'd have wanted Margaret to say to her before she'd left her, if Margaret could have sat down with her and told her what was happening and why she was leaving and what Gladdie should do next. She saw she'd answered her question in asking it. That was just what Susan would want, too, if she could ask for it. She'd want to know as much as possible what was going on and what it was going to mean to her, so Gladdie decided, although it was Hilda's responsibility to speak to Susan, and her right to handle it her way, she'd have a talk with Susan, too.

They must be good people, she told herself while she worked. Susan wouldn't be such a loving child if she hadn't been raised by people who loved her. The day she first saw Susan came back to her, the child running alongside the train with Hilda, her eyes searching the train windows. She'd been looking for her parents, of course. It was their parents children wanted – whether those parents were good or bad or indifferent (which was to say bad) – when they had that look of need in their eyes.

Susan came out to the garden right after Hilda told her. She sat down on her haunches while she watched Gladdie work.

Gladdie couldn't find the words to say anything to the child. She couldn't predict what was going to happen to her, and she couldn't think of any advice that would help her meet whatever unknown was coming. She went on hoeing and Susan went on watching her. She was waiting for a word, anything, as Gladdie would have been waiting if she were her.

She couldn't let the child leave without saying something. "Is it all right if we keep your drawings, Susan?" she asked her. "Hilda and I would like to have them."

Susan nodded.

"You can take your doll with you. Your Mother and Dad will be very happy to see you, won't they?"

Again that shy nod. Gladdie wished she could make Susan promises, but she couldn't. Hilda planned to ask her parents if they could visit them sometime in Winnipeg, or if they would bring Susan to Regina to visit. Gladdie didn't hold out much hope for it happening, regardless of what they said. Susan was only a little girl and would forget them. It wouldn't be long before what they really looked like and were like would leave her memory. She'd try for a picture of them in her mind some day, and they'd be no clearer or more recognizable than her stick people. Gladdie felt sorry to think it, but she knew it would be so. She could tell her things, but they wouldn't matter. She would remember only what was important to her.

Orillia watched Gladdie working below, the sharp hoe biting into the baked clay, until Susan appeared in the garden – without her doll, Orillia noticed – and went right to Gladdie's side. Gladdie stopped hoeing and grinned at the child, then she went back to work. She spoke to Susan now and then. She didn't say much. Orillia wondered where the doll was, if it was already packed away in a suitcase.

She'd heard Hilda come upstairs and go to her room after talking to Susan, and now she remembered the day, early in the summer, when she and Hilda had looked out her window together, watching Susan and Gladdie in the garden. They had both been jealous; they had felt the same sadness, wanting to be the one standing there, partaking in such unconscious love. Now Susan was going to her parents, and Hilda would never see the child again.

Hilda brought the parents into the parlour. They were respectable-looking people in decent travelling clothes. The mother had Susan's colouring, and, as Susan often did, she seemed to drift into the room, looking for an anchor. The father, although he was a young man, looked fatherly.

Susan, before their entry, had gone to Gladdie. She was holding Gladdie's hand when they walked into the room. She was wearing her blue polka-dot dress with the perky ruffles – Hilda's doing, for the parents. Her mother and father, together, said, "Christine."

As naturally as if she'd done it yesterday and all the yesterdays her mind could remember, Susan squealed, a lilt in her voice, in anticipation of the hug her father was going to give her, the swing around and up in his arms. She buried her head in his neck. She nuzzled her cheek into his shoulder. He chuckled, nearly crying. With his free arm, he drew his wife into the circle just as it looked as if her knees were about to buckle, and Susan threw both her arms about her mother's neck. Then she turned and surveyed the women, smug as you please.

Yes, that was that: a little embarrassment on all sides, many protestations and much gratitude expressed. The arrangement, as a possibility if the meeting had gone awry, that Susan could stay on at Mrs. Wutherspoon's another day or two, proved unnecessary. Her parents had brought a suitcase to pack her things. By the time they clicked it closed, Susan was jabbering away to them as unselfconsciously as if she'd never spent a waking five minutes without talking.

The three of them didn't go all the way to the sidewalk with Susan and her parents, but stood in a row on the bottom verandah step. From there they watched the little family roll off down the street. Susan – or Christine, as she was now – was prompted and dutifully waved her little hand out the window for several seconds as they drove away.

Hilda said, "There goes our little girl." She wasn't crying, not yet. Gladdie and Orillia stood either side of her, and she was grateful for their presence.

"I'm going to make us a pot of tea," Gladdie said, but she didn't move. She was remembering the moment the child leapt into her father's arms and then turned and beamed on them like a little queen on a throne. She was thinking of Hilda's grief, and how all the wanting in the world wouldn't get you anywhere, and how Hilda hadn't even lost Susan because she'd never had her. It was her parents she'd needed. Her father and her mother.

Florence and Orillia would make up. The rift between them was temporary, as it had been when Orillia was a child, when she was left with her relatives and felt adrift, waiting for their return.

She couldn't tell Orillia about her past. Over and over again she'd come to the same decision, but she'd never decided like this before. Like shutting a door, like turning your back on a shut door and leaning against it, so it could never open again. But it didn't matter if that door was closed. Orillia hadn't been waiting and watching for her.

after wisdom

They were sitting in a pool of yellow lamplight in the kitchen, just the two of them. The evenings came down earlier now, but Hilda lit the lamp only at quiet times, which was how she thought of those times Orillia left them to themselves. Orillia had gone to her room to read. She'd barely reached the second-floor landing before Hilda had the match flaring over the wick. Gladdie had smiled at that, and reached above her to the wall switch to flick off the electric light. The fat teapot sat between them. Hilda cleared her throat. "Orillia will be leaving soon, I think," she ventured.

Gladdie nodded quite placidly. "Her aunts want her to live with them in Toronto," she said.

"In Toronto?"

"It's best," Gladdie said, with such a tone of finality Hilda was thrown off track.

"You won't go, too, will you?" she said. "I was hoping you'd stay here with me. I don't think I could bear an empty house."

"I'll stay if you still want us to be partners," Gladdie said.

Gladdie liked things businesslike, and it was a help to discuss it that way; it was a relief. "There's a shortage of rooms in the city, you know, since the cyclone. We can take our pick of lodgers," Hilda said. "But maybe I'm being selfish," she said, seeing Gladdie look pensive. "I'd understand if you wanted to go back to Aquadell."

Gladdie smiled and shook her head.

Without any more attempts at transition, because she was never any good at easing into a topic anyway, Hilda blurted the words at the top of her mind. "Oh, Gladdie, don't give Orillia up."

Gladdie reared back in her chair and jarred the table. A shudder of light and shadows flew over them, and Hilda had to grab the lamp to keep it from tipping over. But she couldn't stop now; she'd rehearsed the next part. "I had to give Susan up, and I can't be so selfish as to not be happy for her – I know I must be happy for her, we all must be. But you don't have to give Orillia up."

Gladdie started to speak, but Hilda put her hand out to stop her. Gently, she said, "Won't you go to her and tell her who you are?"

A silence and a stare greeted that question, and Hilda got worried she'd offended Gladdie. She remembered Gladdie telling her about Mr. Riley's storytelling, how people would get mad at him because he knew too much about them. But it was too late to fuss about that now. "I guessed," she whispered. She reached out and patted Gladdie's hand. "It's not so hard to put two and two together, you know." She poured them both another cup of tea, and helped herself to cream and sugar. She felt so much better, getting this out in the open, and she was sure Gladdie would, too. "The wonder is I didn't see it from the start," she went on, shaking her head. "The two of you are as alike as peas in the pod; you'd have to be blind not to see it."

"Alike? Me and Orillia?"

"Not so much in looks, I'll grant you. Her freckles are under the skin, and her hair's so dark you don't see the auburn except in the light, but in other ways, why, I'm just going to say it, if you won't. I told you about my child, the child I might have had. You needn't feel ashamed about claiming yours – not to me, of all people. What are you grinning about?"

"Hilda, dear," Gladdie said. She pursed her lips and put her head down. Why, she was trying to stifle a laugh.

"I'd like to know what's so funny," Hilda said.

Finally Gladdie said, "You're not blind, Hilda, but I have to say, your eyesight's a bit fanciful."

"Fanciful?"

Gladdie just grinned at her, with her head to one side, not even trying to hide her amusement.

"You're not Orillia's mother?"

"No, I'm not. Though I'm pleased as punch you thought so."

"You didn't follow her to Aquadell?" Hah! That got her. She had to put her cup down.

"I did follow her to Aquadell, it's true," Gladdie said. "And I should have told you about it long ago."

"I feel a fool."

"Well, then," Gladdie said. "I'll tell you this for free. I said your eyesight wasn't good, and that was joking, but it was also a lie of a kind. Because you see better than anyone I know. You see straight to the heart of things. You always did, and you always will. I did all I could, this summer, to take her mother's place. You saw that, and knew it was wrong. I had no right to do it."

After that, Gladdie told Hilda the whole story, everything she could never tell Orillia. She started with Jessie Dole, from the wonderful night of her arrival, and went on to Johnnie and the arrangement between herself and him, and how she'd kept watch, all those years, over Orillia.

"But are you sure you shouldn't tell Orillia?" Hilda asked when she'd finished. "Don't you think it would do her good to know who she is – and who you are?"

Gladdie shook her head. "Orillia can be herself without knowing a single thing about Jessie Dole. Or me."

"You would have been a good mother, Gladdie."

"And so would you," Gladdie said.

"I fear Florence Cooper wasn't."

"I don't know, honestly," Gladdie said. "But to be fair to her, I should tell you what happened in Aquadell, that led to Orillia turning against her, and asking for me." So Hilda heard all that story, about the Captain and Florence and Orillia, ending with Orillia's confession that she'd put her mother off a second time, that she'd written to her when Florence was ready to hasten to Regina and told her not to come. "So you see, you were right about that, too. She wanted to come."

"It was you Orillia needed; that's why she did it," Hilda said. "I wish she could know you're the one who watched over her, and kept your promise not to desert her."

"It was just pride in me, wanting that. It's better for us both, to leave things the way they are."

"You know, you sound a bit too much like Mrs. Riley when you talk like that."

"Give me a girl who looks peaked. She'll have resigned herself to life."

"That's right. She was a great one for resignation."

"Resignation's not as bad a thing as I used to think. I figure there's two ways of looking at it," Gladdie said. "One is like sour grapes. You give up what you're never going to get anyway. But the other's a deeper feeling. You lose, but you see the reason behind it. You have to think in layers to grasp it with your mind, but once you've done it, you don't have to think about it." She paused. "I feel like I've been holding my breath for a long time," she said. "I feel better now."

Hilda put her head to the side, studying her old friend. "You look less peaked than you did," she said, in true Mrs. Riley style.

"I'm going to give Orillia that valise. Without the letters. At least she'll have that."

"Go," Hilda said. "Go right now, and do it."

For once, Gladdie took her advice. She nodded, stood up and took off upstairs to her room. Hilda looked up to the ceiling where the lamp's halo glowed, and thought about Susan, who would be asleep by this time of night, in her own bed, in her own room, hundreds of miles away. She thought about the child's little body, curled in that bed, and wished she was of the Roman Catholic religion, and knew how to cross herself to ward off evil and bring goodness down to that little part of the world.

"I want you to have this," Gladdie said. She'd brought the valise to Orillia after emptying its contents.

Orillia stood up from the chair by her bed, where she'd been reading, or maybe thinking, since she blinked a couple of times as if she'd been somewhere deep and had to struggle a bit to come up to the surface. She put her hands up to her hair and tucked in the loose strands. It was a gesture she'd developed recently, as if she was always getting ready to go out into the world. Behind her, the bed was made with the white Marcella counterpane, and the white curtains were drawn across the dark window. Like the hospital, all that white. They'd tried to make it a brave place, but it wasn't a room a grown girl could live in for long. Gladdie held out the valise.

"Oh, I couldn't," Orillia said.

"Its a good quality bag," Gladdie said. "You won't be ashamed to travel with it."

"Oh no, it's a fine bag," Orillia said, looking embarrassed. "But it's yours."

"It's yours," Gladdie said, handing it over.

"Well, thank you," Orillia said, and she took it, though she still looked surprised and held it awkwardly, staring at the clasp and the initials engraved into the silver. Then she wrapped her arms tight around the valise, and hugged it to her breast. "Thank you," she said again, this time with so much feeling it almost seemed she'd sensed whose bag it really was.

"It once belonged to a young woman of good family," Gladdie said.

"I know," Orillia said.

Gladdie was taken aback for a second or two, wondering if somehow or other Orillia did know. Then she said, "Oh, pshaw, you're teasing me."

"I'll keep it always," Orillia said.

Then came the day the day the three of them stood side by side on the verandah steps, looking out to the fields as if they were only taking the air. A succession of dust devils twirling over the summerfallow was the only unusual sight, except for the sky. But they'd already remarked on that. Because of the wind it was not a clean prairie sky, and not the intense blue autumn sky of recent days. No, it wasn't blue. They'd joked about it, saying nothing was going to come at them out of the blue.

At long last the person they were waiting for came walking up their street from the empty end of the block. They all saw her at the same time, and though the wind blustered as if it couldn't make up its mind where to blow, throwing dust in every direction and obscuring her from their vision, they all knew it was her.

Gladdie thought of the story of Solomon's wisdom when she saw Florence Cooper, or Florence Cooper Hagan, as she was now, walking up their street as if she was looking for a fight. You could get your own dander up, Gladdie thought, watching that tight, straight woman march toward you. At the least she'd put you on your guard, especially if you were already feeling you were in the wrong. She came striding through the wind, taking no notice of her flapping skirt and the grit churning around her. She was wearing a wide hat, gripping a big handbag. Looking like she was advertising determination.

Hilda reached behind Orillia and touched Gladdie's arm so they could, for a second, look at one another. Hilda hadn't been surprised when she'd learned Mrs. Cooper Hagan was coming to her house; she'd posted the letter from Orillia, and brought home the one that came in reply. She waited to welcome the woman, wishing it wouldn't be rude to slip into the house before she arrived, with the excuse of putting the kettle on.

As for Orillia, even though she knew her mother was supposed to arrive that day, she experienced a bit of a shock, seeing her in the flesh, walking toward the house, and now, turning up the path to the door. She put a smile on her face. Birds should fly up around her, she thought, as her mother approached. Or fly away and hide. Or the wind should increase, gusts of windowpane-rattling quality, of wake-you-up-in-the-night ferocity, should come out of nowhere and, oh, just tug her skirt, ruffle her starched blouse, pull a strand of hair loose. Toss her hat into the air! For a second, in her mind's eye, she saw it. The hat lifting and spinning off over the fields beyond them. It nearly happened. And what did Florence do? She grabbed the thing, of course, and held it on. And she laughed. That little, unexpectedly apologetic laugh that made you want her forgiveness.

Gladdie saw it too, the hat nearly lifting, the wind that might have sent it spinning, and the pardon Orillia needed before she could go on. And she saw one more thing in that wide open moment, though some time had to pass before she could recognize it for what it was, because Florence Cooper was saying, "You're looking well, I'm glad to see, Orillia," and the two of them were exchanging a wary little hug. Hellos were being traded, Hilda was introduced, and then Florence, who put Gladdie to shame when it came to being businesslike, was saying, "I don't know what you've been told this summer, Orillia, but I've brought you some letters of your father's and the few photographs I have, including one he sent me of your mother." She strode into the parlour and opened her handbag, oblivious to the fact that she had Orillia bewildered and Gladdie and Hilda stunned. "I meant to give them to you on your twenty-first birthday," she said. "But I'm sure by now you have a hundred questions, and I don't suppose a few months will make a difference." And Orillia learned about Jessie Dole and Johnnie, and later, when Florence had gone back to her hotel, she learned about Gladdie. In her happiness then, Gladdie didn't forget the moment she'd thought the wind would blow Florence's hat off her head. In the image of it spiralling upward in a dusty gust and spinning over the fields far away from Hilda's house was the certain thing she knew. She had been right to let go. Florence Cooper was a mother, and love and respect were her due. She was haughty and cranky and less than ideal, but she was there, she was real, as real a mother as you could ever imagine stepping up to the door.

about the author

Connie Gault is the author of two collections of stories and several plays for stage and radio. *Euphoria* is her first novel.

Connie was born in rural Saskatchewan and grew up in Ontario, Quebec and Alberta, returning every summer to visit a small town that has since almost vanished from the face of the earth. She now lives in Regina.

acknowledgements

I first heard of a town moving in D.E. Macintyre's *The Prairie Storekeeper* (Toronto: Peter Martin Associated Ltd., 1970). The quotation by J.R. Miller is from *Strength and Beauty* (Thomas Y. Crowell and Company, New York and Boston, 1899). *Hurlbut's Story of the Bible* was written by Rev. Jesse Lyman Hurlbut and published in 1904.

My thanks to the Saskatchewan Arts Board for financial support during the writing of this manuscript. Thanks also for the use of research facilities at the Saskatchewan Archives Board, the City of Regina Archives, Regina Public Library Prairie History Room, the City of Toronto Archives and Toronto Public Library. I read many texts, both in hand and online, while researching this novel, including town and district histories, personal memoirs and history books, and I'm grateful to all those authors for helping me to imagine a time before I was born. Finally, I want to thank my editor and my readers, for their wise advice, as well as Joanne Lyons for our lifelong deep discussions, and Gordon – for everything.